THE
LUCKY
ONES

THE
LUCKY
ONES
MARK
EDWARDS

 THOMAS & MERCER

Text copyright © 2017 by Mark Edwards

Published by Thomas & Mercer, Seattle

www.apub.com

Amazon, the Amazon logo, and Thomas & Mercer are trademarks of Amazon.com, Inc., or its affiliates.

ISBN-13: 9781477848272
ISBN-10: 1477848274

Cover design by Mark Swan

Printed in the United States of America

Prologue

As soon as she saw the van parked sideways, blocking the narrow lane ahead of her, Fiona knew she'd made a mistake.

She shouldn't have cycled home, should have accepted the lift. But she could imagine the curtain-twitching old guy next door, the one with all the Neighbourhood Watch stickers in his window, mentioning to Trevor that a strange younger man had dropped her off. Besides, she'd wanted to ride home, the wind against her body, legs pumping in time with her heart – *her new, beautiful heart* – gliding through these quiet country lanes, sun low in the just-spring sky, empty fields stretching to the horizon in every direction.

Fiona had felt like a girl again, a teenager riding home from her first boyfriend's house to sneak inside, past her parents' closed bedroom door, to lie on her bed and replay the events of the evening. She thrummed with rediscovered pleasure. Every nerve ending, every hair on her body buzzed with life. The world seemed like it was made for her: the evensong of the birds in the trees was the soundtrack to her second act. The faint, acrid scent of a distant bonfire signified the burning of her old, unhappy life.

Earlier, in his bed, the sheets half-ripped from the mattress, his handsome face on the pillow beside her, an old song playing on the radio, she had experienced a wave of pleasure unlike any she'd ever known.

'I want to run naked out into the street and dance across the lawn, let everyone see how happy I am,' she told him.

He laughed, tracing a line across her belly with his forefinger. 'Why don't you?'

'Because,' she said, kissing and pulling him on top of her again, 'I'm kind of busy right now. Doing . . . this.'

She knew it was crazy. She was forty-nine and he was nearly half that. Twenty years younger! When they met, when she realised he was flirting with her, she had thought he was just being a tease. But back home, a few hours later, she had surprised Trevor by suggesting sex for the first time in months. She had closed her eyes while Trevor made love to her in his mechanical way and thought about that face, those strong legs, the muscles in his arms. It was a delicious fantasy, that was all.

Except now it wasn't. Because he thought she was beautiful. He told her age meant nothing. In her most lucid moments, when they weren't in bed, when he wasn't looking at her in that way, she knew it wasn't serious. Just fun. An adventure. The most wonderful, thrilling adventure. And today it seemed like that adventure would last forever.

Didn't she deserve it?

Good luck comes in threes, everybody said, and her beautiful young lover was the third thing.

She'd been lost in these thoughts, keen to get home to her bath, reliving the afternoon with a glass of wine among scented bubbles, when she'd turned into the lane and seen the van ahead.

Fiona slowed down, suddenly aware that the birds had stopped singing. The sun was already setting, light bleeding from the sky, and the hedgerows crowding the lane had turned from bright green to dark grey. The lamp on her bicycle cast weak light on to the road ahead as she slowed down, straining to see through the dark windows of the van in front of her.

There wasn't enough room to cycle around it. She would have to get off and push.

Why would someone park across the middle of a country lane? Perhaps he had crashed, skidded to a halt and was stuck, needing help. The person inside could be injured or sick.

She took her phone out of her pocket, but she had no reception.

She was torn. She wanted to turn the bike around, get the hell out of there. But what if the driver *was* hurt? There was no sign of life from within. And it was getting darker by the minute.

She couldn't just leave without seeing if the driver needed her help. Somebody had helped her, hadn't they? The universe had bestowed gifts upon her. If she cycled away now, rejecting the chance to be a Good Samaritan, the karmic balance in the world might well shift, and all the good luck she'd experienced recently would drain away, sending her back to the darker days, the days *before*.

She wouldn't risk that.

Gently, she laid her bike on the ground and took a few steps closer to the van. 'Hello?' she called.

There was no response.

Breathing deeply, her strong new heart pounding inside her chest, Fiona strode up to the van and put her nose to the glass.

She jumped back as a man's face loomed up in the window.

He was shrouded by darkness, but she could see his teeth. He was smiling, an odd smile, the kind she'd seen on the faces of born-again Christians, people who knew they were bound for heaven. He didn't appear to be injured, or sick.

Confused, she backed away, and he opened the door, gesturing for her to come closer.

'Hello, Fiona,' he said.

She froze, peering closer. The pallid interior light inside the van had come on when the man opened the door, but his face was masked by shadows.

'Do I know you?' she asked.

With a sudden movement that startled her, he jumped down from the driver's seat and moved towards her. She took another step back.

'Don't be frightened,' he said, still smiling.

'What are you—?'

Her mouth stopped working when she saw what he was holding. She tried to run, but he was too fast, overtaking her and blocking her way. The van was behind her. There was nowhere to go.

'You really mustn't be afraid, Fiona,' he said, arms stretched wide like he wanted to give her a hug – except one hand gripped a shotgun with its barrel pointed to the darkening sky. 'I'm a friend.'

'I don't know you,' she said.

'Does anyone truly know anyone else?'

The oily smile returned. And as he came towards her, lowering the gun in front of him and pointing it right at her beautiful new heart, Fiona realised that the happiest day of her life would also be her last.

ω

They always struggle, right until the end, when the needle slips through their skin and the warmth fills them up, takes away all the pain and sends them off.

As Fiona slipped away I told her, just like I had told the others, 'The art of living well and the art of dying well are one.'

I like to think there was some comprehension – gratitude, even – in the final look she gave me.

The high that hit me afterwards, in the seconds that followed the final beat of Fiona's new heart, was better than anything a needle can deliver. The rush, the buzz, the sheer pulsing ecstasy of it. I touched her face as gently and tenderly as her lover had stroked her just a few hours before.

I kissed her cooling lips.

And I can still feel her looking up at me. Smiling.

It used to be so different, before I discovered the secret. The first time I took a life I was driven by rage. Hatred. I pummelled him with my fists, smashed his face until nose and lips and eyes were nothing but pulp, indistinguishable features on that dirty, ugly face. I snapped his neck with my bare hands, expecting to feel something, some satisfaction, for the fury inside me to abate, the howling to stop.

But it only made me feel worse. And then I was covered in his filthy blood, stinking of his rancid sweat. It clung to me, no matter how I scrubbed myself beneath the pathetic shower in our dark little bathroom.

The second time was the same. And so was the third.

But then I discovered the secret. I learned to do good.

I took one last look at Fiona's body, lying there in the spot that meant so much to her, and I wished we could enjoy the moment for a little while longer. But the world doesn't understand me. They think I'm doing wrong. So I must always be careful, and I was forced to say goodbye.

Still, I consoled myself as I slipped through the darkness, there would be others. And I already knew who was next.

I just wished I could tell him how lucky he was.

PART ONE

Chapter 1

'They've found another one, Ben.' Mrs Douglas gripped the fence that separated my cottage from hers, knuckles white, voice dropping to a stage whisper. 'Another body.'

It was Sunday morning and I was on my hands and knees on the front path, plucking weeds from between the cracks. The grass was getting long and a little cluster of tulips had appeared at the edge of the lawn. The previous evening, checking Ollie had put his laptop away and was getting ready for bed, I'd noticed it was still light outside. Summer was finally here.

But not for all of us, it seemed.

'Where?' I asked, getting to my feet and heading over to the fence.

My former English teacher, Mrs Douglas was in her late sixties now, stout and twinkly, a widow who insisted I call her Irene. I couldn't do it, though. She would always be Mrs Douglas to me.

'Much Wenlock. That's the third one.'

I took my phone out of my pocket. 'Have they announced that it's the same . . .' – I hesitated – 'killer?'

Mrs Douglas waved her hand dismissively at my phone. 'You won't find it on the news, not yet. I've got a friend in Wenlock – she called me, said the police are crawling all over the place.' She glanced around as if a news crew might swoop in at any moment and inter-rogate her. 'And *her* neighbour, who works at the Priory, said that woman was there. You know, that detective with the lovely red hair, the one that was on telly.'

I knew who she meant. I couldn't remember the detective's name either, but like everyone else in Shropshire, I had watched the appeals for information, the press conferences featuring the families of the victims: the parents of the first young woman, the fiancée of that guy who had been next. How long ago was that? I couldn't remember. I had too much going on in my own life.

'It makes me afraid to go out,' Mrs Douglas said, her voice drop-ping to a whisper again. 'Knowing there's someone *out there.*'

I couldn't help but follow her gaze down the hill towards the river and the iron bridge that gave this village its name. This sleepy place, so quiet and green, frozen in time. The place I had left when I was a teenager because nothing ever happened here.

Mrs Douglas might have read my mind. 'Things like this don't happen round here.'

'It's probably unrelated,' I said. 'An accident or something. I expect your friend got the wrong end of the stick.'

A man came out of my neighbour's front door. This was Kyle Vane, the lodger. He was a plumber in his early fifties who had been living with Mrs Douglas for years. His van was always parked outside our cot-tages; he hardly ever seemed to go out to work. 'Irene,' he said. 'You're going to miss the end of the match.'

I looked enquiringly at her. 'The tennis,' she explained. 'Like I'll be able to concentrate on it now.'

'Like I said, it's probably unrelated.'

She headed towards her front door. 'I hope you're right, Ben. I really hope you're right.'

I found Ollie in the kitchen, hunting through the cupboards.

'We've got nothing to eat.'

'There's toast. And cornflakes. Or what about a boiled egg?'

He pulled a face. 'Gross. What happened to that box of Frosties?'

I washed the green weed stains from my hands with my back to my eleven-year-old son. 'I threw them out. There was a thing in the paper about sugary cereals and kids' teeth. Do you know how many—?'

Ollie cut me off with a trademark groan of disgust.

His teeth weren't really my primary concern. Since moving here last year, while I had shed twelve or thirteen pounds thanks to the stress of it all, Ollie had piled on the weight. Megan always made sure he ate healthily, kept snacks out of reach, told him to eat an apple if he was hungry. I had been lax. I wanted to keep him happy, literally sweetening the ordeal of having to leave all his friends behind by giving in to his demands for Coco Pops, *pains au chocolat* and Haribo. I had ignored his evening raids on the larder. There was no delicate way of putting this – my son was getting fat.

And worse, he was unhappy.

'Let me scramble you some eggs,' I said. 'Or how about some fruit? I could pop to the little Tesco.'

'I'll leave it,' he muttered, and skulked off to his bedroom.

I sighed and made myself a cup of tea. I briefly thought about calling Megan, but then dismissed the idea. This was something I should deal with on my own. I wasn't going to give her any ammunition, any reason to say I wasn't looking after our son properly, not that she had shown any signs of wanting custody. Sure, she had protested half-heartedly when I told her I was taking him. But we both knew that an eleven-year-old boy would cramp her style. Make everything less convenient for her and . . .

A flash of what I'd seen that terrible day – white flesh against our blue sofa, her legs wrapped around him, the lip-biting pleasure on her face – invaded my head for the thousandth time. At the exact same moment, next door's German shepherd, Pixie, started barking, and I dropped my mug on the worktop. It wobbled on the edge, rocking from side to side, and I thought it was going to be okay, a little spilt tea, that was all. But as if prodded by a poltergeist, the mug tipped before I could snatch at it, fell to the floor and smashed into a hundred pieces, spraying me with hot liquid. And Pixie continued to bark.

The neighbours themselves, Ross and Shelley, were silent, probably still in bed. They'd woken me at around 2 a.m., singing along to an Ed Sheeran track. Then, when they finally shut up, I hadn't been able to get back to sleep because my nocturnal visitors, the anxiety brigade, had come knocking: Ollie, Mum, Megan, my bank manager. They crowded into my head and babbled at me, talking over one another, telling me all the things I needed to worry about. Now I was so tired I wanted to pluck my eyeballs out.

I mopped up the tea and swept up the broken china, then went to the front of the house, catching a glimpse of myself in the mirror in the hall. There were dark smudges beneath my eyes and my beard needed a trim. I hadn't intended to grow one – I just hadn't bothered to shave. I was thirty-six years old and the truckload of emotional shit I'd been hit by over the last year hadn't done my appearance any favours. Grey peppered my facial hair and the sides of my head – silvery threads that hadn't been there a year ago. I had an insomniac's eyes and my skin was as rough as tree bark.

A noise came from Ollie's room. Had he cried out? I ran up the stairs and opened his bedroom door. 'Ollie?'

He was sitting on his bed, his laptop closed beside him. He was staring at it like it had given him an electric shock.

'What's the matter?' I asked.

'Nothing.' He got off the bed and stared out of the window, where Pixie was still running about, barking her head off.

'Ollie, if something's happened you need to tell me.'

'Nothing's happened, all right? I just lost a build battle, that's all.'

A *Minecraft* thing. But I wasn't sure if he was telling the truth.

'Come on,' I said. 'Let's go and do something.'

'Fine. If we have to.'

My happy, playful son had turned into a teenager two years early.

He left the room and headed towards the stairs. I hung back for a moment, tempted to open his computer and take a peek. But then Ollie called me from downstairs and I decided I needed to believe him. He'd lost at a video game, that was all.

It was nothing to worry about.

ʊ

In the car, I said, 'Let's do some touristy things.'

'Not Victorian Town, please. I'm not a baby.'

Victorian Town was a nearby tourist attraction, a 'living museum' where actors strode around dressed as nineteenth-century ladies and gents and horses pulled carts through the streets. Ollie used to love it there. 'I know you're not a baby. Unfortunately, though, you're not old enough yet to buy your old man a pint.'

He rolled his eyes.

We drove to Ludlow, a pretty market town forty minutes' journey away. On the way, Ollie connected his iPod to the car stereo and played a selection of his favourite tracks: Drake, Tinie Tempah, some highly inappropriate song about doing pills in Ibiza. For at least a year, Ollie had been nagging me about getting a phone. All his friends had them, he'd argued. I'd bought him the iPod – which did everything an iPhone did except make calls – as a compromise, but he still wasn't happy. It was yet another way in which I treated him like an infant, apparently.

I took the scenic route along twisting narrow lanes. We got stuck behind a tractor for five minutes, then had to stop because there were sheep in the road.

'This place is so stupid,' Ollie said as we waited for the creatures to move.

'You miss London so much?'

He didn't respond, just stared at the sheep as the last of them trotted across the rocky ground, allowing us to continue. I lifted my hand in greeting as we passed a farmer with three border collies snaking around his calves. Ollie didn't need to answer. I knew how much he missed his old home, his friends, the school where he wasn't the new boy. I knew, too, how much he missed his mum.

In Ludlow, we parked behind the market and walked towards the castle. Victorian Town might have been too babyish, but Ollie was interested in history, or the ghastly parts of it anyway: the Black Death and medieval torture and people pouring boiling oil over each other. The fun stuff.

At the castle, I read an information sheet aloud: '"The murderous Mortimers . . ." They were involved in the gruesome death of Edward the Second. Hmm, I can't remember how he died. Can you?'

'They stuck a red-hot poker up his bum, Dad.'

I winced. 'Ouch. Thank God we're all more civilised now, eh?'

He had already strolled off and I realised he was heading for the tea room.

'I'm bored,' he said. 'Can we get a cake?'

I sighed. 'Okay, fine. A small one.'

But, of course, the portions were enormous. Sod it, I thought. If you can't beat 'em.

After filling our bellies, we left the castle and found ourselves back in town, exploring the side streets. When I'd moved into the cottage I'd found some leaflets that had presumably been left behind by the previous tenants, including some vouchers giving money off entry to a number of local tourist attractions. One of these attractions had caught my eye. It sounded intriguing. Remembering it now, I looked it up on my phone and found it was only a street away.

'Here it is,' I said a minute later. 'The Museum of Lost Things. Sound interesting?'

He shrugged.

'Great! Let's do it.'

We went inside what looked like a former house and found a middle-aged woman half-asleep behind a desk. She didn't appear to register our arrival. Behind her on the wall was a framed poster declaring this 'one of Britain's quirkiest museums'.

I approached the desk. 'What exactly is this place?' I asked, making the woman jump.

She had the waxy complexion of someone who doesn't go outside very often, but she recovered from her shock nicely and smiled with enthusiasm. 'Everything here was handed in to a lost property office and was never collected.'

'Really? That's cool, isn't it Ollie?'

He grunted.

'How did these items find their way here?'

'Magic.' The woman laughed. 'Seriously, we have arrangements with lots of places – train companies, airports, supermarkets, other tourist attractions . . . you name it. A lot of unclaimed stuff ends up at auction. We buy the items no one else wants.'

I paid our entrance fee and headed up the stairs ahead of Ollie.

The museum was arranged over three floors and was absolutely rammed full of *stuff*, cabinets and display cases containing a random collection of items: a toupee the colour of a ginger cat, a set of dentures, an intricately carved walking stick with a grinning skull for a handle. Beside each item was a little card detailing where and when it had been found: 'Birmingham, March 2011'; 'Falkirk, December 1996'. There was a set of military medals that had been found near Beachy Head, the famous suicide spot, in 1965.

Ollie drifted over to look at a collection of toys: old-fashioned robots, sad teddy bears that made me think of the lost characters from *Toy Story*, Furbies and Cabbage Patch Kids. Beside them sat a Victorian doll, a spiderweb of cracks across her porcelain face, with eyes that followed us across the room. I rubbed my arms, suddenly chilly.

Ollie sat down among a large collection of discarded comics and books, disinterestedly leafing through them. I continued the self-guided tour. There were some bizarre items: an artificial leg, a stuffed magpie that stared at me through dead eyes, a pink dildo that was apparently found in the toilet of a train bound for Plymouth in 1987.

I climbed to the dusty top floor and found myself in a room filled with objects of a more sentimental nature. A locket containing a photograph of a little girl. A cheap-looking engagement ring. A packet of photographs depicting a family seaside holiday. A baby's rattle. An urn that supposedly contained someone's ashes. As I contemplated the urn, a man entered the room. He was tall and slim, with sandy hair. His head was down so I didn't see his face, but from his clothes I guessed him to be in his late twenties. Oddly, he turned and left immediately after he saw me, acting like he'd intruded on something.

Overcome by a feeling of melancholy, I sat down on a wooden bench, surrounded by the detritus of other people's lives, of things that had been loved but never collected. These were all physical objects, most of which could be replaced. But I had lost so much over the previous months. My wife, my home, my job, my self-esteem. Soon, I would lose my mum, too. I had tried hard not to feel sorry for myself, but sitting there in the Museum of Lost Things, my eyes filled with tears and I had to clamp my teeth together and swallow several times.

'You all right, Dad?'

Ollie had appeared and was staring at me with concern. I knew he could see the tears shining in my eyes. I stood and ruffled his hair.

'Yes. Let's get out of here.' I cleared my throat. 'It's boring, isn't it?'

As we entered the stairwell, the hairs prickled on the nape of my neck. I was convinced someone was watching us. But when I turned around there was no one there. I half expected to see the doll with the cracked face dragging herself across the floor towards us, whispering '*Mama. Mama.*'

I shivered, then hurried down the steps and out into the sunshine.

Chapter 2

As soon as DI Imogen Evans heard where the body had been found, she *knew*. Bodies were not discovered in picturesque places like this. They were left in the kitchens and bedrooms where they'd been killed, dumped in rivers or buried in back gardens. She didn't need to know the cause of death. The state of the body didn't matter. The location told her what she feared.

Her first serial killer, the man the tabloids called the Shropshire Viper, had struck – a snake, fangs glistening with venom – for the third time.

Imogen looked around. It was beautiful here, no question. The grandest, most historic of the three sites so far. The entire area, surrounded by fields on all sides and easily accessible via a single narrow road, had been cordoned off, with the volunteers who'd found the body escorted from the premises for questioning. The press hadn't got wind of it yet, and so far no one had put anything on Twitter, thank God, though Imogen knew it wouldn't be long before the news broke.

'Do you know this place?' she asked DS Emma Stockwell as they walked through the cabin that acted as the reception area for Wenlock Priory, complete with a small shop. The shelves were filled with souvenirs: bronze sculptures of squirrels and hares, fancy jars of organic marmalade and chutney, elderflower wine that made her stomach flip as she remembered the bottle of red she'd got through on her own the previous evening.

Emma picked up a leaflet advertising English Heritage membership and flicked through it. 'Yeah, of course. I came here on a school trip. My dad brought us here once or twice, too, when we were kids.' She waved the leaflet. 'We were members. He used to drag us all over the place, visiting boring stately homes and castles.'

Emma, at twenty-nine, was a decade younger than Imogen, with ash-blonde hair pulled back into a ponytail. She wore a khaki windbreaker and jeans, the bottoms of which were splattered with mud. She'd been out walking her dog when Imogen had phoned her this morning, immediately after receiving the call herself.

'Sounds nice,' Imogen said, opening the door on to a path that led up to the Priory. 'My dad used to take me and my sister on tours, too – of the pubs of south London. "Wait here, girls. I'm just going to see a man about a horse." We always got a souvenir – a packet of crisps and Coke in a proper bottle, with a stripy straw.'

Emma smiled uncertainly. Imogen enjoyed the fact that the younger detective never knew if she was joking. On this occasion, she wasn't. Recalling the memory sent Imogen hurtling back in time: the warm interior of her dad's Ford Escort, the taste of salt-and-vinegar crisps, Duran Duran on the car radio, the smell of beer on her dad's breath when he came back, a copy of the *Racing Post* rolled up in his fist. Happy days.

They headed up the path. It was warm, the bright sunshine hurting her eyes. She pushed her auburn hair away from her collar. 'Expert that you are, tell me what you know about Wenlock Priory.'

'Testing me, are you?' Emma said, but her eyes shone like a schoolchild being quizzed about her favourite subject. 'It was a monastery, dating from the twelfth century, I think.' She checked the leaflet. 'Yeah. The twelfth. There's an abbey here, too, which is privately owned and still inhabited, but the Priory is looked after by English Heritage. The town, Much Wenlock, was built up around this place.' She smiled. 'There's a well in the town that is supposed to help women find a suitor.'

'Really? Maybe I'll give it a visit later. *My* well's about to dry up.'

She enjoyed Emma's look of shock.

They neared the end of the path and the Priory came into view. The ragged-edged stone walls of what had once been a monastery and a church stood facing each other across an immaculate lawn. The ruins were about fifty feet high, maybe taller. Arches stretched between some of the buildings, and beyond them stood the abbey, which looked like something from a medieval fairy tale. She could imagine Rapunzel being kept at the top of that tower. It was still inhabited, Emma had said. Imogen tried to imagine what it would be like to live there, contrasting it with her poky flat in Shrewsbury.

Between the ruins were rows of clipped topiary, smooth and green, cut into animal shapes: a mole, a squirrel, a bear. She was sure that the bear was looking at her, and she could imagine it coming to life, springing from its leafy platform, mouth opening, sightless eyes blazing. She shivered. She wouldn't want to come here after dark.

'Why?' Imogen asked. 'Why do it here?'

She didn't wait for an answer from Emma. She had spotted Gareth Davies, the crime scene manager, waiting for her by the edge of the lawn. They made eye contact and Gareth, a slightly built Welshman, held up a pair of white protective suits.

'I think these are your size,' he said as they approached.

'Not my colour, though.'

Imogen liked Gareth. When they'd first met and she'd opened her mouth to reveal a south London accent, the disappointment on his face had been comical. With her name, he'd counted on a Welsh lass.

The two detectives took off their coats and pulled on the suits, as well as gloves and paper shoes, while Gareth entered their names in the log.

'The pathologist is on her way,' Gareth said.

'Karen Lamb?'

He nodded. 'She'll be about half an hour.'

'Who was the first officer?' Emma asked.

Gareth gestured towards a man in his early thirties standing by one of the creepy topiary animals, just beyond the tape that cordoned off the protected inner area. He wore the yellow jacket of a PCSO – a community support officer. This area only had five members of staff, two of whom were PCSOs. They didn't even have a station. Like many of the stations across Shropshire, West Mercia Police had closed it to save money. 'His name's Pete Sullivan,' Gareth said.

Imogen approached the PCSO, wondering if he was always so pale. 'First dead body?' she asked.

The PCSO ran a hand over his bald head. 'Second. The other one was a motorcyclist who lost an argument with a transit van. Nothing like this, though.' His eyes widened and Imogen realised he'd recognised her. The disadvantage of being on TV. 'You think this is his work? The Viper?' he said.

She sighed, irritated that even police staff were using that bloody nickname. 'We don't know yet, Pete. Tell me what happened. Who found the body?'

'One of the volunteers here – a local woman called Moira. She called Bridgnorth and they asked me to come and take a look. I got here at nine fifty, twenty minutes after Moira found her.'

'I'll talk to her, but I take it Moira didn't see anyone near the scene?'

'No. Nothing.'

'Any sign that the scene had been disturbed? By animals, for example?'

Pete shook his head. 'I was careful not to touch the body. I mean, it was obvious she was dead – beyond resuscitation. Her eyes were open, gazing at the sky.'

'Okay.' Imogen patted his shoulder. 'I might need to talk to you again later.'

But he didn't move away.

'Is there something else?' Imogen asked.

'No. I mean, yes. It's just . . . she looked like she was smiling. Like she died happy.'

Imogen stared at him for a moment, then headed back to Gareth and Emma. 'All right,' she said, putting the hood of her suit up over her auburn hair. 'Let's see the body.'

ω

Even though it was a secluded spot and rain seemed unlikely, a tent had been erected over the corpse. Treading carefully on the stepping plates put down to preserve any important evidence, Imogen entered the tent, with Emma just behind her.

The woman was lying on her back, arms by her sides, legs together, as if she were already in her coffin. As Pete had said, her eyes gazed sightlessly at the canvas overhead.

Scene of Crime Officers moved around the victim, taking pictures.

Imogen crouched beside the body. As with the others, there was no blood, no marks on the throat, no obvious signs of violence. The woman was in her late forties or early fifties, white, with mid-length brown hair that looked like it had been recently highlighted. Average weight, about five foot seven. Lightly made up, though the mascara around her eyes had smeared. She was a good-looking woman, well-groomed and wearing casual but expensive clothes: a pair of designer jeans and a light cashmere sweater. She wore white pumps on her feet. And Pete was right: she appeared to be smiling, her lips curled upwards at each corner.

Just like the others.

She wished she could roll up the woman's sleeve to check for what she was sure would be there, but she didn't want to risk incurring the wrath of Karen Lamb or do anything that would jeopardise this investigation.

She got to her feet, taking another look at the body and the grass around her.

'No drag marks,' she said. 'She was carried here. And no sign of a syringe or any other drugs paraphernalia. Just like the others.'

She left the tent, Emma at her heels, and turned slowly in a circle, scanning the perimeter. To the west and north, open countryside stretched as far as the eye could see. To the east, Imogen could see the town, and to the south, the streets where most of Much Wenlock's inhabitants lived, the houses a mix of new and old. Could the killer live there, within spitting distance of this place? It seemed unlikely. The three victims had been found at spots spread out across the county. There was nothing to suggest he was leaving them in his own backyard.

'He can't have carried her too far, not unless he's incredibly strong,' Imogen said. 'He must have parked somewhere nearby before entering the site.'

She closed her eyes and tried to picture it: the man she'd spent so many hours thinking about over the past few months, carrying this woman – like a groom carrying his bride over the threshold? Or over his shoulder? So far, they hadn't found signs of entry at any of the three scenes. It was as if he'd swooped down from the sky and placed his victims gently on the ground before taking off again.

Her phone rang. She took the call, then turned back to Emma.

'That was the station. A guy in Ludlow's reported his wife missing. Five seven, brown hair with blonde highlights. He described her jewellery, too. It matches. Her name's Fiona Redbridge.'

She stepped back through the opening of the tent, hoping Karen would get here quickly so they could at least close the poor woman's eyes. Once more, she crouched beside the body, wishing again that she could roll up the sleeve of that blouse and check for the needle mark she was certain would be there.

Rising and leaving the tent, Imogen stopped as a movement in the middle distance caught her eye. Someone was standing in the field, just beyond the perimeter of the Priory. A man, dressed in black, too far away for her to make out his features. When she took a few steps towards him, he turned and began hurriedly walking away. Imogen approached one of the younger officers with orders to pursue him, but before she'd even finished speaking the man had vanished, as if he'd melted into thin air.

Chapter 3

The atmosphere in the village had changed over the weekend. Nothing one could point to or capture in a photograph, but I could sense it as I headed up Tontine Hill towards the high street, past shops and cafes and B & Bs. To my right, the river was swollen with overnight rainfall. A family of ducks bobbed past. A fat rabbit lolloped up the far bank. Everything was the same.

Everything was different.

This time of year, Ironbridge was experiencing the annual influx of tourists, though numbers were down this year, as they were across the whole county. Serial killers: bad for business. But this was a World Heritage Site, the birthplace of the Industrial Revolution, and under normal circumstances it would fill from Easter until the end of summer. Coachloads of schoolkids would come to stand on the famous bridge, teachers dragging them around Victorian Town or one of the numerous museums that fuelled the local economy. All of this was why I had been so keen to leave here. It felt, to my teenage self, like a dead place, its face turned so keenly towards the past that the present – let alone the future – barely existed.

A cluster of residents stood outside the newsagent's, each clutching a newspaper, the face of the woman who'd been discovered in Much Wenlock on the front page. One of the group, Dave Pilkington – the mechanic who'd recently serviced my car – nodded at me as I approached.

The others simply lifted their eyes to regard me and I felt a tingle of paranoia, as if they suspected me. It didn't matter that I'd grown up here. I'd been gone for over twenty years. I was a born-again stranger, tainted by my years in the big city. There weren't many outsiders living in the village. If the murders hadn't started months before I'd come back, there'd probably be a pitchfork-wielding mob outside my home right now.

Dave held up the newspaper. 'Terrible business.'

'Terrible,' I echoed as I passed.

I entered Effy's coffee shop and sat down. All around me, people sat in pairs, as if it were too dangerous to go out alone, talking – I was certain – of just one topic. Mrs Douglas had been right about the murder: a couple of hours after I spoke to her, while I was wandering around that creepy museum, the police announced they believed it to be the third in a series.

Series. The word caused the temperature in these sleepy streets, along the valleys and across the fields full of sheep, to drop by several degrees. Shropshire had its own serial killer.

I imagined they'd all be talking about it at Ollie's school, where I'd dropped him off an hour earlier. The atmosphere between us was frosty since I'd refused to let him have a second helping of dessert the night before. He had a way of making me feel like the meanest dad on Earth, but I was shocked by his overreaction, the sulk that lasted the rest of the evening. Then, this morning, he'd told me he felt sick, that he was too ill to go to school.

Sure he was malingering, I'd made him go in, even after he'd switched his reason from sickness to fear. 'I'm scared, Dad,' he'd said. 'What if the murderer comes after me?'

I was worried about him, even more than usual. Perhaps he was simply missing his mum and his old friends. There was a chance, I guessed, that he was undergoing some kind of delayed PTSD after the breakup of his parents and the huge disruption to his life. My mother was always telling me that kids were resilient, 'made of rubber', but my son had clearly lost his bounce. Though it might have been best, I was reluctant to take him to see the doctor or a therapist because I was sure what he really needed was time. Time and love.

ᚋ

I was born in a two-up two-down on the outskirts of the village and attended the school that Ollie went to now. My childhood was a happy, bucolic one: lots of building camps in the woods, playing Pooh Sticks over the river. I was an only child, a surprise who came along when my parents were in their late thirties. They were so settled in their way of doing things, so wedded to their careers (her, a lecturer; him, a bank manager) that I was expected to fit in with their adult lives. I was left to my own devices much of the time. Back in the seventies and early eighties, the world felt safer. My friends and I took our bikes and skateboards out without supervision. We used to ride for miles, only returning to our houses when it got dark. I couldn't imagine letting Ollie do the same.

When my teenage hormones kicked in and the appeal of Pooh Sticks waned, I grew to hate this place. It was *boring*. I spent a lot of time in my room playing on my ZX Spectrum. Occasionally, someone would find a porn mag in the woods, which would provide an afternoon of entertainment. Someone's older brother had a motorbike that he'd allow us to ride around the fields. The same older brother would sometimes procure cans of strong lager for us to drink. In the summer, we'd hang around the museums hoping to spot pretty teenage girls whose parents had dragged them here. I met my first 'girlfriend' that way: a freckled, red-haired girl called Sonia who was on holiday. She was from London and knew all about kissing. She left me with sore lips and the promise she would write.

Perhaps it was Sonia I was thinking about when I applied to colleges in London, expecting it to be a city full of girls who knew all about kissing, and more. I will never forget my first night in the city when I was eighteen, taking a bus to Leicester Square and then wandering among the crowds and the lights, elated, convinced this place was meant to be my home. And after I graduated, I stayed, got a job writing copy for a travel agency – something that would pay the rent while I wrote my great novel.

Time was a fast car. I met Megan, moved in with her, got married, had Ollie. I was happy. We weren't rich, far from it. But we had bought a flat at the right time, just before property prices went gaga. We both had decent jobs, and I fully intended to dust off that novel one day. Megan and I loved each other and our little boy. Life was unremarkable but good.

And then.

And then it all went wrong.

After that, I brought Ollie back with me to Ironbridge. It was September, the beginning of the new school term. I rented the cottage from Frank Dodd, an old friend of the family. He also owned the place next door, where the noisy Ross and Shelley lived, along with the dreaded Pixie. After the emotional napalming I'd suffered during the previous six months in London – all the fighting and desperation, the shattering of dreams – coming back had felt like a necessary retreat. I needed to recuperate, to heal. I needed mental and physical space, away from Megan and our flat and the friends who had divided into two camps, mine and hers. Home seemed the obvious place, the memories of my pre-teen years shoving aside the less happy ones. It would, I'd believed, be good for Ollie. And there was a practical reason for coming here, too: my mum was sick. Dad had died a decade ago and I was her only child. She needed me.

I'd underestimated how hard it would be. Perhaps I'd forgotten how bleak this area was in winter, when the tourists stayed away and everyone hunkered down against the cold and the relentless rain. Out here in the countryside, the elements were cruel and the nights were properly dark. And, apart from look after my son, there was nothing to do except watch TV and chew over all the stuff I wanted to forget.

On the darkest nights I lay in bed unable to sleep, my night-time visitors babbling, detailing to me all of the ways I'd failed. All the main players in my life talking to me like Scrooge's ghosts. Megan told me

I hadn't made her happy, that I'd treated her like a picture on the wall that you walk past every day without noticing. Michael made her feel like a real woman. Mrs Douglas dropped by to remind me I'd never written that great novel. My son kept it short: *Dad, you're such a loser.* And Mum shuffled towards me, pale and judgemental, wagging a bony finger. *You're back where you began,* she scolded. *You've failed at life, Ben. Failed.*

ʍ

I flipped open my laptop and logged on to my bank account, checking my balance through my fingers. It was even worse than I'd feared. My savings were running out. I really shouldn't be here, drinking coffee that wasn't out of a jar, but the thought of being alone at home was too grim.

I hadn't realised how hard it would be as a freelance. I'd exhausted all my old contacts now – they'd given me a few scraps of work, but everyone was using in-house copywriters. I tried to calculate how long I could keep going without any work. I had enough for two more months' rent. I couldn't ask my mum for help because all of her savings were going towards the cost of the nursing home.

I had trawled all the job sites – there was nothing available around here for someone with my experience.

I clenched my fists. If Megan would agree to sell the flat . . . My half of the equity would keep me going for a year at least. But she was dragging her heels, saying she needed to find somewhere else to live first. The real reason was that she loved the flat and didn't want to move. I'd asked her to buy me out, but she was pleading poverty, which was ridiculous. Megan had a decent job as a financial adviser, and *he* was loaded. I'd hoped to sort the whole thing out amicably, without the huge costs of lawyers – especially as Megan could afford a much better one than me – but it looked like I was going to have to take her to court. For fuck's sake: why couldn't she be reasonable?

I logged out of the bank site, anger percolating in my veins. That famous thin line between love and hate . . . There was self-loathing mixed up in there, too. I'd taken her for granted. I'd been uncommunicative, wrapped up in my own early midlife crisis, the realisation I was halfway through my life and hadn't achieved a fraction of my dreams. If only I'd realised how lucky I was, if I hadn't been so distracted.

Needing to read about someone who was worse off than me, I pulled the newspaper towards me and turned to the story about the latest murder.

The victim's name was Fiona Redbridge. She was forty-nine years old and lived – *had* lived – in Ludlow, one of the county's larger towns, where she worked as an antiques dealer. There was a photo of her shop on page three, and one of her grinning, posing with a Roman cup that, according to the caption, she had recently sold at auction for ten thousand pounds. There were the usual quotes from neighbours, saying what a lovely woman she'd been: 'down to earth', 'hard-working', 'a pillar of the community'.

My laptop pinged.

It was an email from somebody called Robert Friend with the subject line 'Availability?'.

> Dear Mr Hofland – I manage the marketing team of an Internet start-up in Telford and we are looking for someone to write promotional copy for us. I saw your profile on LinkedIn and as you're local I thought it might be worth a chat . . .

I couldn't believe it. It was an email that had been sent by the gods, answering my prayers at exactly the right moment.

I replied straight away, giving Robert Friend my phone number and telling him that I did have some availability.

Then I sat back. Maybe, just maybe, this could be the start of something. The moment my luck finally turned.

Chapter 4

Imogen left her car outside the hospital and headed through the car park towards the wing of the building where the mortuary was based. As she walked, she noticed a couple of people do a double take when they saw her. It was the hair – it made her too recognisable.

She had been in Shrewsbury for just over a year and had been thrown into this investigation almost as soon as she'd arrived. On the strength of her experience working on one of the Metropolitan Police's murder investigation teams she'd been made senior investigating officer, which had upset the egos of a few of the Shropshire-born-and-bred members of Major Investigations. But the chief inspector, Brian Greene, had chosen her – a non-Salopian – and the rest of the team had to deal with it. However, that was back when they thought this was an isolated murder, that it would be quick and easy to clear up. Imogen wasn't sure if she was being paranoid, but she suspected Greene was beginning to regret his decision.

The first victim was found on 15 February 2015. Her name was Danni Taylor, a twenty-one-year-old receptionist at a veterinary clinic in Craven Arms. At first, the police thought it was a drug overdose, an accident or suicide. But there was no syringe at the scene, and Danni had no history of taking any drugs, let alone the hard stuff. The lack of syringe led them to two possibilities: she had injected herself somewhere else and somebody had moved her body. Or murder.

After talking to Danni's friends and family, Imogen became convinced it was the latter. At first, she thought her death might be related to Valentine's Day in some way: an affair that had gone horribly wrong; unrequited obsession. The murder method didn't fit neatly with that, though, and there was no sign that the motive was sexual in any way. No assault. No semen.

Danni had recently moved in with her boyfriend, a twenty-three-year-old builder called Rob, which made him the initial suspect. The poor guy had undergone hours of questioning, having just learned that the girlfriend he adored was dead. But then a number of witnesses and a CCTV camera confirmed his alibi.

By November, Imogen had concluded they were never going to find Danni's killer. It pained her that her first big case with her new force remained unclosed – back in the Met, her closure rate was right up there with the best.

And then they found another body.

The second victim's name was Nathan Scott. He was twenty-eight, a resident of Bridgnorth who worked at the Jaguar factory in south Staffordshire. He was a good-looking guy, athletic and tall, described by everyone who knew him as the life and soul of the party, a good man who always stood his round at the pub, who went to his parents' place every Sunday for roast dinner.

He was engaged to a hairdresser called Melissa, whose bleached-blonde hair and long legs had led to her being splashed all over the papers after Nathan had been found.

Like Danni Taylor and, now, Fiona Redbridge, Nathan had been found flat on his back, staring at the sky, though in his case the sky was criss-crossed by the bare branches of winter trees. Unlike Danni, who had escaped the attention of the local fauna, rats had gnawed at Nathan's body in the twenty-four hours it took a dog walker to find him.

At first, there was little, besides their postures and the strange humourless smiles frozen on their faces, to suggest that there was any connection between this death and the murder of the young woman on Valentine's Day, until they'd found the hole in his arm. Again, there was no syringe at the scene. Nathan had no history of drug use. He was an athlete, clean living; according to his friends, he'd never even smoked a cigarette. And here he was, his body filled with poison, staring sightlessly into the low winter sun.

ϖ

She entered the mortuary, pushing through the double doors to find Karen Lamb waiting for her.

'You're late,' Karen said.

'No I'm not.'

Imogen figured the best way to deal with Karen, who had less charm than some of the murderers Imogen had put away, was to be assertive. Don't back down because, if you did, the pathologist would push you to the ground and walk all over you.

Soon after they'd met, Imogen had persuaded Karen to go out for a drink. Watching the other woman sip at a small glass of wine, pulling a face like it was pure lemon juice, Imogen had asked Karen why she'd chosen to be a pathologist.

'I don't get on very well with people,' she'd replied. 'Not ones who are still breathing, anyway.' Another wincing sip of wine. 'And the dead rarely disappoint me.'

She had to be taking the piss, surely?

'You're wasting your time,' Emma had said when Imogen relayed this encounter, 'if you think you're going to get her to show her human side.'

Like pretty much everyone else at Shrewsbury nick, Emma was frightened of Karen. It was well known at the station that if you got on the wrong side of her, Karen would simply refuse to talk to you. They called this 'the silence of the Lamb'.

'How's it going?' Imogen asked as she followed Karen, who was tall and stick-thin with curly, greying hair. Imogen guessed she was in her late forties.

'I've completed the post-mortem.'

'I meant, how are you? Anything exciting happening in your life? Any new TV shows you've been bingeing on? Love life looking up?'

Karen turned and stared at her. 'I assume you want to see the body?'

'That would be lovely.'

Five minutes later she stood beside Fiona Redbridge, her body covered by a sheet up to her shoulders. Mercifully, her eyes were now closed. The smile had subsided, too, leaving her with the neutral expression of the dead.

'I assume this is what you're interested in,' Karen said, indicating the woman's left arm, which she lifted from beneath the sheet, holding it so its underside was turned upwards. Imogen moved around the gurney and leaned close to get a proper look.

There it was, just above the crook of her elbow. A tiny mark, surrounded by bruising. The hole into which the poison that'd killed her had flowed.

'Same as before?' she asked.

Karen lowered the arm and tucked it beneath the sheet. 'I'm waiting for toxicology reports, but yes, initial signs are that she was injected with a lethal dose of morphine.'

Imogen nodded.

'As I said, I haven't got the blood tests back yet – though I've asked for them to be fast-tracked – so I can't tell you if the dosage is exactly the same, but the method of administering the drug, directly via a syringe rather than through an IV drip, is the same.'

'Nothing new or different?'

Karen pursed her lips. 'No. There are no other injuries, no sign that she was involved in a struggle. Other than the small puncture wound on her inner arm, there are no visible signs of violence at all.'

'Apart from the fact that she's dead.'

'Quite.'

'What about the position of her lips?' Imogen asked. 'The others were the same. I can't believe they all died with a smile on their face.'

Karen sighed. 'Didn't we talk about this before? Rigor mortis starts to set in two hours after death. It affects the eyelids, jaw and neck first, then spreads to the facial muscles. My guess is that the murderer sat with each victim for two or three hours and held their lips in place until rigor took over.'

Imogen stared at Fiona's body. Karen was right. They had talked about this before. But as with any puzzle, Imogen needed to discuss it, hoping to shake loose the answer.

'But why would he do that?' she asked.

The pathologist shrugged.

It was Imogen's turn to sigh. 'What else can you tell me?'

Karen consulted her notes. 'She was healthy – remarkably fit for her age. She was sexually active at some point in the twenty-four hours before she died. There was a small amount of semen inside her vagina, but no sign of sexual violence.'

They would need to talk to her husband, take a DNA sample to ensure the semen was his. Imogen almost crossed her fingers. If the semen belonged to another man, that could be the break they needed. Or another dead end. The chances were, though, that this was just proof that Fiona had still been having sex with her spouse.

'Let me show you something,' Karen said. She peeled the sheet back, exposing Fiona's chest. Imogen saw it immediately – a prominent vertical scar that ran from Fiona's sternum and down between her breasts, ending a few inches above her belly button.

'She'd had heart surgery?'

'I checked her medical records. She had a heart transplant eighteen months ago. She was fully recovered.' The pathologist shook her head. 'Such a waste of a good heart.'

Imogen watched her replace the sheet. 'So, there's nothing under her fingernails, no foreign DNA anywhere?'

'Apart from the semen, no.'

'What about meals? When did she last eat?'

'Four to five hours before she died. A chicken salad.'

Looked like Fiona Redbridge had been taking care of her new heart.

'Are we done now?' Karen asked. 'I have other clients, you know.'

Imogen did a double take. 'Is that what you call the cadavers? Your clients?'

'Oh, yes. And my customer service is second to none.'

Imogen stared at her, waiting for the smile. She *had* to be taking the piss. But no smile came.

'Do me a favour,' Imogen said, as Karen escorted her out. 'If my body ever ends up in here, God forbid, please don't refer to me as your client. In fact, I'm going to put it in my will. I don't want you anywhere near my body.'

She shuddered as the pathologist looked her up and down like she was imagining her on the slab.

'You'd be in excellent hands, Detective,' she said and shut the door.

ω

It was only a short journey back to the station. Imogen drove in silence, thinking about what the pathologist had told her.

Morphine. As soon as they'd discovered how the first victim, Danni Taylor, had died, Imogen and her team had met with the forensic toxicologist, a man named Kanwar Singh, who gave them a brief chemistry/biology lesson.

'Morphine has a direct effect on the central nervous system,' Singh had told them. 'To put it simply, it blocks the signals between one's nerves and the brain, so pain doesn't get through, or is greatly dulled, at any rate. As well as blocking pain, it can make the subject feel euphoric. It usually causes drowsiness, too, though less so as you build tolerance.'

'Isn't it basically heroin by another name?' Emma had asked.

Singh had smiled at her. 'Apart from one acetyl molecule. They are very similar, but heroin is stronger and crosses the blood–brain barrier faster. The effects are the same, though, ultimately.'

In her time in the Met, Imogen had witnessed numerous deaths by heroin overdose and dealt with many addicts whose dependence on the drug had led them to steal or sell themselves, or even kill. But she'd never come across a single person who'd died from morphine. It was extremely rare as a street drug.

'How much morphine was in Danni's system?' Imogen had asked.

'Two hundred and fifty milligrams. The lethal dose is generally two hundred, especially in those who have never used an opiate stronger than codeine before. From analysing her hair, we were able to get a picture of Ms Taylor's drug history. She was opioid naïve – in other words, she'd never taken heroin or morphine before – so her tolerance levels were low. I would say the person who injected Ms Taylor certainly meant her to die.'

No shit, Imogen had thought.

'How do you know it was morphine rather than heroin?' she'd asked.

'Because of the absence of 6-MAM. It's a metabolite that's unique to heroin.' He'd paused. 'If it's any consolation, and I imagine it would be to the victim's family, she wouldn't have experienced any pain. Quite the opposite, in fact.'

Now, driving back to the station, Imogen continued to puzzle over this. Heroin was easy to get hold of, but morphine was a carefully con-trolled substance, especially since Harold Shipman had employed it to become the UK's most prolific serial killer in the nineties. Where had the killer got hold of it?

Follow the morphine. That's what she had to do. The problem was, she had no idea where to start. There had been no reports of morphine being stolen anywhere in the local area during the last year. Could they really be looking for a doctor?

Imogen went into the Incident Room. Fiona's photo had been pinned up alongside those of the first two victims, Danni and Nathan. There was something in the lives of the three victims, some pattern, that would reveal why the killer had targeted them. Imogen was certain of it.

It couldn't be random. The murder method. The places the bodies were left. The smiles. That was important enough to the killer for him to remain with the body for two or three hours before he dumped it. She didn't believe their serial killer was trying to send a coded message to the police, or create some grand piece of morbid art. But the morphine, the sites where the bodies were left – they meant something to the murderer. She just had to figure out what.

Chapter 5

The kid comes out of the takeaway clutching a paper bag in his podgy fist and sits down on a low brick wall. The smell of hot chips and cheap meat wafts into the alleyway where I crouch in the shadows, half concealed by a black bin. I'm only a few feet behind him, but he's oblivious.

You'd think a kid who grew up in London would be more streetwise. More alert to danger.

He stops and wrestles with the little sachet of ketchup, his hands slippery with grease, squirting the red liquid into the bag before stuffing a chip in his mouth. He takes a bite of what I can now see is a sausage and washes it down with Coke before wiping his palm across the front of his school uniform. He has reddish-brown hair that needs a cut. His cheeks are pink and plump and his eyes are blue and sad.

His name is Oliver, but his dad calls him Ollie.

He's cramming the chips in faster now. Comfort eating – it's obvious. Scratching the itch his pain and anxiety have caused him. A tingle spreads through me, fluttering in my belly and warming my groin. Poor little Ollie is in pain, and I don't think he deserves to be. I think he's a good boy.

And it doesn't take me long to figure out why he's hurting.

There are some other kids, two girls and three boys, around Oliver's age, waiting at the nearby bus stop. Oliver eyes them warily as he eats. They seem too absorbed by one another's company – chucking crisps at each other, hunching over a phone and exclaiming loudly over what is probably a porn video – to notice him. But Ollie has that look, like he's prey, a lamb trembling in a world full of wolves. I wonder if one of these kids is the bully he so fears. It seems unlikely. Oliver wouldn't sit this close. But it's obvious he is a little afraid of them.

He swallows another mouthful of Coke, stuffs another chip into his mouth. I wonder if I was ever like him, back in my previous life, before I found happiness. I recall being hungry, all right. I remember it gnawing at my belly – proper hunger that hurt, that made me weak and desperate. I was never fat like Ollie, though. I was scrawny, ribs sticking out like a starving dog.

Poor Oliver. As hungry as a seagull, shovelling greasy potato into a hole that no amount of food can fill.

He's forgotten what it feels like to be happy.

ω

Nathan Scott was like that when I first encountered him. More than twice Ollie's age, of course, and he was fit and lean, not a blubbery wreck like the boy before me. But behind his blue eyes, I could see it. The disappointment of the perpetual loser; the guy who always comes second.

Being fit and strong – and filled with confidence and inner strength, too, by the time I was almost finished with him – Nathan was the most challenging of my lucky ones. I knew how risky it would be; there was a chance he would hurt me, or get away and expose me. I had to be clever.

He was a creature of habit, so I knew which route he would take that evening. I waited in the van, parked down a side road, and when I knew he was close, I swerved into his path, sending him skidding to a halt, his bike tipping over. He landed on the grass at the side of the road. I was there in an instant, and when he looked up at me, he must have thought I was coming to help, because he smiled. He was dazed, though, momentarily sluggish, and I injected him right there and then, sticking the needle in his arm, just enough to knock him out, send him away on a cloud of bliss. He practically floated into the back of the van.

Later, I was disappointed when he cried, after he realised what was going to happen, that this was the end. He kept banging on about his girl-friend. Melissa, Melissa. He wouldn't shut up about her. In the end I had to threaten him: if he didn't shut his mouth I would go to her next and hurt her. I told him exactly what I would do to those lovely little tits of hers. I showed him my sharpest knife, made him imagine me cutting his beloved wide open, throat to pussy. It worked a treat. He stopped snivelling, but he was shaking hard when I pushed the needle in a second time, giving him the fatal dose. It was fucking irritating and I didn't experience anything near the same high I felt with Danni. Only when he was dead, as the muscles stiffened in his face, did he look right.

Nathan, at the end of the day, was a disappointment.

I'm not going to make a mistake like that again.

ω

Ollie finishes his chips as his bus comes lumbering around the corner, approaching the stop. He'll need to walk past the mouth of my alley to board it, and he'll be alone as he does so, hugging the walls of the buildings, away from the other kids.

I place the bait, setting the brand-new iPhone on the ground at the entrance to the alley, then I retreat farther and conceal myself behind the enormous bin that reeks of rancid frying oil. I've turned the volume on the iPhone up full and disabled the passcode so Ollie won't need a PIN to open it.

I peer over the bin with my own phone, finger poised over the 'Dial' button, which I press the instant Ollie appears. The familiar ringtone fills the air.

Ollie stops, looking around. I see him approach the phone, look around again, confused, then bend to pick it up and answer.

'Hello?' he says in a tentative voice.

I end the call.

He stands there for a moment. The bus is at the stop now. Most of the other kids have got on.

Ollie shoves the iPhone into his bag and hurries to board the bus. I smile. Just like the rabbits I used to trap when I was younger. He couldn't resist.

Chapter 6

Church Stretton was a pretty town, nestled in a valley at the heart of the Long Mynd, part of the Shropshire hills, a designated Area of Outstanding Beauty. As she and Emma drove through the town towards the site where Nathan Scott was found, Imogen couldn't help but admire the green hills that reared up on all sides. But she would've hated to live here. Shrewsbury, she could just about cope with. But God, how she missed seeing faces that weren't white, hearing languages other than her own. How she longed for the crackling, multi-cultural energy of London, the bustle and stink, the anonymity, the *life*. Born and raised in the city, she still found it hard to sleep without constant noise outside her window, so she'd taken to keeping the TV on at night because the silence made her ears whistle.

'Be able to have the top down soon,' Emma said.

'Imagine the headlines. "Lady Cop Drives Topless Through Shrewsbury".'

Imogen's car was a silver vintage Mercedes-Benz SL Pagoda that she'd picked up miraculously cheap at auction. She could still picture the faces of her new colleagues when she'd arrived at work on her first day here, especially the men. A few of them had drifted over to stroke it. She knew that driving around in a vintage soft-top projected an image – that she was a show-off, extravagant, a good-time girl – that didn't reflect who she really was. She'd thought many times about trading it in for something sensible: a VW Golf or a Ford Focus. She could be like the people round here and get a Land Rover. But she loved her Pagoda. Owning it, driving it, made her ridiculously happy. And if people wanted to view her a certain way because of the motor she owned, well, screw them.

They drove to the western outskirts of town and parked in a housing estate on the edge of the countryside. Thankfully, the drizzle had abated, temporarily at least, but the ground was squelchy underfoot as they headed uphill through the trees. After a few minutes, they reached a dirt track that led into a thick copse.

Entering the copse was like stepping into a world of twilight. It was so quiet here – no birdsong, no human noise apart from a tinny buzz in the distance: a plane or distant tractor. Gnats hovered above the churned-up path. A thread of crime tape was still attached to a tree, trailing in the mud, even though months had passed since they'd finished with this place. Imogen grabbed it and tugged it free, scrunching it up and shoving it into her coat pocket.

She stared at the muddy ground as if she could still see the imprint of his body. Nathan had been dressed in mountain biking gear: a black and green cycling jersey and full-length Lycra shorts. Everything except the helmet, which was missing. His girlfriend, Melissa, told the police he'd been for a bike ride but hadn't come home. The bike, an expensive model that was Nathan's pride and joy, hadn't been found, and there were no tyre tracks to suggest that he'd ridden this way. According to Melissa, he'd been planning to cycle along the road from Bridgnorth to Wolverhampton and back, thirteen miles each way.

Did somebody intercept him on that route? Did he change his plan? Or had he been lying to Melissa?

Whatever the answer to that, they had quickly established a connection between Nathan and this place. The Long Mynd was a popular venue for mountain bike competitions, and Nathan had taken part in a number of events here.

Had the murderer known that? Had he watched Nathan take part in a trial here?

She found herself asking this out loud.

'Maybe that's the answer,' Emma said. 'What if he left their bodies in the place where he first encountered them? He spotted Fiona Redbridge at Wenlock Priory . . .'

'And saw Danni in a field in the middle of nowhere?'

'I don't know. It's possible. Isn't it?'

Danni Taylor was found on farmland where sheep grazed and barley grew, just outside a village called Ruyton – or Ruyton-XI-Towns, to give the place its full, fancy name. There wasn't much there apart from a posh prep school on the outskirts, a pub, a church and fifteen hundred people. A farmer had discovered Danni lying beside a dirt track in the now-familiar pose: on her back, gazing at the sky, mouth curled. The farmer had remarked she was lucky the birds hadn't been at her eyes, crediting this great fortune to a scarecrow that stood nearby, warding off corvids. Danni's clothes were soaked through as it had rained in the night, any DNA they might have found on her washed away. They had searched the fields, all the way to the banks of the river, but found nothing. No one in the village had seen anything.

Imogen's phone rang. It was a member of her team, DC Alan Hatton, a newly qualified detective who had a puppyish eagerness to please. Reception was poor beneath the trees, so she headed out into the open, gazing down at the town.

'I've just spoken to Trevor Redbridge, the victim's husband. I told him we need to take a DNA sample from him. Christ, the poor guy's in bits. He made me go through their wedding album. But he said something interesting. He's just got back from a business trip. He hadn't seen his wife for a week before she was murdered.'

'So the semen can't have been his.' She quickened her pace, heading back towards the car. Karen Lamb had been sure Fiona had had consensual sex – there were no signs of violence or a struggle. Had she been having an affair?

'Are you at Mr Redbridge's now?'

'Yeah. I haven't told him about the semen.'

She took a last look at the mulchy leaves where Nathan had been found and gestured for Emma to follow her as she turned towards the path.

'Good man. Stay there. I'm on my way.'

Chapter 7

'Did you remember my chocolates?'

'Hi, Mum.' I stooped to kiss her dry cheek, inhaling her familiar scent. She'd always smelled of lavender. I knew that in the months and years to come, that scent would forever make me think of her.

I took the box of chocolates – her favourites – out of the carrier bag and opened them for her. She popped one into her mouth and chewed. There was nothing wrong with her teeth, or her brain. But her body was ravaged by cancer. It had started in her uterus and spread like a brutal army, invading and pillaging until she had no fight left in her, no resistance. Now it was just a matter of time. The doctors had been saying for the past couple of months that she had only weeks to live, but she kept clinging on. All they could do for her now was make her as comfortable as possible.

'How are you feeling?' I asked.

She pushed the chocolates away. 'I've lost my appetite. Can you raise my bed? I want to be able to see the view.'

I pushed the button that raised her into a sitting position so she could look out across the lawns of the nursing home towards the woods. The grounds here at Orchard Heights were lovely, verdant and well ordered.

'I would have liked to have seen one last autumn,' she said. 'That was always my favourite season.'

'I'm sure you will.' I turned away to the window so she wouldn't read the lie on my face. It was a beautiful place.

'At least the sun will probably shine at my funeral.'

'Mum. Please.'

She sank back into her pillow. She was so thin she was almost skeletal and I was hit by a pang of nostalgia, remembering when I was a child and she used to stride purposefully along the street, with me trying to keep up with her. Of course I hadn't known the happy bride in the photo that stood on the dresser, but my mum had always been energetic, strong. She followed my gaze towards the picture.

'At least I'll be together with your dad again soon. Oh, Ben, come on. There's no point avoiding the subject, is there? It'll be a relief. When I'm gone.'

I stared at the carpet.

'I don't want to be in pain any more, Ben. I'm ready to go, but my bloody body won't give up.' Before I could say anything, she said, 'Now, tell me what's going on with you and Megan. Has she agreed to sell the flat?'

I sighed. 'No. But I've given up trying to do it all amicably. I called a lawyer yesterday.'

'At last! And what did he say?'

'*She* said I can only force the sale of the property with a court order, which I need to apply to the court to obtain. And I can't do that until I've filed for divorce and we've attended mediation. Which could take forever if Megan doesn't cooperate.'

'I tried to warn you about her.'

'Did you? I don't remember that.'

Her breathing was harsh, wet. 'When you were first together. I always thought there was something selfish about her. Cold.'

I shook my head. Mum had never warned me about Megan, and she was wrong. Megan had always been warm, passionate. The coldness was something new, and I was certain it was down to *him*. Michael Stone.

'I saw him on TV the other day,' Mum said, showing off her spooky telepathic abilities. 'I would have chucked something at it if I'd had the strength. He's a smug fucker.'

I couldn't help but laugh. 'Mum!'

I sometimes wondered if the cancer had reached her brain, but the doctors told me it was her medication that made her talk like this. I wished she'd been this earthy when I was growing up.

'Well, I hope this lawyer is good,' she said, her voice weakening.

She closed her eyes and I realised she was in pain.

'Do you need me to call the nurse?'

She held up a hand. 'Wait.' The pain seemed to recede. 'You need to get it all sorted out, Ben. For Oliver's sake. I know how worried you are about him.'

The last time I'd visited, I'd told her my concerns about Ollie's comfort eating, how he was clearly unsettled by the move.

'Oh, I wish I was stronger, so I could help you. I wish your father was still here. He would—' A wave of pain cut her words short. She shuddered and I pressed the button to call the nurse.

A minute later, a young man with curly brown hair appeared. He was tall, in his late twenties, with light-brown skin. Mum touched his forearm as he leaned over her.

'My angel,' she said. 'Ben, this is Emile.'

He smiled, showing off his dimples. 'You must be Ben. Your mum's always talking about you.' He had a French accent.

'She's told me lots about you, too,' I said. This was true. She spoke about this young man as if he were exactly what she'd said when he'd entered the room: an angel. And he did have an angelic air about him, radiating calmness, dressed all in white and with that handsome face.

He reminded me of a friend from college who'd become an evangelical Christian. I could imagine him going to meetings after work, sitting around with long-haired girls wearing beatific smiles, singing about Jesus.

'How are you feeling, Mrs Hofland?' he asked in a soft, kindly voice.

Her breathing was growing more ragged and a sheen of sweat had appeared on her skin.

'Let's make you feel more comfortable, shall we?'

He unfolded the pouch he was carrying, revealing a set of syringes and a number of vials of clear liquid.

'Thank you, Emile.' She turned to me. 'You can go now, Ben. Bring Ollie with you next time, will you? It might be my last chance to see him.'

As I left the nursing home, it started to rain. I sat in the car for a few minutes, watching the wipers swish back and forth. *It'll be a relief. When I'm gone.* I didn't want her to die. She was my mum, my only remaining parent. But I didn't want her to be in pain any more. I was torn between two emotions, one of which I knew to be selfish.

A smug fucker. I laughed to myself. It described Michael perfectly.

I hoped her final words would be equally outrageous.

ʊ

Ollie was in the kitchen when I got home. He had something in his hand, which he quickly stuck in his pocket.

'What's that?' I asked.

'Huh? Oh, just my iPod.'

He carried that thing around everywhere, playing games and watching YouTube videos as he roamed the cottage. Trying to reduce his screen time was one of the many things on my to-do list.

'Good day?' I asked.

'Yeah, it was all right.' He went to leave the room, but I stopped him.

'I was thinking we should go down to London, so you can see your mum. I need to talk to her about stuff.'

'Can I see Jack?' That was his best mate at his old school. They still messaged each other constantly and spoke over FaceTime, which was great, though I was worried that distance would eventually stretch and break their friendship.

'Of course.'

He grinned, and I was glad to see it. I hadn't seen him smile properly for ages.

'I had some good news today,' I said. 'I've got some work. Looks like it could end up being pretty lucrative. Regular, anyway. So we won't have to go and live in the workhouse yet, Oliver. You won't have to go and join a gang of pickpockets.'

'Have you lost the plot, Dad?'

'Sometimes I think I have.'

His iPod Touch beeped in his pocket.

'That might be Jack now. He said he was going to message me when he was online.'

He hurried from the room and a moment later his bedroom door slammed. I went into the living room and turned on the TV, settling on to the sofa with my laptop. Robert Friend had emailed me with details of the job he wanted me to do. It was quite straightforward: a sales letter for a local health spa. And the job came with an unexpected bonus. Robert wrote:

> I've arranged for you to spend a day there so
> you can soak it all up and see what they offer.
> I want you to go as a 'mystery shopper' so
> you get the genuine experience.

I'd offered to go to visit Robert at his office, but he'd said he was always on the road.

I replied to his email now, confirming that I would visit the spa on Thursday and get working on the copy straight away.

Then, deciding to do it while I was in a good mood, I emailed Megan telling her that Ollie wanted to see her, so we were planning to come down to London.

> Also, I've spoken to a lawyer about initiating divorce proceedings. I'm still hoping we can resolve everything amicably, that it doesn't get to the point where we only communicate via lawyers. But that's up to you.

As I hit 'Send', I heard the free newspaper clatter through the letter box. I braced myself because I knew exactly what would happen next. Sure enough, as the paperboy approached the house next door, a machine gun volley of barks shattered the peace, followed swiftly by Ross yelling at the dog to shut up. Then Shelley shouted at Ross: 'Leave my fucking dog alone!'

'Fuck you,' Ross responded. 'Pixie, shut up!'

The barking grew more frenzied, and within seconds the neighbours were having a full-blown row, screaming and shouting at each other, words like *bitch* and *limp-dick* and *stupid* and *whore* coming through the wall.

Ollie came back into the room, eyes wide.

That was it. I'd had enough. I didn't want to have to confront them, but what else could I do? I had to protect my son from this.

I went outside and banged on my neighbours' front door. It sounded like Pixie was doing somersaults inside, going absolutely mental. I looked around at the piles of dog shit on the front lawn, the overflowing rubbish bin. The door opened and I found myself face to face with Ross. Thankfully, there was no sign of Pixie – he must have shut her in the kitchen or living room.

'What?' he demanded, spraying me with spit.

Ross was over six feet tall and looked like he'd swallowed a truck-load of steroids. Now he was staring at me, his face red, a ropy vein pulsing in his forehead.

'I need you to do something about the noise,' I said, forcing myself to ignore the nerves that churned inside me. 'Your dog, and the shouting and swearing. I've got an eleven-year-old son here who can hear every word.'

A door slammed behind Ross and Shelley appeared. She was wearing a grey onesie, hair scraped back in a Croydon facelift. 'What's going on?'

'Ben says we're being too noisy.'

Her face was as red as her partner's. 'What? It's only five thirty.'

Ross kept his beady eyes fixed on me as he spoke. 'Says we're corrupting his son.'

'That fat kid?'

I was speechless.

Shelley elbowed her boyfriend out of the way. 'He goes to Abraham Darby, doesn't he?' That was Ollie's school. 'My nephew goes there. From what I've heard, your precious son will've heard every swear word ever invented already.'

'What do you mean by that?'

She folded her arms and sneered at me. 'It's not easy being the new kid at school. Especially not when you're fat.'

'Are you telling me he's being bullied?'

She rolled her eyes. 'Maybe if you spent less time poking your nose in our business and more time talking to your own kid, you'd already know. Now, do me a favour and fuck off.'

She slammed the door in my face.

Burning with anger, I was about to hammer on the door again – set to let out all my frustration and fury on this *stupid* woman – when I caught a movement out of the corner of my eye.

I turned towards my own cottage and saw Ollie standing there in the doorway, a stricken expression on his face.

'Ollie.'

He disappeared into the house and the anger drained from my body. Oh shit . . . I found him locked in the bathroom. Pixie had resumed barking. Between barks I could hear Ross and Shelley having sex, clearly turned on by their row and the confrontation with me.

'Leave me alone!' Ollie shouted as I tried to persuade him to come out. 'It's all your fault. You made me move to this place. You made me leave all my friends. I hate it here. I want to go back home.' He was crying now.

'Ollie, please, open the door.'

'Go away! You didn't even stick up for me when that horrible cow called me fat.'

'Ollie, come out. Let's talk about it.'

A minute passed. The noises from next door stopped. I put my hand on my chest, concerned by how hard and fast my heart was thumping.

I said my son's name again and, to my relief, I heard the lock draw back. He stood in the open doorway. His cheeks were streaked with tears, which he rubbed at with a grubby hand, smearing grey trails across his face.

'I'm not being bullied,' he said.

'Then what was Shelley talking about?'

He shrugged. 'She was just trying to wind you up, I guess.'

I examined his face, trying to work out if he was telling the truth.

'I'm going to talk to your head teacher.'

'No! Please don't. School's fine, Dad,' he said. 'I just miss my friends. And I miss Mum.'

There was a lump in my throat now. 'I know you do.' I wanted to say that I missed her, too. Because I did, sometimes. I missed the way things used to be. The life we'd had before she'd ripped it apart.

His iPod beeped again. His cheeks flushed pink. 'That'll be Jack. We were halfway through a chat. Can I go?'

'Sure.'

I ruffled his hair – it needed a wash – and watched him head to his bedroom. I wondered why his cheeks had turned pink. Was he really talking to Jack? Or maybe he was chatting with a girl. No, surely he was too young.

Another thump came from next door, another bark. Screw this. If they wanted a war, they could have one.

Chapter 8

The family liaison officer who was looking after Trevor Redbridge invited Imogen and Emma into his whitewashed cottage and saw them into a sitting room where Trevor sat in a stiff-backed armchair. He was in his early fifties, hair streaked with grey at the sides and with the florid complexion of a man who enjoyed a drink. He was wearing a tweed jacket, loose-fitting jeans and a white shirt undone at the collar, through which an unruly thatch of chest hair was making a bid for freedom. Trevor ran an auction house in the centre of Ludlow. He was a successful businessman, well known locally, according to Emma. Now, perched in his chair, tea in a fine-china cup by his side, he seemed utterly lost.

The room, unsurprisingly, was like Aladdin's cave, crammed full of antiques: cabinets and chests and paintings and crockery. A stuffed weasel perched on the mantelpiece, its face forever frozen in a snarl. Imogen was sure it was watching her as she introduced herself to the man who was now a widower.

'I'm sorry for your loss,' Imogen said.

He nodded hopelessly. 'Is there any news? Have you caught him yet?'

There was no point bullshitting him about 'following promising lines of inquiry'. 'I'm afraid not, Mr Redbridge. But we're hoping you can help us.' Imogen took a seat on the sofa opposite him, while Emma chose an armchair in the corner. 'Can you tell us about your wife?'

'What she was like, you mean?'

'That would be helpful. Also, her movements, habits. Her routine. We need to figure out where she might have encountered the person we're looking for.'

He lifted his tea to his lips and winced. 'Bugger, this is stone cold.'

The family liaison officer, who must have been lingering just outside the room, hurried in and took the cup from him. 'I'll make you another.'

'Let's start with the easier stuff, shall we?' Imogen said after the FLO left the room. 'Can you tell me about Fiona's daily routine?' she asked gently.

'Of course. You know she ran an antique shop in town?'

'The Lucky Magpie.'

'That's the one. To be honest, it's more of a bric-a-brac shop. A lot of curios and old junk. But Fiona loved all that kind of stuff, said every piece told a story. The lamest rocking horse, a teapot with a chip in the base, dodgy taxidermy . . . That's where Walter came from.'

'Walter?'

He gestured to the snarling weasel. 'Fiona brought him back one day, said she wanted to give him a home. Ghastly thing. I'll never be able to part with him now, though.'

'You were going to tell us about Fiona's daily routine.'

'Yes. Well, Monday to Saturday we both did the same thing every day: left here around nine and drove into town, sometimes together, sometimes taking our own cars, depending on what our plans were. My auction house is only a couple of streets away from her shop. She opened the Magpie at ten. Sometimes we would meet for lunch at around one, but she usually bought a sandwich and ate it in the shop. She closed up at five and, most evenings, came straight home.'

'Did she travel around much for work? I mean, where did she source the items in the shop?'

'A lot of it came from house clearances, or job lots at auction. Sometimes people brought things in. Most of the stuff that came through the door was low value, but she occasionally got lucky.'

'Like the Roman cup she sold for ten grand?'

Trevor smiled. 'Ah, that was a very fortuitous find. Somebody brought it in and said they'd found it in their mum's attic after she died, sold it to us for a hundred quid. Fiona didn't realise the cup was so valuable, but the moment I saw it, I knew. I auctioned it myself.'

'Shouldn't you have given it back to the original owner when you realised how valuable it was?' Emma asked.

Surprise flitted across Trevor's face. 'That's not how this business works. Besides, he didn't leave a name or address, and he never came forward, even after it was publicised in the paper.'

Imogen still hadn't got to the most awkward part of the conversation. She wasn't looking forward to kicking this poor man while he was down. Plus, there was one other topic she wanted to discuss first.

'Fiona had a heart transplant recently, didn't she?'

He nodded miserably. 'That's what makes this even harder to bear. All the stress we went through, waiting to see if she'd get a heart, wondering if our time together was going to end prematurely, then when it happened . . . We thought we were blessed, that we'd have decades.'

'Was she taking any sort of medication?'

'No. She was fully recovered. She was fitter than I am. Probably fitter than you, Detective. When she got the new heart it was like she was starting her life again, and she really looked after herself. She went to the gym, ate healthily, made me eat all this vegetarian muck. She ran a half-marathon last year, was thinking of doing a triathlon.'

'That's impressive.'

Nathan Scott had been a cyclist. Could that be a connection?

'Had she started training for this triathlon?'

'Not really. But she did join a cycling club.'

Imogen glanced over at Emma, who had obviously picked up on this, too.

'She only went a couple of times, though. She said they all took it far too seriously.'

At Emma's prompting, Trevor went off to get the details of the cycling club.

As he sat down again, Imogen cleared her throat. 'Mr Redbridge, I have a rather sensitive subject I need to discuss with you.' She was aware of Walter glaring at her from above Trevor's head, teeth bared, beady eyes fixed on her, like the guardian of Fiona's memory.

'Oh?'

'I'm just going to come out and ask. Do you know if Fiona was having an affair?'

He stared at her while Emma shifted uncomfortably in her seat. 'Why are you asking that?'

She didn't reply, waiting to see what he would say. Eventually, he pinched his nose and dipped his head again, like a child putting his face underwater at a swimming lesson. When he came back up again he said, 'I don't know. Why? Have you found something out?'

'You told DC Hatton that you were away from the sixth to the thirteenth?'

'That's right. I was at a conference in Tunbridge Wells.'

'And you didn't see Fiona at all during that period? You had no intimate contact with her?'

'Intimate contact?' What Imogen was saying seemed to dawn on him. 'No, I didn't. Are you telling me she was shagging someone else while I was away?' All the colour had left his face.

'We believe she had sex somewhere between twenty-four and forty-eight hours before she died, Mr Redbridge.'

She almost asked Emma to fetch a bowl, because Trevor Redbridge looked like he was about to throw up.

'And I'm sure you can appreciate that we want to speak to this person very much.'

He stood up and moved to the mantelpiece, picking up the framed wedding photo. 'Don't you think it was him? The animal who killed her? He raped her first?'

Imogen could sense his internal struggle. Was it worse for him to think of his wife cheating on him, or being raped?

'There were no signs of sexual violence. And it doesn't appear to be part of the MO of the murderer. We don't think she was raped.'

His Adam's apple bobbed. 'That's . . . good.' He fell back into his armchair, holding the silver photo frame.

'Did you have any suspicions about your wife seeing someone else?' Emma asked, her tone soft.

'No. I mean, I'm away a lot. She was happy recently – happier than I've ever known her. But I thought it was because of the heart transplant.' He made eye contact with Imogen. 'If she was cheating on me, it doesn't mean I'm going to miss her any less.'

Imogen leaned forward and patted his hand. 'You're a good man, Trevor. We'll be in touch about that information we need – the company books and so on. But if you think of anything in the meantime, anything that could help us find your wife's . . . friend, call me.'

ᴡ

'Poor sod,' Emma said when they were back in the car, heading to the station.

'Yeah. Sweet, though, in a way, isn't it? They were married all that time and he was obviously still crazy about her. It almost makes me believe in love.'

Emma laughed. 'Why don't you have a bloke, if you don't mind me asking?'

They pulled up at a red light and Imogen tapped the steering wheel impatiently. 'Where am I supposed to meet one? The only people I meet are other cops – and I won't date anyone at work – and criminals. Maybe I could become one of those women who writes letters to serial killers.'

'What about Internet dating?' Emma asked. 'That's how Steve and I got together.'

Imogen had met Steve a couple of times. He was a salt-of-the-earth sort, a rugby player who seemed to always wear stripy polo shirts. Nice enough, but not Imogen's type. Not that she ought to cling to 'her type'. She'd always been drawn to men who were likely to burn her.

'I can't imagine anything worse,' she said. 'I'd probably get matched up with some sheep farmer.'

'What's wrong with farmers? I know some very sexy young farmers. I should introduce you to a few of them.'

'Farmers do it in wellies,' Imogen said, parroting a bumper sticker she'd seen on the back of a tractor. 'Anyway, I don't want a boyfriend. I'm happy with my cat and my rabbit.'

'I didn't know you had a rabbit.'

Imogen made a buzzing sound.

'Oh! Very funny.'

Imogen smiled. 'Come on, let's get on to the lab. I want to know who Fiona Redbridge was fucking.'

Chapter 9

Frank Dodd's office was located above an estate agent's in a lovely old Tudor building in Shrewsbury. I rang the buzzer and went up. Frank was my landlord and since my row on the doorstep with Ross and Shelley I'd been trying and failing to get through to him on the phone. Fed up of listening to his voicemail message, I made up my mind to visit him in person.

Frank's number two, Adrian, sat behind a desk in the reception area. Adrian was in his late twenties, six feet tall and always dressed in black. I assumed Adrian must be a nephew or the son of a friend because it was hard to see why else Frank had given him a job. In my dealings with him, he had appeared to be incompetent: rarely answering the phone, forgetting to post contracts, and exhibiting a persistently sullen demeanour. Service with a snarl.

'Is Frank here?' I asked.

Adrian lifted his pasty face from his phone screen like it was an enormous effort. He went to close the browser, but not before I saw what he'd been looking at: a photo of a very young-looking girl, naked and bound, grimacing with pain.

The man himself came out of his office before Adrian could muster the breath to answer. I guessed Frank was in his fifties, with black hair teased into a quiff. He wore a black, western-style shirt, matching jeans, a belt with a large square buckle, and black cowboy boots. Frank was a huge fan of country music, particularly Johnny Cash.

'Ben! How the devil are you?' He gestured for me to take a seat in the reception area, then sat opposite me, crossing his boots at the ankle, a warm smile on his face. He had two vertical lines that bisected his cheeks where he'd once had dimples. 'How's your mum?' he asked.

'Comfortable,' I said. 'She doesn't have long left, though.' I broke eye contact, composing myself.

'Ah, that's hard.' Frank nodded, then changed the subject. 'Are you still swimming?'

He always asked me that. Everybody did. When I was a teenager, I'd been the county breaststroke champion. That was how I knew Frank. As a successful local businessman, he was often asked to present medals, which had led to his friendship with my parents. He was in his late twenties back then, but had always seemed much older – though as a fifteen-year-old I thought everyone over twenty-five was decrepit.

I'd gone on to win a bronze in the national championships, which had got me featured in the local newspaper. There'd been some wildly premature talk of me being a future Olympian, but when I was seventeen I'd lost interest, realising I would never be a champion. People still remembered, though. *That's Ben, the swimmer.* It was a label that stuck.

'Only when I go on holiday,' I said, using my stock answer.

'You were like a bloody dolphin. Your mum and dad were so proud.'

I noticed Adrian giving me the once over, as if he could hardly believe that this old bloke could once have been so athletic.

'Anyway,' Frank said. 'What can I do for you?'

'It's a bit awkward,' I said.

'Don't tell me – you've found a body in the basement. Adrian, didn't I tell you to get that out of there before Ben moved in?' He guffawed heartily, but Adrian didn't crack a smile.

'Actually, it's the neighbours. Ross and Shelley.'

'Oh God. What have they done now?'

The previous tenant must have complained about them, too.

'It's noise, mostly.' I told him about the dog, the constant arguments, shouting and playing music in the middle of the night. I left out the part about them having noisy sex. 'They made some pretty nasty comments about my son, too, in front of him.'

'That's not on.'

'So are you going to do something about it?'

'No problem, Ben. I'll have a word. Leave it with me.'

'Thank you.'

As I went to leave I saw a copy of the local paper lying on Adrian's desk. Another front-page headline about the serial killer. 'Police No Closer To Finding Viper.' Frank saw me looking at it.

'Bloody useless, the police round here,' he said. 'Half my tenants have been ringing me, asking me to install burglar alarms and put up CCTV cameras. As if I can afford to do that!'

'People are scared,' I said. 'You can't blame them.'

'At least they don't die in pain,' Adrian said in a quiet voice.

Both Frank and I looked at him.

He flushed pink. 'The killer uses morphine, doesn't he? It's not a bad way to go. Much better than being hacked or tortured to death. Locked in a dark cellar and raped and mutilated.'

Frank rolled his eyes. 'You spend too much time playing those horrible bloody video games, son. They've warped your mind.' He turned to me. 'The other day I came in here and caught him watching one of those terrorist videos – you know, ISIS beheading some poor bastard.'

A smile crept across Adrian's face. 'Like I said, the Viper's victims are lucky. There are far worse ways to die.'

Frank cuffed the back of Adrian's head. 'You're sick. And if I were you, I wouldn't go around saying those things in public. You'll have the police round here, asking if you've got an alibi.' He turned back to me.

'I apologise for my assistant, Ben. You just leave Ross and Shelley to me. I'll tell them to keep it down.'

ɷ

I exited Frank's office feeling like I needed a shower. Adrian was seriously creepy. Since I had my laptop with me, I headed towards Starbucks, intending to work on the copy for the spa and check my emails. Megan hadn't yet responded to my message about filing for divorce, or about my proposed visit to London with Ollie.

I'd lain awake half the night worrying about him. He still seemed upset by what Shelley had said about him. Had it been a mistake bringing him here? Would he have been better off staying with his mum? I wished he would open up to me more, but getting information out of an eleven-year-old boy was like opening an oyster with a paper clip. Was he being bullied at school? The thought of it horrified me, but it was difficult to do anything if Ollie wouldn't admit to it.

I turned the corner and entered one of the city's central squares. A TV crew was setting up in the centre of the square: a cameraman, someone who could have been a sound engineer, a woman holding a clipboard.

And right in the middle of all this was Michael Stone.

I froze. Michael Stone, the man my wife had left me for, here, in my corner of the world. It was like walking into your bedroom and finding someone rifling through your underwear. It was like coming home one afternoon to find your wife having sex on the sofa with the arsehole standing before me now. Except that had been much, much worse.

That day, I'd wanted to kill him. I'd staggered into the kitchen and stared at the knives in their block on the counter, fantasising about plunging one into his chest, or cutting off his balls. I'd stood there, desperately resisting the urge to ruin what was left of my life, until I'd heard the front door slam. Then Megan had come into the kitchen and said, 'I'm sorry you had to see that.'

Later she told me she didn't love me any more.

I shoved the memory away.

Michael stood there now in his trademark long black coat and trendy square-framed glasses. As I got over the shock of seeing him, I realised he was probably filming something about the Shropshire Viper. And if his previous work was anything to go by, he would be focusing on the failure of the police to catch the criminal. Or maybe he thought he could do a better job. He had made his name a decade ago when he tracked down a missing child the police had failed to find and exposed a paedophile gang, turning the whole thing into what was, admittedly, a gripping documentary. Plus, he came from round here. Maybe it was personal.

I took a step backwards because I didn't want him to see me. I still didn't trust myself in his presence – the temptation to throttle him was too strong. We had been friends once. I'd even introduced him to Megan. Oh no, was *she* here? Was that why she hadn't answered my email, because she was too busy traipsing around after her new boyfriend?

Like me, Michael grew up in Ironbridge, though his family's house, on the outskirts of the village, had been much bigger than mine. We'd never been best friends, but we'd been in some of the same classes, gone to the same parties, probably fancied the same girls. In fact, we'd always shared the same taste in women. When I was sixteen, I'd briefly gone out with a girl called Charlotte who'd told me Michael had been pursuing her for ages, but she hadn't liked him because he'd been too pushy. He'd always been a show-off, with rich parents who'd kept him stocked in the latest Air Jordans and bought him a brand-new Mini when he'd turned seventeen.

When we left school, I'd thought I would never see him again. I didn't even think about him for years, until I'd bumped into him in my final year at college. It turned out his girlfriend at that time had gone to the same college as me and she'd brought him to a party on our campus. He had seemed to have mellowed a little since school, and his girlfriend had been lovely, so we'd agreed to keep in touch, meeting for the occasional drink. I'd introduced him to Megan shortly after I'd started dating her, and I remember him whispering to me, 'She's a stunner – what's she doing with you?'

How we had laughed.

I hadn't been surprised when he became famous. We didn't talk often by that point. Megan and I were busy being parents. But then he'd contacted Megan, saying he needed a financial adviser. He was making a lot of money, though Megan wouldn't tell me exactly how much, and she'd gone on to help him set up a pension, invest in stocks and shares and so on, and they'd met regularly to review his finances.

Except, it turned out, that hadn't been all they were meeting for.

The camera started filming, Stone's deep bass tones rolling across the square towards me. I heard the words '. . . serial killer terrifying the sleepy towns and villages of Shropshire . . .' and then Michael stopped. He'd spotted me. Several members of the film crew turned to follow his gaze then exchanged worried glances.

I walked towards him, fists clenched by my side.

'Ben,' he said, coming towards me.

We both stopped, inches apart.

'Is Megan here?' I asked.

He ignored the question. 'How are you, mate? How's . . . um . . .'

'You can't even remember his name, can you? The son of the woman you're sleeping with.' I was trembling with anger.

'Of course I remember his name. Listen, mate, I'm a bit busy at the moment, but I don't, you know, want there to be any bad blood between us.'

The temptation to punch him in the face, break his nose, spray his expensive clothes with blood, was achingly strong.

'Maybe we should get together, have a drink,' he said.

'Yeah, why don't you pop round for a cup of arsenic?'

'If you're going to be like that.' He turned away.

'I assume you're here looking for the Viper,' I called after him. 'I hope you find him. I'd like to see what he'll do to you.'

'Yeah, yeah, whatever,' he said, refusing to look at me. He manoeuvred away until two of his crew were between us and I stood there, still shaking with rage. Then a passing woman bumped into me, breaking the spell, and I walked away, heart thumping, sick with adrenaline.

I knew I wouldn't be able to concentrate on work now. I grabbed a coffee and went back to the car. As I got to the car park, I bumped into Frank and Adrian heading to their van.

'We must stop meeting like this,' Frank said.

'Have you spoken to Ross and Shelley yet?'

'Give us a chance!' He studied me. 'What's up? You look like you're about to blow a gasket.'

I took a deep breath. 'I just bumped into my ex-wife's new bloke.'

'Ouch,' Frank said. 'Do I know him? Want me to send the boys round?'

The tension broke and I laughed. 'I'm not going to answer that. But do you know that reporter, Michael Stone? It's him. I think he's doing a report about the Viper.'

Frank draped an arm around my shoulder. 'Sounds like you're better off without her if she's into a creep like him.'

'I hate him,' Adrian said. 'His programme's shit.'

Frank snorted. 'Ever thought about becoming a TV critic, Adrian?'

As they pulled away in Frank's white Transit van, Adrian stared at me, like a hawk eyeing up a canary.

Chapter 10

Imogen's cat, a grey tabby called Monkey, was waiting in the hallway as she came out of the bathroom wrapped in a towel. Monkey was nine years old now, in retirement from his former life as a tough street tomcat in the mean gardens of south London.

He stretched his mouth wide and emitted his familiar creaking meow.

'All right, all right. Patience.'

She went straight into the tiny kitchen, got out his food and squeezed meat from a pouch into his bowl. She flicked the kettle on and sat at the breakfast bar, gazing out at the quiet, ancient city with its winding, medieval streets, Tudor houses and hanging baskets. A wave of homesickness came over her. It was 7 a.m. Back in Brixton, where she had lived and worked for ten years, the streets would already be noisy. They were *always* noisy. She'd lived close to Electric Avenue, leaving for work just as the market traders arrived each morning and the clubbers left for home, stopping to grab a coffee from a van. Her weekends off she'd spent browsing and shopping in this place that offered all the tastes and smells of the world: ackee and monkfish, noodles and green tea, goat stew and guava. Gangland shootings and stabbings, the constant wail of police sirens, drug dealers rubbing shoulders with commuters, kids pouring out of the Tube station for a gig at the Academy, street traders and vagrants, yummy mummies with designer buggies – there was literally never a dull moment, and she'd loved it.

But she'd had to leave. Because of that arsehole Kevin Moss.

She made a coffee and took it into the bedroom, thinking about the Viper. Always thinking about the Viper. The semen found inside Fiona Redbridge didn't belong to anyone on the DNA database. None of Fiona's friends knew who she was sleeping with. Her computer and phone records gave no clue. Right now, it was another dead end.

Imogen shed the towel and dressed hurriedly in the outfit she had already set out, then downed her coffee. Returning to the kitchen, she grabbed the Tupperware dish containing her lunch. Each dish was labelled with a day of the week and, for a moment, she considered switching today's lunch, tuna salad, for tomorrow's, noodles, because she fancied it more. But if she did that, chaos would surely ensue. She needed this structure, the weekly Sunday night ritual of ironing her clothes and preparing a week's worth of lunches, Monkey watching her while she imposed order on her life.

'It's all right for you,' she said to the cat, who sat blinking at her now. 'You don't have to worry about anything.'

Monkey blinked at her once more, then lay down and licked his back leg, stretched out in a puddle of sunlight.

She left the flat, thinking it wasn't healthy to feel so envious of an animal.

ʊ

Imogen arrived at the station to find Alan Hatton coming out of Greene's office, the older man patting Hatton on the shoulder.

'Ah, Imogen,' Greene said. The smell of bacon sandwiches wafted from the office. Greene was pushing fifty and had succumbed to middle-aged spread. Imogen wanted to tell him to watch his cholesterol. At the same time, the smell of bacon made her mouth water. Beside Greene, DC Alan Hatton was a picture of health and vitality. Tall, strong, good-looking, with a keen desire to please.

'Alan here has found out something very interesting indeed,' Greene said.

'Oh?'

If Hatton had had a tail, it would've been wagging. 'Trevor Redbridge called me at the crack of dawn. He says his wife's mountain bike is missing from their garage.'

'Really? When did he last see it?'

'He says it was definitely there a week ago, just before he went away, because he remembers almost colliding with it when he parked his car. I've got a description – he bought it for her, so he knows exactly what model it was.'

They had two missing bikes now – Fiona's and Nathan's. They obviously weren't looking for the world's most elaborate mountain-bike thief, but if they could find those bikes . . .

'It gets better,' Hatton said. 'Mr Redbridge says the bike has a tracker on it, hidden in the frame. Like a Find My iPhone kind of thing. It's connected to an app, so if it goes missing you can see it on a map. He insisted she get it because the bike was really expensive.'

'And? Have you traced it?'

'Of course. Let me show you.' He gestured them over to his desk and sat down at his computer. Bringing up a map on the screen, he was showing Imogen the location when Emma joined the group.

'There's something else, too,' said Emma. 'You remember we saw a guy lurking around the crime scene at Wenlock Priory?' The man standing in the nearby field, who had run off as soon as he saw Imogen watching him. 'We've got a photo. He's in the background of a couple of the shots the SOCOs took when they were photographing the scene. We blew it up and he's there, as clear as anything.'

Emma handed Imogen a printout of the picture. It showed a young man with sandy-blond hair. He had a weaselly face, not unlike the stuffed animal on the Redbridges' mantel.

'Good work, Emma, Alan,' Greene said.

Imogen nodded. 'Let's get this online. See if anyone recognises him.' She turned to Hatton. 'Alan, you do that while Emma and I go and find this bike.'

ʊ

Bridgnorth was yet another pretty town, split into two parts: the high town and the low. The high town had a ruined castle, a market, a pair of beautiful churches, winding cobbled streets and lovely views over the Severn. The low town had the river itself, but most of the housing was new. A funicular railway connected the two. According to Emma, in the old days the poor people lived in the low town and would break their backs carrying goods up to the rich people on the hill.

They turned on to a narrow, bumpy road in the low town. This was where the red dot had told them they'd find Fiona's bicycle. She checked the map and pulled up to the kerb.

A rickety sign told them this was 'Daunt & Son Scrap Merchants'. A flat-bed truck was parked in the yard.

'Tatters,' Emma said.

'Huh?' Imogen said.

Emma laughed. 'Rag-and-bone men. There are loads of them round here. You must have seen them trundling around in their truck, blowing their bugle.'

'You're kidding me, right?'

'No. I'm amazed you haven't seen them.' She gestured to a loudspeaker on the roof of the truck. 'Except they actually play recordings of bugles now rather than the actual instrument. They go round collecting scrap metal. It's quite a lucrative business, by all accounts.'

They went into the yard, where piles of metal lay in heaps in front of a small red-brick building – more of a shed than anything else. There were pipes, cables, bed frames and old car batteries, copper and lead and iron.

A man in his twenties came out of the shed, walking with the gait of a man who spent a lot of time lifting weights. He wore a black bomber jacket, had a shaved head and looked strong enough to have carried Fiona across that field.

'Can I help you ladies?' he asked, grinning to reveal a gap in his upper teeth.

'Are you Mr Daunt?'

'That's right. Simon Daunt.'

Imogen introduced herself and Emma.

His eyes widened. 'I thought I recognised you. I've seen you on telly.' He seemed amused by this. If he were the killer, he was very cool.

She held up her phone, on which was a photograph of Fiona's bike that Hatton had sent her. 'I'm looking for this mountain bike. We have reason to believe it's here.'

He squinted at it. Imogen expected him to protest, to say he hadn't seen it. Instead, he said, 'Yeah, it's out back.'

He strode off, legs apart like his balls were too large, and the two detectives followed, going down the side of the shed into a larger yard, where scrap metal filled every inch of space. There was Fiona's bike, propped up against a pile of copper.

'Most the bikes we get are old and rusty. Knackered. This one's too good to go for scrap. I was going to stick it on eBay.'

'Where did you get it from?'

He sniffed. 'It was dumped in the front yard.'

Imogen found herself staring at the bike. It was clearly expensive and in immaculate condition.

'When was this?'

'It was here when we came in Monday morning. We don't work Sundays – day of rest and all that – so I guess it must've been left here then. We figured someone must've dumped it here because they couldn't be bothered to drive out to the tip. You'd be amazed at some of the stuff people chuck out. The posh lot up on the hill. Stuff that's in perfect nick, they just chuck it out.'

'And you "stick it on eBay"?'

'Yeah.' He grinned, showing her his gappy teeth. 'We're entrepreneurs.'

'Do you get many brand-new bikes left here?'

He scratched his chin. 'Not adult ones. Kids' bikes, usually. Although . . . hang on.' He went into the shed, Imogen following, where he flipped open a laptop and opened eBay. 'I did sell another really nice bike a few months ago. It was dumped here, like that one.'

He scrolled through the listings of items he'd sold on the auction site. 'Yeah, here it is. Got a really good price for it. It was, like, top-of-the-range, that one. I got five hundred quid, which I thought was good, but then I found out they cost five grand brand new. I mean, how rich do you have to be to chuck out a five-thousand-pound bike? I reckon it was an aggrieved wife, chucking out her hubby's prize possession after finding him screwing her sister.' He chuckled.

She stared at him. 'Didn't you think about reporting it to us at the time?'

He shrugged. He reminded her of Trevor when she'd quizzed him about the Roman cup. Both men had a 'finders keepers' attitude. 'Like I said, in this game you get used to people throwing out expensive stuff. Was it nicked, then? Is that why you're here? The thief must've been a bit bloody stupid to dump it and not flog it.'

Imogen turned her attention to the bike on the screen. It was black and red, with the brand name Merida emblazoned on the side.

'Wait here,' Imogen said, going back out into the yard, where she called Hatton.

'Alan. Nathan Scott's bike – I need the colour and model.'

'Hold on.' She waited while he looked it up. 'Merida, black and red.'

'Fuck me. Is that picture of our crime-scene lurker online yet?'

'Just doing it now.'

She ended the call and strode back into the shed. Simon raised his eyebrows.

'I need the name and address of the person you sold that bike to. And I also need you to come to the station.'

'What? Why?'

'We're going to need to take your fingerprints. Has anyone else touched that bike? The one that's here now?'

'Only my old man.'

'He's going to have to come with us, too. Phone him, will you? Tell him to meet us at Shrewsbury police station.'

Simon Daunt huffed and sighed, but did as he was told. She scrutinised him. It seemed highly unlikely that he was their man. He had been too helpful, although she had encountered criminals who were so cocky they thought they could get away with anything. But her feeling was that he was telling the truth. And that meant the killer must have dumped the bikes here. It was a long shot that Nathan's still bore any fingerprints, but . . .

'You think the Viper left those bikes here, don't you? Why else would you be here?' Simon beamed at her, and Imogen wanted to tell him to spend the money he made flogging stuff on eBay at the dentist's. His next words, however, made her forget all about his dodgy teeth.

'Is there a reward?' he asked.

'Why are you asking that?'

He pointed to a camera that was angled towards the road. 'Because maybe we caught him on our CCTV.'

Chapter 11

'You've got a lot of tension in your back, Ben.'

The masseuse, whose name was Stephanie, pressed down hard between my shoulder blades and the cracking noise made me wince.

'A *lot* of tension. What do you do for a living?'

I couldn't tell Stephanie I was a copywriter because I was supposed to be incognito, so I told her I was a teacher, which was the first stressful job I could think of.

'Just lie still, relax, and let's work on these knots.'

I was finding it hard to let go, but after a few minutes I allowed myself to enjoy it, her hands kneading away the tightness. I closed my eyes. The room was full of scented candles and it was blissfully silent. By the time Stephanie had finished, telling me to remain still for a few minutes, I felt better than I had in a long time.

I sat up. My shoulders felt loose, my back as flexible as a teenager's.

I headed to the steam room, following that with a dip in their warm indoor pool, then had lunch: a superfood salad with a glass of some fancy vitamin water. I didn't think about any of my problems: not my pending divorce, my mum, Ollie, the people next door, the continued existence of Michael bloody Stone. None of it. All I thought about was the sizzling copy I was going to craft to sell the benefits of this wonderful place.

As I emerged into the bright but chilly garden, I saw Stephanie again.

'How are you feeling now?' she asked.

I grinned. 'Like a new man.'

ꞷ

I got back to the cottage just as Ollie was walking up the road from the bus stop, swinging his backpack over his shoulder, shirt half untucked. He pulled his earphones out when he saw me.

'How was school?' I asked.

'All right.'

'I wonder how many times we've had that exact exchange.' I ignored his puzzled expression and went on. 'We can't go down to London this weekend. I finally heard back from your mum. She's here, in Shropshire.'

He stopped. 'What's she doing here?'

'You can ask her yourself. She's coming round to see you tomorrow.'

'That's brilliant. Oh my God, I need to tidy my room.'

Megan had always been militant when it came to ensuring Ollie kept his room neat.

I ruffled his hair. 'Don't worry about it. This isn't her house, it's ours.'

Megan had replied to my email the previous evening, a few hours after I'd seen Michael. So she *was* up here with him – though she didn't mention that fact in her reply. She said she wanted to see Ollie and to get away from London for a few days. Of course, she didn't know I'd spotted her paramour in Shrewsbury.

Thinking about her was seriously endangering my good mood. I was about to change the subject, but Ollie stopped halfway down the path. 'Is she only coming to see me?'

'What do you mean?'

'I just . . . well, I wondered if she's coming to see you, too.'

I caught up with him and put a hand on his shoulder. 'Ollie, your mum and I aren't going to get back together. I know it's hard but—'

Before I could say anything else, he turned away, breaking contact. I sighed. As we approached the front door, Mrs Douglas came out of her cottage. I hadn't seen her since our conversation on Sunday, when she'd told me about the murder at Wenlock Priory.

'How are you?' I called over as I searched in my pockets for my keys.

'Oh!' she cried. 'Ben, you startled me.'

'Sorry.'

She certainly didn't seem herself. She looked greyer somehow. Afraid. She peered around her garden as if she'd forgotten why she'd come outside, then promptly shuffled back into her house.

'Weird,' Ollie said, as I unlocked the door.

'I think everyone's a little on edge at the moment.'

'Because of the Viper? This boy at school, Danny, his dad's a policeman, and he said the Viper removes his victims' eyes and *eats* them.'

'Ollie! That's ridiculous.'

There was a card lying on the doormat inside. Ollie picked it up. Amazon had tried to deliver something. That was strange: I hadn't ordered anything recently.

'Have you bought something using my Amazon account?' I asked Ollie.

'You told me I'm not allowed to do that.'

'Hmm. It's been left next door,' I said. 'With the gruesome twosome. Can you put the kettle on while I go and get it?'

I headed next door, not relishing the thought of coming face to face with either Ross or Shelley, who I hadn't seen since our confrontation. I didn't know if Frank Dodd had spoken to them yet.

Shelley answered. She was dressed in leggings and a long T-shirt with 'Get It Girl' emblazoned across the front. Her face was puffy. Had she been crying?

Before I could ask her about the package, she said, 'Have you seen Pixie?'

'No, I've been out all day.'

'She's disappeared. I left her in the garden while I went to the shops and when I got back she wasn't there. Ross has gone out looking for her.' She chewed a fingernail, looking past me down the road. 'I'm really worried.'

'Can she jump over the fence?' I asked, knowing the answer before I'd asked the question. Unless Pixie had Olympic jumping skills, there was no way she could leap that fence. 'Could she have got through?'

She frowned. 'Yeah, I didn't realise, but there's a gap in the fence behind this, like, shrub. She must have squeezed through. Oh God, what if a vivisectionist gets hold of her? You hear about it all the time.'

As much as I disliked Pixie's constant barking, I hated to think of her being lost, though I thought it was highly unlikely she'd end up in a lab. Shelley obviously loved her. I tried to reassure her. 'I'm sure the dog warden will pick her up.'

She replied with a wet sniff, then spotted the Amazon card in my hand. She went inside and came out with a cardboard box.

'I hope you find her,' I said, turning to go.

'I bet you don't really.'

I turned back. 'What?'

'I said, I bet you don't hope we find her. You hated her.' She glared at me, the tears replaced by sudden anger. 'Did you open that gap in the fence, so she'd run off?'

'That's the most ridiculous thing I've ever heard.'

Shelley burst into tears and slammed the door. Shaking my head, I went back to my cottage, reading the label on the cardboard package. It was addressed to Ollie.

I went into the kitchen, where Ollie was thumbing his iPod, a little smile at the corner of his lips.

'You *have* ordered something,' I said, still cradling the box. 'What is it? How much did it cost?'

'Huh? I haven't, I swear!' Eyes wide with curiosity, he took the box from me and tore it open. 'Oh, awesome!'

He pulled it out of the box. It was a Nintendo 3DS, and the newest model, by the look of it.

I grabbed it from him. 'Ollie, how much did this cost? About a hundred and fifty quid? We can't afford to buy things like this right now. I can't believe you—'

'I swear I didn't buy it, Dad.' He tried to take it back from me, but I set it on the counter and guarded it with my body.

'You must have one-clicked it.'

'I didn't!' He narrowed his eyes at me. 'I put it on my wish list, but I didn't buy it. I'm not stupid. If I did, you would've had a confirmation email, wouldn't you?'

He was right. 'Wait there,' I said. 'And do not open that package.'

I found my laptop and searched through my emails. There was no email from Amazon confirming the order of the DS. I logged on to the Amazon site and checked my order history. Nothing since December, when I'd bought some of Ollie's Christmas presents through the site.

Back in the kitchen, I said, 'Okay, so you didn't order it. Who did?'

'It must have been Mum. Maybe she looked at my wish list and decided to buy me a present.'

That was plausible. But there was one thing I didn't understand. 'Why did you put a 3DS on your wish list anyway? You've got one already. You had it for your birthday last year.'

He found something interesting to examine on the kitchen floor. 'I lost it.'

'What? Where?'

'I took it to school and . . .'

I waited, before realisation dawned. 'Did somebody take it from you, Ollie?'

He still wouldn't meet my eye. 'No. I just . . . lost it. I didn't want to tell you because I knew you'd be mad and lecture me about taking care of things.'

'Are you sure it wasn't taken from you? By a bully?'

He winced. 'Why won't you believe me? I left it on the bus. Please, Dad, can I open the new one now? It's got the new Pokémon game with it. I really want to play it. *Please.*'

I sighed and handed it to him. 'All right, fine.' He sat at the kitchen table, the broad smile on his face making me feel bad for trying to keep the console from him. I felt guilty, too. He shouldn't be afraid to tell me if he'd lost something. Though he was right: I probably would have lectured him about taking care of his possessions.

I had another thing to talk to Megan about now. I took a beer from the fridge and went into the living room. Through the front window I could see Ross coming up the road, with no dog in tow. Shelley ran out of the house and they started shouting, blaming each other for not noticing the gap in the fence.

I was about to sit down when I heard a loud bang.

'Ollie?'

He came out of the kitchen. 'What was that?'

'I thought it was you.'

He shook his head. 'I think it came from upstairs.'

I went into the kitchen and found a heavy rolling pin in the drawer. 'Stay here,' I instructed Ollie, and went upstairs. I checked both bedrooms, then the bathroom. Nobody.

But then it came again. *Thump.*

Ollie, who had disobeyed me and come upstairs, said, 'It came from up there.' He pointed above our heads, to the loft. 'There's somebody up there.'

'I'm going to call the police,' I said.

But as I took my phone out, the hatch opened and someone said, from above, 'Don't call the police. It's just me.'

A head poked through the gap. It was Kyle, Mrs Douglas's lodger, the plumber. He'd been around when I was growing up. I remembered him clearly from when he was in his twenties, with a mullet and an earring, hanging around the bridge trying to chat up tourists. He'd always be sitting on the wall, rolling cigarettes. That same smell of tobacco clung to him now. He didn't wear an earring any more, but his hair was still long at the back, though he was bald on top. I'd found Kyle quite useful since my return. He'd never married or had kids, and sometimes, when I was thinking about all the things that had gone wrong in my life, I'd remember Kyle and feel better. At the moment, though, I couldn't say I was happy to see him.

'Kyle,' I said. 'What the hell are you doing?'

He grinned sheepishly. 'Sorry, mate. We've got a problem with our shower. Air trapped in the pipes. I was trying to fix it.'

'But what are you doing in my loft?'

'They all interconnect,' he said, reminding me of something I already knew. When I'd moved in and gone up to store some junk in the loft, I'd noticed that it ran the length of all three cottages, with just some rudimentary boards propped up to separate each area. 'I dropped my torch and it rolled over into your bit. Sorry. I just came over to retrieve it and then I tripped over a box. Flipping clumsy oaf, I am. I'll clear off now.' He gave me another embarrassed smile.

'Did you clear it?' I asked.

'Huh?'

'The trapped air.'

'Oh. Yeah. I think it's fine now. Cheers.'

He shut the hatch and his footsteps tapped across the space above us and beyond the wall that separated my cottage from next door's.

I went downstairs. Through the living-room window I could see that a white van was parked in front of Ross and Shelley's cottage.

Adrian, Frank's assistant, sat in the passenger seat with the window rolled down, doing something on his phone.

Was Frank talking to them about my complaint? Eager to find out, I went outside and approached the van just as Frank came out of the cottage, muttering to himself. As usual, he was dressed like his hero, wearing a black shirt, jeans and cowboy boots.

'Ah, Ben,' he said, spotting me. He walked over to the van, glanced over his shoulder, then dropped his voice. 'I just came to have a word with Ross and Shelley about noise. They barely listened to me – too busy freaking out over their missing dog – but they've promised to keep it down. Don't worry, I didn't tell them it was you.'

Who else could it be? But I was pleased he'd done it.

'How's everything with you, anyway?' Frank asked. As he spoke, a phone beeped several times. Adrian's, I assumed. 'How's your mum doing?'

'As well as can be expected. She seems to be in good hands, anyway.'

He nodded sympathetically.

'Must be hard,' Adrian said. 'On you, I mean, worrying about her . . . Like, it must be a burden.'

Frank reached through the car window and cuffed the back of Adrian's head. 'Bloody insensitive lout.'

I sighed. 'He's kind of right, though. It is hard.'

'Expensive as well, aren't they, those nursing homes?' Adrian went on. 'When my nan was in one, my mum moaned about how her entire inheritance went on their fees.'

'I'm not bothered about that,' I said. 'I just hate her being in pain.'

'If I ever get like that,' Adrian said, 'I'm going to go to that place in Switzerland. Dignitas. I'd rather be put out of my misery than—'

At that moment, Kyle emerged from his cottage. When he saw Adrian he raised his hand and grinned, and Adrian opened the door, jumped down from the van and slouched over to him. They stood on Mrs Douglas's front lawn, talking.

'Kyle does a bit of work for me,' Frank explained. 'Him and Adrian have hit it off. They probably swap horror videos.' He called out. 'Oi, Adrian! We haven't got all day.'

Adrian and Kyle enacted a complicated handshake before parting.

I watched them drive away, followed a minute later by Kyle in his van. Feeling someone watching me, I turned to see Shelley glaring at me through her front window. A minute later, she put music on and turned it up loud.

I went back inside, sighing. My relaxed mood from the spa had well and truly gone.

Chapter 12

One of my earliest memories is of my dog. She was my dad's dog, really, but she tried to protect Mum and me. She was a mongrel, intelligent and docile as a lamb, but when Dad used Mum as a punchbag, which happened every time he had a drink, the dog would bark and growl at him, even though she knew it would lead to her getting a good kicking and being chucked outside.

That early memory: I must have been three, playing on the floor with my toy, this yellow plastic truck that I'd been given for Christmas, my most prized possession. I left it in Dad's way and the twat nearly slipped on it. He was furious, snatching it up and holding it over my head like he was going to whack me with it. The dog, bless her, made this low rumbling noise in her throat, getting in front of me, and that made Dad laugh and hit her with the truck instead.

So I like dogs. Always have done.

It would have been easiest to kill Pixie. Lure her away, poison her, bury her in a ditch somewhere. Job done, and Ross and Shelley would never have known. But when I looked into those soft brown eyes, I couldn't do it.

Getting her out of the garden was easy. Nice bit of raw meat – dogs are even more predictable than people.

Now, having brought Pixie to this remote farm from the coal shed where I was keeping her, I sit outside in the van and wait for the vet to tell me he's finished. It's all strictly illegal, of course, but this guy owes me – or rather, I know things about him, things that involve little girls, and one day I'm going to rip his eyes out and do things to his testicles that will go some way to making him pay for what he's done. But right now, he's useful, so he can live a bit longer.

Thinking about vets, my thoughts naturally turn to Danni. My first lucky one. She was a pretty girl. Big eyes that reminded me of Mum's and a warm smile. She was – what's the word? – guileless. Another one who deserved happiness, but had found it hard to come by. It was a familiar story, too: fucked up by her mum and dad. I read all about it in her diary.

Danni was the first woman whose life I took, the first person I freed from pain and sent from this mortal coil. She was sweet until the very end. From the moment she realised I was going to kill her she pleaded not for her own life, but the life of the child in her belly. I whispered reassurances: it wouldn't hurt her baby; the little thing wouldn't even know about it and they would always be together. How many parents can say that? Life tears parents and children apart. In death, Danni and her baby will be as one for eternity.

Beautiful.

I expect the morphine made Danni Junior feel pretty special, too.

When she was lying there, after her heart had stopped beating, the temptation to remove Danni's clothes and press my body against hers, to keep her warm for a little longer, was almost overwhelming. Her baby bump hardly showed, but her tits had already grown, big and ripe and round, and I would have loved to suckle on those sweet, dark nipples, to go back in time to the days when I was happy myself.

But I resisted. I felt good enough anyway.

Later that night, I went out and found myself a bad girl. She was young, maybe eighteen or nineteen, had the same dark hair and mournful eyes as Danni. She was rotten inside, though, addled by drugs and drink, and she'd had more men inside her than Wembley Stadium. I took her into the woods and I really wasn't going to kill her, just fuck her, maybe hurt her a little, but I got carried away. I choked her to death beneath my favourite tree, reminding myself that she deserved it. She deserved it because she wasn't Danni. She wasn't good.

And no one would miss her.

I'm not going to do that again, though. I need to stay focused and concentrate on the good people.

ϖ

When the vet comes out to say he's finished, I collect Pixie and take her with me in the van. She looks pretty sorry for herself and I feel bad about it. But it had to be done. Ollie had already texted me, telling me how pleased he was about the dog going missing, how her constant barking drove him and Ben crazy. Well, they won't have to worry about that any more.

Chapter 13

Imogen hit rewind on the CCTV tape for the twentieth time and stared at the image, her face inches from the screen, hoping it would be like one of those old Magic Eye pictures: that some revelation would suddenly spring out at her. But it wasn't happening. She thumped the desk with a curled fist and swore.

At 4.33 a.m. on Sunday morning, a van had pulled up outside the junkyard. On the tape, a man jumped down from the driver's seat, opened the back of the van and hauled Fiona Redbridge's mountain bike out before chucking it into the skip that stood in front of the fence. Then he drove away.

The van's rear registration plate had dirt smeared across it, obscuring the numbers and letters. They had an expert looking at it, trying to enlarge the image, but the quality of the picture was poor. The Daunts had spared every expense when installing their security system, it seemed, and Imogen didn't hold out much hope. It was impossible to tell if it was the same man they'd seen lurking at Wenlock Priory.

They had only been able to ascertain that the vehicle was a white Ford Transit, third generation, manufactured between 2003 and 2013. One of the most common vans on the road. And they knew that the murderer must have driven it from Wenlock Priory to Bridgnorth in the early hours of Sunday morning. A CCTV camera in Bridgnorth had picked up the van leaving town, heading back in the direction of Much Wenlock, five minutes after the bike was dumped. But after that – nothing. He hadn't triggered any speed cameras by driving too fast, so he wasn't captured anywhere else, and the mud-smeared plate meant no other cameras on the ANPR network had picked him up.

So all they knew was that he probably lived somewhere north of Bridgnorth – hardly helpful, when Bridgnorth was in the very southeast of the county.

Imogen scrutinised the picture of the man climbing out of his van and lifting the bike. He was wearing a hoodie and what looked like jeans and black shoes or boots. There were no visible logos or distinguishing marks on his clothes. His face was concealed by shadows, so it was nothing more than a featureless grey smear. All they could tell was that he was just over six feet tall and slim. He was Caucasian, in a county where 98 per cent of the population were also white. It was unbelievably frustrating. Here she was, staring at the man she wanted to find more than anyone in the world, and she still had no idea who he was or where to find him.

But dumping both of the bikes in the same place, in front of a CCTV camera – that had been foolish. A mistake he'd so far got away with. But he would slip up again, she was sure. Or he had made other errors already. They just had to find out what they were.

Emma came into the office holding two Starbucks cups, one of which she handed to Imogen, followed by a muffin.

'You're an angel.'

'Have you heard who's in town?'

Imogen bit into the muffin, then started talking with her mouth full. 'Not Brad Pitt? Oh God, he's tracked me down, broken the restraining order again.'

'He can't resist a woman who can fit a whole blueberry muffin in her mouth.'

'I've got pro skills.' She laughed. 'Come on then, spit it out. The gossip, I mean, not your coffee.'

'Michael Stone.'

'Oh. Now I've lost my appetite.'

Emma sat down in a chair that squeaked as it swivelled. Imogen hated that chair almost as much as she loathed the Viper.

'I've got bad news. He's making a programme about the Viper. Camille called him.' Camille McDaris was the media relations officer. 'He wants to talk to you. He mentioned someone called Kevin Moss.'

Imogen put her head in her hands. 'Oh, that wanker. He's going to try to make me look incompetent, like it's all my fault there's "a killer on the loose".' She'd waggled her fingers and put on a stupid voice, imitating Stone's.

'Who is Kevin Moss?' Emma asked.

Imogen placed the half-eaten muffin on her desk, then reached behind her and switched off the screen showing the frozen CCTV image.

'I'll understand if you don't want to tell me,' Emma said.

'I don't want to. But it's probably better if you hear it from me, before that toerag Stone broadcasts it to the whole country. I'm just trying to work out where to start.'

ᖬ

Kevin Moss had been a newly qualified detective constable who'd joined the Murder Investigation Team shortly after Imogen was promoted to detective inspector. Imogen had taken an instant dislike to him. He was too cocky – thought he was God's gift not just to women but to the whole police force. His father had been a detective, a well-known figure in the Met with a reputation for being a hard man, the type who believed women had no place in the front line of the fight against crime. Moss Senior had recently retired, and Kevin had clearly been brought up in his father's mould. He was twenty-seven years old, good-looking with chocolate-brown eyes and dark hair. Imogen was sure he'd only got his detective's badge because of his contacts. He was all mouth: lazy, not particularly intelligent and careless. In his first month, he had almost screwed up an investigation by mishandling evidence, and he'd tried to pin the blame on his female partner. The superintendent, an old friend of Moss Senior, had given Kevin a bollocking and asked Imogen to mentor him.

'Keep an eye on that little twat,' had been the super's exact words. 'His dad was an excellent detective.'

'And a massive misogynist,' Imogen had responded.

'He was old school. But he was good, Imogen. The trouble is, Kevin's been brought up to think that being a great cop runs in his blood. He needs a short, sharp shock, that's all.'

'So you want me to bring him down a peg or two?'

'I didn't say that. Just make sure he understands the reality of being a good detective.'

But she had gone away remembering the words 'short, sharp shock'.

A week later, Imogen had been working late. She was in a bad mood. A rape investigation had fallen apart. She was certain she knew who the rapist was – a scumbag called Piotr Nabora with priors for sexual assault and narcotics – but the victim, a young Romanian woman named Maria Albu, had suddenly announced that she wouldn't testify against him. Somebody had got to her. Imogen had spoken to her that afternoon; the poor girl was practically hyperventilating with fear. She had a three-year-old daughter and Imogen was certain that Nabora – or, more likely, one of his associates – had threatened Maria and her little girl. Maria was now saying that the sex was consensual.

Imogen had seen the injuries Nabora had inflicted on this tiny, twenty-four-year-old woman. She knew there was no way Maria had consented. They had photographs of her bruises. She had internal injuries. But without Maria's testimony, they stood little chance of getting a conviction. It was intensely frustrating. Imogen knew that Nabora – a nasty little shit who looked like a rat that had learned to walk on its hind legs – would do it again.

As she was banging at the keyboard, finishing her report, Kevin Moss had wandered over and peered over her shoulder.

'What are you working on?' he'd asked. 'Oh, the Maria Albu case. I heard about that. Sucks.'

'Yeah. It does.' She'd turned back to her computer, hoping he'd go away, but he'd loitered behind her. 'Why don't you go home, Kevin?'

He'd ignored her, continuing to read over her shoulder. 'I was thinking, maybe someone should pay Nabora a visit, let him know we're keeping an eye on him.'

'Is that what your dad would have done?'

He'd shrugged. 'Dad probably would have given him a good kicking. You can't get away with things like that any more, though, can you?'

'Fortunately not.'

Kevin had perched his bum on the desk across from Imogen's. 'Don't tell me you wouldn't like to see that tosser get what's coming to him?'

'I want to see him behind bars, Kevin. That's justice.'

'Hmm.'

A silence had fallen between them.

'So, what do you say? Should we have a word with him? So he knows he's being watched?'

She had been about to say, 'What? And have him do us for police harassment?' but then a wicked thought had crawled into her head. The more she'd seen of Kevin, the more convinced she'd become that he would never be a good detective. He had been poisoned by the 'old-school' ways of his dad.

She'd found herself saying, 'Why don't you go and talk to him?'

The thought that had crept into her head had been, *If Kevin gets done for harassment, he'll be off my back. And maybe Nabora will get the message. Maybe it'll stop him doing it again – at least for a while.* Either result, in that moment, had seemed good to her.

Kevin had stared at her, obviously shocked that she'd agreed, before nodding and saying, 'I think I will.'

He'd swaggered off across the office.

The next time she'd seen Kevin, he'd been in a hospital bed.

ω

Emma's eyes were wide. 'What happened?'

Imogen rubbed her face. Telling the story made her feel sick with regret. Why hadn't she told Kevin to forget about his stupid idea and go home?

'He went down to the place where Nabora lived. He was in a house on the edge of this rough estate in Brixton. We were told to only go there in pairs. Anyway, Nabora was there with various members of his gang. There was a drug deal going down when Kevin knocked on the door.' She paused and let out a big sigh. 'Nabora shot him.'

'Shit.'

'The bullet caught his spine, here.' She touched her lower back. 'They left him for dead, but a neighbour heard the gunshot and called the police. The next thing I knew, Kevin was in hospital. He survived but . . .'

Emma waited.

'He was paralysed from the waist down.'

'Oh, Imogen.'

'And, of course, he told everyone that I had ordered him to do it, told him to go and put the frighteners on Nabora. I had his dad, the famous Gary Moss, screaming at me in the hospital, calling me a bitch and a stuck-up slag who'd ruined his son's life. It was horrendous. I was hauled in to see the super . . . He knew exactly what Kevin was like, told me that I should deny it – it was my word against his, no one who knew me would believe that I'd ordered him to do something so stupid. But I felt so guilty. It was my fault. I didn't stop him.'

'But you had no way of knowing he'd get shot.'

'That's what the super said. But I knew Nabora. I knew what he was capable of. I should have known there was a good chance he'd have a gun. I just didn't think . . . I was stupid.'

'So what happened? Did you deny it?'

Imogen nodded, feeling wretched. 'Yes. I couldn't bear the thought of my career being over. I love doing this. It's what I've worked for my whole life. And I suppose I didn't see any point in throwing it all away. I mean, I didn't put him up to it. It was his idea. I just failed to stop him. That's what I tell myself, anyway, when I'm lying awake at night, picturing that poor bastard in his wheelchair.' She sipped at the cold dregs of her coffee. 'He could have stayed in the police, got a desk job, but he quit.'

Emma was quiet for a moment. 'So is that why you left the Met to come here?'

'Yeah. I couldn't bear it there any more. The guilt was eating me up. And a lot of my colleagues believed Kevin – I could see it on their faces. Rooms would fall silent when I entered them. So I put in a transfer request. I wanted a quiet life. If only I'd known.'

Emma put a hand on Imogen's shoulder. 'If it's any consolation, I'm glad you didn't confess. Because then you wouldn't be here. You're a brilliant detective, Imogen.'

'Do you think so? Then why are we no closer to catching the Viper?' Imogen had given up trying not to use the killer's tabloid name.

'Because he's clever, and lucky. But we will find him, I know it. You'll find him and stop him.'

Imogen chucked her empty coffee cup into the bin. 'If I'm not kicked off the case. God knows what Kevin's doing now, but it sounds like Michael Stone has tracked him down, found out what I did. He's going to broadcast it on BBC1. *Viper Detective's Tragic Error.*'

'You'll just have to deny it again.'

Imogen realised she was late for a meeting with Greene. 'I'm too busy for this shit. I'm going to ignore Stone for as long as I can. And if he tracks me down, well, I'll just have to appeal to his better nature. If he has one.'

Chapter 14

Michael Stone loved coming home to Shropshire – it reminded him of everything he'd achieved in life. Oh, if his friends could see him now! The funniest thing was, they *could* see him – prime time BBC1, *No Stone Unturned*, the highest-rated current affairs show on TV, award winning, critically acclaimed, untouchable. And now, on top of all that, he had the woman he'd coveted for the last decade on his arm and in his bed.

Except Megan was in a right mood with him.

'I told you, it wasn't my fault,' Michael said over breakfast in their hotel room. 'I barely said a word.'

Megan was looking hot in a white bathrobe, her hair damp and pinned up. She prodded her scrambled egg with her fork. 'I bet you wound him up. You know I don't want Ben to be hurt any more than he has been already.'

He reached across and stroked her cheek with his knuckles. 'You're a good person, Meg.'

'Hmm. Hardly.'

'Annette said she thought he was going to punch me.'

Her face darkened and she got up and crossed the room to grab the hairdryer. She hadn't eaten any of her breakfast and he was tempted to help himself until he remembered how many pounds the camera added.

Michael knew that Megan wasn't only thinking of her estranged husband's feelings. She didn't want to piss Ben off because she was worried he'd try to stop her from seeing wotsisname, their son. Any minute now he expected her to start blaming him for encouraging her to let Ben have custody.

He went over to Megan, who was now sitting at the dressing table. He leaned in close and nuzzled her neck, her hair wet against his cheek.

'Michael, not now.'

He kissed her cheek, glancing at himself in the mirror. 'Listen, you don't need to worry about Ben stopping you from seeing him. I can afford a top lawyer. We'll fight for custody, if that's what it comes down to. Or joint custody, whatever you'd prefer.'

She turned her head and gave him a quick peck on the lips, giving him a moment of hope before she turned back to the mirror and switched the hairdryer on.

Fine. Whatever. She was nervous about seeing her son. He understood that. He was an understanding guy. But later he'd get her to put on the expensive lingerie he'd bought her for this trip and he'd bend her over the bed and she'd look over her shoulder at him in that way that drove him crazy and . . . and . . .

'I'm going to take a shower,' he said.

ω

'. . . terrifying to picture something so brutal happening in this beautiful setting. And the police are still no closer to finding the man who committed this unspeakable act. The great writer PG Wodehouse called this county "the nearest earthly approach to paradise". Let us pray that Danni Taylor, Nathan Scott and Fiona Redbridge really are in paradise now.'

Michael strode over to speak to the director, Louis. 'How was that? Too over the top?'

'No, that was great. Nice work.'

Michael turned and surveyed the field. In the distance he could just make out the buildings on the outskirts of Ruyton-XI-Towns, the church steeple rising through the mist. Behind him, the River Perry and more farmland. It was going to look great on camera. A picturesque place to die.

Michael took a snap on his phone and posted it to Twitter. *At the spot where the #shropshireviper's 1st victim was found. V moving. That poor lamb.*

He knew it would get hundreds of likes.

After shooting a couple more takes, they went into the village to find a pub where they could have lunch before heading to the next location. In the Land Rover, Michael asked if DI Evans had called back yet.

'Not so far,' said Annette Lawrence, one of the researchers. It was Annette who had tracked down Kevin Moss and heard the story of what Imogen Evans had persuaded him to do. The poor bastard. Annette was in her mid-twenties with lustrous dark hair that fell almost to her waist. She looked a little like Whitney Houston before the crack got her, and the men on the crew spent half their working lives gawping at her. 'I'll chase that media woman again.'

'That's no use,' Michael snapped. 'We need to go straight to Evans herself. Can't you find out where she lives?'

Annette frowned. 'Are we allowed to do that?'

'Well, we want to give her a chance to tell her side of the story, don't we?'

He had nothing against Imogen Evans personally – in fact, he had a thing for redheads – but she and her team had thus far failed to find the Viper. And the public were going to love the story of what had happened to Moss. They hadn't filmed the interview yet, but Michael knew it would be a thing of beauty, Moss in his wheelchair, the brave young detective, career ruined before it had begun. Would the public really want a woman who wrecked the life of this poor young man in charge of the biggest manhunt in years?

'Find her address,' he said. 'At the very least, I want a shot of her trying to evade the camera. If we're lucky, she'll try to grab the lens or tell us to fuck off.' He laughed.

Driving into the village, they encountered a bus by the side of the road, the driver standing beside it holding a road map, looking lost. He flagged them down and Louis, who was driving the Land Rover, pulled over and rolled down the window.

The bus driver approached the car. 'Any idea where Boreatton Park is?' he asked. 'It's an outdoor activity centre. My bloody GPS has bust and I've got a coachload of fed-up Brownies here.'

A dozen ten- or eleven-year-old girls peered out at them.

'Sorry, mate,' Louis said. 'We're not from round here.'

They drove on, spotting a pub a minute later. Michael had a thought. 'Maybe we could use that. If there's an activity place round here for kids, we could get some shots of the innocent little Brownies riding horses or whatever it is they do. Juxtapose it with a dramatization of Danni Taylor's murder. Innocent babes playing, the shadow of death hanging over them.'

'Yeah, nice,' said Louis.

Michael gestured to Annette as they got out of the car. 'Give this Boreatton place a call,' he said. 'See if they're happy for us to film there.'

Over lunch – the rest of the crew had ploughman's, while Michael picked at a salad – they discussed the murders again. Michael had to admit it had become something of an obsession. How he would love to crack this case, or at least put together a plausible theory that would get the hairs on the napes of his viewers' necks standing on end. Of course, he didn't have the resources the police had, but he was a storyteller. He glanced round the typical country pub, with its exposed oak beams and brickwork, and wondered if anyone here knew of any interesting rumours he could use to spice up his report, ideally about police incompetence. Might be worth chatting up some of the regulars, though none of them looked too friendly. He was reminded of that scene from *An American Werewolf in London*, when the travellers enter The Slaughtered Lamb pub. Still, he was a local lad made good. They might help him. And he had noticed a guy at the bar, with greasy blond hair and dressed head to toe in black, who kept staring at him like he wanted to approach, but was too shy.

Michael headed over.

'Michael Stone,' he said, sticking out his hand.

The man's handshake was surprisingly firm.

'Adrian,' he said. 'I've seen you on TV. I'm a big fan.'

Michael smiled modestly. 'I'm back on my old stamping ground. Looking into this dreadful business.'

'The Viper?'

'Exactly. The police don't seem to be any closer to catching him, do they?'

Adrian downed half his pint in one go. 'They're bloody hopeless. I called them, you know. They just ignored it.'

Michael tilted his head. 'Called them?'

'Yeah.' Adrian swallowed another mouthful of beer. 'The night that girl was killed, the first one, my neighbour—'

He stopped suddenly.

'Go on,' Michael urged.

But Adrian shook his head. 'I can't. I have to go, get back to work.' He got down from his stool and went to leave.

Frustrated, Michael stepped in front of him. 'What were you going to tell me about your neighbour?'

'It's nothing. I don't want to get anyone into trouble.'

'But you said you called the police.'

Adrian glanced over at the table at Annette, Louis and the rest of the crew. 'If I tell you, you'll want me to be on TV. I don't want to be on TV.'

'We won't, I promise. Just tell me what you know. Maybe I could pass it on to the police. They'll take me seriously.'

But Adrian put his head down and stepped past Michael. He headed through the exit and Michael followed.

'Adrian! Look, take this.' Michael caught up to him and pressed a business card into the other man's hand. 'If you want to talk to me, in confidence, call me. Please. I promise I won't make you appear on TV. I won't even use your name.'

Adrian examined the business card and shoved it deep in his pocket. Then he jogged away.

Michael watched him go. An oddball who probably didn't have real information. Michael went back inside to finish his salad.

Chapter 15

I was awoken by a squeal from next door, followed by a crashing sound – like someone knocking over a table – and the *thump-thump-thump* of footsteps hurrying down stairs. The back door banged and I heard Shelley's voice, high pitched and excited. 'Pixie!'

I went to the back window. Shelley was attempting to catch her German shepherd, who was bouncing from fence to fence, mouth opening and closing, though I didn't hear any barks. The dog seemed to be in some distress. Ross appeared in his dressing gown and Shelley turned to him, her face pink and scrunched with confusion. I couldn't make out what she was saying.

I ran downstairs and into my own garden, eager to know what was going on. Ross had managed to catch the dog and was holding her by the collar, crouching and inspecting her throat.

Pixie barked. Except what came out wasn't a bark – it sounded more like an asthmatic cough.

'What's happened to her?' Shelley was in tears now, on her knees beside the dog, who was trembling, tail between her legs. She tried to rear up on to her hind legs and emitted another of those strange non-barks.

'Is she okay?' I asked. It was a stupid question, I admit. But I didn't know what else to say.

Ross glared at me as he dragged the dog into the house. Shelley followed, slamming the door behind her.

It looked like Pixie had fallen ill while she was missing, probably from spending a day and night outdoors. What was it called – kennel cough? As much as I disliked the dog's incessant barking, I was relieved nothing terrible had happened to her. I went back inside, made myself a coffee and woke Ollie up, telling him he needed to get ready for school. I soon forgot Pixie. I was too distracted by what was going to happen that evening.

Megan was coming round.

ω

When I got back from the school run, Ross and Shelley were putting Pixie in the back of their car. Shelley's expression reminded me of Megan's that time we thought three-year-old Ollie had meningitis. Ross simply looked angry.

I spent the rest of the morning working on my copy about the spa. Writing about it brought back a sense memory of the bliss I'd experienced the day before. I vowed to make it a regular occurrence, especially if Robert Friend continued to give me regular work, as he'd promised.

I finished the first draft and went to the front window. It had turned into a beautiful day, the sky a clear and cloudless blue, and I took my coffee out on to the step. Sitting in the sunshine, I decided I'd done the right thing bringing Ollie here. It was a lovely part of the world. The school break was coming, my son's first in the countryside, a summer without the grit and fumes and oppression of London. He was going to love it – though I might need to persuade him not to spend the whole time shut in his room with his iPod and new DS.

I was about to go back inside when the neighbours pulled up, Pixie gazing mournfully out of the rear window.

Shelley got out of the car, banged the door behind her and strode straight over to me with a face of thunder.

'It was you!' she screeched, jabbing her finger towards me.

I stood up. 'What are you talking about?'

Ross had followed her into my front garden. He was trembling with barely suppressed rage, fists clenched by his side. 'We've just got back from the vet's. Someone fucking debarked Pixie,' he said, his voice low and menacing.

I stared at him blankly. 'Debarked?'

'They cut her vocal cords.'

'What?'

Shelley was right in my face now, her own face red with fury. 'Don't act all innocent. That twat Frank Dodd said someone had complained about us. It was you, wasn't it? Moaning about Pixie's barking.'

There was no point denying it. 'Only because when I tried to talk to you reasonably you wouldn't do anything about it.' The two of them moved closer to me, Godzilla and his bride. My front door was open and it wouldn't be hard to nip inside and shut the door, but I wasn't going to run away from this pair, even if they did want to murder me. I was done with running. 'But I didn't do anything to your dog.'

'Then who the fuck else would have done it?' Ross demanded, his face growing redder by the second.

'I have no idea. But I like dogs. I would never do anything to hurt one. I mean, debarking – that's illegal, isn't it? Even if I was the kind of person who would consider doing that to a dog, I wouldn't have a clue how to go about it.'

It was Shelley's turn to speak. 'The vet reckons it must have been done in some backstreet place.'

'A backstreet vet's? I didn't even know places like that existed.'

'Well, they do.'

But it looked like they might finally believe I wasn't responsible, as Ross unclenched his fists and Shelley turned her head to gaze at Pixie through the car window.

'My poor baby,' Shelley said, eyes filling with tears. 'Someone hurt her. When I find out who it was, I'm going to kill them.'

'I'll rip *their* fucking vocal cords out,' Ross said, eyes fixed on me.

'But is she going to be all right?' I asked. I looked at their car to see the dog gazing over with doleful eyes.

'Yeah,' Shelley said, turning back to face me. 'But she won't ever bark again.'

'Have you called the police?' I asked.

'Yeah. They're on their way round,' Ross said. 'Not planning on going out, are you? They'll want to talk to you. Come on, Shell.'

He tugged at her arm and they headed back to their car, letting Pixie out and leading her into the house. I stared after them, then looked around at the other nearby houses and cottages. Mrs Douglas's living room curtain moved. She must have been watching.

I went back indoors, mulling over the puzzle. But it was too weird. I had no answer.

ʊ

'Can you get changed, Ollie? We're going out.'

'But . . . what about Mum? Has she cancelled?'

'No. But she doesn't want to come here. She wants to meet for dinner so we're going to Bridgnorth.'

He huffed. 'I wanted her to see my room.' He dropped his school bag on the floor and scuffed his feet all the way to his bedroom.

I hadn't been too surprised to receive the text from Megan. I had a feeling she'd want to meet in public. She probably thought if we were at my place I'd do or say something to embarrass her, cause a scene. I knew how low her opinion of me had sunk, and in fairness to her, I had been pretty vile the last time I'd seen her. Justifiably so, I'd thought at the time.

I'd been picking Ollie up from the flat after he'd spent a couple of nights with Megan over Christmas. Halfway through saying good-bye to Ollie, she'd been distracted by a text message as he'd tried to thank her for his presents. This had been a common theme of our last months together, before I'd discovered her affair: she'd always been on her phone, unable to watch TV or eat dinner or have a conversation without checking it. Seeing her look at it now, ignoring her son, had brought all the rage I'd managed to conceal to the surface, and when Ollie had left the room to collect his bag, I'd got up in Megan's face and hissed, 'You're a bad mother.'

It was as if I'd stuck a knife between her ribs. And I'd enjoyed it. I'd liked hurting her. I'd grabbed Ollie and hustled him out of there before she could retaliate.

Now, driving to Bridgnorth, I told Ollie about Pixie. He just grunted like the topic was too boring to react to.

Dinner with Megan was going to be the third out-of-the-ordinary encounter of the day. First, there'd been the confrontation with Ross and Shelley. And then, as the neighbours had promised, the police had come round. It was actually one of those community support officers, a young blonde woman, who'd asked me lots of questions about my relationship with the couple next door. She hadn't seemed particularly interested, but had written down everything I'd said before going off to talk to Mrs Douglas.

I parked in the centre of Bridgnorth, by the library.

We'd arranged to meet in a fish restaurant on the high street. The streets were unusually quiet. Was this because of the Viper? As I wondered this, a man appeared from an alleyway with a dog on a lead and I jumped, heart banging.

'You're acting weird,' Ollie said. He had his hood up, despite the mild weather.

I tried to make light of it. 'That's because I *am* weird.'

He almost smiled. 'Yeah. True.'

'Don't forget to thank your mum for the DS.'

'Of course I won't. I'm not six.' There was a long pause, during which I could sense him struggling to speak. We were almost at the restaurant. 'I miss her.'

Three little words that broke my heart. I pulled him into the alleyway, between two shops. 'I know you miss her, Ollie. I understand how hard it is.'

His hood hid his face. 'I keep having dreams. That we're back in London, all together in our old flat. Mum's cooking dinner and the two of you are happy. And then we sit down on that red sofa and *Britain's Got Talent* is on TV and we're all laughing and joking and you and Mum are, like, being nice to each other. And it's all good, like how it used to be.'

'Oh, Ollie.'

'And then I wake up.'

He was crying now, the sleeve of his hoodie pressed against his eyes, shoulders heaving gently, and I wanted to pick him up like when he was a baby, comfort him, make it all better. But all I could do was put my arm around his shoulder and wait for the tears to stop. Which they did, quickly. Even when he was a baby, Ollie had never cried for long.

He swiped at his eyes with his sleeve, sniffing. I handed him a tissue. I didn't know what to say. That time would heal his wounds? That now he'd get two Christmases, two birthdays, all the rubbish people usually say to kids to make them feel better?

'I didn't want her to see me like this,' he said, after blowing his nose. 'I want her to think everything's cool. That I don't give a shit. Sorry.'

'It's fine. You have retroactive permission to swear.'

That got a small laugh.

'Do you feel ready to go in?'

'I suppose so.'

I pulled his hood down and ruffled his hair. 'Come on, then. Let's show her how well we're doing without her.'

ω

Megan was seated at a table in a dimly lit back corner of the restaurant, a half-empty glass of white wine before her. I had expected to see her staring at her phone, but she was watching out for us. She lifted a hand and Ollie hurried over to see her. She stood and they hugged. I noticed her eyebrows go up as she saw how much more of him there was to hug now, all the weight he'd piled on since Christmas.

'Ben,' she said, as I reached the table.

'Hi, Megan.'

We all took our seats, chair legs scraping in the awkward silence.

'This is a nice place,' she said. 'I didn't expect—'

'There to be decent restaurants out here in the boonies?'

'Dad!'

'Sorry.' I forced a smile. 'You look well.'

In fact, she looked great. Painfully so. She'd grown her hair and looked more groomed than usual. She wore a soft green sweater that brought out the flecks in her eyes. She'd lost a few pounds too . . . probably from all the sex she was having. A bitter taste flooded my mouth and I forced myself to think about something else.

I avoided Megan's eye. It was going to be difficult to talk about anything important, like selling the house, with Ollie here. Maybe that was why she'd wanted to meet in a restaurant. Here, I couldn't send Ollie to his room so the grown-ups could talk.

Megan and Ollie chatted for a while and we ordered dinner. I could sense Megan wanting to tell Ollie to order something that wasn't too calorific, but she bit her tongue. She looked relieved when he asked for Diet Coke. I was surprised. But perhaps this was a result of overhearing Shelley insulting him.

'Something weird happened next door to us,' I said after the food arrived, going on to tell her about the dog being debarked.

'That's terrible!'

'At least we won't have to listen to the bloody thing barking all the time now,' Ollie said.

'That's not very nice,' Megan said, but she was smiling. 'Wow, another whodunnit in Shropshire.'

I spoke before I could stop myself. 'Maybe your boyfriend could make a documentary about it.'

Megan flinched. 'Please. Not now.'

Ollie announced that he needed the toilet. As soon as he was out of earshot, I said, 'I saw Michael yesterday, in Shrewsbury. I assume he's making a programme about the Viper?'

She stared at her plate, poking at the remains of her plaice with a fork. I couldn't work out if she was simply reluctant to talk about him with me or if something was wrong. Was everything in their garden less than rosy? Something was definitely amiss. I could read her. Although I'd been blind to her affair, hadn't I? I obviously didn't know her as well as I'd thought.

'Okay, if we're not going to talk about him, we need to talk about the flat.' But before I could say any more, Ollie returned. 'Can we meet again, while you're here, just the two of us?'

'Sure.'

As she said this the light struck her in a particular way and it was as if I'd been punched in the stomach. She looked exactly as she had when we were first married, back in those glorious days when we couldn't stop talking, when everything the other person said was interesting. When we couldn't keep our hands off each other. I had a flash of Megan beneath me, naked, gazing up at me, flushed across her collarbone, the warmth of her naked body. I remembered how she'd looked at me when we brought Ollie home from the hospital that first time. I recalled her resting her head on my shoulder on a long train journey home.

It still hurt, and I prayed she couldn't see it on my face.

Ollie returned to the table and sat down. 'I forgot to say thank you,' Ollie said to his mother.

'What for?'

'For sending me that DS,' Ollie said.

'You've lost me.'

'Someone sent him a new Nintendo DS,' I said.

'Well, it wasn't me.'

'Are you absolutely sure?' I asked. 'You might have been looking at his wish list and clicked by mistake.'

'I'm not an idiot, Ben.'

I had already double-checked my bank account so I knew that Ollie hadn't done it himself.

'Do you promise it wasn't you?'

Taken aback, she said, 'I swear.'

I looked at Ollie. He looked back at me. 'Who the hell did buy it, then?' I asked.

Chapter 16

I want to high five myself when I see Ollie at the bus stop with his new DS. Public wish lists are wonderful things. It's a shame the gift box didn't have a camera concealed inside so I could have seen the happy expression of surprise illuminate his face. I was worried Ben wouldn't let Ollie keep the Nintendo, that he would be suspicious of where it came from. But, as I suspected, he was too kind. Or too wrapped up in his own problems.

I watch from the mouth of the same alleyway I waited in the week before. No chips this week, which I'm delighted to see. He hasn't been doing himself any favours, filling his body with all those crap empty carbs. That stuff doesn't make you happy.

He's taking my advice. Listening to me much more than he listens to his dad.

Does he suspect that his new friend sent him the DS, too? Perhaps, but he hasn't said anything about it to me. Mostly, he messages me about the bitch next door, her dim-witted boyfriend and the now-barkless Pixie. And he messages me about the bullies at school.

Here they come now. Jake and Aaron. They swagger down the road, spouting shit at full volume. Ollie must hear them because I see his shoulders stiffen and he immediately shoves the games console into his backpack.

But it's too late. They've seen it.

Jake is the worst of the two, I can tell. The mouthiest and most vicious. The one who most deserves to be crushed beneath the wheels of the bus that could arrive at any moment. Tall for his age, a twelve-year-old with hints of bumfluff on his face and a voice that threatens to break at any moment. I've seen photos of his bedroom on Facebook, the big TV with an Xbox plugged into it, photos of topless babes all over the walls. Parents too busy earning money and filling the recycling bin with wine bottles to pay attention to the scum they are failing to rear properly.

Aaron is his wisecracking sidekick, not that his wisecracks are funny. A budding psychopath who spends his spare time on Twitter, trolling female celebrities. He lives with his mum and sister on a housing estate near Jake and spends the money they extort from other kids on weed. The world would be a much better place without him.

'What did you just put in your bag?' Jake asks, stopping by Ollie.

'Nothing.'

'He's lying,' Aaron says. 'Looks like his daddy's bought him a new DS already. What happened, Blob? Did you run home crying? Tell Daddy some mean boys took your toy away?'

Jake laughs. 'Yeah, Blob. Let's have a look. We won't take it this time. We just want to look at it.'

I can't hear Ollie's response. But the bus has turned the corner and is shuddering to a halt. Ollie jumps up, keeping a tight hold of his backpack, and dodges the vile pair, boarding his chariot home. Jake raps on the window where Ollie sits and makes a throat-slashing gesture while, behind him, Aaron puffs out his cheeks and stomps around, mimicking a sumo wrestler. Some of the other kids on the bus laugh. As it pulls away, I can just make out how red Ollie's face is.

The two bullies stride away, laughing.

I follow.

ꞵ

After a few minutes, the boys turn off the main road on to a footpath that leads to the housing estate where they live. On one side of the path, woodland. On the other, a playing field, where a game of football is taking place.

As the boys step on to the path, I slip into the woods and walk alongside them, concealed by a line of trees.

I pull my balaclava on.

There is a jogger on the path, twenty yards ahead of the boys. As soon as he pulls out of sight, I leap out of the woods like a ninja, landing in front of the two bullies.

It's time for them to know how it feels to be on the receiving end.

Aaron cries out in shock. Jake's eyes widen. Before they can react further, I punch Aaron in the solar plexus and deliver a swift kick to Jake's balls.

Both boys crumple to the ground.

I stoop and grab them by their throats, one in each hand. They are so small, so pathetic.

'Make a noise and you're both dead,' I hiss.

A trickle of liquid runs across the path, wetting my shoes. Aaron has pissed himself, the pathetic maggot.

'This is a warning,' I say. 'Leave Ollie Hofland alone. Go near him again, I'll kill you.'

Their eyes nearly pop out. They are just children, really. Weak, scared little children.

'In fact, if I hear anyone has given him grief, I'll kill you. First, I'll make you suck each other's little cocks. Then I'll cut them off. Then I'll shove them down your throats till you choke. Understand?'

They nod in tandem.

'Good.'

I let them go and slip back into the trees. I watch them for a moment, helping each other up. Aaron is crying, staring at his soaked trousers, and Jake has gone as white as a lily. These boys are destined for a life of unhappiness, of dissatisfaction and pain. Maybe one day, in the future, I will track them down and do what I threatened.

If they don't leave Ollie alone, that day will come very soon.

Chapter 17

'Excuse me? Detective?'

Imogen had been coming out of her front door, deep in thought, and looked up, startled.

The young black woman smiled. 'DI Imogen Evans?' She was pretty, wearing a tight-fitting red jacket and black knee-high boots, an umbrella held over her head. She came closer, dodging the puddle that always greeted Imogen on days like this.

Imogen was in a foul mood. She'd slept badly, details of this fucking impossible case flipping and churning around her head all night. Her alarm went off ten minutes after she finally sank, exhausted, into sleep. And now she was getting doorstepped. In the pissing rain. By a woman who looked like she'd stepped out of a fashion magazine.

'Who are you?'

'My name's Annette Lawrence. I work with Michael Stone.'

'Oh, for God's sake.'

'I was hoping to talk to you about Kevin Moss.'

Imogen put her head down and strode away, sticking close to the buildings that provided a modicum of shelter. Annette followed, falling into step with her, seemingly gliding across the surface of the puddles that splashed Imogen's ankles.

'Please, Detective, it'll only take a few minutes. We want to get your side of the story.'

Imogen stopped, jabbing a finger in the other woman's face. 'I have a murder investigation to conduct. I don't have time to talk to you.'

'It'll only take a few minutes.' Annette checked over her shoulder. 'Listen, it's in your best interests, honestly. If you don't talk to us, well . . .'

'What? What exactly will happen?' Imogen took a step towards the other woman, who, Imogen was pleased to see, had the good sense to appear nervous. 'I have nothing to say to you. But you can give a message to Stone from me.'

'Yes?'

'Tell him to fuck off back to London.'

She turned her back on the woman and stormed away, the rain and wind whipping her damp hair into her face. She knew she was going to regret that comment, but right now she didn't give a damn.

ɯ

Imogen's mobile rang as she was about to enter the station.

It was Emma. 'We've had a call about the guy who was lurking at the crime scene. The caller said our guy's name is Adrian Morrow. He's a local.'

'What do we know about him?'

'He's twenty-six, born and bred in Shrewsbury. Listen to this: last year, a young woman called Katie Booth made a complaint against him for harassing her. Stalking her. They went on a couple of dates and she said he wouldn't leave her alone, kept calling her, hanging around outside her flat, texting her dozens of times every day. I dug out the report. She said he was, quote, "creepy, obsessed with serial killers and horror films." She said that when she told him she was going to report him to the police if he didn't leave her alone, he said he didn't care because he'd always wanted to be notorious.'

'Gosh, you think he's still single?' But the fact was, Imogen's blood stirred. She pressed the phone against her ear. 'So what happened?'

'One of our officers had a word with him and that was the end of it. They followed up with Katie a week later and she hadn't heard from him again. The file was closed.'

'A bit anticlimactic,' Imogen said. 'Still, interesting. Does he work?'

'Yeah, for Dodd's Property Management. It's in the town centre. He should be there now.'

'All right. Let's go and have a word with him.'

She met Emma at the address in the centre of Shrewsbury. On her way there, she'd called the station and explained that she needed backup. It seemed unlikely that Adrian Morrow would be armed or try to make a run for it – he probably wasn't involved at all – but what had happened to Moss made her extra cautious. Feeling her adrenaline surging, she positioned the three uniformed officers who'd responded around the building, blocking the exits.

'I'm assuming you haven't come across Frank Dodd before?' Emma said as they climbed the narrow staircase. 'He's the biggest landlord around here.'

'The name rings a bell.'

They entered the office to find a man in his fifties sorting through a pile of paperwork at a desk, frustration evident on his face. He had black hair teased into a quiff that was threaded through with grey.

Imogen and Emma introduced themselves.

'Take a seat,' he said. 'My bloody assistant's gone AWOL and I've got tenants ringing me every two minutes.' He appeared to find what he was looking for and came around the desk, joining them on the sofas. Imogen couldn't help but stare at his cowboy boots.

'So how can I help you ladies?' he asked.

'We're looking for Adrian Morrow,' Imogen said. 'I'm assuming he's the assistant who's gone AWOL.'

Dodd raised his eyebrows. 'What's he done now? Not been bothering more young women, has he?'

Imogen exchanged a glance with Emma. 'You know about that?'

'Oh, yes. His mum told me. She's been a tenant of mine for years. She actually begged me to give Adrian a job shortly after the whole thing happened, help keep him on the straight and narrow.'

'And when did you last see him?'

'Day before yesterday. I've been calling him, but he isn't answering. I assumed he'd been on a bender and was holing up in his flat, recovering.'

Hearing he'd gone missing, Imogen found herself more and more interested in talking to Adrian Morrow, to get the measure of this 'creepy' young man.

'I was about to head round his flat, see if he's there,' Dodd said, getting back up.

'We'll come with you,' Imogen said.

ω

Fifteen minutes later, they stood outside Adrian's place. Imogen pressed the buzzer to his flat, but there was no reply. While she thought about what to do next, a man in his sixties appeared with a bunch of keys in his hand. A resident of the building.

'Have you seen Adrian Morrow?' Imogen asked.

'Not for a day or two. It's been blessedly quiet. He normally has this dreadful music on all night, or horror movies turned up full volume. Sometimes it sounds like he's murdering someone in there.'

'I'm going to need you to let us in,' Imogen said.

They left the three uniforms outside watching the building, and followed the man up to the second floor. Imogen rapped on the door and waited a few seconds. It was cold and dank here in the hallway, the smell of mildew thick in her nostrils. She had that taste in her mouth, coppery, like blood.

'I've got a key,' the neighbour said. 'He left the spare with me in case he locked himself out.'

Imogen mulled this over. 'Okay. Thank you.'

The neighbour fetched the key and handed it to Imogen. She gestured for Emma to follow her and told Frank Dodd, who had remained quiet throughout, to wait, sending the neighbour back to his flat.

She stepped into the dim hallway as quiet as a cat, Emma right behind her. The smell here was different, but equally unpleasant: the odour of damp clothes that have been left to dry mixed with something nastier – the stink of rubbish bins and stale alcohol fumes.

The flat was small, with three doors leading off the hallway. The first door stood open, revealing a grimy bathroom.

She crept along the corridor. The flat was silent, the only sound Emma's breathing behind her. She turned the handle of the first closed door and pushed it open at arm's length, pressing her back against the wall.

No noise or movement, so she entered the room. The room stank of stale sweat and cigarette smoke. The unmade bed was empty. Imogen gestured for Emma to remain in the hallway and quickly checked beneath the bed and in the closet. No one was hiding there.

Back in the hallway, she listened at the final door. Again, all was quiet, and she repeated the routine she'd used to open the bedroom door.

'Holy . . .' She trailed off, the swear word remaining under her breath, and entered the living room. There was a galley kitchen on the far side of the room. The curtains were closed, but enough sunlight came through the gap to reveal what could only be described as a shrine.

A shrine to evil.

It was like a museum dedicated to serial killers. Books were piled on tables, the faces of famous murderers adorning their covers: the Yorkshire Ripper, Fred West, Gary Ridgway, Ted Bundy. Many more true-crime books were crammed into an IKEA bookcase. DVDs on the same theme were stacked in front of the TV. Imogen took this all in before her attention turned to the wall.

It was covered with posters and cuttings from magazines, the type Imogen had seen in the supermarket, with titles like *Real Crime* and *True Crime Stories*. Lurid accounts of mass killings and savage murders. Rapists, stalkers and serial killers stared into the empty room, along with gruesome photos of their victims.

Imogen did a cursory check around the room and the kitchen, but there was nowhere Adrian could be hiding.

'Look at this,' Emma said.

Between the pages of a glossy magazine were cuttings from newspapers featuring pictures of Fiona Redbridge, Danni Taylor and Nathan Scott, with headlines like 'Viper Strikes Again' and 'Police Clueless, Claims Mother of Viper's Second Victim'. There was a photo of Imogen leaving a press conference, frowning as a photographer stuck his camera in her face.

On another wall was a map, very similar to the one in the incident room at the station, with the places where the three bodies had been found marked with red pins. Imogen felt that familiar tingle, a quickening of the pulse.

'I knew he was into his true crime stuff,' Dodd said, making Imogen jump. She hadn't heard him enter the flat. 'But I didn't know he was *this* into it.'

He stared around him at the piles of murder paraphernalia before turning his attention to the map. 'Fuck. Is that where the Viper's victims were found, on those spots?' He rubbed the bridge of his nose. 'His poor mother.'

Imogen crossed the room to the computer. Pulling her sleeve down over her hand, she prodded the keyboard so that the screen sprang to life. She found herself staring at another picture of herself. This one had been taken from a distance. She was coming out of the tent at Wenlock Priory, where Fiona Redbridge's body had lain.

She called the station, escorting Frank Dodd out of the room while she waited for them to answer. They needed forensics down here, sharpish. Outside the flat, she told Dodd to go back to work. She handed him her card, scribbling her mobile phone number on it.

'If he turns up, or contacts you, don't tell him anything, okay? Just call me.'

'You mean, act normal?'

'Exactly.'

'You don't want me to make a citizen's arrest?'

'No, Mr Dodd. I definitely don't want that.'

He walked away, shaking his head. She went back into the flat and, as she spoke to the forensics team, telling them what she needed, she studied the newspaper cuttings on the wall. Certain words detailing how the victims had died had been highlighted with a yellow pen.

Then she spotted something else. Beside the photos of Fiona, Danni and Nathan, Adrian had drawn a little picture using the yellow highlighter. A circle, two dots and a curl. A smiley face.

Chapter 18

The screaming and shouting started at just after 8 p.m. on Monday night.

I hadn't seen or heard much from Ross and Shelley over the weekend. In fact, Saturday and Sunday were quiet overall. Ollie went out with Megan, who had declared at the end of our meal that she wanted to take him out to do something fun: bowling, the cinema, shopping for new games for his DS.

I spent most of this peaceful time working. Robert Friend had declared himself delighted with the work I'd done for the spa and sent me a new assignment, writing a mail-order brochure for a farm shop that specialised in local, organic produce. I'd received a huge hamper full of honey, jam, chutney and all sorts of treats, which I chewed my way through, like the Hungry Caterpillar, as I worked. This was turning out to be a dream job, and I wished I could meet Robert to thank him.

At the back of my mind, though, was the niggling question of who had sent Ollie the Nintendo. I contacted Amazon customer service, who told me that the DS had been bought using a gift card, which allowed the sender to avoid using a billing address, and that they were unable to tell me who had sent it 'for reasons of confidentiality'. I argued with them, but it was like being stonewalled by a robot.

I was sure there was something Ollie wasn't telling me, but he insisted he had no idea who had sent it. On the drive back from Bridgnorth, I asked him if he'd been chatting with anyone online whom he didn't know in real life. He swore he hadn't been, apart from some chats with other kids in *Minecraft*. We had the conversation, again, about how you couldn't trust people online, that adults sometimes pretended to be kids.

'Dad, I know all that. They go on about it at school all the time.'

'What about these people you chat to within *Minecraft*? Are you sure they're kids?'

He huffed. 'Yeah. Well, I'm pretty certain. I don't know their real names, do I? And they don't know mine, or where we live, so there's no way any of them could have sent me the DS.'

It made no sense. So while he was out with Megan on Saturday, I searched his room and checked the history on his computer and iPod. But there was nothing to suggest he'd been chatting with anyone, no mysterious messages. All I could do, for now, was delete his Amazon wish list and vow to be more vigilant about his online behaviour.

Monday, when he came home from school, he bounced through the door like he used to when he was a few years younger.

'You're in a good mood,' I said.

A strange little smile crept on to his face. 'It was a good day,' he said. 'A better day.'

I had no idea what that meant. Before I could ask, he went to his room and I heard him fire up the computer.

Something was definitely going on. But then an email arrived from Robert Friend and I got drawn into a long exchange with him. At dinner time, Ollie came out, still beaming, and told me he wanted something healthy for his tea. 'Just a baked potato or beans on toast.'

'Did your mum say something to you over the weekend?'

'What, about me being fat?'

'Ollie . . .'

'No, she didn't. I just decided . . . Being overweight makes me vulnerable to things that will make me unhappy. It causes me pain.'

I stared at him. What an odd thing to say. But he was in such a good mood that I didn't want to spoil it by interrogating him, so I left it.

And then, after we'd eaten and Ollie went to his room to do his homework, the yelling started.

Shelley kicked off with a cry of 'You fucking bastard,' followed by 'I hate you!'

Ross shouted back that he hadn't done anything. 'You're a fucking lunatic!'

'Then what the fuck is this?'

I went into Ollie's room and told him to put some music on. He was staring goggle-eyed at the wall as Ross called Shelley a frigid bitch and a slut.

'How can I be both?' she yelled back. Which was a fair point.

'At least the dog's not barking,' Ollie pointed out.

The shouting carried on, back and forth.

'For God's sake,' I said. 'I'm sick of this. I'm going round there again.'

'Dad, leave it. Maybe they'll do us a favour and murder each other.'

I smiled despite myself. 'You shouldn't say things like that.'

'Or maybe, if we're really lucky, they'll rip out each other's vocal cords.'

It had gone quiet next door. I went into the living room and put the TV on. An hour later, the shouting started again. I turned the TV up so I couldn't make out what they were saying. Shelley's voice was loudest, growing ever more strident and high pitched, while Ross's voice alternated between a low rumble and a sudden, sharp insult. I expected them to start having noisy make-up sex at any moment. But then they fell quiet again.

It was ten o'clock. Ollie was asleep and, with nothing on TV, I went up to bed. What an exciting life – going to bed at ten, on my own. I still wasn't used to having a bed to myself. I picked up the book I was reading, the autobiography of a nurse who'd been accused of killing her patients before winning an appeal. She seemed as guilty as sin to me – but I couldn't concentrate. I kept thinking about Mum, whom I hadn't visited for a couple of days, which made me feel horribly guilty. I worried about Ollie and the Nintendo DS and his weird comments. Most of all, I thought about Megan.

Ever since our meal on Friday evening, my wife's face kept popping into my head. Seeing her brought back all the pain of the break-up, the shock of seeing her fucking Michael Stone, the grief I felt for our marriage. I'd read loads of articles online about how, when a serious relationship ends, it's like suffering a bereavement: a bereavement without a funeral. The death of love. Sometimes, in my darkest moments, it seemed even worse than having one's partner die. Dead people don't keep showing up to remind you of what you've lost.

Close to midnight, as I was finally drifting into sleep, the arguing next door started yet again. I groaned and pulled the pillow over my head. All I could hear was Shelley shouting, 'How could you? How could you do that?'

And then they were quiet and I fell asleep.

ω

I was woken at five by a blue flickering light inside my room and the sound of voices from the still-dark street. There were two police cars parked outside next door's house. As I watched, an ambulance trundled up the road.

I pulled on some jeans and a T-shirt and headed downstairs.

I found Mrs Douglas already in her front garden, holding a mug of tea and watching as uniformed police officers went in and out of Ross and Shelley's cottage. Kyle stood in the doorway, watching.

'What's going on?' I asked her.

She was pale, but it was clear she found the situation exciting, too. 'I thought it was him,' she said. 'You know. The Viper. I thought he'd got someone round here. But the policeman I spoke to said it was a domestic.'

Ross and Shelley's front door opened and two paramedics carried someone out.

In a body bag.

They manoeuvred the body into the back of the ambulance while more police officers, including a couple in plain clothes, milled around.

'Oh my God,' I said to Mrs Douglas. 'I heard them arguing last night. I had no idea . . .' Nausea hit me. Had I heard Shelley's final words? 'I should probably go and talk to the police, tell them what I heard.'

'Good idea.' She lowered her voice. 'See what you can find out, too.'

I headed down the path to speak with an officer, fully awake now thanks to the sight of the body on the stretcher. Half of the neighbourhood had emerged from their houses. Ollie, thankfully, was still asleep.

I was in shock. Shelley – dead. I knew Ross had a history of violence, but—

I was stopped in my tracks by the sight of the police emerging from next door with someone in handcuffs.

I had been wrong to assume. It wasn't Ross they were leading out of the cottage, and it hadn't been Shelley in the body bag.

She was the one in handcuffs.

ʊ

A little later, a flashy vintage sports car pulled up outside and two women got out. The one who emerged from the driver's side had a shock of red hair. I recognised her. She was that cop, the one who had been on TV appealing for information about the serial killer. I couldn't remember her name. The other woman, who I assumed was also a detective, had a runner's physique and wore a dark grey windbreaker. They went into the cottage next door.

I tried to concentrate on work for a while, but then the doorbell rang.

It was the two detectives.

The redhead held up her police badge. 'Ben Hofland? Detective Inspector Imogen Evans. This is Detective Sergeant Emma Stockwell. Do you mind if we come in and ask you a couple of questions about your next-door neighbours? You told one of the constables that you heard them arguing last night.'

'Yes. Come in.'

I led them into the kitchen. It was a new experience, having detectives in my house. Quite exciting. 'Do you want a drink? Tea? Coffee? I've just got a new Nespresso machine.'

'Very flash.' DI Evans laughed. 'Go on, then. Anything's better than the swill we get at the station.'

'Not as flash as your car,' I said. She was better looking than she seemed on TV, with that flame-red voluminous hair and bright blue eyes. I made coffee for the three of us and we sat at my kitchen table.

'Did you hear anything last night?' DI Evans asked.

I recounted what I'd heard as well as I could remember. DS Stockwell wrote it all down.

'They fell quiet just after midnight. I guess that's when she did it.' I imagined she must have stabbed him.

Evans sipped her coffee. 'Did you ever see Ross receive any female visitors while Shelley was out?'

'Is that what it was about?' I asked. 'Ross was having an affair?'

'That's what we're trying to find out.'

I shook my head. 'They were a nightmare couple. But they seemed devoted to each other. Made for each other, if not in the best sense.

I certainly never saw anything. And I hadn't heard them argue about infidelity before. I'd remember if I did.'

'Why's that?' DS Stockwell asked.

I immediately regretted saying anything. 'Just . . . personal experience.' I cleared my throat.

'You called them "a nightmare couple",' she said.

'Yeah. Noisy. Aggressive. I actually complained about them to my landlord the other day. He's their landlord, too.'

'Really? And who is this landlord?'

'His name's Frank Dodd.'

The two detectives exchanged a glance. DS Stockwell said, 'Have you ever encountered Mr Dodd's assistant, Adrian Morrow?'

'Yeah. Unfortunately.'

Another exchanged glance. What was going on?

'Why did you say "unfortunately"?' DI Evans asked.

'Just . . . he's a bit strange. Why are you asking?'

'Oh, we're hoping to talk to Mr Morrow in connection with something else. Anyway, back to your neighbours. You definitely didn't see any women sneaking in or out of their house?'

'No. But you should talk to Mrs Douglas on the other side,' I said. 'She's the archetypal nosy neighbour. I'm sure she'd know if any women sneaked in to see Ross. She has a lodger, too – Kyle. He's always at home – at least, his van's always parked outside.'

'We will talk to Mrs Douglas, thanks. You've been very helpful, Mr Hofland.' She got up, her colleague following suit. I watched them go, heading next door to talk to Mrs Douglas and Kyle.

Later, I read the reports about Ross's murder online: 'Woman Stabs Boyfriend in Jealous Rage'.

Apparently, Shelley had discovered a string of texts between Ross and a 'mystery blonde', including numerous naked selfies and 'lewd' messages.

Shortly after midnight, according to the 'police source', Ross had received a message from his unnamed lover:

Must be lovely and quiet there without the dog barking . . .
Or is the other bitch yapping on as usual? ;)

That's what had made Shelley snap. And suddenly, after the dog warden came to take Pixie away, there was no one living next door.

Chapter 19

Adrian Morrow still hadn't turned up. None of his friends or drinking buddies had seen him, nor had his mum, a jumpy, skinny woman who chain-smoked her way through her encounter with Imogen and Emma. Mrs Morrow seemed mostly concerned that her son – who didn't have an alibi for any of the murders – had let Frank Dodd down.

'Frank did Adrian a huge favour giving him a job after . . . that trouble with that girl. Why would he vanish like this? I bet it's another girl. Adrian's always been like this. He forms attachments to people really quickly. He disappeared before, a couple of years ago. Turned out he was holed up with this awful punk who works in the Rose and Crown. Called herself Rebel, as if that's a real name. She had piercings *all over*.'

Imogen wasn't sure how Mrs Morrow knew that.

'As soon as you find him, you tell him to call me,' said Adrian's mum as they left. 'If his dad was still alive, he'd give him a good hiding.'

Imogen made a note of that. Had Adrian's dad been violent? It was an oversimplification, a huge leap from being smacked by your parents to becoming a serial killer, but was that the root of all this? Violence amplified through the generations? She thanked Mrs Morrow and left. She had somebody else to visit.

ω

Anthony Lester owned a house in a tiny village called Ashford, close to Ludlow where Fiona Redbridge had lived. This morning, he had phoned the station and told the cop who answered that he'd been having an affair with Fiona. She was with him on the evening she was killed.

Imogen had instructed Emma to carry on with the search for Adrian, visiting the girl his mum had told them about, the one with piercings everywhere. She drove out to Lester's alone, her mind wandering to the events of the day before: the murder of Ross Yates by his girlfriend, Shelley.

That was a weird bit of business. After visiting the scene and carrying out a couple of informal interviews with the neighbours, Imogen had passed the lead on that case to DS Cohen, briefing him on what they'd learned so far, including from the guy next door, Ben Hofland.

When Imogen found out Ross and Shelley rented their cottage from Frank Dodd, she had done a mental double take. Could Adrian somehow be involved in this, too? No, it had to be a coincidence. As Emma had said, Dodd was the biggest landlord in the area.

A few hours into the investigation, it didn't look like it was going to be as straightforward as it initially seemed. The texts and selfies Ross received had come from someone who didn't appear to exist. The phone number used was from a 'burner', a pre-paid phone with no registered owner. And no one knew who the woman in the photographs was, though it seemed likely the pictures had been ripped from a soft porn site.

Imogen was pleased she'd been able to pass it on. It was the one perk of leading the Shropshire Viper investigation.

She arrived at Anthony Lester's house and a sheepish-looking man in his late twenties let her in. As she entered the house, a text arrived from Emma. She'd spoken to the punk girl. She hadn't seen Adrian for months.

Anthony Lester was tall with broad shoulders. His nose was crooked like it had once been broken, probably playing rugby or falling off his bike. She knew he had studied sports science at Loughborough University and worked as a physiotherapist specialising in injured athletes. She also knew that he was twenty-nine years old and single and lived alone. He had been a member of Ludlow Wheelers, the same cycling club Fiona belonged to, for three years and had no criminal record, though he had once spent a few hours in a cell after he and some university friends had got shit-faced and caused a ruckus after a rugby match.

He offered her a cup of tea, which she declined.

'Why didn't you come forward earlier?' she demanded the moment they sat down.

He had the good grace to look embarrassed. 'Because of her husband.'

'You're scared of him?'

He laughed. 'Hardly. He's a lot older than me.'

'As was Fiona.'

Now his eyes blazed with indignation. 'You think there's something wrong with that? It's the other reason I didn't come forward. I thought you might try to pin it on me, find it impossible to believe our relationship was above board. Fiona never told any of her friends about us because she knew what people would think. That I had some ulterior motive, was after her money or something.'

He was on a roll now, had clearly been thinking about this a lot. 'It's amazing how society thinks it's perfectly normal for young women to have affairs with older men, but if it's the other way round all the old jokes come out. Cougars and toy boys. But so what if she was twenty years older than me? She was beautiful. An amazing, vibrant, sensual woman.' His voice got louder, his eyes misty. 'Nobody knows how much I've been hurting since it happened. Since she was taken away from me.'

'But not hurting enough to want to help us find out who did it.'

'I told you—'

Imogen cut him off. She believed him, had seen it many times before. Important witnesses not coming forward until after they'd agonised over it for days. They had already checked Lester's alibis for the murders of Danni and Nathan. They were rock solid. So unless he'd killed Fiona and set it up to look like she was the third victim of the Viper – which seemed highly unlikely – he was guilty of nothing more than hiding the truth.

'Did you have sex with her on Saturday the twelfth?'

That was the last day Fiona was seen alive, before her body was discovered the morning of the thirteenth.

He swallowed hard and it took him a couple of attempts to get his words out. 'We spent that afternoon in bed together.'

'At your place or hers?'

'Here.' He glanced around, as if he could still smell Fiona, see her imprint in the air.

Imogen leaned towards him. 'And then what happened?'

'I offered to drive her home, but she said she wanted to cycle. She insisted, in fact. She was worried about her neighbours seeing us. I was concerned because it was nearly dark, but she said she'd be fine. I should've argued. I shouldn't have let her ride home alone, down those country lanes.' He stared into the past and his eyes misted over. 'It's my fault she's dead.'

'Tell me more about you and Fiona.'

It took so long for him to speak that Imogen was about to repeat the question. But then he said, 'I met her when we were both out riding our bikes. She had a puncture and I helped her. I invited her to join the Wheelers.'

'When was that?'

'Last summer. July, I think. It was shortly after she'd recovered from her heart transplant. She didn't want to waste any more time. She said she wanted to live life to the full.'

'So you took advantage of that?'

He shot her a look. 'We both did.'

'And what? Was she planning on leaving her husband for you?'

He laughed. 'Why would she do that? The situation was perfect as it was. Trevor was away a lot, which gave us plenty of time to have fun. We didn't only spend our time in bed. We went out, spent the money Fiona got from selling that Roman cup. We had to be careful, but, well, that added to the excitement. The fear of getting caught. Have you ever had an illicit affair, Detective? Nothing else makes you feel so alive.'

'Not so thrilling for the one who's being cheated on, is it?'

'True. But Fiona was the one who almost died. Trevor was happy with his auction house and his stuffed weasel. Fiona didn't want to hurt him. We just had to make sure he didn't find out. That's the main reason I didn't come forward. I didn't want to hurt Trevor.'

Big of you, Imogen thought.

'But there's another reason why I thought you might try to pin it on me. I knew another one of the victims. Nathan Scott.'

Imogen sat up, even though they had already checked out Lester's alibi. Could he be the elusive connection between the victims?

'We were both on the mountain-biking circuit,' he said. 'I competed against him loads of times.'

'You were rivals?'

He barked out a laugh. 'Hardly. Nathan was way better than me. The second best in the county. There's a guy called Finlay who always beat him. Except for one time. I was there for that. Best day of Nathan's life.' He frowned. 'That was shortly before he was murdered.'

Something stirred inside Imogen, the seed of an idea. But it was too slippery and vanished before she could examine it.

'Do you think . . . Finlay could have held a grudge against Nathan?'

'Finlay?' Anthony laughed. 'Nah, he was cool about it. He actually seemed pleased for Nathan. Finlay is one of those annoying people who's really good without being a massively competitive dickhead.

Finlay wasn't on top form that day, though. He seemed knackered, like he hadn't been training properly.'

Imogen tried to grasp the fleeting idea she'd had a moment ago.

'What about Danni Taylor? Did you know her, too?' She leaned forward, eager for him to say yes.

'The first victim? No. I hadn't heard of her till she was murdered. I actually double-checked all my patient records to make sure, after I realised I was connected to two of the victims.'

Shit. 'We'll be checking that out ourselves. And one more question: Have you ever met anyone called Adrian Morrow? He's a few years younger than you.'

Anthony shook his head. 'Never heard of him. Why, is he a suspect?'

'Just someone we want to talk to.' Imogen got up to leave. 'We're going to have to take a proper statement from you,' she said. 'And we need to work out the route Fiona took home.'

'She would have gone the quiet way, down the lanes. She always did that because it avoids the traffic.'

'Did you ever notice anyone watching you? Maybe driving a white Transit?'

'No.'

She was about to go when Anthony said, 'I wish . . .' He fell quiet.

'You wish what?'

He blinked away tears. 'I gave her a present, the last time I saw her. A necklace with a pendant in the shape of a bicycle. I thought it was, you know, symbolic of how we met. She was wearing it when she left. She said she'd tell Trevor she bought it herself, if he ever asked. I wish I could have it back to remember her by.'

Imogen paused. She had no memory of seeing a pendant around Fiona's neck. She would have to check.

Outside, she punched the Redbridges' address into her satnav. She drove the route slowly, avoiding the A road as Lester had suggested. She soon found herself driving along a quiet lane, hedgerows on both sides, no houses or farm buildings nearby. How easy it would be for someone to lie in wait hidden from the road.

She stopped her car and got out, staring across the fields at the patchwork of green and yellow, postcard perfect in the afternoon sunshine. A fat bee came looping out of a hedgerow, nearly colliding with her face. Wisps of smoke rose into the pale-blue sky from a distant bonfire. A trio of horses played together in their paddock. There were no people around. She could have been the last woman on earth.

There were no cameras down these roads. If Lester had come forward straight away, they could have scoured them for tyre marks or signs of violence. But it had rained since then, and dozens if not hundreds of cars would have driven up and down here. Any evidence would have been erased days ago.

They needed to find Adrian. He was still their only suspect.

Chapter 20

Michael, Annette and Louis, the director, were camped out in Michael's hotel suite, poring over the footage they'd shot so far and pulling together a pre-pre-edit to figure out how much more material they needed. The sense of triumph Michael had felt when he first came back had melted away. Now he was itching to get out of this godforsaken place and head back to civilisation.

Louis hauled himself out of his chair, rubbing his back. 'I'm going to call it a night, if that's okay with you. You two going to carry on?'

Annette said, 'Won't Megan be back soon?'

Michael checked his watch. 'Nah. She's taken her kid to the IMAX in Telford. Let's carry on for a bit.'

'Come on, Mike,' Louis said. 'Give the poor girl a break. She looks knackered.'

'I'm fine. And I'm not a girl,' Annette replied.

'That told him,' Michael said, after Louis had gone.

'Yes, well, I know I'm only a lowly researcher and I'm supposed to suck up to the director, but . . .'

'I like your style. You'll go far, Annette.'

'I intend to.'

'What did you do before you started working in TV? I don't think you've ever told me.'

She avoided his eye. A secret? Intriguing. 'Oh, nothing much. I hung around with losers.'

Fifteen minutes later, Michael said, 'Sod this, let's go to the bar, get a drink.'

He let Annette go ahead of him down the corridor so he could enjoy watching her bum in the tight little skirt she was wearing. The truth was, he was a little intimidated by Annette and women like her, this new breed of strong women who weren't afraid to call themselves feminists. He'd checked out Annette's politically outspoken Twitter feed, on which she and her contemporaries policed the world for racism, misogyny, transphobia, xenophobia, social injustice, you name it. It had put him on notice, but he admired her for it. He liked ballsy women.

He'd never try anything on with her, though. It would be all over the web within minutes.

And more to the point, he already had a gorgeous, strong-willed girlfriend. One who probably wouldn't be too chuffed to come back to the hotel and find him alone with Annette in their room. Megan was already suspicious of Annette, had accused Michael of having 'mentionitis'. He guessed that this was an unfortunate by-product of cheating: you started to tar everyone with your own unfaithful brush. Megan wasn't in a good way at the moment: she was torn up with guilt now that the initial reckless rush of their relationship had abated. She was regretful, racked with shame over how easily she'd let Ben take their son. Now she was talking about fighting Ben for custody. Michael had gently tried to dissuade her; he really didn't want a kid around cramping their style. But she seemed even more determined since she'd been spending more time with Ollie. Maybe bringing her to Shropshire hadn't been such a great idea.

'What are you thinking about?' Annette asked with a little smile as they exited the lift on the ground floor.

'Oh, nothing. Life.'

'Deep thoughts, huh?'

'I have them occasionally. Actually,' he lied, 'I was thinking about the documentary. Maybe we should drop the part about Imogen Evans and Kevin Moss.'

'What? You're kidding.'

'I think it's a distraction from the main story. And it could back-fire. The public seem to like Evans. It's the hair. She reminds people of Fergie.'

Annette looked confused. 'From the Black Eyed Peas?'

'No, the Duchess of York. Sarah Ferguson.' He barked out a laugh. 'Christ, sometimes I forget how young you are.'

They reached the bar and Michael ordered a bottle of sauvignon blanc.

'I disagree. It's part of the narrative. Incompetent cop unable to stop killer.'

Michael pushed a glass towards her. 'Doesn't it go against your principles? Crapping on another woman?'

Annette blanched. 'I don't see it like that.'

He found this exchange amusing. 'It just doesn't seem very sisterly to me.'

Before Annette could respond, Michael's phone beeped. Probably Megan, letting him know she was on her way back.

But the text wasn't from Meg.

This is Adrian. Do you still want to talk to me about my neighbour?

He showed the message to Annette.

'Who's Adrian?'

'Remember when we were in the pub the other day, that weird guy at the bar, the one who legged it halfway through our conversation? He told me he'd called the police about his neighbour after the first murder, but they wouldn't listen to him. Then he got spooked and ran off.'

'A time waster?'

'I don't know. What if he actually knows something? This would be just what we need – some crucial bit of testimony the police ignored.'

Annette took a large gulp of her wine. 'Seems like a long shot.'

But Michael was already texting Adrian back.

Yes, I'd love to talk. Can I call you?

While he waited for a response, he took a deep pull of wine. His phone beeped, and in his haste to get to it, he splashed the front of his jacket. 'Bollocks.'

Annette picked up a napkin from the bar and dabbed at it. 'Lucky it's not red. Hey, look out, we're being watched.'

A barmaid was staring at them.

'Give them something to gossip about.' Annette leaned in and placed a hand on his chest, whispering in Michael's ear. 'Pretend I'm telling you I want to fuck you.'

He jerked away, flustered. He had a hard-on – well, a semi – and the barmaid was really gawping at them now.

'Annette!'

'It's just a bit of fun.'

He was so surprised by what she'd done he'd temporarily forgotten about the text from Adrian. He snatched up his phone.

No. We need to meet f2f.

'Face to face,' said Annette.

'I know what it means. I'm not eighty!'

He texted back. Where and when?

139

The reply came immediately. Now. Followed by a link to a location on Google Maps. Michael studied the map. The address was in the middle of nowhere.

He finished his glass of wine. 'So. Fancy a trip out into the boonies?'

ᵚ

'Where the hell are we?' Annette asked. They had pulled off the road and found themselves deep in the countryside, driving down a narrow, twisting lane in the dark. The open fields on either side of the road vanished as they entered a wooded area. It was like driving into a black tunnel, illuminated only by their headlights. 'I don't like it. It's like the bloody *Blair Witch Project*.'

Finally, Michael had found something that scared her. 'This is Hopton Wood. The place we're looking for isn't much further.'

Michael wasn't scared at all. He'd been in much worse situations: the dens of dangerous criminals in London and Manchester, a paedophile ring, amongst people traffickers and drug dealers. He'd come face to face – f2f, indeed – with some of the biggest scumbags in the country in some truly dark places. Also, he'd grown up around here, been camping in these woods, sneaked off into the trees at night to drink and smoke and have sex.

And even if he had been a little afraid, he wouldn't show Annette. He wanted her to think he was a big man. To *know* he was a big man.

They drove on. Mist hung between the branches of the black trees and drifted across the surface of the road like a cloud fallen to earth. Michael went slowly, in case another car came speeding around a corner.

'Why would anyone choose to live in a place like this?' Annette asked. 'There aren't even any shops.' She checked her phone. 'And no mobile signal.'

'Some people like solitude. Or maybe our friend Adrian is a farmer.'

'Or a survivalist.'

'Or a serial killer,' Michael said in a horror movie voice.

'Don't. Please.' She paused. 'Did he seem like a serial killer?'

'Well . . . he was wearing a vial of blood around his neck and had a jar of death's head moths in his pocket.'

'Very funny.'

'Almost as funny as what you did back in the bar. When you whispered in my ear about wanting to fuck me.'

'I didn't! I was telling you to pretend I'd said it.' She was still fiddling with her phone, holding it up and trying to get reception. 'I was feeling mischievous, that's all. Sorry if I crossed a line. How is Megan, by the way? You act cool, but I can tell you really love her.'

'Now you're going to make me blush.'

She laughed.

They were deep inside the woods now. 'This had better be worth it,' Annette said. 'If Adrian turns out to be a time waster I'm going to be pissed off.'

'It won't be a waste of time. This trip has already made me realise what the film is missing – we need more creepy night-time shots, the woods in the dark. That's where the first two victims were found, wasn't it? Their bodies were left out in the countryside in the dead of night. Imagine the killer dragging his victims into the woods . . .'

'Please, Michael.' But he saw a glint of excitement in her eyes. She knew how good it would look, re-enacted on TV.

'Here we are. According to the map, anyway.'

'But there's nothing here.'

'Hmm.' Michael pulled over on to a dirt track and got out of the car, leaving the headlights on. Annette followed. A little way along the track was a wide metal gate. Behind the gate, more woodland, trees crowded together, making it impossible to stray from the path that led through them. It was silent, apart from some faint rustling among those impenetrable trees.

'There's a light, look,' Annette said. She'd recovered her compo-
sure – or, at least, was showing her bravest face. She was right: there
was a pale yellow glow on the other side of the trees. Adrian's house,
presumably.

Michael went back to the car and switched off the lights, plunging
them into almost complete darkness. He could feel the tension coming
off Annette. He touched her arm lightly and she flinched.

'Don't worry,' he said. 'I'll protect you.'

'I think it might be the other way round.'

'Come on, let's go and find out what he has to say.'

Annette hesitated. 'Are you sure it's safe?'

'Yeah, of course.'

They went through the gate and headed along the narrow path
until a small stone cottage came into view. A single light burned in the
front window.

'What big eyes you have, Grandma,' Annette said.

'It is a bit like that, isn't it?' Michael approached the building and
peered through the window into a poky room. There was a fireplace, an
armchair, a bookcase. No television. And no sign of life. He knocked
on the door and waited.

Almost immediately, the door opened. It was the man from the pub.

'You came,' he said. 'Come in.'

The light inside the little house was dim, as if Adrian had bought
the lowest-watt bulbs available. He led them into a little kitchen. The
walls were streaked with dirt, and a strange, sweet smell hung in the
air. Filthy crockery was piled high in the sink, and a jar of coffee lay
upended on the counter, granules spilled across the surface. A calendar
hung on the wall showing a photo of a puppy above the dates, and
Michael noticed it hadn't been turned over since April. The stove top
was covered with mummified scraps of food.

'I'd offer you a cup of tea, but the milk's gone sour,' Adrian said.

'No worries,' Michael assured him, thinking he wouldn't accept a drink made in this kitchen even if he witnessed Adrian clean the cup with antibacterial wipes. Annette was looking around like she'd been drawn into a house of horror. 'Do you live here alone?'

'It's just me now,' Adrian said. He kept glancing towards the window that faced out into the garden. Michael could see nothing but his own reflection in the glass.

'So what have you got to tell us?' Annette asked.

'Come through to the living room and I'll show you,' Adrian replied. 'It's just along here.'

Michael badly needed to pee: he'd been holding it for the last half hour. Wine always went straight through him. 'Can I just use your toilet first?'

Adrian's lips curled into a thin smile. 'Of course. Second door on the right.'

Annette shot him a 'don't leave me' look, but Michael had to go. He mouthed, 'You'll be fine,' behind Adrian's back.

The loo was even grottier than the kitchen. Maybe that was why the bulbs were so dim – to conceal the filth. He could almost smell the limescale. A framed square of cross-stitch tapestry hung above the loo – a phrase spelled out in curling script, 'There Is Nothing Terrible in Not Living'.

'Weird,' Michael said to himself. He finished and headed down to the living room at the front of the house.

There was no sign of Annette or Adrian.

'Hello?'

He headed back along the hall to the kitchen, thinking they must have gone back there. As he went through the kitchen doorway, he sensed a presence behind him.

He turned, just in time to see a blur of movement in the dim hallway, a black shape descending at speed towards his head. Then a flash of blinding white pain.

The object struck again, and Michael entered a deeper darkness.

Chapter 21

I picked Ollie up from school and took him to see his grandmother. On the way, I told him I'd booked guitar lessons for him, beginning at the start of the school holidays. I thought he'd be pleased – he'd been saying he wanted to learn to play for ages – but he pulled a face. I was sure he'd enjoy it, though, once he got started.

The weather was filthy, the late-afternoon sky crowded with evil-looking clouds, wind attacking the trees in the grounds of Orchard Heights like it wanted to destroy anything pretty and alive. So much for summer. The sky opened at the very moment we reached the front door of the nursing home and I hurried inside, but Ollie held back.

'Come on,' I urged. 'You're going to get soaked.'

'Can't I wait in the car?'

I had no choice but to go back out into the rain.

'She really wants to see you, Ollie. She might not get many more chances.'

Maybe this was a little too honest, as it made Ollie burst into tears. I was shocked, and put my arm around his shoulders, ignoring the greasy raindrops that battered us, talking into his ear in a soft voice.

'Come on, mate. I know it's hard.'

'I can't stand it. It's horrible.'

I had put his reluctance to visit down to a normal eleven-year-old aversion to hospitals and old people. I pulled him closer, wishing I could protect him from everything: from sickness and divorce and death.

'Seeing you makes her feel better, though. Plus, she's on some really good drugs.'

His eyes widened. His dad – talking about drugs! He was still young enough not to think I was being horribly naff.

A blast of wind almost knocked us off the step. 'Let's go up before we're swept away to Oz.'

As predicted, Mum was delighted to see Ollie, and he spent twenty minutes showing her how to play *Minecraft* on his iPod. Then he told her all about the few days he'd spent with Megan and a film she'd taken him to see the previous evening. Mum looked at me over his shoulder as he recounted the plot and showed her a clip from the movie – he'd managed to connect to the nursing home's Wi-Fi – and her eyes shone with sadness. I could tell, too, by the slight tremor in her hands, the set of her jaw, that she was in pain.

'Do you want me to call that nurse?' I couldn't remember his name.

She glanced at Ollie. She clearly didn't want him to see her being medicated. 'I'm fine.' But her voice had changed, become more breathy, and the tremor in her hands was more pronounced.

'Let me find someone. We should probably get going anyway. Ollie has homework to catch up on.'

He groaned. 'But I wanted to show Nan this video.'

'And I wanted to see it,' she said. 'Maybe I should get myself one of these gadgets.'

I left her room and immediately spotted the man Mum called her angel. Emile, that was his name. He was coming out of another patient's room.

'Emile? Mum seems to be in a lot of pain.'

He nodded, again reminding me of someone who has recently discovered God. It was that smile.

'I'll be there in two minutes,' he said, then hesitated. 'Ben, your mum keeps saying that she wants to go out, to see some of the places that are special to her. The church where she and your father got married. Your former home. The village where she grew up. She knows it might be her last chance. I thought I should mention it.'

'You think it would be okay?'

'It can't do any harm. I'm sure she would like you to take her. I can come along, too, in case she needs medical attention.'

'Okay. Thank you. I'll talk to her about it.'

He blessed me with a beatific smile. 'Wonderful. But we shouldn't leave it too long.'

ʊ

I pulled up outside the house to see somebody sheltering in the porch. The car windows were so awash with rain that it was hard to make out who it was. But then Ollie said, 'Is that Mum?' and I realised he was right.

What was Megan doing here?

We dashed up the path, jackets over our heads. Megan was pacing back and forth, like a polar bear in the world's tiniest enclosure.

'Are you all right?' I asked, cramming into the porch beside her and scrabbling to unlock the front door.

As soon as we got inside, she said to Ollie, 'I need to talk to your dad a minute.'

'Fine.' He skulked off to his room.

'We've just been to see Mum,' I explained. 'It's hard for him. All of this is hard for him.'

I gestured for her to follow me into the kitchen. I had no idea what Megan wanted to talk to me about – the flat sale, hopefully – but I needed a drink. I opened a bottle of merlot. 'Want one?'

'I shouldn't . . . I'm driving.' She eyed the bottle thirstily. 'Oh, go on then. I'll get a taxi, charge it to Michael's production company if I have to.'

We sat at the kitchen table and Megan took a large gulp of her wine. She wasn't wearing make-up and her hair hung loose. Again, I thought how thin she was. But, apart from that, she looked good. For a moment, it felt like we were still together – sitting in the kitchen, a bottle of wine between us, Megan dressed down like she always was at home. She pushed her fringe out of her face and sighed.

'What did you want to talk to me about?' I said.

'It's Michael.' She needed more wine to get her next words out. 'He's gone AWOL.'

'What do you mean?'

'When I got back to the hotel last night, he wasn't there. I assumed he'd gone out with some of the crew so I went to bed, expecting him to come crawling in in the middle of the night. Sorry.' She shook her head. 'You don't want to hear this, do you?'

I had flinched when she'd mentioned Michael crawling into bed. But I said, 'It's fine.'

'Are you sure? It's just . . . I don't have anyone else to talk to.' Her glazed eyes told me the wine had gone to her head quickly. She had always been a lightweight. 'We are still friends, right?'

Were we? Until this week, I'd only thought of us as a couple in the throes of a divorce. We had barely exchanged a civil word since I'd left London. Now she was acting like we'd been separated for years, moved on. Or was something else going on here? It was hard to read her.

'Just tell me the rest of the story,' I said, struggling to keep my voice even.

She refilled her wine glass, right to the rim. 'He wasn't there when I woke up. He hadn't come to . . .' She stopped herself from saying 'bed' and instead said, 'He hadn't come back. I guessed he must have crashed on someone's sofa. Or maybe he was working all night. He does that sometimes. I sent him a text asking where he was, but he didn't respond. Anyway, at about ten I got a call from Louis – he's the director of *No Stone Unturned* – asking me if I'd seen Michael. They were supposed to be shooting some more footage and he hadn't turned up.'

I had a brief image of Michael lying injured in a ditch somewhere and suppressed a smile.

'Then Louis said, "And Annette hasn't turned up either."' Megan winced like she'd tasted something bitter.

'Who's Annette?'

'She's this drop-dead gorgeous researcher who works with Michael. Mid-twenties. Super-confident. Did I mention she's gorgeous? Michael never stops talking about her. I went downstairs to reception to ask if they'd seen either of them and the smirking woman behind the counter said she'd seen them leave the hotel together last night. Louis said neither of them are answering their phones. Then, about an hour ago, I got a call from *The Sun* asking if it was true that Michael was having a fling with his researcher?'

'You're kidding.'

'Christ knows how they got my number.'

'It's on your website, isn't it?'

She frowned. 'Not my mobile. Anyway, the point is that this journalist had a tip-off from someone who works behind the bar at the hotel. This person must have heard from the receptionist about Michael going AWOL and called the paper with their juicy gossip. This barmaid saw Michael and "an attractive black woman" acting like a loved-up couple at the bar. And no one's seen or heard from them since. They're probably holed up at another hotel somewhere, shagging each other's brains out.'

She knocked back the last of her wine – she was drinking it like it was water – and looked around for another bottle.

I fetched one from the rack, opened it and refilled her glass.

'Wanker,' she said. 'Not you. Him.'

I was still on my first glass. 'Megan, do you really expect me to be sympathetic?'

She waved a hand, hair falling over her face. She blew at the loose strands and they stuck to her lips. She was well on the way to being drunk. 'You don't have to tell me. It's my own stupid fucking fault.' She stared into space, eyes glassy.

I didn't respond because I had no idea what to say. Part of me was punching the air, glad she'd got her comeuppance. Another part of me felt sorry for her. A third part was trying to figure out why she was here, telling me all this.

And a final part was yelling at me: *This is it. It's over between her and Michael. This is your chance to get back together, to be a family again.*

'Maybe there's an innocent explanation,' I said.

'Oh, God,' she said, taking another big mouthful of wine. 'Tell me something else. Talk to me about something to take my mind off that prick.'

So I told her about the next-door neighbours, happy to get off the topic of Michael and his probable betrayal of my wife, at least temporarily. I was sick of the voice in my head shouting at me.

'First, a couple of female detectives came to see me, including the one with the red hair who's always on TV . . .'

'Imogen Evans? Michael's got a bee in his bonnet about her.'

'Really? Well, anyway, then another detective came round, to ask exactly what I heard that night. He wanted to know if I'd ever seen Ross with another woman, which I hadn't. They're having problems tracking down the woman they were supposedly fighting over.'

'Wow. High drama.'

'I know. It's been weirdly quiet the last couple of days with them gone. The landlord, Frank, came round, too. He said he's having to fend off enquiries from potential new tenants because he can tell most of them just want to gawp at the murder scene.'

'People are sick.'

'I know. And on the subject of weird shit going on, I've taken Ollie's DS away from him.'

'Why'd you do that?' Her voice was beginning to slur now.

'Because I have no idea who bought it for him. What if it's some pervert who's trying to groom him?' I lowered my voice. 'He chats with people online through the games he plays. He swears he's never given out his real name or address to anyone, but there are ways of tracing people, aren't there? IP addresses and so on.'

Megan looked thoroughly alarmed.

'I don't feel comfortable with him keeping the DS, so I've confiscated it till we find out who sent it.'

'Let me talk to him.' She stood up so quickly that she staggered, arms windmilling comically, and I instinctively got up to catch her. She fell against me.

There was a long pause, our faces inches apart.

She kissed me.

It was a sloppy kiss, all lips and tongues and spit; she hadn't kissed me like that for years. Her mouth was warm and spiced with wine. She wrapped her arms around me, her breasts soft against my chest, her bony hips pressing into me. My body reacted automatically and she must have felt me grow hard because she moaned and gave me a look, again like something from the beginning of our relationship. Her hand was suddenly there, on my jeans, squeezing me. I wanted to lift her on to the table, hitch up her dress and pull her underwear aside, enter her, fuck her like I used to, fuck the pain away.

I broke free of the kiss.

She looked confused for a moment, then leaned forward, trying to kiss me again. I put my hands on her shoulders, holding her back. I was still hard. My body wanted to do it.

But I couldn't. I *shouldn't*.

'What's the matter?' she asked.

I caught a movement out of the corner of my eye and dashed into the hallway to see Ollie's bedroom door shutting. He must have seen us. Oh, shit . . .

Megan came out of the kitchen, holding on to the door frame. Her hair was all over the place, her eyes red. My erection had dwindled, but my heart was still thudding.

'I'm going to call you a cab,' I said.

She sighed and went back into the kitchen. I was still tempted to take her by the hand and lead her to the bedroom. I knew her body. It would be so easy, so familiar. I knew how good it would feel, but I also knew that the moment it was over I would regret it. Because as she'd kissed me and pressed herself against me, I'd realised for the first time that I didn't love her any more. It was over. Broken. And all I could see ahead of us if we got back together was mess and resentment and disappointment, for me, for her and for our son.

Maybe I was making too much of it. Maybe all she wanted was a drunken shag, revenge on Michael. But as I called the taxi, I felt sure I'd done the right thing.

That night I had an erotic dream, a sweaty, filthy dream of entwined limbs and mouths and whispered dirty words, a woman with red hair astride me, under me, a porn movie of the subconscious. I awoke feeling hot and strangely embarrassed. Because it wasn't Megan I'd dreamt of. It was that cop, the one who'd come round to talk to me about Ross and Shelley. DI Imogen Evans. I went back to sleep, but I don't remember what I dreamt about next.

Chapter 22

When he came to, the room was dark. There were no windows, just a line of narrow vents cut into what must have been the outside wall, high on the ceiling. The light that crept through these vents was diminishing, making it eight or nine at night. In the dim light, he could just about make out the outline of the solid wooden door that kept him here. He tried to move but he was tied to a chair behind what looked like an old school desk, with another chair on the other side. His hands were cuffed behind his back, the metal digging into his wrists. He shouted Adrian's name, then Annette's. Nobody responded.

Without being able to check his phone or watch, Michael had no way of telling how long he'd been here. It must have been almost twenty-four hours.

He was cold, hungry, thirsty and terrified. On top of all that, his skull was sore where Adrian had struck him and his head ached.

He'd been so stupid, coming out here without telling anyone. But there had been two of them, and Adrian had seemed so harmless.

He hadn't thought for a moment that the guy in the pub might actually be dangerous.

That he might be the Viper.

Megan would be going out of her mind with worry. He could picture her pacing their hotel suite, wringing her hands, pale and beautiful with fear. The crew, too, would know this was unlike him. He was always contactable. Surely they would have spoken to the police by now, put out a description of his car? He had to assume that, unless Adrian was stupid, he'd have moved it by now, concealed it somewhere.

Nobody knew where they were.

And he had no idea what had happened to Annette. If she was still alive.

His cheeks felt wet and he realised he was crying. He imagined himself being interviewed on TV, recounting his ordeal, and he would claim that he'd cried because he was so worried about his young female colleague.

But really, he was crying for himself.

ω

He sat like that for a long time, light draining from the room, drifting away into a reverie about his funeral. Megan would be there, all in black, sobbing for the future they never got to share, the head of BBC factual content would stand up and give a eulogy about how Michael was the best investigative journalist he'd ever worked with and there would be thousands of people on Twitter sharing their grief. He would be trending, and his face would be on the front cover of every newspaper. 'Killed In The Line Of Duty'.

He was so absorbed in his thoughts that when he heard a key turn in the lock and the drawing back of a heavy bolt, he didn't react until the door had opened and a figure stepped through.

Adrian. And he was holding a shotgun.

Michael tried to struggle, to free himself from his bonds, but Adrian pointed the gun at him and said in a low voice, 'Don't bother.'

'Adrian. Please.'

The other man laughed, clearly finding something amusing. 'Call yourself an investigative journalist. You couldn't even investigate my real name.'

Beyond the thick walls of the room, Michael heard a noise. A woman shouting. Annette? Almost immediately, she fell silent.

'Your name's not really Adrian? Who are you?' Michael's voice came out shaky and pathetic.

The man didn't respond to the question. He crossed the floor of the cellar and sat at the desk, opposite Michael. He propped the shotgun against his chair and produced a small bottle of water from his jacket pocket, placing it on the desk.

Michael licked his dry lips, determined not to plead. His tongue felt like a dried-out slug in his mouth. All he could think about was how good the water would feel on his lips, slipping down his throat.

'Want it, do you?' The man nodded at the bottle. There was a sneer in his voice, so different to the meek man Michael had met in the pub.

Michael's resolve broke almost immediately. 'Please.'

'You can have it. But I need to ask you some questions. Do you promise to answer fully and honestly?'

Right now, Michael would have sold out his own mother for a drink. 'Yes. Anything. Please.'

The man whose name wasn't really Adrian smiled and raised the bottle of water to Michael's lips, allowing him to drink. The water was the best thing Michael had ever tasted. He sucked at the bottle like a baby, liquid running down his chin and splashing the desk.

His captor threw the empty bottle to the floor and placed a phone on the desk. He opened an app and tapped what looked like a 'Record' button.

'Tell me what you know about Imogen Evans,' he said.

Chapter 23

I leave the house and drive into Shrewsbury, park in the city centre and walk through the dark streets until I reach the address I'm looking for. An old house, converted into one- and two-bedroom flats. There's a light on in the window, but I know there's no one home. I've already made sure of that. I slip on a pair of gossamer-thin gloves.

Getting inside is easy — these old locks are a doddle to pick. You'd think a detective would know better, especially one who'd lived in London. She's left the lights on in her haste to get out.

Oh, Imogen. You're making it too easy for me.

Michael has confirmed my fears, going on about her fantastic clear-up rate at the Met. God knows he's given to hyperbole, but I believe him. She's one of the best.

'If you hurt me,' Michael had said, finally gathering some courage, 'the whole country will be outraged. The police will try a hundred times harder to catch you.'

And I have to concede, part of what he said is right. Taking Michael and Annette has upped the risk level considerably. And I can't afford the risk — the risk of being prevented from finishing things with my next lucky one. If there's a chance that DI Evans could stop me — and Michael's words have made me worry that she could — well, I figure removing her from the scene will set the police back long enough to give me time to do what I need to do.

And I have the perfect method.

I want to have a look around her flat first, though. I can't help it. I'm a student of humanity. I want to know who Imogen is.

I peek into the bathroom, where it's dark. Light from the hallway illuminates the womanly lotions and potions on the side of the tub: bath bombs and shampoo and conditioner for that lustrous hair of hers. I picture her in the bath, pink nipples rising above soapy water. How sweet it would be to stay here, to watch her undress. Such a shame I won't be able to do that.

As I enter the bedroom, something comes towards me, darting across the floor like a shadow. I brace myself – but it's just a cat. It brushes against my leg and I fight back the urge to kick it. I loathe cats. Vile, selfish beasts; witches' familiars. I'd like to wring its neck, but I don't want Imogen to be distressed. I want her to think everything is absolutely normal.

I shoo the cat from the room and stand before Imogen's bed. It's a lonely place. A king-sized bed, but a dent in only one pillow. Imogen is careful to sleep on one side, as if she's waiting for a man to come and claim the other. That makes me sad for her. I gently pull back the duvet and press my nose to the sheets, inhaling the smell of her sweat. I imagine her lying here, pleasuring herself, all alone, probably picturing someone like me: someone strong, capable, dominant. A man who knows about pleasure and pain. A man who knows exactly how to make a woman happy.

I'm turned on now, and I force myself to think about something ugly and rotten to quell the desire. I'll save it for later.

Save it for when she's cold.

I look around, opening the wardrobe, impressed by how organised she is. There are three empty hangers and three outfits hung in a line. Thursday, Friday, Saturday.

Aware of time getting on, I head into the kitchen. Her dinner plate is still on the table. The cat threads around a chair leg and, once again, I resist the temptation to hurt it. A lone woman with a cat. Poor Imogen is a living, breathing cliché.

It's time I did something about that.

I open the fridge, expecting to find it full of microwaveable meals for one, which could be a problem. But I'm surprised to find that Imogen cooks for herself. The fridge contains fresh vegetables and meat, and several Tupperware containers stacked on the middle shelf.

Each Tupperware dish has a label on top. 'Thursday', 'Friday', 'Saturday'. This is perfect. I imagine her standing here on a Sunday evening, preparing her lunches for the week, just as she lines up her clothes. Again, it makes me feel sorry for her, but also confirms that I'm right to be wary. If she's that dedicated, if her life is so dominated by her job that she's prepared to spend Thursday and Friday lunchtimes eating food she'd prepared days before, then she is an adversary worthy of my respect.

And that's why she has to go.

I pull out the Tupperware dish marked for tomorrow and prise the lid off with my gloved fingers. A pasta salad: penne with red peppers and sweetcorn and – ah, what's this? I grin.

It's almost as if fate wants me to do it.

Chapter 24

Imogen was drying her hands in the ladies when the media officer, Camille McDaris, came in and grinned at her.

'Just the woman. Sounds like your friend Michael Stone's unlikely to bother you any more.'

Imogen had told Camille, a brunette with blonde highlights, about that woman from Michael Stone's show doorstepping her.

'What do you mean?'

'It's all over the Internet this morning,' Camille said. 'Apparently, he's run off with one of his researchers. They absconded the night before last. With any luck they won't come back to finish the documentary.'

As soon as she reached her desk, Imogen checked the *Mail Online*. There was the story, halfway down the home page. It showed a photo of Stone along with a history of his love life – apparently, he was seeing his financial adviser, who was staying at the hotel in Shrewsbury – and a number of photos of his 'new love', Annette Lawrence, the woman who'd been waiting for Imogen outside her flat the other morning. Imogen didn't blame Stone for running off with her. Hopefully, lust had driven them both half-crazy and they were halfway to Belize or somewhere, their documentary, and the story of Kevin Moss, forgotten. She couldn't imagine the programme being completed without Stone.

So that was one piece of good news.

She fetched herself a coffee from the machine, rubbing the back of her neck as she went, trying to massage some of the tension from her muscles. She had slept badly, being unable to shut down her brain. At nine o'clock that night, they'd received a call from an anonymous member of the public saying they'd seen Adrian at a communal squat in Telford. He was drunk and boasting about how the police were looking for him but would never find him. Imogen had been informed and had rushed over to Telford. It'd been a wild goose chase. There had been no sign of Adrian, and the squatters had been so unhelpful that she couldn't tell if the call had been genuine or not.

It had been after midnight before she'd got home, and of course she'd been unable come within half a mile of sleep. Finally, she'd fallen into a dream in which she was locked in a coffin, thumping the lid and screaming as dirt was shovelled on to it. When she'd woken up, she'd found four long, angry scratches on her belly, self-inflicted. The sheets had been soaked with rank-smelling sweat. She'd stood beneath the shower for a long time, the scratches burning, allowing the pain to bring her back to life.

Getting out of the shower and going into the bedroom, Imogen had shivered, even though it was a warm morning. She'd had the feeling she was being watched, eyes roaming over her body clad only in a towel. She'd shut the window, closed the curtains and chided herself. She was being ridiculous. But the room hadn't felt right. Was that why she'd had bad dreams? Had she been able to detect someone had been in here? She'd sniffed at the air, catching a faint odour of stale smoke. But then she'd reminded herself that she often smelled smoke in here; it drifted up from the downstairs neighbour's flat. She'd shaken off the feeling and found today's outfit in the wardrobe.

Sitting at the little table with her single bowl of muesli and cup of coffee, a wave of loneliness had hit her. She missed her friends in London. She missed her family, even her old colleagues. Monkey had scoffed his breakfast and slunk off to the bedroom, where he would spend the day sleeping. She'd stood up, the coffee cup rattling on the table, and cursed herself and her self-pity.

Before leaving, she'd grabbed the labelled Tupperware dish of pasta salad. More evidence of her lonely life: lunch for one, waiting for her in the fridge in the station's communal kitchen for when she'd finished up the notes from her conversation with Anthony Lester.

Her fingers hovered over the keyboard as she remembered what Lester had told her about the bicycle pendant he'd given Fiona that she'd been wearing when she'd left his place. Imogen had checked the report: the pendant hadn't been on Fiona's person when her body had been found.

Did that mean the Viper had taken it? Was he collecting souvenirs? Again, the cycling connection was there, because Nathan Scott's helmet was missing, too. Imogen had immediately phoned Danni Taylor's mother and then her boyfriend to ask if they could think of anything Danni might have had with her when she'd been taken. Neither of them could offhand, but they said they would check. There had been no sign of any souvenirs at Adrian's flat, but he could be keeping them somewhere else.

Was Adrian Morrow the murderer? There was something niggling at the back of Imogen's mind. Would he really be so foolish as to allow himself to be spotted hanging around the crime scene, especially when he'd been so careful before? He had a record when it came to harassing women, but one of the victims was a strong, fit male. Could Adrian have overpowered the super-fit Nathan Scott? Perhaps if he'd had a gun . . .

And what was his motivation for doing this? Where had he got hold of morphine? Right now, the only thing that made Adrian the prime suspect, apart from his evident interest in the murders, was the fact that he'd gone missing after the police had released his photo. It made him look like he had something to hide.

They needed to find him. But Imogen had reminded the team at that morning's briefing: they couldn't assume Adrian was guilty. It was vital to keep an open mind. Because she was convinced the Viper was cleverer than Adrian Morrow.

She ran through the possibilities. One: Adrian was guilty and was hiding because he knew the police were on to him. Two: Adrian was simply a ghoul with an obsession with serial killings, and he'd gone missing for some other reason; for example, he might be holed up with a girlfriend or be worried that the police would think he was involved. The latter seemed unlikely – they had spoken to everyone Adrian knew. No one had seen him since the weekend, when he'd been in his local pub, drinking cider and playing on the fruit machines as normal. His Internet history hadn't revealed any secret contacts or plans either. And his phone was switched off and therefore untraceable.

Halfway through writing up the notes, she stopped dead when she reached the point in her conversation with Lester where something had niggled at her.

Anthony Lester, Fiona's lover, had been talking about how he knew victim number two, Nathan Scott.

There's a guy called Finlay who always beat him. Except for one time. I was there for that. Best day of Nathan's life.

She stared at the screen where she had typed this statement, tapping the desk with one hand, the other idly stroking the scratches on her belly.

She picked up the phone.

'Anthony, I need to ask you about the race you told me about. When Nathan Scott beat his biggest rival.'

'Yeah, Finlay,' Lester replied.

'Where was the race?'

'The Long Mynd.'

She nodded to herself. She had known for a long time that Nathan took part in races across the place where his body had been found, but they hadn't been able to find any significance in this. Nathan had competed in lots of different places across Shropshire. Imogen had filed this fact away, in case it turned out not to be a coincidence.

'And you said that day was the best of his life. Was that your interpretation?'

He was silent for a moment, so she wondered if he'd understood the question. 'No, it wasn't an interpretation. He told me. In fact, he told everybody.'

'Everybody?'

'Yeah, loads of us went to the pub after the race to celebrate with him, including Finlay.' Anthony had said Finlay was happy for Nathan, but Imogen had checked his alibi just in case. It was solid. 'Nathan was buying everyone drinks, talking about how it was the happiest day of his life.'

'He used those words?'

'Uh-huh.'

She hung up and immediately searched for Trevor Redbridge's number at the auction house.

Trevor breathed heavily into the phone. 'Detective. Have you got some news?'

The desperate eagerness in his voice made her heart sink. He had loved his wife. It crossed her mind that perhaps he, the cuckolded husband, was responsible for her murder, that he'd made it look like she was the victim of the Viper to put the police off the scent. But she dismissed the thought immediately. Like Finlay, Trevor had an alibi. 'Sorry, sir. I just need to ask you a question about Wenlock Priory.' This was the place where Fiona's body had been found. 'Had Fiona been there before?'

'Hmm. Yes.'

'With you?'

He thought about it. 'Once, a long time ago.'

'And was it a significant event in any way?' She was hoping he would say he'd proposed to her there.

'No. As I recall, it pissed down and Fiona kept complaining about her shoes being too tight.'

Damn. 'And had she been there since?'

He thought about it some more. 'Actually, yes. I think she went with her friend Jane. That must have been shortly before she had her transplant. I remember Jane taking her, hoping it would cheer her up. Fiona was in a pretty dark place back then.'

'Have you got Jane's number?'

'Yes, at home. But, Detective, I don't understand—'

'I'll explain later.' She got Jane's surname – Sturridge – out of him, along with her address, and she looked up Jane's number.

Jane Sturridge sounded very well-to-do, unless she was one of those women who put on a telephone voice. She was able to answer Imogen's question straight away.

'Yes, I remember it very well. Fiona got a call on her mobile while we were there. From the hospital.'

Imogen rubbed at her scratches.

'They told her they'd found a heart for her. It was amazing, actually. A very special moment. I've never seen Fiona look so relieved . . . and happy.'

Jane Sturridge made a snuffling sound. She was crying.

Imogen thanked her and put the phone down. Her heart was beating fast.

She had one more call to make, her second call to Danni Taylor's mother, Samantha, in as many days.

Imogen waited a moment, gathering her thoughts, before dialling. If there was one person she longed to give good news to, it was Danni's mum. Even if catching and punishing the man who'd taken her daughter from her wouldn't bring Danni back, Samantha – who was long divorced from Danni's dad and who had no other children – craved some sort of justice. In the months since Danni's death, Imogen had witnessed the decay of Samantha's soul: she appeared thinner, greyer and more brittle every time Imogen saw her. She had complained to the press about the police's failure to catch her daughter's killer, but Imogen didn't hold that against her. She understood the compulsion to lash out.

Imogen spoke softly, gently, when Samantha picked up the phone. 'Samantha, it's Imogen Evans.'

'Oh. Detective. I haven't thought of anything yet . . . I've been racking my brain.' She was referring to Imogen's earlier question about an item going missing.

Imogen made a reassuring noise. 'Samantha, I need to ask you something. The area where we found Danni, near Ruyton-XI-Towns – did that place have any special significance for her? Any memories?'

Samantha was bright, and Imogen could almost hear the other woman's brain ticking, trying to work out why she was being asked this.

Her voice was flat. 'I don't think she'd ever been there before. Not that I knew of, anyway.'

'Can you do me a favour, Samantha? Are you near a computer? I'm really sorry to ask you to do this.'

'It's okay. Yes, I'm on the computer now. What do you want me to do?'

'Open Google Maps. Now, search for Ruyton-XI-Towns.'

She knew how painful this would be for the other woman.

'Okay, done.'

'Thanks, Samantha. Now, can you zoom out a little?' She knew Samantha's eye would focus in on the field where Danni's body had been found. 'Look around the map. Can you see anywhere, anyplace that Danni visited?'

She waited while Samantha followed her instructions. Imogen could hear blowing noises at the other end of the line and guessed Samantha was smoking.

'No, there's nothing.'

'Are you sure? Maybe zoom out a little further.'

'Okay.' Her voice was still flat, almost dead. 'There's . . . wait.'

'What is it?' Imogen tried to suppress her eagerness. She was also on Google Maps, looking at the same area.

'Boreatton Park. PGL. She went there when she was a little girl.'

'PGL? What's that?' But as she spoke, she spotted it on the map and clicked the link to the PGL website. It was an outdoor activity centre. Kids could go and stay there overnight, try canoeing, orienteering, all that sort of stuff. Mountain biking? Imogen frantically clicked around the site trying to find out.

'She went there with school when she was in year seven. I remember because it was just before me and her dad split up. We spent the weekend she was away trying to work through our problems. Ha! We told her when she got back.'

'That you were getting divorced?'

Imogen heard her take a deep drag on her cigarette. 'Yeah. Well, we told her Daddy was moving out. That it was just going to be me and her from now on.'

'Was it hard on her? Sorry, stupid question.'

Samantha snorted. 'Yeah, it was hard. She got back from PGL all excited, talking about how they'd been on pony rides across the fields and through the woods, asking if we could get one, could the three of us go on a pony-trekking holiday together. Then we hit her with the bombshell.' Her voice quivered. 'For a long time, Danni said that was the last time she was ever truly happy, that weekend before her dad left.'

Imogen thanked Samantha and hung up, then stared at the map.

Fiona finding out about her heart transplant at Wenlock Priory.

Nathan finally beating his great rival at the Long Mynd.

Danni riding ponies across the Boreatton estate before finding out her parents were getting a divorce.

That was three out of three.

Could it be a coincidence? All three victims' bodies had been left at the places where they were happiest while they were alive. Was the Viper doing this by design?

It seemed so fantastical, so neat – when crime was usually so messy, so chaotic – that she wanted to reject the idea. But there was something in it. There *had* to be.

Realising it was lunchtime – already! – Imogen got up and went through into the kitchen, still deep in thought. She found DC Alan Hatton studying a sorry-looking sandwich, his nose wrinkled.

'Does this smell off to you?' he asked, holding it out so she could get a whiff of it.

It smelled like rotten eggs. 'Definitely. Don't eat it. How long has it been in the fridge?'

He thought for a moment. Made a face. 'About a week.'

She laughed and took out her own pasta salad. But as soon as she prised the lid off she realised she wasn't hungry. The stink of Alan's sandwich had stayed with her; her stomach recoiled at the sight of her salad. But Alan was gazing at it like a dog staring at a sausage.

'Do you want this?' she asked.

'Are you sure?'

'Yeah, take it. *Bon appétit.*'

'Thanks, guv.'

She left him tucking into the salad and headed to the incident room, all the while thinking through her theory. Then she studied the map on the wall, a pin showing where each of the bodies had been found.

The places where Danni, Nathan and Fiona had been happiest.

Imogen shuddered and scanned the map of the county, imagining its woods and rivers, its farms and pretty towns, its roads and churches. She pictured him out there, waiting, watching. Somewhere, she knew, he was planning to kill again.

Would the next victim be found in *their* happy place?

She scribbled notes on the whiteboard as she thought it through.

The souvenirs.

The happy places.

The painless, morphine-induced deaths.

Lips curled into a twisted approximation of a smile.

She was circling the answer, she knew it. The Viper's crimes weren't messy, weren't chaotic. There was rhyme and reason to them, evidence that he was working to a plan. And that ought to make it easier to figure out what he would do next.

Chapter 25

Ollie came into the kitchen where I was working at the table, honing the copy for the second client Robert Friend had sent me, the farm shop. It was the first day of the summer holidays and Ollie was off for six weeks.

He plucked an apple from the fruit bowl. He'd definitely lost weight, just a couple of pounds I estimated, but I was pleased he was heading in the right direction. There'd been a programme on TV the night before about kids Ollie's age being referred to obesity classes, with a succession of shame-faced parents interviewed about what they'd allowed their children to eat. I would still need to keep an eye on him, but it was one less thing for me to worry about.

'What's going on with you and Mum?' he asked.

I closed the laptop and employed a delaying tactic. 'What do you mean?'

He stared at the floor tiles. 'I saw you the other night.'

'Ollie . . .'

'Are you getting back together?' The hope that had been bubbling beneath his words sprang to the surface. 'Are we going back to London?'

I got to my feet. When he was little, when he scuffed his knee or was frightened by a clap of thunder, I could scoop him up and cuddle him, make the pain and fear go away. I wanted to do that now. But all I could do was be honest.

'Ollie, I'm sorry, but that's not going to happen. Your mum and I are going to get divorced. And we live *here* now.'

His eyes narrowed – just as they'd done when he was a toddler about to throw a tantrum – and I expected him to say, stereotypically, 'I hate you.' Instead, he said something much worse.

'You hate me.'

He tossed his half-eaten apple on the counter and fled the room. I hurried after him, but he was too fast, slamming his door shut and locking it. I banged on the door, wishing I'd removed the lock when we moved in.

'You're a loser,' he shouted. 'That's why Mum doesn't want you any more. A stupid loser.'

I took a long, deep breath. 'Come on, Ollie, let's talk about it.'

I pressed my ear to the door. I couldn't hear a thing.

I gave up. He needed some time to cool down.

I went out to the front garden. The sky was a sheet of solid blue and the rain of the previous few days had left the garden looking fresh and verdant. For a moment, standing there with the sun on my face, I felt at peace. The street was quiet now without the incessant noise from next door. I felt so much better than I had a couple of weeks ago. Megan had texted me earlier to apologise for how she'd acted the night before and to say that she would talk to the estate agent about selling our flat as soon as she returned to London. I actually wanted to thank her. The previous night had been cathartic: it made me realise exactly how I felt about her now. I knew I was ready to let her go. Ollie would come round, I was certain.

I was ready, at last, to move on with my life.

ω

Lunchtime came and went and Ollie was still locked in his room, despite my efforts to tempt him out with the smell of soup cooking. By two o'clock, I'd had enough. I banged on his door.

No response.

'If you don't come out in the next minute I'm going to fetch my tools and drill through the lock.'

I could hear him moving about.

'Forty-five seconds.' I checked my watch. 'Thirty.'

The door opened and he scowled at me.

'Come on,' I said. 'It's time for your guitar lesson.'

'Oh, I don't want to go. I'll be rubbish. And why do I have to do it in the school holidays?'

'Because I don't want you spending six weeks playing video games. You'll enjoy it, I'm sure. I wish I'd learned when I was a kid. I might have been a famous rock star by now.'

He rolled his eyes.

'Grab your guitar and I'll buy you an ice cream on the way.'

He disappeared back into his room. He picked up his iPod, glanced at it, then chucked it into a drawer. He came out wearing a new hoodie Megan had bought him at the weekend and carrying his new guitar.

We walked down the hill towards the centre of Ironbridge. Ollie's head was hanging low, lips pursed, but as I talked stream-of-consciousness nonsense about ice cream, running through all the flavours I could think of or make up – raspberry ripple, white chocolate ginger, moonbeam and stardust – his frown lifted. Just a little.

'This is a lovely place to live, isn't it?' I said as we headed down Madeley Road. When the sun was shining and you could hear birds twittering in the trees as a fat moggy strolled unhurriedly across a quiet road, I wondered why I had ever moved away from this place to London. But, of course, that was my forty-something self thinking; the teenage me had been stifled and bored. And Ollie was brought up in the big city. The very air here must taste strange to him.

'It's all right,' he said.

'Everything okay at school?' I asked.

'Yeah, it is actually.'

'You've seemed happier recently.' I decided not to bring up what Shelley had said about him being bullied. Not when his mood was so delicately balanced.

'I guess.' A little smile appeared. 'It was a lot better last week. Dad, when can I have my DS back?'

'When I find out who sent it to you. Listen, I'll buy you one myself. We're going to be selling the flat now and—'

His face fell again and I inwardly slapped myself.

'So there's, like, definitely no going back?' he asked. We had reached the ice cream shop now, just across from the river, and the sun was behind Ollie, shining in my eyes. He appeared to be ringed by a halo.

'Let's get that ice cream and talk about it. We've got fifteen minutes before we need to get to your lesson.'

I knew he wouldn't be able to resist. He chose toffee fudge while I went for caramel praline. We walked on, past a group of children on an outing to see the bridge, down the steps and turning left on to a path that ran alongside the Severn. The previous days' rain had caused the water level to rise, but now the river was calm, flowing languorously towards the distant sea, and the whole scene was tranquil, not far from idyllic. The opposite bank was crowded with tall trees, their reflections rippling on the murky green surface of the water. A small family of ducks glided past as we watched, drifting away from the bridge that dominated the landscape. 'So,' I began. 'About your mum and me.'

He winced. Here we were, two males, about to have an uncomfortable conversation about grown-up stuff. I ploughed on. 'Sometimes the best thing for two people, even two people who love each other, or used to love each other, is for them to be apart. Because—'

He wasn't listening. Instead, he was looking over my shoulder, up at the bridge.

'What's that guy doing?' he said.

I turned, squinting into the light.

There was a man – sandy-coloured hair, late twenties, tall and slim, though too far above us for me to see his face – standing on the very edge of the bridge at its central point, facing the river. He had climbed over the metal barrier and was clinging on to it, his hands behind him. Instinctively, I took a step forwards in his direction.

A woman, who must have just walked on to the bridge from the car park on the other side, shouted something. The man didn't react. Instead, he turned his face, and I was sure he was looking at Ollie and me.

And then he jumped.

His arms windmilled as he plummeted feet first towards the river, his shirt billowing up around him, exposing the flesh of his belly.

I shouted, 'No!' But as the word left my mouth, he hit the water and went under.

There were other people nearby, but all the locals turned to look at me, the former swimming champion, and the tourists followed their cue.

I didn't have a choice. I climbed over the low railing that separated the path from the riverbank, yelling at Ollie to stay where he was as I tugged off my shoes and threw my phone and wallet on the ground. My ice cream, already discarded, lay melting on the path.

I dived in, head first, the coldness of the water stunning me, the shock of it momentarily shutting down my system as I surfaced. I sucked in air and shook my head as I trod water, looking around. Ollie was shouting at me, pointing. I swivelled and saw the man. He had come up thirty feet downstream, his arms flapping in a kind of desperate doggy paddle. He gasped and went under.

I struck out towards the man, who had surfaced once more and was being carried slowly downstream. He thrashed, cried out, and I realised he couldn't swim. This was not a jape. It was a suicide bid. But now instinct had kicked in, the natural desire to survive. His head went under, then resurfaced, panic in his eyes. If I didn't get to him very soon he would tire, go under. Drown.

I was twelve or thirteen feet from him now, trying to ignore the intense cold, my breathing ragged, but all I could think was that I needed to save him, this stranger.

He disappeared again, briefly, then reappeared. He turned towards me, splashing the water around him as he tried to stay afloat, so I got a good look at his face. At that moment, something weird happened, something that would stay with me afterwards.

He grinned.

Then he submerged yet again.

My clothes were heavy, making it hard to move without being sucked under. It had been a long time since I'd got my lifesaver badge, pyjama clad in the warm water of the indoor swimming pool. A long time since I was a young, strong swimmer. For a moment, I feared for my own life. I imagined Ollie's future, forever haunted by what he'd seen, his dad drowning, having to go and live with Megan and Michael. My mum would die alone in her room. All this flashed through my head in an instant and gave me new strength. I ignored the heaviness of the T-shirt on my back, the jeans that clung to my legs, and pushed on towards the man, reaching the spot where he'd been treading water.

I couldn't see him.

'There, Dad, there!' Ollie pointed to a spot a few feet downstream where the water churned. I swam towards it and, after filling my lungs with air, dived under. There he was, sinking towards the riverbed, a dark shape that was, mercifully, still moving, arms waving weakly.

I grabbed him and tugged him upwards. He was heavy, but he kicked his legs, helping me and himself, and after what felt like a hundred years we broke the surface, just as the air in my lungs ran out.

I yelled at him to stay still, to stop thrashing. He did what I said, going limp as I took hold of him from behind, my forearm over his chest, gripping him tightly. We were closest to the far bank, opposite where Ollie stood. I could see other people, including the woman who had shouted from the bridge, making their way towards us along the bank. It wasn't easy for them, as there were several fences to negotiate, and the sloping front garden of a house.

The man I was holding on to suddenly twisted round and grabbed hold of me, what I assumed to be a last-minute panic that pushed my head under the water. I swallowed several mouthfuls of the stuff before surfacing again and getting hold of him, screaming at him to calm down, that he was going to be fine. He went limp again, closing his eyes.

We were close to the bank now and I looked around for a good spot to climb out. There was a flat, rocky area ahead of us, just past the edge of the garden in which the onlookers now stood. I tugged the man towards it and, crawling on to the hard ground, pulled him after me with my last ounce of strength.

I sunk to my hands and knees, spitting out brackish, foul-tasting water on to the rocks. My freezing clothes clung to me. It was cold here, in the shadow of the trees, and I began to shiver uncontrollably. I fought the urge to vomit and lifted my head to look at the man I had rescued, my vision blurry, head swimming. He lay still, wet clothes clinging to his skin, revealing his muscular arms. Gathering strength from some deep well, I crawled towards him, ignoring the pain in my knees, ready to do CPR.

He opened his eyes and looked back at me.

'You're a good man,' he said.

To my astonishment, he got to his feet and, as if he'd just been for a pleasant swim in a pool, climbed up the bank into the trees, leaving a trail of water behind him. He vanished from sight.

I collapsed, stunned, and lay still, heart thumping, unable to stop shivering until the woman from the bridge finally made it across to the rocky platform and wrapped me in her coat. Other people arrived. I stared at the sky through half-open eyes, the sun a watery haze above me.

The next few minutes were a blur. They got me to my feet and helped me across to the garden, where I lay in the light, recovering. Somebody said, 'Where did he go?' and another person said they'd called an ambulance. Ollie was there, looking down at me, and the woman from the bridge said, 'Your dad's a hero. He was always a brilliant swimmer.' The anxiety on my son's face changed to pride, and then I closed my eyes.

Chapter 26

Michael slumped forwards on to the desk in what he had come to think of as his cell. With little natural light to go by, time had blurred, augmenting his fear. The lack of food as well as dehydration had rendered him weak and sluggish. The empty bottle of water lay across the room, taunting him. He kept nodding off, then jerking awake suddenly, certain that spiders the size of hands were climbing up his back, burrowing into his flesh. He dreamed that a spider laid eggs beneath his skin and the eggs hatched, a million tiny baby arachnids bursting from a hole in his arm. He could see them on the walls of the room, filling the basement, and knew he would drown in a sea of scrabbling, furry legs, wrapped like prey and eaten.

When he was fully awake, he vacillated between the certain belief he was going to die there and the hope that his captor would set him free. Escape seemed impossible and rescue unlikely. Who knew where to look?

The thin light that trickled in through the air vents had ebbed away and now it was dark again. In the distance, he heard a car engine, followed shortly by footsteps above his head.

The door opened and the man from the pub came in, closing the door behind him.

'When are you going to let me go?' Michael demanded, his mouth so dry the words emerged as a rasp. 'They will find me, you know. I'm famous. Do you think no one is looking for me?'

'Actually, they think you and the girl have run off into the sunset, hand in hand.' The man's voice bounced off the cold brick walls.

'Annette? Where is she? Have you hurt her?'

He laughed. 'She's a good person, so I won't make it hurt.'

The man was close to him now, a damp, sour smell coming off him. He took the chair opposite Michael and leaned forward. 'You shouldn't have fucked Ben's wife.'

Michael was stunned into silence. 'What?'

'I think you heard me. If you'd kept it in your pants, you wouldn't be here now.'

'Ben? I don't . . .' Michael's mind raced.

'I can almost hear your brain whirring,' the man said. He affected a whine. '*What's Ben got to do with it?*'

'Did he put you up to this?' Michael said. 'Is he here? Outside that door?' He raised his voice. 'Ben? Are you there?'

That earned him a slap across the face. His neck snapped back, the chair almost tipping. Michael's vision flashed white.

'Ben's a good man,' the man said. 'Just a lost soul who needs saving.'

'I don't understand.' Michael was almost in tears now. 'Is Ben paying you? I have more money than him. A lot more money. Whatever you want, you can have it.'

'You think money is the answer? That says it all. That really says it all.'

Michael whimpered.

'You want to know why you're still alive, Michael?' The man leaned closer. His breath was sour. 'You wanted an exclusive, didn't you? Well, you're going to get one. The scoop of the fucking century.'

He left the room.

Michael laid his head on the desk and closed his eyes, exhausted. He must have drifted off, because it felt like only seconds had passed when the door opened again and there was something wet on his cheek. Saliva – or tears.

He lifted his head, and thought he must still be asleep. Asleep and dreaming.

Chapter 27

Imogen was back in the incident room with Emma. It was 9.30 a.m. And, once again, she hadn't slept. All night, details of the investigation had churned inside her head, going round and round: happy places, souvenirs, morphine. At one in the morning, she had got out of bed and gone out into the empty streets, needing to walk, to clear her head. She had passed a pair of drunk teenage boys who sniggered, no doubt in response to a lewd comment one had made about her. The look she'd given had silenced them.

'Okay,' she said now, perching on the edge of a desk. 'Danni Taylor's boyfriend, Rob, called me last night. You know how I was trying to find out if the offender took an item from her, like the helmet that was taken from Nathan Scott and the pendant from the third victim? After I spoke to Mrs Taylor, she called Rob and asked him to search his and Danni's flat, to see if anything was missing.'

Emma waited.

'He says her lucky teddy isn't there. It's a tiny blue bear, about six inches high, that she'd had since she was a little girl. Rob said she'd been carrying it around with her in her handbag since she found out she was pregnant.'

Emma's mouth dropped open. 'And he's only just noticed it wasn't there?'

'To be fair to him, he says he hasn't been able to bring himself to touch any of her stuff since he got it back. It was too upsetting.' Danni's bag was discovered next to her body. It had passed through forensics before being sent back to Rob. 'But he checked the bag last night. Everything else, including her purse, is in there.'

'It doesn't help us much, though, does it?' Emma said.

'Not unless we make an arrest, no. But we are finally starting to build a picture of our killer.' She turned to the map. 'This is what we know. One: Danni Taylor's body was found in the place where her mother says she was last truly happy – the field where she went horse-riding as a girl. Two: Nathan Scott was left at the site of his happiest moment, the Long Mynd, where he was victorious over his greatest rival. Three: Fiona Redbridge's body was left in the place where she learned she was going to get the heart transplant she needed. Her friend says she had never seen Fiona so happy.' She let that sink in.

Emma stared at Imogen like she'd just told her she believed the killer was an alien from another planet.

'I know it sounds nuts,' Imogen admitted. 'I've been doubting it myself. But they all offered up the same information about the crime scenes. The friends and relatives of our victims haven't got together and cooked this up. They really were all found in a place that was exception-ally meaningful to them.'

'But . . . if that's the case, how did the killer know? You think he got that information from them, just before he killed them?'

'That was my first thought,' Imogen said. 'But then we'd have to accept the premise that he made no advance preparations. I can't believe that he wouldn't have scoped out the dump sites, checked out how to access them, made sure there wasn't going to be anyone around, that he wouldn't be caught on camera.'

Imogen continued. 'I think he knew exactly where he was going to leave his victims before he took them, which means he gathered information about them ahead of time. Somehow, he found out where they had their happiest moments. But how? Did he talk to them? Spy on them? Talk to people around them? Was it something they'd posted online? We need to go back and interview anyone who might have known where our victims were happiest. Did they pass that information on to anyone? I've asked Tracey Snelling to go over all the victims' phone and Internet records again.'

That had been her first call this morning. Tracey, the team's data analyst, had arrived at the station soon after, and began cross-tabulating all the data she could find, looking for patterns.

'Alan was supposed to be helping her,' Imogen said. 'Have you seen him? He should be here by now.'

'I'll text him.'

Emma tapped out a message on her phone.

Imogen was annoyed with Hatton. He was shirking his duty, right when he was most needed. When she saw him, she was going to remind him there was no room for slackers on her team.

Imogen was about to resume the debriefing when another member of the team, DC Ian Robertson, burst into the room. He was out of breath, his face red.

'We've just taken a call from a farmer. He's found a body.'

ᚹ

Imogen and Emma were first to the scene, which was halfway between Shrewsbury and Church Stretton, thanks to Imogen's car and her disregard for the speed limit. Her heart had pounded all the way there. Another body. So soon? It was only two weeks since Fiona Redbridge.

'We don't know it's the Viper,' Emma said as they walked toward the farm.

'Can you try Alan again?' Imogen said. 'We're going to need all hands on deck.'

Emma tried. 'He's still not answering.'

'For God's sake. Okay, call Ian and get him to go round, get the lazy sod out of bed.'

The farmer met them at the gate. He was in his mid-forties with a ruddy face, flyaway hair and wearing a check shirt and wellies. His expression was grim.

'David Knox,' he said, introducing himself. 'I found her when I was heading out to mend a fence. She's in the farthest pasture. Come on, it's easiest to get there by tractor.'

A part of Imogen, the part that didn't feel like it was being squeezed in a vice, wanted to take a snapshot of this, of her sitting in a huge red tractor as it trundled towards the crime scene, to send to her old colleagues in London. It was so bizarre, so different from her previous life. The stink of manure and the rumble of the tractor were alien sensations to her. Her nose tickled from hay fever and the roof of her mouth itched. David Knox turned his head to look at her.

'This is an organic dairy farm, so the livestock roam free through the meadow. She's lying among them, in the middle of the field.'

'Among the cows? They won't . . . nibble at her, will they?' Imogen replied.

He laughed. 'They're strict vegetarians, Detective. They were steering well clear of her.'

They reached the farthest field and Knox brought the tractor to a halt. He jumped down and gestured for Imogen and Emma to follow. The field was indeed full of cows, quiet and slow moving, grazing on lush grass. They lifted their heads to regard the approaching humans, decided there was nothing to fear, and went back to eating. Imogen edged past them, feeling uneasy.

Emma rolled her eyes in response to Imogen stepping delicately around a cowpat, but Imogen didn't care. Because, just ahead of them, was the body.

As Knox had implied, the cows were treating the area where the body lay as if the ground were poisonous.

It was a woman – that much was easy to tell from her shape and the clothes she wore: a short skirt, black boots with a chunky heel, a striped shirt. She lay in the same position as the other victims had, on her back, arms by her sides, legs straight and together. As Imogen got closer, she realised the woman's skin was brown.

'I know her,' she said as Emma arrived by her side, looking down at the body. 'Oh my God. I know her.'

Behind Emma, an ambulance trundled across the field towards them, along with more police, who were making their way on foot. David Knox stood nearby, watching the drama play out on his land.

Imogen knelt by the woman's side.

'Her name's Annette.' She groped in her brain for the woman's surname. 'Annette Lawrence. She works with Michael Stone.'

'The one who doorstepped you?'

Imogen nodded, thinking hard. This didn't fit. All the victims so far had been local. And it seemed highly unlikely that this was Annette Lawrence's happy place. Furthermore, there was no 'smile' frozen on her face.

This one didn't fit the theory. Had she been wrong? Maybe it was the bright sunshine or the stench of cow shit, but her temples throbbed.

The ambulance reached them and a pair of paramedics, a man and a woman, got out. The male paramedic ran up to them and threw himself on to his knees beside Annette.

'She and Stone were supposed to have run off together,' Imogen said, gazing out across the fields, past the ambling cows, as if she might see another body: Michael Stone's. Or had *he* done this? She felt cold inside. But before she could say or think anything else, the paramedic stood up rapidly.

'There's a slight pulse,' he said. 'She's alive.'

'What?' Imogen said, wheeling around to face him.

But he was already running towards the ambulance, gesticulating at his colleague. 'Narcan,' he yelled.

Imogen watched as both paramedics returned to Annette and knelt beside her. One of them had a syringe in his hand.

DCI Greene had arrived on the scene and now stepped in front of Imogen, blocking her line of sight.

'Tell me everything.'

She repeated what she knew about Annette. The whole scene was so bizarre it made her dizzy: the cows wandering around, the sight of the guv with mud stains on his trousers. But Annette Lawrence was *alive*.

And that meant she must have seen the man who did this to her. She would be able to confirm whether it was Adrian.

The paramedics had Annette on a stretcher now. Imogen watched as they carried her into the back of the ambulance, and then she and Emma headed back to the car, trudging across the field, half-blinded by the sun.

Emma's mobile rang.

'It's Ian,' she said to Imogen.

'Is he with Alan? Get him to tell Hatton to—' She stopped. Emma had gone as white as the clouds that scudded overhead. 'What is it? Emma, what's happened?'

But Emma was making another call, her hands trembling. 'I need another ambulance. What? I don't give a crap about that. Get it there *now*.' She spelled out an address. 'The patient's name is Alan Hatton. Yes, DC Hatton.'

'Emma, tell me what the fuck is happening,' Imogen demanded.

Tears shone in the eyes of the younger detective. Imogen had never seen her like this before.

'It's Alan. Ian said . . . Ian said he thinks he's dead.'

Chapter 28

I dreamt I was standing on the Iron Bridge, overlooking the river. The sky was pink and the water beneath me was as red as blood. A couple strode across the bridge towards me. It was Megan and Michael, hand in hand. They were laughing, and I was sure their laughter was directed at me. Ollie walked behind them, holding his iPod. I tried to attract his attention, but he ignored me. In an instant, the dream shifted and Megan and Michael were replaced by Detective Evans, her red hair loose, wearing a short black dress with a tattered hem. She mouthed something and pointed towards the river. I gazed down. Someone was thrashing in the water. Flowers surrounded them, floating on the surface: poppies and crocuses, tulips and daffodils.

I craned my neck to see who the drowning man was, ready to jump, to save him.

It was me.

I thrashed in the water, swallowing mouthfuls of river, heavy clothes weighing me down, and as I sank towards the riverbed, I heard a scratching, scraping sound, a muffled thump that may or may not have been my heart.

I jerked awake. I was sodden with sweat, gasping for air, gulping it down in the darkness. I could still hear the scraping, shuffling noise. It was coming from above me.

That was the last thing I needed. Rats in the attic.

I climbed out from beneath the stinking sheets and headed for the shower, washing the night and the dream away. It lingered, the sensation of drowning in that red water, the sight of Detective Evans leaning over the railing, watching me. A detail from the dream came back. She had yelled, 'I'll save you,' and started to pull her dress over her head, revealing pale skin, a second before I woke up.

I laughed at the memory of it. Why would I need saving? The dream felt like a final purge, a cleansing of the anxieties that had plagued me for months. The washing away of my fears.

Everything was good.

I was happy. For the first time since I'd seen Megan and Michael together, I was actually happy.

PART TWO

Chapter 29

The Royal Shrewsbury Hospital. Imogen waited in the corridor outside the private room in which Annette Lawrence was currently being examined by a doctor. She was desperate to talk to Annette, but the medical team were keeping the police away from her.

Downstairs, Emma and most of the other cops who had come here directly from the farm waited anxiously outside the intensive care unit where Alan Hatton was being treated. Like Annette, he was still alive when the ambulance had reached him, but barely. He was unconscious when Ian had found him after busting into his flat, where he was greeted by a scene out of hell: the carpet and bed awash with vomit and diarrhoea, Alan lying among it, drained of colour, slimy with sweat and impossible to rouse.

The first paramedic on the scene thought it might be norovirus. But yesterday Hatton had seemed completely fine, the picture of health.

'He looked like he'd been poisoned,' Ian had told Imogen when they'd met at the hospital. Now they had Alan attached to a life-support machine. According to the doctor, Alan's internal organs were shutting down. This wasn't norovirus. Was Ian right? Had Alan been poisoned? All they could do was wait. And hope.

And pray.

While they waited, Imogen paced from one end of the hospital corridor to the other, going out of her mind with frustration.

Finally, the consultant dealing with Annette – an Indian man in his forties with a neatly trimmed beard, a proper 'dishy doctor' – came out of Annette's room, and Imogen stepped into his path. His name badge read Ramesh Sankhar.

'How is she?' she asked.

'She's doing okay, actually. The Narcan given to her by the paramedics at the scene saved her life.'

A save shot. Imogen said a silent prayer to modern medicine. 'Was it morphine, like the others?'

'Morphine or heroin. Certainly an opioid, but without thorough tests, we can't say right now.'

'Morphine,' Imogen said. 'It must have been.'

Sankhar blinked at her.

'Do you know how much she was given? And how she survived?' Imogen asked.

He looked past her, obviously keen to get on with his rounds. 'Regarding the dosage, we will have to run tests, but it can be hard to tell.'

'Can I see her?' Imogen asked, determined not to take no for an answer.

'That should be fine.'

But Imogen was already heading for the door.

She found Annette lying flat on her back, her face turned to one side, staring into space. But as soon as Imogen came in, Annette pushed herself up into a sitting position and propped a pillow behind her back. There was a tube in her arm, probably fluids to rehydrate her.

The first thing she said was, 'Where's Michael? Is he here? The doctor wouldn't tell me anything.'

Imogen pulled a chair to the side of the bed and sat down. 'We don't know where Michael is, Annette. I was hoping you could tell me. Can you take me back . . . tell me everything you remember.'

Annette collapsed against the pillow and closed her eyes, allowing Imogen the opportunity to study her properly. Annette's skin was dry and her cheeks sunken. Her fingernails and cuticles were bitten. In her hospital gown, she looked very different from the glamorous woman Imogen had encountered a week ago. But, with her eyes still shut, she told Imogen what had happened.

'Michael met this guy in a pub. He said his name was Adrian . . .'

A jolt of electricity went through Imogen's body. 'Adrian Morrow?'

Annette opened her eyes. 'I don't think he gave Michael his surname.'

So it *was* Adrian. Imogen gestured for Annette to continue.

Annette recounted what had happened. Her eyes were open again, but she was looking into the middle distance, picturing what had happened.

'Michael went to the toilet and I went with Adrian into the living room. Then I felt something, like a wasp sting. I looked down and saw he was holding a needle. He'd jabbed me with it. I blacked out before I could speak or shout to warn Michael.' She paused. 'I woke up in a basement.'

'With Michael?'

'No. But Adrian told me Michael was in another part of the basement, that he was safe.' She took a deep breath.

'I understand how terrifying it must have been—'

'It wasn't. I mean, *he* wasn't scary. Adrian. He seemed so normal. I mean, he was intense, and he wouldn't come close to me. He had me chained to a chair, but he stayed at the edges of the room, except when he brought over food or water and put it on the table for me. Stale sandwiches and crisps. A bruised apple and an overripe banana when I complained about the lack of nutrition.'

Imogen leaned forward. 'Did he talk to you?'

'He hardly said anything. He just kept reassuring me he wasn't going to hurt me. "I don't want to cause you any pain," he said. And, I don't know why, but I believed him. At first, I was scared he would try to rape me or kill me. But as time went on, I started to think he was going to let me go, that I'd be okay.'

'And he didn't say anything more about Michael?'

'No. I mean, I can't remember. It's like there's a black hole in my brain where the memories should be.'

'They'll come back,' Imogen said. 'You just have to give it time.'

'I don't know. Maybe I don't want the memories to come back.'

Imogen could understand that. 'What happened at the end, Annette?'

'I don't know. I was asleep. He put a mattress in the corner of the room and told me to lie down, get some rest. So I did. I was exhausted.' She paused, thinking about it. 'I have this vague memory of waking up, of a prick of pain, and then of being enveloped by warmth, a feeling of bliss. I recognised the feeling.'

Imogen was confused. 'Recognised it?'

Annette met Imogen's eye, unashamed. 'I was a very different person when I was a teenager. I hung around musicians a lot. Rock bands. When I was sixteen or seventeen, I went out with this guy who thought he was the new Jimi Hendrix. He got me using heroin. I wasn't an addict – it was a recreational thing.' She chewed her lip. 'That's what I told myself, anyway.'

Imogen was surprised. She'd met Annette Lawrence only once before, but she was very different from the heroin addicts Imogen had encountered in the line of duty. Drugs like cocaine were, of course, prevalent among people who worked in the media, but it was hard to imagine Annette nodding off with a needle in her arm.

'The doctor, the one who was here before you came in, told me that's how I survived today. If I was opioid naïve, as he called it, the dose would almost certainly have killed me.'

'And you didn't tell Adrian you'd done heroin before?'

'Of course not.'

'Annette, we need to find the place you were being kept. Michael could still be there. Do you think you could find it again? Draw me a map?'

'I think so.'

Imogen produced a notepad and got Annette to recount her and Michael's journey. Imogen wished she could take Annette out in order to pinpoint exactly where they'd stopped, but there was no way she would be allowed to leave the hospital yet.

Then she remembered she had Adrian Morrow's photograph saved on her phone, a picture his mum had given them. For confirmation, she brought up the picture and showed it to Annette. 'I just want to double-check this is the man who abducted you.'

Annette took a long, hard look at the picture.

'That's not him.'

Imogen made certain she was showing Annette the correct picture, that she wasn't going crazy. 'Are you sure?'

'Yes. I'm sure. He was about the same age as this guy, probably a bit older. His hair was a similar colour, kind of sandy blond. But that isn't him. One hundred per cent, it's not him.'

Imogen stood up. Every time she thought she was getting somewhere in this investigation, the ground shifted beneath her.

'But he definitely called himself Adrian?'

'Yes. I mean . . .' She rubbed her forehead. 'That's what he said when he met Michael in the pub. He didn't use a name in the basement.'

Imogen turned away from the bed. Adrian was a common name . . . but no, that was too much of a coincidence. It couldn't be another Adrian.

Had they jumped to conclusions?

Her mind raced. They knew that Adrian had been at the third crime scene, and they also knew he had a record of stalking, and that he had an unhealthy interest in serial killers. That wasn't so uncommon, though. Sometimes, flicking through the TV schedules or browsing in a bookshop, it felt to Imogen like the whole world was obsessed with serial murderers.

The more she thought about it, the sicker she felt. But then she returned to the main reason they suspected Adrian. His disappearance.

Was somebody else responsible for that?

Was Adrian being set up?

What if the Viper had seen the police's appeal to identify Adrian and spotted an opportunity? Here was a chance to distract the police, send them looking in the wrong direction. Adrian hadn't run away. He was dead, his body hidden somewhere. And, if this were all correct, they had fallen for it. *She* had fallen for it.

'When did Michael meet Adrian?'

Annette told her, and Imogen checked the dates on the calendar on her phone. It was after they'd released his photo. Then what had happened? An anonymous caller had phoned in to identify him. The Viper. It had to be. Imogen paced the hospital room. That meant the Viper had to be someone who knew Adrian, although that hardly helped. Through work, he came into contact with hundreds of tenants and prospective tenants, and he was well known in the pubs around Shrewsbury. He'd gone to school around here, too.

So, the real Viper had set the police on Adrian's trail. But why had he introduced himself as Adrian when he met Michael? He obviously wanted to conceal his identity, but he could have used any fake name. He must have thought there was a chance Michael would talk to the police, tell them about the man he met in the pub.

But the most important thing was that the Viper had screwed up. Perhaps Annette's pulse had been too faint to detect when he left her. Maybe something had spooked or disturbed him. Whatever the reason, he had inadvertently given the police their first break. Because here she was, alive. And she had seen the killer's face.

ʊ

She met Emma downstairs, outside intensive care.

'Any news on Alan?' Imogen asked.

Emma was still pale, her eyes wide with anxiety. 'The doctor just came out. They're still running tests, trying to work out what's happened to him. They say it's his kidneys and liver . . . I'm scared, Imogen.'

'Has someone called his parents?'

'They're on their way.'

Imogen nodded. 'Listen, I know you probably want to stay here, but we need to find Michael Stone.' She explained about the map, and discovering it wasn't Adrian who took Michael and Annette. 'I can go on my own, but—'

'I'll come. I'm going crazy here. And we've got a job to do, right?'

'Right.'

Imogen asked Emma to drive so Imogen could talk to Greene. She told him what she'd found out so far, though she didn't tell him about her theory that Adrian had been set up. She wanted to talk it through with Emma first. She also asked him to arrange for a sketch artist to visit Annette.

'When we get there, we need to go in quietly,' she said to Greene. 'We can't turn up mob-handed, sirens blaring and scare the perpetrator off. Agreed? The moment we find the place, we'll call.'

'And you'll wait for backup to arrive,' DCI Greene said.

'Of course.'

ʊ

Hopton Wood was on the border with Wales, to the far west of the county. There was no other traffic on this narrow country lane, and Imogen could imagine how spooky this place would be at night. Even now, while it was still light, there was something creepy about it. Imogen was reminded of fairy tales, of Little Red Riding Hood, the big bad wolf waiting among the silent trees. Emma, in her trainers and outdoor gear, with that fresh face and her hair tied back, looked at home here. A country girl. But to Imogen, raised in the concrete jungle, places like this were familiar only from horror films and nightmares.

She consulted the map she'd drawn with Annette's help.

'It's somewhere around here,' she said. 'Annette told me there's a black gate to the left, just after a bend in the road.'

'Like that one?' Emma asked, her voice hushed. Imogen's intensity was contagious.

They pulled over into the space in front of the gate and killed the engine. Imogen peered past the gate into the woods. Annette had said the house wasn't visible from the road.

Imogen's skin tingled. This was the place. She was sure of it.

She got out of the car and checked the ground for tyre prints, but it was as smooth as if the earth had recently been swept.

'I'm going to take a look. I don't want him to hear all the commotion and run.'

'You told Greene you'd wait for backup as soon as we found the house. I think that's a good—'

Imogen wheeled around. 'What if he's injecting Michael Stone right now?'

'Imogen, I think you need to relax. You're not thinking straight.'

'My thinking is as straight as a fucking arrow.' Imogen strode towards the gate, aware of her pulse pounding in her ears, of Emma pausing behind her, then following.

She squeezed through the gate and, treading lightly, headed down the path, which was about the width of a car. Emma caught up and fell into step beside her.

'There's no phone signal here,' Emma said, checking her mobile. Imogen ignored her and quickened her step.

At the end of the path, a small stone cottage came into view.

Imogen approached the front door and pressed her ear against the wood. She couldn't hear anything. She moved to the front window. The curtains, which looked ancient and moth-eaten, were closed.

Imogen headed round the side of the house to the right. It was so quiet. The curtains were drawn closed at every window. Was this place deserted? Maybe that made sense . . . the Viper could have lured Michael and Annette to this abandoned building, a place where he wouldn't be disturbed. At night, it wouldn't have been so easy to tell the cottage wasn't currently inhabited. It would have looked more like a home. But then she reached the back of the house and found a bare window, which allowed her to see into the kitchen. A plate and a mug sat beside the sink; the plate had toast crusts on it. Someone *was* living here.

Emma, who had been looking around the garden, appeared at Imogen's shoulder, making her jump.

'Jesus,' Imogen hissed.

Emma's eyes were wide. 'There's a garage over there.'

Imogen followed her over. It was a basic red-brick structure, a lot newer than the house, with a corrugated iron door that was padlocked shut. Imogen glanced back at the house, checking there were no signs of life, and said, 'Did you hear something? A voice, coming from inside here.'

'No. I—'

But Imogen had already gone off in search of something to use to break the padlock, almost convincing herself that she'd heard a voice, that she wasn't making it up so she'd have a good reason to break into the garage.

There was a little shed nearby. It was unlocked. Imogen poked her head inside and saw a number of tools hanging from rusty nails. She picked up a hammer and returned to the garage.

'I really think we should go back to the road and wait for backup,' Emma said.

'I need you to keep an eye on the house. If you see or hear anything, or anyone, tell me immediately.'

Imogen repeatedly tapped the side of the padlock, using a technique a senior detective had taught her, and it popped open. Easy when you knew how.

She pulled the garage door open, wincing at the grating noise it made.

'Bingo.'

Inside the garage was a black Audi. It matched the description of Michael Stone's car. She didn't need to check the plates; it had to be his.

Imogen walked to the back of the Audi. There was nothing else in the garage except for a carrier bag close to the rear wall. The floor was covered with a sheet of tarpaulin. She knelt and, using a fingertip, opened the bag and peered inside. Empty sandwich wrappers, a half-drunk bottle of water, a mouldy banana.

A wasp came buzzing out of the bag, flying at Imogen's face, and she fell backwards, landing on her bum with a thump that rang out around the garage.

'You all right?' Emma asked.

Imogen stared at her. 'Did you hear that? The ground – it sounds hollow.'

She got to her feet and pulled the sheet of tarpaulin aside to reveal a hatch. In the doorway, Emma watched the house, glancing over her shoulder every few seconds to see what Imogen was doing.

Beneath the hatch, Imogen found a flight of steps going down into the earth.

'Imogen, don't go down there.'

'I have to. Stay at the door, keep a lookout. Okay?'

Imogen went down backwards, holding on to the wooden steps. Halfway down, she swore as a splinter pierced her finger. And then she was on solid ground again, standing in near-darkness. The only light came from the open hatch above. She knew she should go back to the car, fetch her torch, but she was too desperate to know if Michael Stone was down here.

There were two doors. She tried the one on the left first and found it was unlocked. It opened into a dark room. She felt around the edge of the door and, sure enough, found a light switch on the outside of the room. Shielding her eyes, she flicked it on. The room was empty, except for a chair and table at the centre.

She left that door open and tried the other. Again, it was unlocked. She stepped inside and found the light switch.

She immediately wished she hadn't.

'Oh God. Oh fuck . . .'

She forced herself to stay calm, to ignore the stench and the buzzing sound. She needed to look, even though she knew she would never be able to unsee it.

Michael Stone lay on his back on the floor, in the same position Annette and the other victims had been found in.

But there had been nothing peaceful about Michael's death.

There was a ragged slash across his throat, the flesh gaping open. That was how he'd died. But that wasn't his worst injury. His face was black and purple with bruises, his lips swollen, a sickening lump on the side of his head.

One eye was still open. The other had been cut out, leaving a black hole in his face. Thick, dark blood had run down over his face, but had dried now to form a crust. Flies buzzed around him excitedly.

As she watched, a fat black fly emerged from Michael's bloody eye socket and took flight, bouncing off the fluorescent light.

Imogen fled the room.

Chapter 30

My phone woke me up. I ignored it, burying my head beneath the covers. It was the weekend and I had promised myself a much-needed lie-in. But then the phone started ringing again and, reluctantly, I reached out for it. It was Megan. She was crying.

'It's Michael . . .' The rest of her sentence was unintelligible, her words shivery and tear soaked.

'Megan, slow down. I can't understand you.'

I guessed it was to do with him running off with that researcher. Megan had a bloody cheek, calling me about it, like I'd provide a shoulder to cry on.

'Michael . . . he's dead.'

I must have misheard. 'Meg, calm down. Talk slowly. What's happened?'

'*Michael's dead.*'

I withdrew the phone from my ear like it had bitten me. *Dead?* At the same moment, my bedroom door burst open and Ollie came in, wide eyed and panting with horrified excitement, carrying his laptop. 'Dad, have you seen the news?'

I held up a hand. 'Hang on, your mum's trying to tell me something.'

Through her sobs, she told me what she knew, while Ollie held his computer in front of my face, displaying the headline on the BBC website. Michael had been murdered. The police had found his body in a house in Hopton Wood yesterday. They wouldn't tell Megan very much at all, but the media were convinced he'd been killed by the Viper.

'What about the researcher?' I asked, when Megan fell quiet.

She blew her nose. 'Annette Lawrence. She's alive. They found her on a farm, I don't know, somewhere out in the boonies. Oh, God, this place . . . It's *evil*. How can you live here?'

I ignored that. I was reeling. I had known Michael a long time. We had been friends once. But after what had happened with Megan, I'd hated him.

I was relieved to find that I wasn't glad he was dead, but I wasn't sad either. I mainly felt shocked, as if the celebrity Michael Stone, the one everyone knew from TV, had been murdered, not the man I knew. More than anything, I felt sorry for Megan – how could I not, hearing her sobs? Despite everything, she was still my wife, the mother of my son.

'Do you want to come round?' I asked.

She sniffed. 'Yes. Please. I need to see Ollie.'

She ended the call.

I had a quick shower, then grabbed my laptop. As expected, the story was everywhere: the lead item on all the news sites, trending on Twitter, everybody talking about it on Facebook. It was media catnip, a high-profile journalist killed while investigating a serial killer who was still at large. There were few facts about what had happened to Annette Lawrence, although *The Sun* claimed to have an exclusive interview with the farmer who had found her. According to *The Guardian*, the police were going to hold a press conference at 1 p.m.

I closed my laptop and made breakfast for Ollie and myself.

'Do you think . . .' he began, then stopped.

'What?'

'Nothing. It doesn't matter.'

But I knew what he was going to say: he wanted to ask if Megan and I were likely to get back together now Michael was dead. I was glad he wasn't going to make me answer that question again. Since Wednesday, when I'd pulled that guy from the river, Ollie's attitude towards me had completely changed. He seemed to look at me in a different light – a *better* light. I'd done something that he saw as heroic. As I'd walked home, wearing dry clothes a local shopkeeper had lent me, it had felt good to see the admiration on my son's face.

Megan turned up mid-morning. It was a fine day again, so I invited her into the garden and put the kettle on. She sat there in her sunglasses, pale and shaky, sipping sweet tea, while Ollie sat nearby. The whole thing was painfully awkward. I didn't know what to do or say.

'It could be worse,' Megan said at one point. She looked at me through the dark glass of her shades. 'It could have been you.'

I had no idea how to respond to that.

At just before one, I suggested that we watch the press conference, which was being broadcast live on BBC News. We went into the living room.

There was DI Imogen Evans. She had dark circles around her eyes and frown lines on her forehead that hadn't been there when I'd met her less than a week before. Evans's superior, a big guy called DCI Brian Greene, sat to her left. Two other cops flanked them.

Ollie came into the room to watch as DI Evans talked. She confirmed that they believed Michael's death was linked to the murders of Danni Taylor, Nathan Scott and Fiona Redbridge. Cameras flashed and reporters tried to interrupt. Evans and Greene watched them impassively until everything calmed down.

'We have a witness,' DI Evans said, 'who had close contact with the man we are looking for. I'm now going to show you a photofit that has been created with the help of this key witness. If anyone recognises this man, I urge you to call us on the number shown here. Do not approach him. We believe him to be extremely dangerous.'

The photofit filled the screen. He appeared to be in his late twenties or early thirties, Caucasian with short, sandy-coloured hair, narrow blue eyes and thin lips. He gazed out at us, daring people to recognise him. Beside me, Megan stifled a sob, just as Ollie gasped.

He pointed at the TV. 'It's him. Dad, it's *him.*'

It dawned on me what he meant. 'Oh my God. You're right.' I scrambled to find my phone and punched in the number on the screen with shaking fingers.

'What are you talking about?' Megan asked.

Ollie answered while I waited for someone to pick up the phone at the other end.

'That's the man Dad saved. The one he pulled out of the river.'

Chapter 31

Imogen left the press conference to find Emma waiting for her. Emma wore a grim expression, and as Imogen caught her eye, the younger woman raised a trembling hand to her lips, as if trying to stop the words from escaping.

'It's Alan. He's gone.'

Imogen laid a hand against her chest, her heart fluttering beneath her palm. She'd known this was coming, had been prepared by the doctors at the hospital. But there had still been a chance of a miracle, a thread of hope.

That thread had now snapped.

'Oh,' she heard herself say.

'I've just come from the hospital. Karen Lamb is going to perform the post-mortem. She was about to start when I left.' A tear rolled down her cheek. 'His body was still warm and now that . . . that woman . . .'

Imogen put her arms around Emma. She was stiff at first, but soon relaxed into the embrace, allowing herself to be held. Imogen hadn't realised how much Emma cared about Alan Hatton until he was taken ill. She had since learned they were good friends, that they hung out together outside work. How had Imogen not known that?

She let Emma leave her embrace.

'Did Karen say when her report would be ready?'

Emma's reply was faint. 'Later today. I . . . Imogen, I don't know what to do. The lads are all talking about going to the pub, having some kind of wake. It just doesn't . . .'

'Go home, Emma. Take the rest of the day off.'

'But the investigation. Alan wouldn't want us to stop trying to catch the Viper.'

'We're not going to stop. But you need to rest. I bet you didn't sleep last night, did you?'

Emma shook her head. Imogen didn't mention that she'd barely slept either, once again. Partly because she was worried about Alan, but mostly because every time she closed her eyes, she saw the fly crawling from the hole where Michael Stone's eye had been. She was running on adrenaline.

'Go home, see your boyfriend, try to rest. I'll call you once I've spoken to Karen, okay?'

'No.'

'Pardon?'

'I don't want to go home. I want to stay here, be with other people who knew Alan. And I want to do my job. People need us, Imogen.'

She walked away, holding her head high.

ϖ

Imogen headed straight to the hospital. Karen hadn't finished, so Imogen called in to see Annette. Another grieving woman, though she still seemed more shocked than anything else, in a post-traumatic state.

Imogen sat with her for a while, asking her if she'd remembered anything else, anything that might help them find the Viper. She showed Annette more photographs of Adrian, to double-check she hadn't been mistaken. The man in the sketch, though sharing some of Adrian's features, was clearly a different person. And Adrian Morrow still hadn't shown up. Nobody had heard from him; nobody had seen him. Imogen was convinced he was involved, but she couldn't figure out exactly how.

Annette drifted off to sleep and Imogen headed down to the mortuary. She found Karen Lamb in her office. The pathologist was tapping away at her computer with one hand and eating what looked like a roast beef sandwich with the other. The room smelled of meat, and Imogen thought, not for the first time, that if she spent her days cutting up bodies, it would almost certainly turn her vegetarian.

'Have you finished examining Alan Hatton yet?' Imogen asked.

Karen smiled. 'Just. I'm still awaiting some results that I've sent off to the lab, which will take—'

'Do you know what killed him?'

'Oh, yes.'

Her fingers flickered over the keyboard.

'And?'

'*Amanita phalloides.*'

'Which is?'

'This.' Karen swivelled her computer screen so Imogen could see it. A Wikipedia page was open. *Amanita phalloides.* The death cap.

Imogen was incredulous. 'He ate poisonous mushrooms?'

'The most common of all poisonous mushrooms, yes. They grow in the woods around Shropshire. Very easily mistaken for edible fungi. Was Mr Hatton a forager?'

'I never heard him mention it.'

Karen nodded. 'Well, it's definitely what killed him. It shut down his liver and kidneys. And there were still remains of the mushrooms in his stomach, along with everything else he ate yesterday – not that there was very much of that. It looks like he had a couple of slices of toast for breakfast and some pasta.'

Imogen went cold.

'Pasta salad.'

'Yes, possibly, though it's hard—'

'No, I know he had pasta salad. It was mine.'

Karen tilted her head, studying Imogen with amused eyes. 'Did you eat any of it?'

'No, I gave it to him.' She explained what had happened at the station two days ago.

'Okay. Well, we need to find the container it was in and get it analysed,' Karen said.

'It was in the communal fridge at work,' Imogen said, half to herself.

'Ooh,' Karen said, her eyes shining. 'Maybe there's a murderer at the station.' She leaned forward. 'And you were their target.'

Imogen's legs had gone weak. She remembered the feeling she'd had the other morning – sure someone had been in her flat. She'd dismissed the idea. But could it be possible that someone had come into her home and poisoned the salad? It seemed more likely than the idea of someone doing it at the station.

'I need to go,' Imogen said.

'Looks like you had a lucky escape,' Karen said, gesturing to the report she was working on. 'I almost got to work on *your* body.'

Imogen left the room, exhaustion and shock combining to send her reeling.

Karen's voice seemed to come from far away. 'Another time, Detective.'

A lucky escape. If she hadn't encountered Alan in the kitchen, she would be dead.

And he would still be alive.

Chapter 32

I sat in the reception area of Shrewsbury police station. Ollie was at the house with Megan. I'd told her she could stay the night, in the spare room, if she wanted. I hoped Ollie wouldn't interpret this as a sign we were getting back together. But, right now, I had other things on my mind.

Had I saved a serial killer from drowning? I wasn't stupid enough to think this meant I was responsible for Michael's death. I mean, how was I supposed to know the guy I'd pulled from the water was the Viper? But I shivered as I recalled the way he had grinned at me, and the words he'd spoken after I'd pulled him out. *You're a good man.* What did that mean?

There was a strange, subdued atmosphere at the station. A young woman with blonde hair in a ponytail came out. She had red eyes, like she'd been crying. 'Ben Hofland? Can you follow me, please?'

She took me to an interview room and sat me down. 'Detective Inspector Evans will be along in a moment.'

I waited, my leg swinging restlessly beneath the table. The door opened and the first thing I saw was that mane of red hair. Instinctively, I stood up, ready to shake her hand. I remembered the dream I'd had about her the night before; the way she'd pulled her dress up to reveal her pale body. That wasn't the first time I'd dreamt about her, was it? The first one had been filthy. And it had been so real. I was embarrassed, as if she could see into my head.

She took hold of my outstretched hand. Her grip was firm, but her demeanour had changed since the first time I'd met her. She had the air of someone who'd just received terrible news, a halo of grief surrounding her. There were dark smudges beneath her eyes and her skin was so pale it was almost translucent. I had an urge to put my arms around her, to comfort her, an urge I pushed away immediately.

She gestured for me to sit. 'I thought I recognised your name. It seems like you're having an interesting month.' Her voice was flat.

'You could say that.'

She leaned back, folding her arms. 'How long have you lived in Ironbridge?'

'I grew up there, but moved to London when I was eighteen. I only just came back after I, ah, separated from my wife.'

'I'm sorry.'

'Oh, it's fine, we're . . .' I trailed off, unsure what to say.

'I meant I'm sorry you had to leave London and come here.' She produced a copy of the photofit I'd seen on TV. 'You say you believe you know this man.'

'I don't know him. I pulled him out of the river in Ironbridge on Wednesday afternoon. He was trying to drown himself.' I described what had happened.

Her pen froze on the page. 'I wasn't told any of this. Are you absolutely sure it was him?'

'I'm certain. Assuming this is an accurate likeness, it's definitely him.'

'Did you report this at the time? Did the police or an ambulance attend?' She was leaning forwards now, sleeves pushed up, pen poised over her pad.

'No. Nothing like that. As I said, as soon as I got him out of the river he ran off. I didn't think about reporting it and we didn't need an ambulance. I mean, he was fine. So was I, once I'd recovered.' This was true, though I was sick later that night, my body purging itself of the nasty water I'd swallowed.

She stood up. Sadness had been pushed away by determination. 'Take me there.'

'Pardon?'

'To Ironbridge. I want to see where this incident happened.'

Chapter 33

The Severn was calm beneath them. Imogen noticed how Ben Hofland shivered as he looked down at it. A coach had just deposited several dozen history buffs in the car park and here they came, trip-trapping over the bridge, holding their phones aloft. It was so noisy that when Ben pointed to a rocky ledge on the right-hand bank, Imogen could barely hear him. She leaned closer as one of the tourists bumped into her from behind, sending her stumbling into him.

She quickly extricated herself. 'Sorry.' She took a deep breath, aware of how he was looking at her.

'I had a . . .' He closed his mouth, eyes shifting away.

'What?'

'It's nothing.'

She waited, but he didn't say any more, giving her a quick flash of a smile instead. It was a nice smile, one that threw her out of the situation for a second and led her to appraise him. He was a bit too skinny, tired around the eyes, but she liked his unkempt beard and his hair that needed a cut. Nice arms, too.

She immediately slammed a door on that line of thought. She was tired, too, physically and emotionally drained. She was barely thinking straight – at a time when her thinking needed to be clearer than ever.

At that moment, a forensics team was combing her apartment, looking for signs of an intruder, the person who had poisoned the salad in her fridge by adding death cap mushrooms to it. They had found the Tupperware container in the dishwasher, and that had been whisked off to the lab. Alan had eaten the whole thing. Later, after the forensics team had finished, someone was coming round to fit new locks and install cameras and a state-of-the-art burglar alarm.

Just the thought of someone being in her home made Imogen sick, even if it hadn't led to Alan's murder. She couldn't feel happy about her lucky escape. A young man, someone she had liked and respected, was gone. And she was sure she'd caught a couple of her colleagues looking at her like it was her fault.

Could it be the work of the Viper?

Right now, she found it hard to believe it could be anyone else. Who else wanted her dead? It couldn't be Kevin Moss. And she had checked: death cap mushrooms were common in Hopton Wood, close to the house where she'd found Michael's body.

It fitted with the Viper's method of killing, too, didn't it? Another kind of poison, but one that caused excruciating pain and suffering.

'It will be easier to show you from the path,' Ben said, bringing her back to the present and leading her across the bridge and down some concrete steps. Soon, he was recounting exactly what had happened: the feet-first plummet, the rescue, the aftermath.

'There were three weird things,' Ben said. 'The biggest one is that after I dragged him out he ran off into the trees, there.' He pointed.

'Did anyone go after him?'

'No. The others seemed more concerned about helping me than pursuing him. And I could barely move, let alone chase him into the woods.'

She examined the dark green water. She wouldn't fancy jumping in there. 'Weren't you concerned for your own safety?'

'I'm a strong swimmer. I used to compete in swimming competitions when I was at school. Took life-saving classes.'

She nodded.

'To be honest, I didn't stop to think.' He rubbed his arms. 'Now I wish I'd let him drown.'

'We don't know for certain that it was the killer,' Imogen reminded him.

'I haven't told you the other odd stuff yet. One of them is just a small thing, but when I was trying to get him over to the bank, he grinned at me. Like it was all a joke, or a game. Then, when I pulled him out, and I was lying exhausted on the rocks, he told me I was a good man.'

'Tell me exactly what he said.'

'"You're a good man." That was it. It seemed like it was all a game to him. Or a test. He did it deliberately, jumped in, knowing he would be okay. He wanted to see if I would save him, if I was "a good man," or if I would stand there and refuse to risk my own safety.'

A sudden dizziness made Imogen's legs weak. She had to sit, perching on the low railing. The vision of what she'd seen in that basement came back to her. Michael, his eye missing, the fly crawling from the socket.

'Are you all right?' Ben peered at her with concern.

'I'm fine. I skipped breakfast, that's all.' Her heart was doing that skittering thing again.

Ben crouched beside her. His hand wavered close to her shoulder before he withdrew it. 'Do you want some food? There are a few cafes just over there.'

She blinked, shaking the nightmarish image of Stone away, and tried to think straight. Ben was still crouching and she could sense the heat coming off him, could almost see it, a red shimmer that surrounded his body. She blinked again, rubbed her eyes.

'No,' she said, too harshly. 'Stop worrying about me.' She pushed herself off the railing. Flashes of light danced before her, but the red shimmer had gone. 'Let's go back to what you were saying. It seems extremely risky on his part, to jump from such a height. I mean, how high is it?'

He stood. 'Fifty-five feet.'

She raised an eyebrow.

'We have all this stuff drilled into us at school around here.' All traces of mirth vanished as his attention returned to the water. 'I think he must have been confident he'd survive. He's probably a strong swimmer like me. The more I think about it, the more I'm convinced he was pretending to drown. But why, Detective? Why me?'

'I think you're being a little paranoid, Mr Hofland.'

He winced as if stung. 'Paranoid?'

'Yes. What makes you think he particularly wanted *you* to jump in after him? There were other people around. One of them could have jumped in.'

'Except they didn't. Everyone expected me to do it. You know how I said I used to be a strong swimmer? I was a local champion. Everybody around here knows about it. The guy I pulled out of the water must have known, too. I mean, he's too young to remember my swimming days, but anyone could have told him.'

She pondered this. 'How would he have known that you would be passing by at that exact moment?'

'I have no idea.'

'Did you see anyone following you?'

'No. I'm pretty sure he was already on the bridge when we got here.'

'You hadn't updated Twitter or Facebook? *Going for a walk by the river.*'

'No, I'm not on Twitter and I hardly use Facebook.'

She barely heard his reply because she was deep in thought. Was this how the Viper chose his victims? He put himself in a difficult or dangerous position and waited to see who helped him? She needed to find out if the first three victims had performed any heroic acts or helped any strangers. Had they put themselves in the firing line by playing the Good Samaritan?

And was Ben Hofland next?

He was watching her, waiting for her to speak.

'Could you come back to the station, answer some more questions?' she asked.

He pulled a face. 'Can it wait a little while? I've got my wife to deal with . . . My estranged wife. She's in a state about Michael.'

'Michael Stone?' That was weird. 'Big fan, was she?'

Incomprehension flitted across his face. 'Fan? No . . . didn't I tell you? She was having a thing with him. She was his girlfriend.'

Imogen stared at him. But before she could say anything – *What the fuck?* for example – her phone rang. Emma.

'Greene wants you back at the station.'

Imogen hung up and studied Ben. He was connected to the Viper through that staged suicide attempt, and through his wife and Michael. Not only that, but he had lived next door to a woman who had murdered her boyfriend.

She found herself regarding Ben in a different light, her mind ticking over.

She pulled up the picture of Adrian on her phone. 'Do you recognise this man?'

'Yes, that's Adrian. My landlord's weird assistant. Why? What's he got to do with it?'

Another connection with Ben Hofland. She must have been giving him an odd look because he shifted, uncomfortable beneath her gaze. Dots of information bounced about in her head, but none of them would connect.

'I'll need to talk to you again very soon. Your wife and son, too. I assume you can walk home from here?'

She jogged back to her car, not waiting for his reply.

ω

Imogen and Emma fell into step as they headed towards the incident room. Emma was being brave.

'How did it go with the witness?' Emma asked.

Imogen recounted what Ben had told her. 'And get this – his missus was shagging Michael Stone. I want a couple of officers watching him.'

'Why?'

'Because he's connected to this. I don't know how exactly. He doesn't look like the man Annette described to us, so I'm not saying Ben Hofland is the Viper or that he's lying about pulling the man who killed Michael Stone out of the river. But he's mixed up in this somehow.'

She stopped walking, making sure she had Emma's full attention. 'We assumed the Viper killed Michael Stone and attempted to murder Annette Lawrence because they were investigating him. But what if that's not the real reason, or the only reason?'

Emma had no answers.

'We have to believe that the murderer screwed up, that he didn't know Annette would survive. If Annette had died, we'd have no description of him and we wouldn't know that Ben Hofland had pulled him out of the river. We need to find the witnesses to this dramatic rescue and confirm that he looked like the man in the photofit. And I want a full background check on Ben Hofland.'

'Leave it with me,' Emma said.

They reached the incident room, where DCI Greene was waiting along with the rest of the team. What remained of them. The space where Alan Hatton had always stood was conspicuously empty. All heads turned as Imogen came in. Frowning faces.

Greene had taken Imogen's spot at the front of the room. She stood beside him, resisting the urge to barge him aside. She wasn't going to let him take her place at the centre of the investigation.

A publicity photo of Michael Stone had been added to the wall behind Greene, incongruous alongside the pictures of the non-famous victims. If today's media coverage was anything to go by, Stone's death had rendered the others unimportant, as if the life of a celebrity was worth far more than an ordinary civilian. Imogen knew that even if – God forbid – the Viper went on to kill twenty people, in future, Stone's name would always appear top of the list of victims. Unless one of those victims was more famous.

'Emma has been looking into the provenance of the house where Stone's body was found,' Greene said. He gestured for her to speak.

'The house belongs to an Eileen Rowland,' Emma said. 'She's owned it for a long time – since 1966, in fact, according to the Land Registry.'

'Fifty years,' said Greene, and Imogen wanted to congratulate him on his grasp of maths.

'Where's Ms Rowland now?' she asked.

'Nobody knows,' Emma replied. 'There's no death certificate for her. Her state pension is still being paid, straight into her bank account. We are waiting for access to her account now so we can check if any withdrawals have been made. But I spoke to the utility companies – the gas and electricity bills are being paid by direct debit.'

'She's Victim One,' Imogen said, and everyone looked at her. 'I bet you. He killed her and took over the house.'

'Could he be her son? Or grandson?' another member of the team asked.

'She has no children,' Emma said. 'She's never been married. It seems she's lived alone all her life. We're trying to track down other members of her family, but as far as we can tell, she led a hermitic existence. And there are no neighbours for us to talk to. The nearest residence is a mile away.'

'The perfect place for a serial killer to base himself,' Imogen said, almost to herself, ignoring the way DCI Greene looked at her.

'Anyway,' Emma went on. 'We're going through the house now. His DNA must be in there.'

That would only be useful if his DNA was on file.

'And Eileen Rowland's medical records should be with us soon.'

'We should dig up the garden, too,' Imogen said. 'I bet we'll find her.'

Greene nodded. 'Let's talk about that when forensics have finished. They're pulling the place apart. DNA, fingerprints, tyre marks, footprints . . . there must be something in there that'll tell us who he is. They've finished at your place, by the way, Imogen.'

As soon as the briefing was over, Greene pulled her aside.

'You seem tired, Imogen. Strained. Perhaps you should take a few days off, after everything that's happened.'

She remembered Emma's reaction to a similar suggestion earlier.

'I don't need to do that, sir. I have a new line of inquiry I'm following and I can't afford to lose any momentum.'

'Oh?'

She told him about Ben Hofland and his wife, but his attention wandered halfway through.

'Hmm. Well, I'm sure we're going to have our man soon.' He smiled a cool smile. 'In forensics we trust.'

'Did they find anything at my flat?'

'I was about to tell you. They believe they've found traces of death caps on the counter in your kitchen. It looks like they were added there and whoever did it dropped a few tiny fragments.'

'Did they find any sign of a break-in?'

'Apparently not. Have you left your keys unattended anywhere recently?'

She thought about it. 'I'm certain I haven't.'

'Hmm.' He frowned, and she realised how tired he looked. All of this was getting to him, too. 'You know, in all my years as a cop, nothing like this has ever happened. No serial killers. None of my men or women have been murdered. Sometimes I wonder if you brought some of the poison with you from London. Metaphorically speaking, I mean.'

She stared at him, open-mouthed.

He waved a hand. 'Go home, chill out, stroke the cat, whatever it is you do to relax. I'll see you back here tomorrow, hopefully refreshed and ready to show us some of the brilliance we were expecting when you came here.'

He turned away, leaving her biting her tongue, fighting the urge to yell something at his retreating form.

Someone had tried to kill her. They had failed, but a young man lay in the morgue instead, and maybe Greene was right. First Kevin Moss, now Alan Hatton. People around her got hurt. Or died.

A wave of self-loathing threatened to wash her away – but even as it hit her, she was able to push back, take the hatred and turn it outwards. It was the Viper who had done this; she was suddenly certain of it. He had killed again. And she knew what she needed to do: take the rage that burned inside her and use it.

Use it to catch him.

She was certain the answer lay somewhere among the tangle of threads in her head. The happy places. The souvenirs. The connection between Ben Hofland and the latest victim. What couldn't she see?

She wished her own happy place – a playground in London where she'd spent many joyful afternoons with her dad – wasn't so far away. If she could go there now, maybe she could clear her mind and find the answer. In the meantime, instead of happiness, she had rage.

And that would have to do.

Chapter 34

'Ollie, hurry up. Your mum's going to miss her train.'

Megan was going back to London, to our old flat. She'd decided she couldn't hang around Shropshire any more, even though she wanted to be near Ollie. She wanted to be at home, and had insisted she had work to do. She'd already talked to the police, though she didn't think she'd told them anything useful.

'I don't know what he's doing in there,' I said. 'It's getting harder and harder to prise him away from his various screens.'

'He's a good boy though,' she said. 'I'm going to miss him.'

'I'll bring him down to London soon.'

While we waited for Ollie, she put her arms around me. We held each other and it felt different. There was no sexual stirring. No bitterness either. It was like we were two survivors of a disaster, free of the wreckage, parting with a smile. We'd been through a lot together, but now it was time to move on. Megan had her own grief for Michael to deal with. I also knew she was going to miss Ollie badly. We were going to have to find a way to share custody. Maybe he could stay with her during school holidays. We would figure it out.

After dropping Megan off at the station in Telford, I took Ollie shopping. I surprised him by taking him to Game and buying a new

DS. Then, in the park, Ollie saw a couple of kids from school and joined them in a game of football while I watched from a bench.

I couldn't stop thinking about my conversation with Imogen by the river, the stunned look on her face. I needed to talk to her, had left messages for her to call me, but she was busy. I kept going over it in my mind, trying to work it out. Imogen seemed to think it was a coincidence, that I had rescued the man who'd killed my wife's lover. Except that was before I'd told her about Megan and Michael. I felt confused and sick. How had I got mixed up in this? What was going on? The most likely explanation, I was sure, was that for some reason Michael had told the Viper about me while he'd held him prisoner. Or maybe the Viper had been following Michael, knew he was seeing Megan, and had tracked me down. But why?

Ollie finished his game of football and I was able to put it from my mind, temporarily, at least. Ollie seemed worried about something.

'Dad . . .' he began when we were almost home.

'Yes?'

'Nothing.'

I assumed it was something to do with Megan. Obviously it was hard for him, saying goodbye to her, knowing that this was it now. His new life. I wanted him to talk, but knew from experience that if I probed, he would clam up.

'There's something . . .' He fell quiet again.

'What is it, Ollie?' He had the new DS box in his hand. 'Is it to do with the other DS? Do you know who sent it to you?'

He shook his head and said again, 'It's nothing.'

I didn't push it.

Back at home, I got a beer out of the fridge and took my laptop into the living room to check my emails. The first one I noticed was from Robert Friend, marked 'Urgent'.

> Hi Ben. Sorry for the short notice but my
> other main copywriter is sick and I have an

urgent piece of work that needs doing (brief
attached). I need it by end of play tomorrow.
Would that be possible? I'll pay you extra.
Cheers, Robert.

I skimmed through the brief. It would be tough, but was definitely doable. I replied and said I'd be happy to do it, and he responded immediately. You're a life saver!

The next email in my inbox was headed Congratulations, you're a winner!

I was about to consign it to the junk folder until I realised that the sender's name, Global Insight, was familiar. I opened the email.

'Oh my God.'

Back in February or March, I had been called by this market research company, Global Insight, asking me to complete a questionnaire. I would have told them to sod off, but they were offering £20 for my time and trouble, along with entry into a prize draw to win a further £1,000. I had been hard up, so I'd done it. Twenty quid was twenty quid. The survey had been all about personal fulfilment and ethics, and there had been some quite high-brow questions about the nature of happiness. I remembered getting stuck on a question asking me where and when I'd been happiest. I had considered it for ages, discarding answers about when I'd met Megan, because those memories were sour, before finally choosing a memory from my teenage years.

It had taken me several hours to complete, and the £20 had been deposited in my bank account the next day.

Now, the email read:

Dear Mr Hofland, I'm delighted to tell you
that you are the winner of our prize draw and
£1,000 has already been deposited into your
bank account. Congratulations!

I didn't believe it. Surely it was a con of some kind? But I logged into my bank account – and there it was. A thousand pounds, deposited this morning.

I stared at the screen. A thousand pounds wasn't a huge amount of money, but it was still very welcome. And I'd never won anything like that before.

It was amazing. From being at my lowest point a month ago, everything had turned around. My son was much happier, I felt settled here, the issues with Megan and the house sale were sorted and I was getting regular work now. Even Lady Luck was smiling on me.

So why did I feel so uneasy?

It wasn't just because of everything with Michael and the man I'd pulled out of the river. It was Mum, too. How could I enjoy any good fortune when she was suffering so much, when she was so close to death?

Ollie appeared in the doorway. He looked excited about something. 'Dad . . .'

'Hi, Ollie.'

'I need you to look at something.'

'Is this the thing you were going to tell me about in the car?'

He shook his head. 'No, this is something else.' He had his iPod in his hand. I gestured for him to sit down next to me. 'What is it?'

'You know the guy who you pulled out of the river? The one the police are looking for?'

'I do.'

'Well, when I woke up this morning I had a thought . . . that I'd seen him before. I mean, before that day by the river. You know like when you wake up in the middle of a dream because your brain is trying to tell you something?'

I nodded. I knew the sensation well.

'That happened to me this morning,' he said. 'You remember that weird museum we went to? The Museum of Lost Things? I was dreaming about that, and there was someone watching me.' He shivered at the memory of the dream.

'Go on.'

He opened the photo album on his iPod. It had a camera, just like an iPhone. 'When you were looking round the museum I took some photos of some of the exhibits. I was going to send them to Jack to show him the lame stuff they have here in Shropshire. Anyway, look at this.'

He showed me a photo he'd taken of a glass cabinet containing a pink dildo. I remembered hoping Ollie wouldn't see it or know what it was. Naïve of me. Now, he seemed too excited to be embarrassed by the dildo in the picture.

It was a pretty terrible photo. It was almost all reflection. Ollie was clearly visible in the glass, holding up his iPod.

There was someone behind him.

'I remember turning around, catching him watching me,' Ollie said. 'He left the room immediately. But it was him, Dad. The guy you saved.'

I took the iPod from him, scrutinising the picture. The reflection was dark, so it was impossible to make out the man's face. But as I studied it, I remembered seeing a guy in his late twenties enter one of the rooms and exit immediately.

'Are you sure, Ollie? Sure it was him?'

'I'm not, like, one hundred per cent sure. But I knew I'd seen him before. This must be him, Dad. It must be.'

Chapter 35

Imogen was at her desk at eight, poring over the report Tracey had sent her. For months they had been trying to establish a link between the first two victims, combing through records of their movements, cross-checking lists of acquaintances, scanning phone and Internet usage records. Then Fiona was added to the mix. Still nothing.

Imogen had asked Tracey to create a timeline, a kind of potted biography, for Danni, Nathan and Fiona. She didn't bother with Michael Stone or with Annette Lawrence, who was still in hospital but recovering well.

During the night, Imogen had tried to figure out how Ben Hofland fitted into this. He had no criminal record, and they had confirmed with witnesses that the river rescue had happened exactly as Ben had said. There was no reason to think he was guilty of anything . . . but he was involved in some way. The question was how? And right now, she didn't know the answer.

The next question was: why did the Viper kill Michael Stone? Was it because he feared Michael and Annette were going to expose him? Had the TV reporters got closer to uncovering the truth than the police?

She needed to talk to Annette, find out exactly what she and Michael had uncovered.

The other possibility – an outlandish one – was that the Viper had murdered Michael because he was having an affair with Ben's wife. But why?

Her phone rang.

It was Gareth Davies, the crime scene manager. 'We need you to come to the house in Hopton Wood,' he said, slightly breathless. 'We've found something.'

ɯ

Imogen parked in front of the gate in Hopton Wood, swatting at gnats as she got out of her car. She walked up the path toward the cottage. Yellow tape was strung between the trees.

Gareth was waiting in the shade outside the little house, a cigarette in his hand.

'What have you found?' Imogen asked.

'It's best if I show you.'

He led her into and through the house. It looked like one of those neglected places you see on estate agents' sites, the kind of house that's been occupied by the same couple for forty years and hadn't been redecorated in all that time. Horrible flowery wallpaper, nasty green carpets, framed Athena posters on the wall: a clown squirting water from a flower, a topless man cradling a baby, a naked couple beneath the outstretched wings of a swan.

'My God. Some of these must be collectors' pieces,' Imogen said.

'For collectors of eighties tat? Look at this.' Gareth pointed at a familiar painting of a young boy with tears trickling down his cheeks.

'I remember this,' she said. 'There used to be all this stuff in the paper about this picture. They said it was cursed, that it would make your house burn down.'

'Shame this place hasn't burned down. It gives me the creeps.' He wrinkled his nose. 'It stinks, too. Dust and boiled cabbage. You should see the state of the kitchen.'

They went upstairs. There were two bedrooms and a small bathroom. Imogen poked her head inside and recoiled from the filthy toilet, caked with limescale, and the porcelain bath ringed with ancient dirt. Dozens of insect corpses filled the plastic light fitting. She looked away.

'This is the master bedroom,' Gareth said, pausing outside the room. 'One of my team noticed something weird. If you look up at the house, there are two windows on this corner. But there was only one inside.'

Imogen waited.

'Turns out there was a false wall with a secret room behind it. If you go up into the loft, there's a hatch that opens into this secret room. But we don't need to go through the hatch because we've knocked the wall down.'

Imogen entered the room. Behind the bed was a plasterboard wall that had been half torn down. There were more old-fashioned, tacky paintings on the other walls, along with a framed cross-stitch that hung above the bed. A quote or aphorism had been embroidered on a sheet of fabric: 'The Art of Living Well and the Art of Dying Well Are One'.

It sent a shiver down Imogen's spine.

'So what did you find?' she asked.

She fully expected him to say they'd found Eileen Rowland's body. Or Adrian's, as she was now convinced the Viper must have disposed of him. Adrian was probably already dead when Imogen had visited his flat.

She was braced for some horror, but Gareth surprised her.

'A drugs lab.'

She raised her eyebrows.

'I know you've been trying to work out where the murderer got liquid morphine from. Here's the answer. He's been extracting it from tablets. Morphine sulphate pills, to be precise. Strong painkillers. We found prescriptions for them, made out to Eileen Rowland.'

She held up a hand. 'Hang on. Tell me more about the morphine. How did he extract it?'

'It's pretty easy. It's something addicts do. You crush the tablets into a powder, put that into a tube, add water and shake it till you create a suspension.' Imogen, no scientist, was lost already, but let him carry on. 'Then you filter it . . . You end up with about seventy per cent of the morphine that was in the tablet, in liquid form, ready for injection.'

'So you don't need to be a chemist to be able to do this?'

Gareth laughed. 'No, it's a piece of cake. All the equipment is dead easy to get hold of and instructions are readily available online.'

'And can you tell how recently the equipment was used?'

'Last week, I'd say. We've taken fingerprints. I mean, this whole house is full of hair, dead skin, bodily fluids. It's a dream of a crime scene. We've already sent a load of samples to the lab for analysis. It's priority one, so should be with you very soon. Also, Ian's been trying to get hold of Eileen's doctor.'

Imogen went back downstairs and found Ian.

'Did you get hold of the doctor?' she asked.

'I didn't need to. We managed to get an emergency court order to access her medical records. Her doctor's been prescribing her painkillers for years, off and on. Strong stuff: tramadol, fentanyl, morphine sulphate.'

'For what ailments?'

'You name it. Stomach pains, arthritis. She had a hip operation a few years ago that went wrong and she was given morphine while she was recovering from that. Then, a year ago, she called the doctor out saying she'd injured her hip falling down the stairs and was in agony. He prescribed morphine sulphate.'

Imogen shook her head. She felt bad if she took paracetamol or ibuprofen more than two days in a row. When she was younger, she'd suffered from awful period cramps and had taken codeine, but it'd made her so spaced out she'd vowed never to touch it again. There were, though, thousands of people addicted to painkillers. She'd watched a documentary about it. Dodgy doctors dishing out opioids like sweets.

'What do we know about Eileen Rowland, apart from her love of painkillers?'

Ian consulted his notepad. 'She was born in 1948, which makes her sixty-eight now. She bought this place in 1966. Her parents both died the year before that, in a car accident, and apparently left her enough money to purchase this house and to never have to work. She's never claimed any benefits, never married, had no children and, apart from going to the doctor, she appears to have led a completely secluded existence.'

'Did she pick up the prescriptions herself?'

'Yes. From a number of different pharmacies; I guess so no individual pharmacist noticed how many painkillers her doctor was dishing out. The one she used most was at a big supermarket in Ludlow.'

'Have we got a photograph?'

'No. There isn't a single photo in the whole house. She didn't have a passport or driving licence. This woman appears to live completely off the map. It's incredible, isn't it? That in this day and age, someone can do that.'

A cloud passed over the sun, casting the house in shadow. Goosebumps prickled the skin on Imogen's arms.

'Somebody must know her. She must have bought groceries. Used the library? We need to talk to the doctor, get a full description of her.'

'That's already in hand.'

She nodded. 'Does it look like she really was living here alone?'

'Yes. We've searched the entire place. There's no sign of anyone else living here. The only incongruity was a box full of comics in the attic. Boys' comics: *2000 AD*, war and science fiction stuff. But maybe that's something she picked up somewhere. Perhaps she found it in a junk shop and bought it thinking she could sell it on. Who knows? Hopefully, we'll know more when the DNA results come back.'

Imogen's phone rang. It was Ben Hofland.

And what he told her had her running to her car.

Chapter 36

Eileen's in her favourite armchair, that tatty piece of shit she insisted we bring from the Homestead, telly turned up so loud it gives me an instant headache. I scoop up the remote and turn the volume down.

'Hello, darling,' she says, but she doesn't tear her eyes from the TV. She's like a toddler who's just discovered the gogglebox and got herself a new addiction.

She takes my hand and presses it against her cheek, turns it and kisses my palm. Her skin is thin, lips dry, but her eyes are as beautiful and intelligent as they always were. Her wisdom still shines.

'I brought all your favourites,' I say, opening the grocery bags so she can have a peek.

Jaffa cakes and Bakewell tarts and steak and kidney pies. A bag of Granny Smiths and a bottle of Gordon's gin. Her eyes roam over the bags. 'Never mind all that stuff. Did you bring my pills?'

'Eileen . . .'

She lets out a wail of disappointment and distress, clutching her hip and squeezing her eyes shut.

'I've got paracetamol. Ibuprofen. Or I could get some Solpadeine from the chemist's.'

She thumps the arm of the chair. 'None of that stuff works.' She tries to get up, but cries out in pain. Her eyes water like I'd slapped her, though

I'd only thought about it. I want to shout at her, tell her to stop being so weak, so pathetic.

Weak. Pathetic. *The words trigger a memory. I see Dad standing over Mum, fist raised, blood on her lip, terror and resignation in her eyes. Hearing me crying, cowering in the corner of the tiny room, he spins round. 'Shut up! You're pathetic. A weak, spineless little shit.* Shut up!'

In my fantasy, I pick up the knife he uses to skin rabbits and drive it into his face.

But he was right. I was weak. Back then. I was pathetic.

'Let me take these to the kitchen,' I say to Eileen as she moans.

In the kitchen, I put the shopping bags on the floor and lean against the counter, head in hands. Eyes screwed shut, the world black and red. Dark drying blood. The hole in Michael Stone's face. I calm myself with a song, humming, tapping my fingers on the worktop.

That bitch reporter. Why didn't she die? It was meant to be a lethal dose. Stupid stupid stupid boy. Should have waited, stayed till she stopped breathing. Not run away when a light came on in the farmhouse. I bang my fist against the counter, furious with myself.

I take a fork from the cutlery drawer and press press press it into the softer flesh on the underside of my arm, dig it in. Learn from the pain, let it help you focus. In my head, I see them right now: the police are crawling all over the Homestead like ants on a bun. They must have found my secret place. And that means they've found the medicine. Even if they haven't yet, there's no way I can go back there. Not now. Not ever.

It's an inconvenience.

Finding my phone, I start tapping out a text to Ollie. It feels risky now, more so than before. Since the river, since his mum's boyfriend was found. But I need to know what's going on in that house. And Ollie still thinks I'm his friend and guardian angel.

Hey Ollie. Just checking in. How's it going?

No immediate response. I pocket the phone. My heart's still banging away, not helped by the moaning noises coming from the other room. Snivel snivel. Shut up, woman. Shut the fuck up.

Dad punching mum in the face. Shut up, woman.

Deep breaths. Deep. Fucking. Breaths.

I put the shopping away and hesitate when it comes to the gin. Maybe it'll help. I grab a glass and pour a triple measure, hurrying back into the living room.

'*Here, drink this.*'

She's on her feet, holding herself up with her stick, trembling, white with the effort of it. How old is she? Sixty-eight? Christ, she looks older than that. Ancient. Worn out.

Like it's time to go to a happier place.

I shake the thought away, take hold of her and help her sit. She winces, sweat beading her brow.

'*It hurts,' she says, her voice a harsh whisper. 'I need my pills.*'

'*But there aren't any left.*'

'*Then I'll have to go back to the doctor,' she says. 'Get some more.*'

How can I tell her she can't go to the doctor? That she'll never be able to go and see him, or any doctor, ever again.

'*You can't,' is all I can say.*

'*I need it!' Screeching; fingernails scraping my brain.*

I put my hand around her throat. How easy it would be to put her out of her misery.

I squeeze.

ʊ

Michael Stone was, if I'm counting correctly, the fifteenth human being I have killed.

Three of them were my lucky ones.

The other twelve were simply unlucky. Unlucky because they brought to mind my dad. Were my dad, for their last few seconds of life.

The first was when I was eighteen. I stumbled on him camping out in the woods near the Homestead. He was homeless, filthy, stinking of the same foul liquor my dad used to breathe all over us. He asked me for money, offered to blow me for a tenner. I stared into his eyes and could see it there: the harm he'd done others, the stains on his soul. That was the first time the fury came upon me, and as I brought the rock down on his skull, once, twice, twenty times, I saw his face, his pleading face. And it soothed my soul.

Once he was dead, though, he ceased being my dad, like flicking a switch. As I buried him there in the woods, using a shovel I'd fetched from home, I felt simultaneously purged and sullied. I heard her voice, Mum's voice. You're wicked just like him. You'll dance in hell together, you two, father and son. *Such* a disappointment.

One night, a month or two after that, I returned under cover of night to the place where I last saw my parents. Of course, the workers were long gone. There was a housing estate on the site now. Had they gone looking for me? How long had they hung around after I'd vanished? I imagined Dad being pleased I was gone, even though it meant there would be no skivvy other than Mum to pick up dog shit and scrub the caravan. No one else to take his temper out on. Did they go on to have other children? Unlikely. That was one of the things he screamed at her about: her inability to bear him more sons. Like he so cherished the one he had.

I returned to the Homestead with an itch deep inside me, one I could not reach. It tormented me. It was always there, like tinnitus – barely noticeable most days, other times unbearable.

There was only one way to scratch that itch.

They were always homeless, vagrants, criminals. The kind of men no one would miss. And as I beat them or throttled or stabbed them, I saw his face on theirs, a shifting mask that begged for mercy and received none.

A few years later, when I got Internet access, I discovered what had happened to Mum and Dad. She died when I was seventeen. Accidental death, it said. I couldn't find any other details. But I knew. That bastard had killed her.

Two years after her, he was dead, too. He drank himself to death.

I had missed my chance to kill him myself, and in the twelve months after that, I spent long periods in the red grip of the Fury. I barely remember them, was hardly conscious of my acts, but I remember my dreams. Dreams in which Mum was drowning in a lake of blood, reaching out, a dark shape in red water. Dad held her head under and I tried to push him away, desperate to save her.

Never able to.

ᚦ

I loosen my grip on Eileen's throat after only a second or two. Her eyebrows knitted together while I squeezed, but when I release her, I see her choose to take it as a caress. I couldn't do it, not like this. But I can't allow her to die in pain. Not after everything she's done for me. I stroke her hair, kiss her damp brow.

'I'll get you something,' I say. 'Leave it with me, okay?'

'Okay.' She closes her eyes. 'But hurry.'

Chapter 37

The museum smelled of dust. Or maybe the odour was coming off the woman behind the desk, who appeared to Imogen to be semi-comatose, eyes closed, a crumb stuck to her lower lip from a cookie she'd half eaten before she'd dozed off. She jerked to life as Imogen approached like someone had plugged her in. Before her lay a visitors' book, open to show the names and email addresses of people who had come here recently, along with their comments.

Imogen had rushed to the museum immediately after receiving the call from Ben telling her what Ollie had remembered. Ben had sent her a copy of the photo, which had been forwarded to the lab so they could enhance the shadowy image, though it was of such low quality that Imogen wasn't sure if this would achieve much. On the way, she had asked Emma to meet her here. Emma seemed to be bearing up well, as determined as Imogen to avenge Alan's death by catching the man responsible.

'Welcome to the Museum of Lost Things,' the woman behind the desk said.

Imogen and Emma showed her their IDs. 'Can I have your name?'

'Janet Burgess. How can I help?'

Imogen produced the photofit of Annette's abductor and laid it on the reception desk beside a stack of leaflets. 'Do you know this man?'

'Yes, he works here. That's Craig.'

'Well, blow me.'

Janet Burgess gave Imogen a puzzled look, then said, 'He's not in today. He called in sick.'

'What does he do here?'

'He works in the back office. There are only a few of us here – Craig does most of the cataloguing, fixes things that need fixing, is in charge of security. All the behind-the-scenes stuff. And there's a guy called Adrian who pops in occasionally to check everything is running smoothly.'

'Adrian Morrow?'

'That's him.'

Imogen was tempted to punch the air. Here was proof that the man who had abducted Annette knew Adrian. His name was Craig, and he had to be the person who had set Adrian up.

'What's Craig's surname?' she asked.

'Rowland.'

Imogen's blood was pumping now. 'As in Eileen Rowland,' she said to herself.

Janet heard her. 'Yes, that's his mum. Well, that's what he calls her. He told me once that she adopted him, because his real parents didn't want him. Poor little lost soul, he is.'

'Does he have an office?' Imogen asked.

'Yes. Let me show you.'

Imogen turned to Emma. 'Can you take a look around while I check out the office?'

Imogen followed Janet up a staircase, cabinets containing lost property on each level. The cabinet on the first floor contained a bald mannequin's head that stared sightlessly out from behind glass. Beside it was a stuffed rodent that reminded her of the weasel on Trevor Redbridge's mantel, with its beady eyes and its mouth frozen in an eternal snarl.

'Here it is,' Janet said, showing Imogen into a tiny, windowless room. It was stuffed full of cardboard boxes and padded envelopes, piles of paperwork, tools, stacks of old magazines and assorted toys.

Imogen picked up a toy cowboy from the desk. It was Woody, the character from *Toy Story*, arms and legs flopping.

'We get a lot of items like that sent to us,' Janet said. 'All those careless children . . . Craig loves toys, so some of them end up staying in here rather than going out on display. He particularly loves cowboys or anything to do with the Wild West. He's a big kid, really.'

Imogen put the cowboy back on the desk. If only Janet knew what this 'big kid' had done.

At that moment, Emma burst into the little room. 'Imogen. You need to come and look at this.'

She followed Emma up another staircase and into one of the exhibit rooms, Janet following behind.

'It's over here,' Emma said, gesturing to a tall cabinet in the corner. Imogen wondered how many visitors this place got. It was musty and depressing. All these lonely objects. Imogen had lost her favourite doll when she was eight, leaving it in a park. It hadn't been there when she went back; she'd cried for days. Passing a display of once-loved teddy bears, she remembered what it had felt like back then, how the replacement doll her dad had bought her never filled the hole in her heart.

'Look,' Emma said, pointing to the bottom shelf of the cabinet.

It was labelled 'Lucky Charms'. There were just three items on the shelf.

A cycling helmet. A small blue teddy bear. And a pendant in the shape of a bicycle.

'Craig found those items himself,' Janet said from behind them. 'He was proud of himself. I'm not sure why he labelled them that way though.'

ω

Imogen sent Emma back to the station to brief the rest of the team on what they'd found and run checks on Craig Rowland, and got a couple of uniforms to come and guard the museum in case Craig showed up.

She also called the forensics team out so they could take away the souvenirs along with Craig's work computer and his personal belongings. Imogen had an appointment to keep.

In the car, blood still thrumming with excitement at this breakthrough, she thought about the ramifications. Now they had a name to go with the face, although Janet Burgess, who had been warned against speaking to anyone about what had happened at the museum today, didn't have any photos of Craig. Nevertheless, they knew how he was connected to Eileen Rowland and the house in Hopton Wood, and they knew that he must be the person who had attempted to frame Adrian. Imogen was willing to bet Adrian was dead; probably buried somewhere in those woods.

It was important that Craig didn't know they were on to him, though she guessed he was being more careful since his likeness had appeared on TV and he'd realised Annette was still alive. That's why he hadn't gone to work. Maybe, now his face was out there and the police were crawling all over his base, he would give up, flee the county, perhaps even the country. But she didn't really believe he would do that. He had tried to kill her – almost certainly to jeopardise the investigation – which meant he must be planning more murders.

Somehow, they had to find out who his next target was, and draw Craig out of his hiding place.

ᘂ

Imogen ran into the hotel where Annette was staying to find her waiting on the reception sofa, a suitcase by her feet. She held her back straight, but there was an air of suffering that hung around her, creating a kind of exclusion zone, and the other hotel guests were giving her a wide berth.

Imogen sat beside her. 'Heading back to London?'

'Yes, I'm waiting for my taxi to the station.'

'Looks like I caught you just in time, then.'

'I heard about that young cop getting poisoned. Is it related to what happened?'

Imogen decided to lie. Annette was still a reporter, after all. 'We have no reason to think so. Do you mind if I ask you a couple more questions?'

'Okay. I guess. But I've told you everything I know.'

This meeting almost felt pointless now that they knew the Viper's identity, but he might have let slip some piece of information that would help them find where he was hiding.

'I need to know what your captor talked to you about,' she said. 'Has anything come back to you?'

Annette stared at the shiny floor. 'Parts of it . . . He was talking about happiness.'

Happiness. With everything that had happened, she'd almost forgotten her theory about the victims' happy places. She leaned forward. 'Go on.'

'It was weird. He asked me if I knew the secret of happiness.'

Imogen waited, impatient.

'He said something about there being two types of people. Good people, who deserve happiness, and bad ones, who need to be punished.' She paused. 'It's all so blurry. I was hungry, dehydrated. I'm sorry, Detective, but that's all I can remember.'

Annette stared into space, frowning like she could see the place where she'd been kept. 'I know there's more. Memories that I can't access. I think another part of my brain has built up a barrier, is stopping them surfacing.'

Imogen stood up. Then sat down again. On impulse, she gave Annette a hug. Annette stiffened at first before relaxing. She hugged Imogen back.

'Take care,' Imogen said as she got up. 'You're going to need to talk about what happened to you, so you should see a counsellor. Promise me?'

'Guide's honour.'

Chapter 38

Janet Burgess's name flashes on my mobile screen. What does that old bat want? I almost let it go to voicemail, but the ringing is as persistent as her shrill voice.

'The police are at the museum,' she says. 'They sent me home. They were asking all sorts of questions. I don't understand—'

I interrupt her, trying to keep my voice calm. 'The police. Did you get their names?'

'Yes. Evans was the main one. Her off the telly with the hair.'

Rage has been bubbling deep inside of me since I'd discovered that not only was Annette Lawrence still alive, but that I'd poisoned the wrong cop. Janet's words turn up the flame, so the rage grows, faster and harder, a rush of bubbles now, on the way to boiling point. Two big mistakes. Sloppy, stupid, careless. It must be tiredness, the stress of looking after Eileen, of trying to ensure everything works out with Ben. The rage is aimed at myself. But as Janet witters on about how the police had found the 'Lucky Charms' exhibit – 'Why were they so excited? I didn't understand, and that red-haired policewoman was practically punching the air' – my fury finds another target.

'Are you at home?' I ask. 'I'm coming over.'

ω

When I put my hands around her throat, doing what I couldn't do to Eileen, her eyes almost pop with shock. She tries to speak, to say my name, but all she can do is poke out her tongue and hiss like a snake.

I squeeze so hard I think her head's going to come off.

Afterwards, panting like a lover in a post-coital glow, I roll her body up in a rug and carry her out to the van. Janet lives down a quiet country lane; there's no one around. The adrenaline deserts my body and I feel a stab of regret. Janet's the first woman I've killed in anger, unless you count the little tart I murdered after sending Danni to a better place. But I remind myself I did it for a reason.

'You knew too much,' I murmur to her surprisingly heavy corpse as I heave it into the van. I giggle, then immediately tell myself to get a grip. There is still so much to do. The police, lovely Imogen, probably think that I'll stop now, run away, scared off by what they've found, the way they've moved into my territory.

'What am I going to do about Eileen's pain?' I ask Janet's corpse. The moment I ask, the answer hits me.

'Thanks, Janet,' I say. And I drive away. I'm tempted to leave her in the back for a while. It's good to have someone to talk to.

Chapter 39

Imogen found Emma waiting for her by her desk, holding a wad of paper.

'Imogen, look—'

'What have we found out about Craig Rowland?'

'Nothing. He hasn't got a national insurance number. No tax records, no driving licence, medical records. Zero Internet presence. Nothing. It's as if he doesn't exist.'

'How can that be possible?'

'I don't know. I called Eileen's doctor to ask if Eileen had ever mentioned Craig or taken him in to see him. He says that as far as he knew Eileen lived alone.'

Imogen tapped the ends of her fingers together, thinking. 'Janet Burgess said Craig called Eileen his adoptive mother. Where did she find him? We need to go through reports of all children who went missing in that area between, let's see, nineteen ninety and ninety-five.' She noticed Emma ruffling the sheaf of paper she was holding.

'What have you got there?

'This is what I wanted to talk to you about, before we got sidetracked. Tracey has found something. Remember when you asked her to go through all the victims' Internet and phone records, looking for a mention of their happy place?'

Imogen nodded eagerly.

'Well, look at this.' She laid a sheet of paper on the desk. 'Tracey searched through the email records looking for the words "happy" and "happiest". There were loads of hits, which is why it's taken so long, but nothing that seemed significant. So Tracey decided to go through all of the files on the victims' computers, all the attachments they'd sent and received. She found this.'

It was a printout of a survey headed Global Insight, with Danni Taylor's name and address at the top. Lots of questions about 'what makes you happy?' along with 'what would you do?'-style questions, clearly designed to test someone's ethics. One of the questions leapt out at her: *What would you do if you saw someone drowning?* Danni had answered that she would call for help.

Emma turned the page. 'Look at this.'

Imogen read the question. 'Where and when did you experience your happiest moment?'

Danni had answered: *Horse riding at PGL when I was eleven. It was just before my parents got divorced . . .*

'Holy fuck,' Imogen said.

Emma's eyes shone. 'And that's not the only one.' She produced two more printouts. 'Nathan Scott completed one of these surveys, stating that he was happiest when he beat his greatest rival in a mountain bike event in the Long Mynd. And Fiona Redbridge's—'

'Says she was happiest at Wenlock Priory when she learned about her heart transplant?'

'You got it. I spoke to Trevor Redbridge. He remembers Fiona completing the survey. He said she was paid twenty pounds for doing it and was entered into a prize draw, which she won. The exact same thing happened to the other two.'

This was it. Imogen had that taste in her mouth, the taste of a case cracking open. 'We need to find this company: Global Insight.'

'I've already done it,' Emma said. 'Guess who the registered owner is?'

'Tell me!'

'Eileen Rowland.'

'Craig, using his adoptive mother's name as cover.'

Imogen picked up a pen and tapped it on the desk.

'Happiness. That's what it all comes down to.' She told Emma what Annette had said. 'He told her there are two types of people – good ones who deserve to be happy, and evil ones who need punishing.'

'And he targets the good ones?'

Imogen stared at Emma, not really seeing or hearing her, looking instead at the answers that had been eluding her.

'Good . . . happy . . . Oh my God. I think I've got it.'

She hurriedly sat back at her desk and pulled up the timelines that Tracey – God bless her – had produced, detailing the victims' lives.

She started with Fiona Redbridge. 'Look at this. In the months leading up to Fiona's death, all this happened to her. She had a heart transplant that saved her life. She came into loads of money after somebody brought that Roman cup into her shop, the one that turned out to be worth £10,000. She had an affair with a much younger man. Anthony says she was at her happiest, that she had a new lease of life.'

She opened Danni Taylor's timeline. 'Danni had experienced good fortune, too. She was pregnant, that was the big one. I know she and her boyfriend were delighted. They'd just found a really nice flat, as well. And they'd got a pet cat, a stray they'd taken in. According to Danni's mum, that made her really happy.'

Finally, she went over Nathan Scott's timeline. 'Nathan won that race, beating his long-term rival, Finlay.' Imogen thought back to her interview with Nathan's girlfriend, Melissa. 'He'd recently moved in with Melissa, the girl he'd been in love with his whole life. She told me that before they were together, she and Nathan were really good friends, but that she'd friend-zoned him because she was going out with someone else.'

Emma nodded. 'Then she found out this boyfriend was cheating on her.'

'Yes. Nathan was there for her, a shoulder to cry on . . . and soon they were an item.' Melissa had sobbed as she'd recounted this tale because they'd had so little time together. And Nathan's friends all talked about how Nathan had been on a huge high since getting together with Melissa. One of his mates had said he was walking on air.

'They were all happy,' Imogen said. 'They'd all had good fortune. That was what all their families said: everything was going well for them. I should have seen it, Emma. Should have made that connection.'

Emma frowned. 'How could you have? It's not something we look for, is it? It's not the kind of thing that comes up when we look for links. *They were all happy.* If you'd gone to the guv with that he would have laughed you out of the building.'

There was a long pause, after which Emma said, 'So he targeted people he knew to be happy. Or . . . *he made them happy.*'

Emma blinked. 'How could he have done that?'

'I don't know. Maybe that's crazy . . .' But she was already trying to work it out. *Could the murderer have somehow manipulated his victims' lives?*

'How did he choose them?' Emma asked. 'And how did he know what needed fixing in their lives?'

'The questionnaires.' She picked up Nathan's questionnaire. One of the questions was *Name three things that would make you happy.* Nathan had answered with just two points: *To be the county champion!* and *To persuade the woman I love that it's me she should be with.*

She showed Emma. 'I bet Rowland sent out loads of these questionnaires, looking for the perfect target, people who would answer honestly, with problems he could do something about.'

'And how did he get their email addresses?'

The answer came instantly. 'I bet they all went to the Museum of Lost Things and signed the visitors' book.'

Emma grinned at her. 'Bloody hell.'

'Let's come back to that. There's another thing that doesn't make sense,' she said. 'Michael Stone and Annette Lawrence. Why did Rowland kill Stone and try to kill Annette? Unless . . .' Butterflies looped the loop inside her belly. 'Unless he was doing it to make someone else happy. His next victim.'

She stared at Emma.

'What is it?'

But Imogen didn't reply. She grabbed her phone, searched for the number she needed and hit the 'Call' button.

He answered almost immediately.

'Hello?'

'Ben? It's DI Evans.'

'Oh, hi. Did you go to the museum? Did you find him?'

'I'll get to that.' She kept her voice as even as possible. 'Something's come up in the investigation. Can you tell me if you've ever heard of a company called Global Insight?'

He didn't hesitate. 'Yes. I did a market research questionnaire for them. I won their prize draw, actually. A thousand pounds. I was—'

'Did you answer a question about when and where you were happiest? And another about things that would make you happy?'

'Yeah . . . What's this about?'

She was already heading to the door, Emma at her heels. 'Are you at home? Okay, good. I want you to stay there. Don't answer the door to anyone. Make sure your windows are shut and locked. No, don't be alarmed. I'll be right round.'

She stopped at the door and turned to Emma. 'You stay here. Tell Greene everything we've found out. I'll call you from Ben Hofland's.'

'You think he's the next target?'

She hurried out, calling out the answer over her shoulder. 'I'm certain of it.'

Chapter 40

After the call from Imogen, I couldn't sit still or concentrate on work any more. I went round the cottage twice, checking the windows. I put the chain on the door. I even poked my head into the loft to double-check there was no one lurking up there. I was already feeling uneasy, knowing the Viper knew who I was, but Imogen's words, the urgency in her voice, had flat out scared me.

I was alone in the house. Ollie was with Mum. It was the day of her outing with Emile, her tour of places with happy memories. Our old family home. The church where she'd got married. The village where she'd lived when she was a girl. Now I felt glad I hadn't been able to go along and had sent Ollie in my place.

I didn't have to wait long before Imogen's fancy little car screeched to a halt outside. She slammed the door and thirty seconds later was standing in my hall, the chain back across the door.

'Are you on your own?' She waved for me to sit at the kitchen table.

'You're really freaking me out,' I said.

She waited for me to sit then joined me, sitting opposite. The air of sadness that had clung to her last time had dissipated. Now, she seemed determined, focused. A little intense, maybe, but that was reassuring. If I really was in danger, I was going to have to put my trust in this woman. And, instinctively, I found I did.

'I'll explain everything, I promise, but before you bombard me, I have to ask you some questions. Firstly, where's your son? It's the summer holidays now, isn't it?'

'He's gone out with my mum and her nurse.'

A puzzled frown.

'My mum has terminal cancer and is in a nursing home. Her nurse, Emile, arranged for her to go on an outing. I couldn't go because I agreed to do some urgent work. I completely forgot about the whole thing.'

'You forgot?'

'I know. I'm a terrible son. But it's fine because Ollie has gone instead. She'll like that.'

'So when is your son due back?'

'Not till teatime.'

The tension in her shoulders dissipated a little. 'Okay. Good.'

'Can I bombard you with questions yet?'

That brought forth the tiniest of smiles, revealing a gap between her front teeth. 'Not yet. I need to ask you something that might seem odd, but humour me.'

'Consider yourself humoured.'

'I want you to detail all the good things that have happened to you recently. Any good fortune you might have had. Anything you can think of, big or small.'

She was right. It *was* an odd question.

'Good things. Blimey. Until recently, my life had been one shit event after another. I found out my wife was shagging my so-called friend. My mum got cancer. I had to move back here and . . . I didn't feel welcome. Everyone's been so paranoid with the serial killer at large and it seemed like half the village were looking at me suspiciously. My son didn't want to be back here either, and he blamed me. On top of that, my neighbours were a total nightmare. I had no money or job and Megan was refusing to sell our flat. I was at the lowest ebb I can remember.'

'And then?'

I rubbed my face. 'A lot has happened over the last month or so. Some of it pretty horrible or weird. I mean, you know parts of it anyway. Like one of my neighbours killing the other. Pulling that guy, the fucking Viper, out of the river. Michael's murder.'

She had her notepad open in front of her. She wrote down what I'd said. 'Let's come back to those. Tell me the uncomplicated good things that have happened to you.'

I went through it all. 'First, I got a regular supply of freelance work. It's well paid, comes with perks like a visit to a spa and is actually pretty easy. Although I might not have that any more if I don't finish the piece I'm meant to be working on today.'

She asked me for the details of who had given me the work, noted it down and gestured for me to continue.

'Things have improved between Megan and me. It hasn't been straightforward . . .' I couldn't figure out how to tell her my estranged wife and I almost ended up in bed together, so I skipped it. 'She's devastated by what happened to Michael. But before that, she'd already agreed to sell the flat. We can have a conversation again now. It's amicable, and I guess that's the best I can hope for.'

Imogen wrote that down, too.

'What else?'

I thought about it. 'Ollie is much more settled now. I was pretty sure he was being bullied at his new school because of something Shelley next door said, plus the way he was acting. But he seems fine now. He's looked at me differently, too, since the whole thing with the river rescue. Like I'm some kind of hero.' I smiled, embarrassed. 'And he appears to accept that Megan and I aren't going to get back together and that it's not all my fault.' I paused. 'There was one weird thing, though. Somebody sent him a Nintendo DS – a games console – and I still haven't found out who.'

'Really?'

I explained about the wish list and she said, 'I'll get someone to look into that. Anything else?'

'Nothing major. The thing with the river rescue has meant people around the village look at me differently. I won a grand after doing that questionnaire, though I'm sure you're going to set me straight about that being a good thing.'

She didn't respond.

'The only thing that's still keeping me awake at nights is the worry about my mum. But she's in good hands. And today will cheer her up.' The sun came out, flooding the kitchen with light, as if this scene was being orchestrated by God. 'Yeah, it's all turned around. There are only two things that would make it all perfect. My mum getting a miracle cure and recovering from cancer. But obviously that's not going to happen.'

'And the other thing?'

'Ha. Yeah . . .' Now I felt too embarrassed to say anything.

She raised an eyebrow. 'Come on, spit it out.'

I cleared my throat. 'Well . . . it would be nice to have a woman in my life.'

'Hmm. Would you really want that?' There was a hint of a smile around her lips. 'All the mess and complication? You've only just broken up with your wife.'

I was trying to decide what to say next when she said, 'Anyway, that's not important.' Her expression had grown serious again. 'Ben, there's no easy way to say this, but I am almost certain you are in danger.'

The way she said it chilled my blood. 'I'd already gathered that.'

'What I'm going to tell you . . . you mustn't share it with anyone else. I'm only telling you because I think it's important that you understand and take it seriously.'

I swallowed. 'Okay.'

She explained how three of the victims had taken part in the same survey about happiness, and had all won the prize draw.

I stared at her. 'Michael as well?'

'No, he and Annette Lawrence are different. I'll come back to that. Though you might work it out yourself.'

I opened my mouth to ask what on earth she meant, but she held up a hand. 'Here's the other thing. All three of the main victims – by which I mean Danni Taylor, Nathan Scott and Fiona Redbridge – died after enjoying a spate of good fortune. They were all killed when they were at their happiest.' She gave me some examples. Despite the sunshine pouring through the window, I grew colder with every word she spoke. 'And their bodies were left in the place they named in their survey. Their "happy place".'

'Holy. Shit.'

'Like I said, it's vital you don't share this information.'

I got up from the table, not knowing what to do with myself, and sat down again.

Imogen reached across and touched my hand. I was so surprised, I pulled mine away.

'Ben, you've gone white. Are you okay?'

'Am I okay? Jesus, Detective. You've just told me I'm in a club I really don't want to be part of. The Shropshire Viper Victims' Club.'

'You won't be. Because we're going to protect you. Now we know all this, we can catch him. We're so close. We know who he is; we just don't know where to find him. But you're going to help.'

'I need a drink.'

She checked her watch. 'It's a little early . . .'

'It's one o'clock. Liquid lunch.' I stood and fetched a beer from the fridge. 'I assume you can't drink because you're on duty.'

'Afraid so.' She watched as I popped the cap off and took a slug from the bottle. It didn't make me feel any better. She was still staring at me intently. There was a dark gleam in her eye and her breathing was heavy. She made me think of a hunter, one that had the scent of its prey.

'So . . . you think all the stuff that's been going on, the things that have made me happy – the killer is behind it? How can that be possible?'

'I don't know yet, Ben. That's why we need to go through everything you've told me in as much detail as possible.'

I took another swig of beer. My mind was racing, skipping back through all the events of the last couple of months. A macabre image flashed in my mind's eye: me, lying dead in the place I'd named in my survey.

'Ratlinghope.'

'What?'

'That's the place I was happiest. It's what I put in my survey, anyway. The real answer is the place where I got married to Megan, in London, but that's tainted now. All the happy memories that involve her are. So I put Ratlinghope.' I fiddled with the label on my beer bottle. 'I was originally going to put the place where I won my first swimming race, or my bronze medal. But thinking about all that doesn't really make me happy these days.'

She waited.

'When I was sixteen, seventeen, I was in a band with a few school friends. I was the singer. We weren't very good. We were terrible, actually. But we managed to wangle a slot at this little festival they have just outside Ratlinghope every year, on the nature reserve. It's called The Devil's Ball.' I smiled at the memory. 'It was amazing. We did a load of cover versions and the crowd were really into it, probably because they were drunk or high. It was just such a great feeling, being on stage on a gorgeous summer night, all these people singing along. And afterwards this really hot red-headed girl took me back to her tent and . . . Well, it was a great night.'

'It sounds it.'

'I really don't want you to find my body there.'

'We won't, Ben. Like I said, we're going to look after you. We'll protect you.'

'You personally?'

She looked at me. 'Yes.'

'What you were saying.' I swallowed. 'Do you think . . . do you think he killed Michael to try to make *me* happy?'

'I think that's a distinct possibility.'

I put my head in my hands, hardly able to take it in.

'I'm certain he threw himself into that river to give you a chance to impress your son and the people who live around here. I also think he might have had something to do with your neighbours.'

'Shelley and Ross? But how could he have?'

'I'm not a hundred per cent sure. But that thing with the dog having its vocal cords cut. Hadn't you been unhappy about the dog barking all the time?'

I was about to ask how she knew that, then remembered that I'd mentioned it to the first officer who'd interviewed me. Imogen must have read the report.

'The whole thing with the next-door neighbours doesn't make sense,' Imogen continued. 'We haven't been able to find this mistress of his. The texts were sent from a burner. We don't think the mistress really exists.'

Meaning the texts were sent by the Viper.

'Have you met this guy who's been giving you work?' she asked.

'Robert Friend? No, he said there was no need. You think . . . ?'

'It seems highly likely.'

I was reeling. Then I remembered the first question I'd meant to ask her. 'The guy in the photofit, from the museum. Is it him?'

She hesitated.

'Come on, Imogen. You have to tell me. If I'm his next target . . .'

She nodded once, and before I could ask anything else – like who the hell was he? – Imogen's mobile rang.

She took the call, listened. The colour drained from her face.

'I need to go.'

'What's happened? Can't you tell me?'

She stared into my eyes. 'You're going to have to come with me, for your own safety.'

Chapter 41

I'm parked on the corner of a narrow lane that leads on to a slightly wider road, green all around me, a flock of sheep bleating in a nearby field. I travel these pathways like a fox. And though my den – the Homestead – has been taken over by my enemies, preventing me from returning there, today I am a hunter.

I wait for my prey.

Silent. Patient.

Today, I am going to kill two birds with one bite.

My mind strays to Eileen, waiting in pain at the flat.

I was nothing when she found me. A wretch. A snivelling ten-year-old runaway, living in the woods, trying to catch rabbits, stealing apples from orchards, living off scraps.

I knew I couldn't go back – not after what I'd seen from the doorway of their tiny bedroom: Dad with his hands around Mum's throat, the fury in his eyes. When he'd cast her aside, he'd stormed out into the main living space of the caravan, knocking me aside like I wasn't there.

'What the fuck are you staring at, boy?' he'd demanded, pulling off his belt as he spoke. I knew what was coming. He took hold of my hair and pulled me up towards his red face, almost lifting me from my feet. 'Feel sorry for that bitch, do you?'

I could see Mum peering at me from the darkness of their room, imploring me to run, to save myself. When he wasn't around, she was kind and sweet and she would sing to herself — old songs that made me laugh. She told me stories and stroked my hair and told me not to hate my father; he couldn't help it, he was a good man deep down and he loved me really. Sometimes I would see her crying as she cooked, tears dripping into the dinner. She always saved some food for the dog, feeding her when Dad wasn't around. She was a good person. The best person.

Dad pushed me to the floor beneath a painting of Christ and his crown of thorns. 'Stay there. I want you to hear her. You need to learn what happens when you disobey me.'

As if I hadn't learned that many times before.

Somehow, from somewhere deep inside, I found the courage to say, 'Leave her alone.'

There was disbelief in his eyes. I had dared to speak up. He ran a hand through his sweaty black hair. From behind him, I could hear my mother — her spirit so broken she could no longer stand up for either of us — sobbing.

Dad held the belt inches from my face. 'When I've finished with her I'll be back for you.'

He smiled the smile of the Devil, then turned his back on me and stalked back into the bedroom.

I couldn't bear it: her screams, the begging, the smack of the leather on her flesh. I ran around like a trapped fly, snotty and half-blind with tears, searching for a weapon. A boiling kettle? A rolling pin? My eyes fixed upon the biggest knife, the one Dad used to carve meat. My hand trembled as I crept back to their bedroom. I was going to ram it between his shoulder blades, slit his throat, stab him in his fucking evil eye.

Save her.

But I froze in the doorway. She wasn't screaming now. She was panting and he was grunting. Like an animal. Our dog was running about in the dark outside the caravan, barking madly and growling. I stood there and trembled, willing myself to be a man.

Be her man. Her saviour. I prayed to the picture on the wall. I need courage to fight against the Devil, against terrors and troubles and, above all, fear. I need Your help.

I couldn't do it. I couldn't go in there.

I was a coward. A worm, a maggot. Dad was right. I was a pathetic waste of space.

I dropped the knife, Dad's grunts and Mum's sobs echoing in my ears as I fled that place. I ignored the dog, ran into the woods, into the darkness, and I never saw them again.

I was lost, alone, until Eileen found me.

And saved me.

ω

The car I've been waiting for comes past, doing thirty, and I start the engine and turn the corner, following them down the narrow lane. The nurse is driving. From the glimpse I got of him as they cruised past, he's tall and broad. Handsome. Mrs H is in the back and Ollie is next to her.

I follow, staying back just enough to keep them in sight. Another car comes along in the opposite direction and I pull over to let them past, looking down to conceal my face.

I catch up with my quarry easily. I am calm, heartbeat slow and steady.

The boy who used to be a chicken, now a fox.

We reach St Andrew's Church and the car pulls over. This is the place where Mrs H got married. A lovely venue. A good place to be happy. This is an old Roman site, Viroconium. A seat of ancient wisdom, a place of wine-red blood and blood-red wine. The river is close by, but little else: a hotel a short distance away, a smattering of country houses.

I pull up a little way back and watch them. The nurse – Emile, that's the name Ollie used in the messages we exchanged last night – gets out and opens the hatchback. He takes out a foldable wheelchair and helps Mrs Hofland into it. Ollie stands beside the car now, scratching his head.

You know you can never tell people about our friendship, *I repeated yesterday afternoon.* There are a lot of perverts out there. Your dad will think I'm one. He already took away the DS I sent you. If he finds out you've got a phone and we've been chatting, he'll take it away. Probably your iPod and your computer too.

He's a good boy. Even now, accompanying his dear old grandmother on this trip. Because somebody, a Friend, made sure his dad was too busy to come.

There are a couple of other tourists at the church nosing around. But they're coming out as my quarry goes in. They drive away as Emile pushes Mrs H up the path towards the place where she was happiest. I guess she lost her cherry that night; that's how it worked in the old days. Stupid people denying themselves pleasure. Dumb morality. The fear of God. The world might be fucked up now, but at least most people no longer believe in all that nonsense.

I pull the balaclava over my head, pick up the shotgun and step into the sunshine. They're at the entrance to the church, gazing up at its stone facade. I run through the churchyard, past scattered gravestones.

Ollie sees me first. He cries out and Emile turns. The old woman remains facing the church; she tries to crane her neck, to see what's going on.

I raise the gun and Emile lifts his hands. He really is handsome. Ollie is staring at me, seemingly in shock, probably thinking he's fallen into one of his stupid video games.

I point the gun at the nurse. 'Where is it?'

'Where is . . . what?' His accent is thick, French.

I jab the gun towards him. 'The morphine. The fucking morphine.'

'I haven't—'

I don't let him finish. 'Don't lie. I know you must've brought it with you. Where is it? Come on.' I swivel the barrel of the gun towards the old woman. 'Answer now or I'll blow her fucking head off.'

He swallows. 'It's in the car.'

I point the gun at him. 'Let's go.'

I tell Ollie, 'Don't move or I'll kill him.' He's already crying.

I march the French nurse towards his car. 'Where is it?'

He swallows. 'On the back seat.'

'Get it. Come on.'

He bends to put his head and shoulders into the car and I see the bag that the morphine must be in. I glance around to check no one is coming.

Emile comes out of the car holding the bag, which I tell him to throw to me. It lands at my feet.

'The key, too.'

He tosses it to me and I snatch it up. He's a good man, a nurse, and there's no need for me to kill him.

'Kneel,' I say.

'Please . . .' He starts babbling in French and I shout at him, order him to kneel and look at the ground. He finally obeys and I turn the shotgun around and smack the stock into the back of his head. He goes down face first, out for the count.

I need to get out of here before someone comes, but there's one more thing to do.

Something I need to do for Ben.

I stride back into the churchyard. Ollie shrinks away from me as I drop the bag between my feet and swivel the wheelchair around. Mrs Hofland looks up at me. She's frail, clearly sick, the life ebbing from her body day by day. But her eyes are defiant. The old bird's still got spirit.

Unfortunately, spirit never protected anyone from a shotgun.

'I'm not scared of you,' she says. 'What are you, a junkie?'

I smile beneath the balaclava. 'Not me.' Then I point the gun towards her. 'You're a burden. Hanging on to life, making your son worry. He won't be truly happy till he's free of you.' I glance up at the church. A vision of that picture of Jesus that used to hang in the caravan flashes in my mind. I hear Mum muttering Hail Marys. 'Need to say a quick prayer first?'

'Yes. I pray that you burn in hell, you bastard.'

I put my finger on the trigger.

And Ollie throws himself in front of the gun, between me and his grandmother.

'Get out of the way, Ollie,' I say.

His eyes widen when I say his name. 'Who are you?' His voice is squeaky.

I can't shoot Ollie – that would undo everything. All my careful planning, gone to hell.

'Move, you little shit.'

'No.'

The red mist comes over me. I raise the gun, ready to strike him with the stock, knock him out so I can get this done, when Mrs H yells 'Help!' She's yelled it at someone, behind me.

I look. There's a middle-aged man by the lychgate, peering at me through his sunglasses. Where the fuck did he come from?

Ollie is clinging to the wheelchair, making it impossible for me to get a clear shot at his grandmother.

Fuck this. I snatch up the bag and sprint towards the gate. The bloke in sunglasses doesn't move as I approach – clearly scared of the gun – but he's got his mobile out and is no doubt calling the police.

I step towards him and shoot him in the chest. He falls backwards, an O of surprise frozen on his face. I run out of the churchyard and back to my car, chucking the bag on to the passenger seat as I get in. I fire the engine and screech away, cursing because Mrs H is still alive. But at least I got the medicine. As I drive, I unzip the bag and search inside it, steering with one hand. I find a syringe and a little bottle of clear liquid.

Just one tiny bottle. Twenty milligrams.

I thump the wheel and scream a curse. I'm tempted to turn around, go back, shoot that nurse in the head, kill Ollie and overturn the wheelchair, make the old bitch beg on the church path before putting a shot in her brain.

But I keep driving.

Chapter 42

'Wait here,' Imogen told Ben when they reached the station reception area. She asked the duty manager to keep an eye on him – 'Don't let him go anywhere' – and hurried off to find the rest of the team.

'What's going on?' she asked as soon as she entered the incident room. Greene was there, along with Emma and most of the others.

'I was going to ask you the same thing,' said Greene. 'Emma's been filling me in about your theory.'

'It's not a theory.' She forced herself to add, 'Sir.'

'No?'

'I've spent the morning with Ben Hofland. Everything fits. You can't deny it: all of the victims, apart from Michael and Annette who were targeted for a different reason, got one of these questionnaires, which originated from a company supposedly owned by Eileen Rowland.'

'I'm not denying that. It was excellent work on Tracey's part.' The data analyst, who was present, turned a shade of pink. 'But this idea about the killer trying to make everyone happy? It's . . .' He groped for the right words, failed to find them and went with, 'Airy-fairy nonsense.'

Imogen glared at him.

'It doesn't matter why he did it anyway, does it?' Greene went on. 'We know who he is. Everyone is looking for him. He's not going to try anything else.'

She was incredulous. 'How can you say that? After what just happened at the church?'

Greene chewed air, then pointed a finger at her. '*You* need to calm down,' he said to her. 'You're practically bouncing off the walls.'

He wasn't wrong. She felt like someone had plugged her into an electric socket. She had completed the journey from Ironbridge to Shrewsbury in a crazy twenty minutes, treating the speed limit with contempt, overtaking on bends, running red lights. She'd found she simply hadn't cared, which was ironic considering that her number-one priority at that moment was keeping Ben alive. He'd sat beside her, clinging to the seat with white knuckles.

She forced herself to take a breath. Two more members of the team had come in while she was arguing with Greene, both of whom were staring at her, goggle-eyed.

Greene nodded to Emma. 'DS Stockwell, can you bring the latecomers up to speed?'

'Yes, sir. We've got one fatality. A man called Oscar Wheatley, who stopped outside the church and was calling 999 when the perpetrator shot him in the chest with a shotgun. He died on the way to hospital.'

Craig's fifth victim. Six if you included the foetus inside Danni.

'What about Mrs Hofland?' Imogen asked. 'How is she now?'

'She's fine, but they're keeping her in hospital, with an officer on the door. It seems that, along with the morphine Emile was carrying, Mrs Hofland was the target. But the grandson saved her. He stood between her and the gunman, refused to move out of the way. A very brave boy.'

'It all fits,' Imogen said quietly, ignoring the daggers Greene sent in her direction. 'He thinks Ben will be better off if he doesn't have to worry about his mum. Where is Ollie now?'

'He's in an interview room with a female uniform looking after him,' Emma replied. 'We didn't have anywhere else to put him.'

'I need to talk to him—'

'In a minute.' Greene was a snappy bastard today. 'Let's go through the rest of it first. Emma.'

'Sir. The suspect was driving a dark-blue car. Ollie is pretty sure it was a Volkswagen. But they only saw it as he was driving off, and they were too far away to see the reg plate. We will, of course, be checking any CCTV in the area.'

'So he has this blue car as well as the white van,' Imogen said. Emma nodded.

'Any change in his appearance? New haircut or colour? Beard?'

'We don't know. He was wearing a balaclava.'

Ian piped up, 'That's weird, considering we already know what he looks like.'

'Not really. We only have a photofit. And he doesn't know we've been to the museum and found the souvenirs.' Imogen addressed DCI Greene. 'You can't deny he's targeting Ben Hofland. Even if you don't believe my *theory*.'

Greene stroked his beard and sighed. 'The questionnaire and today's incident do seem to back that up, yes.'

Imogen forced herself to pause, chewing over her next words. 'Sir, I'm convinced my theory is correct. I don't know why he's doing it, what twisted logic he's following, but he wants his victims to be happy when he kills them.' She cast her eyes around the room and was gratified to see she had everyone's rapt attention. 'He's patient. He spends a lot of time setting things up. I'm sure he killed Michael Stone because he was having an affair with Ben's wife. He risked his own life to make Ben look like a hero in front of his son. I'm sure that if we look at all the other things that have gone right for Ben recently, our man will have had a hand in them.'

'Ben, is it?' said Greene. 'Not Mr Hofland?'

Imogen wanted to punch DCI Greene in his smug, pink face, but she ignored him and carried on. 'The attempt on Mrs Hofland was the next stage. He must think that having a mother with cancer is a problem Ben wants solved. Probably the final problem. I think he's approaching his endgame, as he's cleaned up nearly every area of Ben's life he could hope to influence – he's punished the man who cuckolded him, he's sending work Ben's way, I'm sure he's responsible for what happened to the neighbours, too. Tough luck not being able to get his suffering mum out of the way. But by now he's surely feeling the pressure, and he's going to want to strike soon in any event, while Ben – *Mr Hofland* – is still happy.'

'Except Hofland isn't going to be that happy any more, surely?' Emma said. 'Not now someone's tried to off his mother. So maybe the killer will feel the need to do something else to raise his happiness levels.'

Imogen glanced quickly at Greene, who looked like he'd just caught a whiff of a noxious fart.

'Perhaps he'll think Ben will be relieved his mum and son escaped unscathed,' Emma added.

'Like I said,' Imogen continued, 'my feeling is that he's going to want to strike soon. But we have an advantage.'

'Which is?' Greene asked.

'He doesn't know we've figured out that Ben is his next target.'

'Right. So what are you saying?'

'That we need to protect Ben – but we have to be subtle about it. We can't have panda cars parked outside his house, uniformed officers on his front lawn. We want the killer to come forward, so we can catch him.'

Greene raised a greying eyebrow. A little smile crept on to his face and he licked his lips. 'Use Hofland as bait, you mean?'

'Not bait. He's already the next target.' She made an upturned claw shape with her hand. 'We wait, he comes.' She squeezed the claw shut, a Venus fly trap closing on a bug. 'We get him.'

ʊ

Imogen walked with Emma to the reception area. Ben jumped up when he saw them.

'I want to see Ollie.'

Imogen touched his shoulder. 'I'm going to take you to him right now.'

They led him through a door and down a long corridor. 'Have you spoken to him yet?' Ben asked.

'No. I thought it would be best if you were there. Besides, we can't interview a child without an appropriate adult being present. Here we are.'

Imogen opened the door to the interview room and gestured for Ben to go in. Standing in the doorway, she watched Ollie leap up from his chair – an echo of his dad in reception – and Ben threw his arms around him, pulling him close and stroking his hair. She heard him say, 'It's okay now. It's okay. I'm here.'

The little scene tugged at something in Imogen's heart. It could so easily have been different. Ben could've been identifying his son's body in the morgue at this moment. His mother's, too. As she pulled the door closed to give them a minute of privacy, she silently renewed her vow to protect this family. She also found herself wondering: how could Ben's wife have left them? Especially for Michael Stone. She knew she shouldn't think ill of the dead, but Ben was ten times the man Stone had been. If this were her family—

'Sweet, aren't they?' Emma said, appearing behind her and saving Imogen from the contents of her head. 'What do you think Craig's going to do next?'

'I'm not sure exactly.' She clenched her fists. 'He keeps coming into the open then slipping back into the shadows. That's why we need to follow my plan. To be there when he next steps into the light.'

Emma nodded. 'If Craig intends to do to Ben what he did to the others, he's going to need more morphine, because according to Emile

Clement, the twenty mil of morphine stolen from the bag isn't enough for a lethal dose. He said they're only allowed to carry that much morphine with them.'

'Thank God for that,' Imogen said.

Emma went on. 'We've put out a bulletin to every doctor, pharmacist, clinic and hospital in the area telling them to be on high alert. We're talking to our drug dealer contacts, too, making sure they've seen the photofit.'

Imogen was impressed. Amidst the horror of this case, Emma had been the one shining light. Imogen was definitely going to recommend her for promotion when this was all over.

'With mention of a reward, I assume?' Imogen said.

'Yep. So if he approaches any dealers to buy morphine or heroin . . .'

'That's good. Okay, I'll talk to you later.'

Imogen knocked on the door of the interview room and went in. Ben and Ollie sat beside each other on the far side of the table. Imogen took the seat opposite them.

'I hear you've been a very brave boy,' she said.

Ollie grunted. 'I did what anyone would've done.'

Again, he was echoing his dad. 'I don't think many boys your age would have been so heroic. You saved your gran.'

Ollie glanced at Ben before meeting Imogen's eye. 'He knew us. He used my name. Is he after us? Me and Dad and Gran?'

'Ollie . . .' Ben began, but Imogen interrupted.

'You don't need to worry. We think he was just after the medicine Emile had in his bag. Maybe he overheard your gran say your name.'

It was obvious Ollie didn't believe her. He wasn't stupid. But he nodded, not brave enough to challenge a police detective.

'I was thinking . . .' Imogen glanced at Ben before addressing his son. 'Perhaps you'd like to go and stay with your mum for a few days, just while we sort all this out.'

'No way. I want to stay here, with Dad.'

Ben had turned his chair around so he was facing Ollie. 'It might be a good idea, Ollie. You've had a shock. It would be good for you to get away for a little while. You can hang out with your old friends.'

Ollie shook his head vehemently. 'No! I'm not going anywhere. You can't make me.'

Imogen raised her palms. 'No one is going to force you to do anything, Ollie. Listen, why don't I get you something to drink? How about a hot chocolate? Are you hungry? I can send someone out to get some sandwiches and crisps.'

'I'm starving, actually.'

'Ham and cheese?' The boy nodded. 'Great. And in the meantime' – she stood, gesturing for Ben to follow her – 'I need a word with your dad.'

She took Ben to the adjacent interview room.

'I honestly think it would be a good idea for him to go and stay with your wife for a few days. It will be safer,' Imogen said.

'I thought you said you were going to protect us?'

'I am. I mean, we are.'

Ben folded his arms. 'It doesn't seem like the Viper wants to hurt Ollie anyway. He had the chance to shoot him and didn't do it. And we know why that is, don't we? He knows how unhappy it would make me. He clearly doesn't think my son is a burden.'

Imogen thought about it. Ben was right. The Viper's logic might be twisted, but it was getting easier to follow. Ollie was a source of happiness for Ben. In fact, from what Ben had told her, it seemed Rowland had done everything he could to remove Ollie's problems so Ben didn't have to worry about him. Imogen made a mental note to find out who had been bullying Ollie at school, to see if they'd had any visits warning them to stay away from Ollie.

'I've made my mind up,' Ben said, arms folded. 'He stays with me. If we're under police protection, this must be the safest place to be.'

She nodded. 'All right. Have you got a spare bedroom?'

'No. It's only a two-bedroom cottage. Why?'

'I'll sleep on the sofa then.'

'Eh?'

'I'm coming to stay. And that's non-negotiable.'

Chapter 43

'Is that you?' Eileen calls as soon as she hears the door shut.

'Yeah, it's me. Just going to take a shower.'

'But—'

I ignore her entreaties and lock the bathroom door behind me, stripping off and removing the clothes that stink of sweat. While I scrub myself with Eileen's carbolic soap I run through everything in my head.

The car is in the garage, plates changed back to the originals, in case Mrs H or Ollie got a good look at them. The gun is concealed in the boot. The spent cartridge is still inside the gun.

I'm certain no one followed me or saw me enter the garage. CCTV coverage on those roads is scant, but that hardly makes me feel better.

I bang my head against the shower tiles, deserving the pain because I fucked up.

Mrs H is still breathing.

And I have barely enough morphine to take the edge off for Eileen, let alone send Ben off in a state of bliss.

It's all Ollie's fault. After everything I've done for him. Everything I've done for his dad. I think Ollie needs to be taught a lesson about gratitude when I've finished with Ben. I'll tie concrete blocks to his ankles and chuck him off the fucking Iron Bridge. He'll have the time it takes to drown to think about what he did.

I count to ten to calm myself, to quell the rage. The police don't know as much as they think. Everything is still on with Ben. It would be better if his mother was dead, no longer a burden on him. But maybe, having almost lost her, he will be glad she's still around. A close shave can make you feel grateful for what you've got, can't it? Yes, that makes sense.

I could have used that with the others. I could have made Danni worry about the baby in her belly, made her sick, so she was flooded with relief when it turned out to be okay. There's so much more I could have done.

I knew how she longed for a baby because it was in her secret diary, the one she kept hidden from her boyfriend. It didn't take me long to find it after I broke into her flat. It was concealed in a box beneath her bed. It also didn't take long to switch her contraceptive pills for placebos that I'd made myself. That, and the cat I left in her garden – after removing it from someone else's house – was all it took to make her happy.

Nathan was easy, too. Poisoning his great rival the morning of their race. It was easy to get into Finlay's flat, too, to slip half a tranquilliser into his sports drink – just enough to slow him down. It was reasonably straightforward to remove Melissa's boyfriend, too. Paid an attractive call girl to seduce him, then ensured Melissa knew all about it. Beating both his sporting and his love rivals – that was all Nathan needed.

I had such high hopes for Fiona. I'd been forced to play a long game with her. She was the first I encountered, and in the worst state. That first time, watching her, I wondered if I could find a heart for her, deliver a donor. But it was too complicated. I was about to give up on her, move on, when she got the heart she needed. And then I had to wait for her to recover, get fit, get happy. The Roman cup and the money it brought helped. But the most important part was to find a lover for her. A man who would make her feel young and vibrant again.

That was a challenge. I thought about hiring someone, a male escort to play the role. But that would have been too risky. I needed to find someone especially attracted to older women. I found an online dating site that caters for that demographic, set up a fake profile and posed as a fifty-year-old woman. There were a lot of young men in the area who were looking for an older lover. I was impressed. And then I hit gold: a young man called Anthony who listed his main interest as cycling. Fiona had recently started cycling. I tracked Anthony to a forum on which he boasted about his ability to seduce any woman he took a fancy to. If I could just get them to meet . . .

In the end, it was easy. I phoned The Lucky Magpie saying I was a member of Ludlow Wheelers and that we had some old trophies that they might be interested in buying. I knew that when she got there no one would know anything about these trophies – but next time I went along to spy on a Wheelers' meet, there she was, standing close to Anthony, looking at him in that special way.

People are so easy to manipulate.

When I turn off the shower, I can hear Eileen moaning in the other room, desperate for what I've got in my bag.

She can wait.

I stand naked before the mirror.

My father stares back from the steamy mirror, mocking me, taunting me with his eyes, his teeth, the lines on his/my face. You look like me, *he says.* You *are* like me. And no matter how hard you try, you'll never make amends. As if you could!

You *left* her with me, you weakling, *he says.* Little boy or no, you knew what that meant. You left her to die, miserable, scared and in pain. No matter what you do, no matter how many people die happy and pain-free because of you, that will never change.

I grasp the little cup that sits on the basin, the one Eileen keeps her toothbrush in, and I'm squeezing it, arms trembling, fingers stiff, and it takes every ounce of strength, all my self-control, not to smash it into the mirror. To grip the shards and rip apart my reflection, splatter myself and him with our shared blood.

ω

As I emerge from the bathroom, Eileen rolls her head in my direction and says, 'At last. I thought you'd drowned in there. Then I heard you talking to yourself, like you used to when you were a boy.'

I hate her in that moment. Her weakness, the grasping way she clings to me, makes demands of me, expects me to do her bidding. You owe me, *she always says. But I never asked her to take me in. And I've been so good to her. Supported her, procured medicine for her. I have provided. Repaid my debt a thousand times.*

But I bite back my irritation and ask, 'How are you feeling?'

She looks terrible. Pale and sweaty and trembling, gnarled fingers clasping at the arms of her chair. Her hair is grey and her skin is going the same way. Beads of sweat stand out on her upper lip. I can hardly look at her.

'I need my medicine,' she says, and I fetch the bag I took from the nurse and unzip it.

Eileen licks her lips as she watches me. 'Oh, you good boy. Such a good lad.'

I perch beside her with the loaded syringe and she turns her arm over, the veins blue and prominent. She doesn't really like needles – Eileen has always preferred to kill her pain with pills – but she's in too much pain to care right now. She hasn't seen how little there is in the syringe. I push the needle into her flesh and depress the plunger.

She sighs in anticipation and waits.

Opens her eyes and stares at me.

'It still hurts. I need more.'

I fail to keep the irritation out of my voice. 'I don't have any more.'

She tries to heave herself out of the armchair, but I push her back. It's easy – she's so skinny and light; pain has stripped the flesh from her bones.

'I have to go to the doctor, then,' she mewls. 'Get a new prescription.'

'You can't, you stupid bitch!'

Her eyes go wide with shock. I've never spoken to her like this before. I'm wringing my hands. They want to seize her throat, to squeeze and shake her. You won't feel pain then, I want to shout.

'After all I've done for you,' she says in a weak voice.

I have to leave the room. In the kitchen, I find the gin and pour myself a full tumbler, swallow it down. The alcohol helps me think straight. She's right – I need to get more medicine, and not just for her.

And I have an idea.

I take my phone out of my pocket and shut the kitchen door, muffling Eileen's desperate, irritating pleas.

ᴡ

A little later, after I've made the call, I text Ollie.

Hello. How was your day?

He replies almost immediately. **OMG, you won't believe it.** *He goes on to recount everything that happened at the church from his point of view.*

Thankfully, he doesn't suspect anything. He has no idea that it was his new friend who pointed a shotgun at him today.

But what he says next is interesting. Very interesting.

After finishing the conversation, I fix dinner for Eileen and take it to her on a tray, along with a tumbler and the bottle of gin.

'I have to go,' I say as she ignores the food and pours herself a large glass. I take a final look at her, trying to think kind thoughts – but unable to shake a new image, that of her decapitated skull swarming with maggots – then head out to the van and drive home.

Chapter 44

I found Imogen in the kitchen. She had her hair pulled back in a thick ponytail and was wearing a black vest top, leggings and trainers. She looked like she was about to go to a yoga class. Her face was free of make-up and she smelled clean, floral, like she'd just got out of the shower. A lock of hair hung loose, clinging to her cheek, and I had a sudden urge to reach out and tuck it behind her ear.

'I've made coffee. Do you want one?'

'That would be lovely.'

She bent to get the milk out of the fridge. It was jarring to find an attractive woman in my kitchen first thing in the morning. Jarring, but certainly not unpleasant. But then I reminded myself why she was here: to protect me. As well as Imogen, there were two police officers in a van that was parked across the road. Others were, Imogen assured me, very close; near enough to reach the cottage within a couple of minutes if anything happened.

She had also assured me this was all very irregular. Her boss, DCI Greene, had given me a very odd look when he'd seen me at the station. The police don't normally guard non-VIPs, especially in their own homes. But I got the impression they were so desperate to catch the Viper they were willing to bend some rules.

Imogen put two mugs of coffee on the table and sat across from me, glancing at the window behind me.

'It's going to be hot today.'

I nodded. I could already feel it, the temperature creeping up, the sky that lovely shade of blue that makes England so appealing in summer. But it was humid, too, the stickiness making me feel even less comfortable in my skin, less able to relax.

'How did you sleep?' I asked.

She smiled. 'Not bad. Your sofa is actually pretty comfortable.'

'It's not mine, not really. All the furniture, apart from a few bits and pieces, belongs to my landlord, Frank.'

'The one who dresses like Johnny Cash?'

I raised an eyebrow. 'You've met him?'

'Yeah, he came into the station moaning about the mess next door. I think he expected the police to clean it up, but it's not our job.'

'What's the latest? Any progress finding Rowland?' Imogen had told me what they'd found at the museum, that they'd identified the man as Craig Rowland. I'd been asked if that name meant anything to me. It didn't.

'We're still looking for him. And we'll find him.'

I drained my coffee and placed the empty mug in the dishwasher. 'I'd like to go looking for him myself. I mean, I like having you stay here' – blurting this out earned not a flicker of response from her – 'but you can't stay here forever. And—'

It struck me – why they were really here, why Greene had given me that peculiar look.

'You're not here to protect me at all, are you?' I said. 'You're using me as bait.'

'Ben, no—'

'Okay, maybe it's both. And it's fine, really. You want to catch him. I want you to catch him. But if I'm bait, why don't you let me go for a walk down a quiet country lane? You could give me a panic button, put a GPS device in my shoe.'

'We wouldn't put you at risk like that.'

'And what's the plan if, as I suspect, nothing happens? If he doesn't come because I'm stuck at home with a bodyguard.'

'He doesn't know we're here.'

'Are you sure? He seems to have a god-like power to know where everyone is at all times. How did he know I was going to be walking past the bridge? Or that my mum and Ollie were going to be at that church?'

'I don't know.'

Yesterday, someone had been round checking the cottage, our phones and our computers for bugs, including Ollie's laptop and iPod. They found nothing. The police had also spoken to Mrs Douglas and Kyle next door, asking them if they had seen anyone hanging around, telling them it was part of the continuing investigation into Ross's murder, that they were trying to confirm that it was indeed Ross who had taken the dog to be debarked.

I carried on. 'Going out into the open has to be better than sitting around like a mouse cowering in a hole. If you and the rest of West Mercia police are there to protect me, surely it will be fine.'

'No. We don't take risks with civilians' lives.' She took a step towards me. 'Listen to me, Ben. This isn't just about you. It's about catching the man who has already killed six people, possibly more.' Earlier today, she'd told me that they'd discovered that one of Rowland's colleagues, a woman called Janet, was missing. Adrian was still missing as well. And I knew, too, that Imogen was including her colleague, DC Hatton, in that number, though they had no proof it was the Viper who'd killed him. This was personal – for both of us.

'It's about their families,' Imogen said. 'And it's about stopping him. If you go off on your own, force us to reveal that we're protecting you, it could – almost certainly would – mess everything up. Do you understand that?'

'I do. But I want you to understand that I'm willing to do whatever it takes to help you get him. He was going to kill my mum. I want the bastard to rot in jail. And surely if you'd let me go out there—'

'No. He'll come to us,' she said. 'He'll come. And when he does, we'll be ready.'

ω

I went upstairs for a shower. When I came back down, I checked Ollie was okay – he was playing *Minecraft* in his room – and found Imogen talking to someone on her phone.

'Any news?' I asked when she'd ended the call.

'Not really.'

'Was his car recorded on CCTV yesterday?'

'Unfortunately not. And it wouldn't surprise me if he was using fake plates anyway.'

'What about the gun? Can't you trace that by, I don't know, matching it with the bullet?'

'You've been watching too many thrillers. First, shotguns use cartridges filled with shot. If we had the cartridge and found the gun, we might be able to match them by how the firing pin hit the cartridge's primer. But it's only useful as evidence, not in helping us find him.'

In real life, the police appeared to be a lot less powerful than they were on TV. 'I thought, with CCTV everywhere and DNA, it was much easier to catch criminals these days.'

She laughed.

I went over to the window.

'I need to go out,' I said.

'Ben, we already—'

'I need to go to Orchard Heights to see my mum, check she's okay. You can't stop me from doing that. I'm sure Ollie will want to see her, too.'

She sighed. 'Wait here.' She left the room with her phone, to check with her boss I assumed, and returned a few minutes later. 'Okay, that's fine. But I'm coming with you.'

My car had been parked in the sun all morning and was stifling inside, the seats hot to the touch.

As I got in the car, Kyle came out. He raised a hand when he saw me watching him, then got into his van and drove off.

'Everyone in this county either seems to drive a four-by-four or a white van,' Imogen said.

I raised my eyebrows and waited for her to continue.

'Rowland doesn't have a driving licence, but we know he's been driving a white van as well as the blue Volkswagen he was in at the church. It's risky driving around without a licence, and those vehicles can't be registered to or taxed by him. I've been trying to figure it out.'

'Hmm.' I didn't have the answer but also couldn't see why it was important. It couldn't be that hard to get a fake licence. The vehicles he was using were probably stolen.

I started the engine and cranked up the air conditioning to full. In the back seat, Ollie listened to music on his iPod. Beside me, Imogen was quiet and tense, eyeing everybody we passed, sitting straighter every time we stopped at lights.

I glanced at Ollie in the mirror. He fiddled nervously with his iPod. Perhaps I should have made him go to stay with Megan after all. I wondered if he was eager to tell his friends about what had happened at the church. Although the press had reported the incident, they hadn't been allowed to mention Ollie by name because of his age.

When we next stopped at traffic lights, it struck me that the people on the street looked scared. I knew if I turned on local radio they would be talking about it. The serial killings. The murder of Michael Stone. And now, a fatal shooting at, of all places, a pretty village church. This part of the world had been turned upside down, and here Ollie, Imogen and I were, right at the centre of it.

Chapter 45

Jasper Bube lives in a garden flat in the Whitmore Reans ward of Wolverhampton, one of the cheapest areas of the city. I shake my head at the overgrown front garden, a broken child's pushchair lying among the weeds and the paint peeling off the door. God knows who the pushchair belongs to. As far as I know, Jasper doesn't have any kids, unless he's managed to knock up one of his fellow skagheads.

All last night, I struggled with the question: where can I get more medicine?

Morphine is one of the most heavily guarded drugs out there. I've seen shows on TV where a criminal dons a white coat and walks through a hospital, smiling at nurses, all the way to the storeroom where the drugs are kept. The fake doctor then fills his pockets with jars of pills. But in reality, the stuff is kept locked in a safe. And how likely is the white coat trick to work? The whole idea is laughable.

Same with trying to rob a pharmacy. It's too risky. The likelihood of it all going tits up is off-puttingly high. At the very least, they'd probably catch me on CCTV. Or some have-a-go hero of a chemist would end up getting himself shot.

I've thought about robbing an ambulance. It wouldn't be too hard. Make an emergency call in the middle of the night from an empty property. Greet them with a shotgun. Maybe if I was lucky I'd get one of the solo

*response vehicles with a single paramedic on board. But I did a little dig-
ging and found that ambulances only keep a small amount of morphine on
board; barely more than Mrs H's nurse had in his bag. I'd have to rob a
whole fucking fleet of ambulances to get the amount I need. I have an image
of myself lurking on country roads, gun in hand, a modern-day highway-
man yelling 'Stand and deliver' at paramedics.*

*There was only one answer, a solution I'd tried to avoid. Heroin is a
dirty word, not a respected medicine but a street drug, used by prostitutes
and lowlifes and decadent rock stars. But it's so easy to get hold of, and I
know from my online research that it's almost identical to morphine . . . It's
not heroin's fault that it has a bad reputation. All along, I had this stupid
feeling that using smack would somehow sully what I was doing. Eileen
always said H was for losers. She railed against drug addicts even while she
kept herself dosed up on the pills the doctor dished out, and I went along
with it. I have been foolish.*

But now I have a solution.

*Jasper takes forever to answer the door, but finally he's there in front
of me, a skeleton with white flesh hanging off it, eyes peering at me from
dark purple pits.*

'What are you doing here?' he says. 'Is there a problem?'

'Everything's fine, Jasper. I want to ask you for a little favour, that's all.'

*He sniffs and plucks at the sleeve of his baggy cardigan. He's definitely
still using. 'What favour?'*

'Let me in and I'll tell you.'

*Reluctantly, he opens the door so I can push past him into the living
room.*

*'Jesus Christ.' The place is a tip. Overflowing ashtrays, old polystyrene
kebab cartons, clothes piled everywhere, stains on the carpet and on the sofa.
It stinks, too, of stale farts and vomit and McDonald's. There's a bottle of
what looks like piss on the mantelpiece.*

'I was about to clear up,' he says.

'Yeah, I'm sure.'

'Do you, er, want a cup of tea?'

'I'll pass.'

He looks relieved and slumps on the sofa. There used to be a TV here, a pretty decent widescreen one, if I recall correctly. No doubt he sold it to pay for gear.

'So what I can do for you?' he asks.

I'm about to sit beside him, but spot a suspicious damp patch and have second thoughts.

'I won't beat around the bush. I want to score some heroin.'

The surprise on his face is delicious. He licks his parched lips. 'Why are you asking me?'

'Come off it, Jasper. Everyone knows you're a smackhead. Jasper the Junkie. Even the little kids around here call you that.'

He looks hurt. But he doesn't say anything.

'Here's what I want you to do. Call your dealer. Tell him you want to buy five grams. You can keep a gram for your trouble.'

Jasper's eyes almost pop out of their pits.

He gets up from the sofa and gestures for me to put my arms in the air so he can reach under my jacket and pat me down, suspicious I'm wearing a wire.

'I'm not working for the police, you moron,' I say as he finishes.

'Tell your dealer I want good shit. As pure as possible. And I need it today. In fact, I'm going to wait here till he arrives.'

Jasper searches around the room till he finds his phone. It's an ancient Nokia, a real museum piece. He leaves the room, clutching it with white knuckles.

After he's gone, I pick up the glass ashtray and empty the contents on to the carpet. The ashtray is good quality faux crystal with a decent heft to it. Jasper probably nicked it from somewhere. I stick it in my pocket.

ʊ

He comes back ten minutes later and tells me the dealer is on his way. Shortly afterwards, the doorbell rings and Jasper jumps up, carrying the cash I gave him while we were waiting. A minute later, he's back, licking his lips, desperate to shoot up.

'Hand it over. Don't worry, you'll get what's coming to you.'

He passes it to me, as reluctantly as a child playing pass the parcel. 'I won't ask what you need it for,' he asks.

'No, you won't,' I say, and I hit him in the face with the glass ashtray. His nose cracks and he cries out so I hit him again, this time on the side of the head, just above the ear. He goes down like a sapling in a hurricane. It's stinking and hot in the room and I'm covered with sweat. I hit Jasper in the face with the ashtray repeatedly until I hear a soft crunching noise. He emits a final, rasping breath and lies still. I wait a few moments and then check his pulse to ensure he's dead. The ashtray is smeared with blood and there's a crack down one side. Shame. I put it back in my jacket pocket to dispose of later.

I'm confident no one's going to come looking for him. Not today. Probably not for a week, until the neighbours notice an extra-rank smell and flies on the windows. By then, this will all be over. And Jasper the Junkie's death will be nothing but a footnote in my glorious tale.

Chapter 46

We reached the nursing home and went inside. Weirdly, the incident seemed to have perked Mum up, as if standing up to the man pointing a shotgun at her had given her some of her fire back, put spots of colour back in her cheeks. She gazed at Ollie with adoration.

'He was foolish standing in front of me like that,' she said. 'But he's a hero.'

We didn't stay long. On the way back, Ollie closed his eyes and dozed off, his iPod on his lap. The heat, which had continued to creep up as the day went on, made me sleepy, too, so I wound down the car windows, hoping the breeze would wake me up.

'There's going to be a storm,' Imogen said.

The sky was clear now, the most gossamer of clouds streaked across it, but I knew she was right. The air was thick, torpid. It needed to break.

Imogen glanced back at the sleeping Ollie. 'I was expecting your son to be more traumatised by what happened,' she said.

'He's been through a lot recently,' I said. 'He's grown a thick skin. I'm sure it'll hit him though, before long.'

'Hmm.' She looked back at him again. 'I'm surprised you let him have his own mobile phone. Or am I out of touch? Do most eleven-year-olds have them these days?'

I pulled up at a red light. 'It's not a phone, it's an iPod. It does everything a phone does except—'

She interrupted me. 'No, I've seen his iPod. We checked it for bugs. That looks like a phone.'

'But Ollie doesn't have a phone.' We were still stuck at the lights. 'Pass it to me. I'll show you.'

She grabbed it off Ollie's lap and turned it over. Even before she gave it to me I could tell something wasn't right.

'It says "iPhone" on the back,' she said.

'What?' The lights turned green and I had no choice but to keep driving. 'Ollie,' I said in a loud voice. He stirred and I said his name again. He opened one eye and groaned.

'Ollie, what the hell are you doing with an iPhone?'

The other eye opened and he sat forward, trying to snatch it off Imogen, but the seat belt tugged him back.

I spotted a petrol station and pulled in, unbuckling my seat belt as soon as we stopped. I took the phone from Imogen.

In the back seat, Ollie had gone pale. 'He said I mustn't tell you.'

'What the hell? Who said? Where did you get this?' I pressed the button to bring the screen to life. It was protected by a pin. 'What's the PIN? Tell me!'

Imogen put her hands between us. 'Ben, calm down.'

I sucked in bitter air. Ollie looked like he was about to be sick.

'Ollie,' Imogen said gently. 'Where did you get the phone?'

'My friend gave it to me.'

'What friend?' I demanded.

Imogen gestured for me to stay out of it. She repeated my question in a calm voice.

'He calls himself Epicurus. That's, like, his screen name.'

Imogen said, almost to herself, 'There was an Epicurus quote on the wall at Eileen Rowland's.' Then, 'What's the passcode for the phone, Ollie?'

'Zero zero zero three four one.'

She tapped it in and went straight into the messages app, scrolled up and read some of the messages before closing the phone and pressing the button to switch it off. 'Rowland could be using this phone to track our movements,' she said, getting her own mobile out. 'I'm going to call for backup. He could be following us right now.'

I poked my head out of the window and looked around, focusing on faces in passing cars, half-expecting the Viper to loom up at any moment, shotgun in hand. Or would it be a syringe?

'Ben,' Imogen said, 'roll your windows up. We need to stay in the car.'

While we waited for the police backup, Ollie told us that he'd found the phone in an alleyway near the stop where he catches the bus home. He'd brought it back and, almost immediately, 'Epicurus' had messaged him.

'He said he was my guardian angel,' Ollie said, his voice so quiet I had to strain to hear him, 'and that he was going to help me deal with the bullies at school. At first I thought it was actually one of them, that it was, like, a prank. But then he must have done something because they stopped hassling me. And he said he was my friend, that I could tell him stuff and he'd help me with my problems.'

'Why didn't you tell me any of this?'

'Because he told me not to. He said you'd confiscate the phone like you took away my DS.'

'He sent you the DS?'

He nodded. 'Yeah, though I didn't know that straight away. I asked him if it was him after Mum said she hadn't bought it for me.'

'Oh God, Ollie, you should have told me.'

He wouldn't meet my eye. 'You were too wrapped up in your own problems.'

I let that go for the moment. 'But you know about all the dangers of talking to strangers online.'

'Yeah. But this wasn't online. And I knew he wasn't, you know, a pervert. He wanted to help me, that's all.'

'This is how Rowland knew your whereabouts,' Imogen said to me. 'If Ollie was carrying this phone around with him . . .'

'Did you tell him about your guitar lessons?' I asked.

He nodded miserably.

'That's how he knew we were going to be passing the bridge at that exact time,' I said.

For the past few weeks I'd seen Ollie playing with what I thought was his iPod numerous times. I hadn't looked closely enough. And I should have pressed Ollie more about the bullying, dealt with it myself. Then my son wouldn't have needed to rely on this stranger to help him. This bond of trust wouldn't have formed between them. It was all my fault.

Ollie stared at the floor of the car. He swallowed, and I was sure he was going to cry. The words rushed out. 'Dad, I'm sorry, I'm really sorry, but I didn't want to tell you about the bullies and everything because, you know, you had so many other things to think about like you kept saying every night and I knew how worried you were about Nan and money and . . .' He broke down and I climbed into the back of the car and held him, his face against my shoulder, and told him it was okay. And while he sobbed I made a promise to myself. I would be a better father. Attentive. On the ball.

I would be the dad he needed me to be.

If I survived.

ω

At the station, Imogen insisted that Ollie should go to stay with Megan for a few days, and this time I agreed. I called Megan, giving her the scantest of details, and explained that a couple of police officers were going to bring Ollie down to London that night. She had a million questions, but I told her I'd explain later. Imogen told me she was going to talk to her old colleagues in the Metropolitan Police to ensure someone watched Megan's flat.

The police took the iPhone away, presumably to examine the messages that Ollie and Rowland had exchanged.

Imogen sent Ollie into a waiting room so we could talk in private for a moment.

'In one of the messages,' Imogen said, 'Ollie wrote that you have a policewoman staying with you and, I quote, "the feds" are watching the house.'

Feds, I knew, was teen slang for police.

'Now we know why he hasn't come near you yet. You were right, Ben. The plan isn't going to work. He knows you're being protected, so he's not going to come.'

I ran both hands through my hair. 'I'm furious with myself.'

'There's no need. This phone could be just what we need to catch him.'

Driving up the hill a little later, I was aware of people watching us, the hidden police officers, their cameras and eyes trained on the car. Kyle's van was back in position outside the house next door and I was sure I saw their curtains twitch. The sensation followed me into the house. The feeling of being watched.

I paused just inside the front door. Imogen's phone rang and she went off to take the call. Ollie was about to slink off to his room when I said, 'Wait.'

'What is it?' he asked.

'Does it feel like someone's been in here to you?'

He looked around. 'No . . . Hey, Dad?'

'Yes?'

'I promise not to keep secrets from you in future.'

'Even when you're a teenager?' I sighed. 'Listen, I'm not angry with you. I blame myself. You've been through so much recently, moving here, me and your mum splitting up. I promise it's going to get easier. Okay?'

He nodded, embarrassed. 'I'd better go and pack.'

'All right. But first, come here.' I gave him a hug, noting again how much weight he'd lost recently.

After he'd gone to his room, I went through the cottage, room by room. Nothing was out of place. There were no mysterious footprints. After checking the kitchen, where Imogen was having a heated discussion on the phone, I stopped looking. It must have been my imagination. After all, if the person who wanted to harm me knew the police were watching the house, there was no way he'd risk coming here. And how would he get in without being seen anyway?

I went to the window. The horizon was black with storm clouds.

Chapter 47

Imogen tugged at the strap of her bra and rocked her head from side to side, wincing at the pop and crunch of her vertebrae. It was 10 p.m. and the storm hadn't broken yet. The house was filled with a filthy heat and her clothes stuck to her skin. She longed to take a shower, to get out of these clothes and into a cool pair of pyjamas. She wanted to open all the windows and find a spot where there was a breeze.

But she couldn't do any of those things. Greene had told her to stay put. There was 'no need' for her to come in to work on the plan for tomorrow. It was all in hand. Her role was to watch Ben, keep all the doors and windows locked, not to let him go anywhere or call anyone or do anything that might make Craig suspicious.

'I thought it was what you wanted,' Greene had said in that supercilious tone of his. 'To be Hofland's babysitter. So what are you complaining about?'

'That was before,' she'd protested. 'I'm still the lead detective on this investigation. I should be there, in the incident room, making sure the plan is idiot-proof.'

'Don't worry, Detective. We country bumpkins have got it all under control. Stay there, watch Hofland, make sure he gets a decent night's sleep. I'll call you if anything changes.'

He'd hung up, leaving Imogen prickling with anger. She'd wanted to call him back, seek reassurance that when they got Rowland in custody she would lead his interrogation. But she'd had a sickening feeling Greene would want to do that himself. He wanted to take credit.

And he didn't trust her not to fuck it up.

Well, screw him. She was going to be the one to make the arrest. She'd made a promise to the victims' families. There was no way she was going to let Greene muscle in at the last moment.

She opened the fridge door and let the chilled air waft over her, closing her eyes as she felt the sweat dry on her skin. 'He's mine,' she muttered to herself.

'What's that?'

She jumped and slammed the fridge door as she turned. Ben stood in the doorway, wearing jeans and a fresh T-shirt. He'd trimmed his beard, too.

She sat at the kitchen table. 'I was giving myself a pep talk,' she said. 'And trying to cool down.'

'Horrible, isn't it? I keep thinking the weather's going to break at any moment, but it's just getting worse.' He opened the fridge and took out two bottles of beer. Beads of condensation slid down the green frosted glass. Imogen licked her lips involuntarily.

'Want one?' he asked. His mood appeared to have lightened since Ollie had gone. He held out one of the bottles and his T-shirt rode up an inch, revealing a slice of flesh. She looked away.

'I can't.'

'I won't tell, I promise.'

The temptation was physically painful, but she shook her head, and regretfully watched him put the second bottle back. 'Come and sit down. How are you feeling about tomorrow?'

He took a long swallow of his beer and she watched his Adam's apple bob.

'I was going to say "nervous", but I don't know if I am, not really. It's more like restlessness. Or being in a state of high tension. I can hardly sit still and my heart's going like this.' He tapped his fingers rapidly against his chest. 'It's been a surreal couple of days.'

He took another swig of beer and she noticed how the bottle brought out flecks of green in his eyes. She looked away again, trying to find something else to focus on. This stupid heat was doing weird things to her brain, to her body.

'It must be exciting for you, I guess,' he said.

'Huh? Exciting isn't the word I'd use. I just want it to go smoothly.'

'He might not turn up.'

'I'm pretty sure he will.'

The fridge hummed in the silence between them. Imogen checked her watch. It was ten fifteen. She ought to go to bed soon, but she knew she wouldn't be able to sleep.

'Don't let me keep you up,' she said. 'You should get some rest.'

'It's too hot.' He paused, picking at the label of his bottle. She could tell he was trying to gather the courage to say something.

She stood up and crossed to the counter where Ollie's phone was plugged in. She was careful to check it every fifteen minutes in case Rowland sent a message. They didn't want him wondering why it hadn't been responded to.

There were no new messages, not since his response to the texts Imogen had sent pretending to be Ollie, setting everything up for tomorrow. That was good. There were no signs that the Viper had realised he was being played. He had fallen for it, she was sure. Fallen for it because he was as desperate for this to be over as they were.

'Be right back.'

She went to the downstairs loo, then found herself going into Ollie's room to double-check the window was secure.

It was cooler in the boy's bedroom, away from Ben. She would wait here on Ollie's single bed for a few minutes, let her body temperature fall, but her legs had different ideas, and a moment later she found herself back in the kitchen. Ben had finished his lager and was fishing in the fridge for another.

'Sod it,' she heard herself saying. 'I'll have one.'

He smiled as he opened it and handed it to her, and the glass was so cold, dotted with beads of condensation, she couldn't resist holding it against the curve where her neck and shoulder met. She was aware of Ben watching her. She closed her eyes and raised the bottle to her lips. When she opened her eyes, Ben was still staring at her. She matched his gaze for a moment before a voice in her head asked her what she was doing. She made herself go to the opposite side of the room, to stand by the back door. She took a number of deep breaths and put her face to the glass panel of the door. It was too dark in the garden to see much apart from the dark silhouettes of shrubs and the trees that overhung the rear boundary. But then a movement in the far corner of the garden caught her eye.

It looked like someone exiting over the back wall.

She unlocked the door.

'Wait here. Lock the door behind me.'

He was beside her immediately, his shoulder brushing against hers, peering into the darkness. 'What did you see?' His voice was thick with concern.

'Probably nothing. A cat or a trick of the light. But I want to take a look. If anything happens, if you can't see me for more than three minutes, press the alarm.' They had given Ben a personal alarm that connected directly to the police station, and that would alert the cops out front as well.

'Detective, I don't think—'

But she opened the door and crept out, waiting to hear the click of the lock behind her before continuing into the garden. She headed straight for the back wall where she'd seen the movement. *If I was an American cop*, she thought, *I'd have my gun drawn right now.*

She sneaked across the garden, under cover of darkness.

There was no sound apart from the wind rushing through the trees, like an advance party announcing the impending storm. She reached the wall and peered over. No sign of anyone or anything. She sensed a movement to her left and looked up. A light had come on in the cottage next door. She made a quick circuit of the garden, satisfied herself no one was there and headed back to the door.

Ben let her in. 'Well?'

'Nothing to worry about.' She picked up the beer from where she'd left it and took a sip. 'Feels like the storm's about to hit though.'

'It's felt like that for hours.'

He was standing too close to her. She forced herself to take a step away from him.

'Let's go into the living room,' he said. 'It's cooler in there.'

They sat opposite each other, Imogen in an armchair, Ben across from her at the end of the sofa. She sipped at her beer. Ben had carried in two more bottles, along with the opener.

'What part of London are you from?' Ben asked, breaking the silence that thrummed between them.

'Brixton. Well, I was born and brought up in West Norwood, but I lived and worked in Brixton. Right in the heart of the action, near Electric Avenue. How about you? Where did you live?'

'Highbury.'

She raised an eyebrow. 'Nice. I thought you were one of those trendy north London types.'

'Ha. Yeah, that's me. The kind who'd rather die than go south of the river.' He winced. '*Rather die.* Huh.'

'You're going to be fine, Ben. I promise.'

'You keep saying that.'

'Because it's true.' She felt her phone vibrate in her pocket and glanced at it. A message from DCI Greene, asking her to call him. For one irrational moment, she thought he was going to tell her off for drinking on duty. Well, he could wait a minute.

'Do you miss it?' she asked.

'London? I did. When I first came back here I felt like a failure. Marriage over, career on the ropes. Coming back to the village where I grew up. It's hardly a great success story.'

'But now?'

'Well, I did feel a lot better until you turned up and told me all the good stuff that's been happening is down to some psychopath who wants to kill me.'

She laughed at that – more snort than laugh, which touched off another round of laughter. Ben joined her, at least.

God, she was so tired.

'Yeah, well,' she said when she'd settled down. 'I can see how that would take the shine off. But least you've got someone you know cares about you, haven't you?'

That broke loose a fresh bark of laughter from him and he raised his beer to her. 'You've got a positive genius for finding the silver lining, Detective Evans.'

He had finished his beer and reached forwards, laughing again, to pick up another from the coffee table. But, maybe because he was laughing, or because he was looking at her as he reached out, he knocked the bottle over and it rolled across the table on to the floor.

Trying to act cool, as if this hadn't happened, he grabbed the beer and popped off the cap.

Beer exploded over his shirt.

Imogen couldn't help it. The look on his face, the puncturing of his male pride, his attempt to act cool – she spluttered with laughter.

'Whoops,' Ben said.

And then they fully lost it.

All the tension of the past few weeks roared out of her as Imogen bent over, unable to stop the hysteria from bursting forth, and Ben the same, leaning back in his chair, clutching his belly, groaning, 'Stop it, please, stop it.'

'Oh, my stomach.'

'Mine, too.'

'I can't—'

Another torrent of laughter escaped her. She hadn't laughed like this since she was a teenager, experimenting with weed round her best friend's house, and every time she thought she could stop, she pictured Ben spraying himself with beer and it started all over again.

They laughed for five minutes straight, wiping tears from their faces, holding their middles, until Imogen realised her phone was ringing. She checked the display. Oh hell. Greene. She hadn't called him.

Forcing herself to keep a straight face, Imogen said, 'I'd better get this.'

When she stood, her legs were weak. Her stomach muscles ached. It was actually a little frightening, the way she'd lost control. But she felt better now, with some of the tension that had been building up inside her released.

Ben got up, too. 'Detective . . . Imogen . . .'

'Yes?'

'Listen. I really like—'

The phone was still ringing. She put a finger to her lips and shook her head. 'Nah. Don't, okay?'

'But—'

'Not now. Maybe when this is all over. Okay?'

He looked ridiculously pleased. 'Okay.'

She left the room, light-headed and slightly delirious, and finally answered the phone. She glanced back into the living room as Greene harangued her, demanding to know why she'd taken so long to answer. Ben was sitting down again, cradling his beer against his damp chest. He was smiling. Maybe, she thought, something good would come of this fucked-up situation. But they had to catch the Viper first.

Chapter 48

I drive to Eileen's and her eyes light up when she sees what I've got. I prepare the heroin and carry her through to her bed. I have a feeling she's going to be out of it for a while after this, and I'm right. The needle slides into her vein and she sighs and sinks back against the pillow. It's good stuff. Jasper's dealer came through.

I leave Eileen in her happy place and go into the living room. On a shelf, I spy the book she used to read aloud from, The Great Lessons: Philosophers and Philosophy. *It's yellow and falling apart now, pages stained with grease. I skip to the chapter on Epicurus and read a few of my favourite passages.*

We must, therefore, pursue the things that make for happiness, seeing that when happiness is present, we have everything; but when it is absent, we do everything to possess it.

And.

It is better for you to be free of fear lying upon a pallet, than to have a golden couch and a rich table and be full of trouble.

I think of Eileen now, lying on her filthy mattress, free of fear and pain.

I find my favourite quote, the one that used to hang on the wall at the Homestead:

The art of living well and the art of dying well are one.

Dying well. Dying happy.

Something my mother was never able to achieve.

ɷ

I sleep on the sofa, sweating in the heat of the night, and wake up just in time for the TV news. They're talking about me, showing the last press conference again, Imogen Evans holding up the photofit. I have to admit, it's a good likeness. Annette did well, damn her.

I hit 'Pause' and study Imogen on the screen. Get closer and trace her image with a fingertip.

When I unpause, the reporters are standing outside Janet's house, talking about how she's missing. I smile. She's not missing; I know exactly where her body is. She's providing some lucky worms with a feast.

As I switch the TV off, the phone I use to contact Ollie beeps. The message is very interesting indeed. I text back and soon we're chatting. My hatred of the stupid boy subsides. I'm feeling good this morning. Because I know today is going to be the day.

I pack up my things, including the remaining heroin, check Eileen is still in a slumber, and head off.

Chapter 49

I hadn't felt so nervous getting behind the wheel since I'd taken my driving test twenty years before. My palms were slippery and I stalled the car immediately after starting the engine.

As soon as I got the car off the drive, sense memory took over and I was able to get out of Ironbridge without swerving into a lamp post or stalling again. I knew there were armed police waiting at my destination; there were also two car-loads of plain-clothes cops – including Imogen, wearing a baseball cap to hide her highly recognisable hair – following me now. There was a helicopter on standby, though it would only be deployed if the 'target', as Imogen referred to him, was alerted to the police's presence and tried to escape. She had told me all this over a breakfast I couldn't eat.

'And I'll be right there, watching you,' she'd said.

'You don't have a gun, though, do you?' I'd asked.

'No. I'm not trained.'

'So what if he points his shotgun at me and the other cops can't get to him in time?'

'He's not going to shoot you, Ben. He wants you alive.'

'Temporarily alive, you mean.'

The tension that had been relieved the previous evening, when we both collapsed in a heap of giggles like stoned students, was back. All that remained from that crazy five minutes was this new understanding between us, a bond forged in laughter.

Just before I'd left, I'd watched Imogen send the texts from Ollie's phone that the police hoped would draw the killer out of his lair. The police had worked out a script using Ollie's previous texts as a model, creating a lexicon of words and abbreviations he normally used.

I'm pissed off. Dad's gone out and left me with the old lady next door. Like I'm a baby!

The reply had come back less than thirty seconds later.
Really? Has he gone with that policewoman?

Nah, she's gone off somewhere.

Why?

I dunno. Some TOP SECRET thing going on in Shrewsbury!!

That sounds intriguing.

Yeah! LOL. Anyway, she's gone. She said something about how they were all needed there, and that's not all. Dad says we're gonna have to move tomorrow.

There was a delay before the next reply. Imogen had chewed her thumbnail.

What do you mean, move? Where are you going?

IDK. That fed said they can't afford to keep watching us here. She was well angry about it. They're going to take us somewhere tomorrow. A safe place.

Another delay. I'd watched Imogen's face, the rapt concentration, jaw muscles working as she waited for the response, clearly praying the Viper would believe all of this. They needed him to believe that today was his only chance of getting me, that tomorrow Ollie and I would be in a safe house, that right now all the police had been called to some big incident in Shrewsbury.

So where's your dad going now?

To visit the place where his dad's ashes were scattered.

Your grandad?

Yeah. I never met him. But my dad goes there every year on Grandad's birthday which is actually next week. But he might not be able to go then so he's doing it today.

The previous evening, after finding Ollie's secret phone, the police had asked me to think of a location that meant something to me, a secluded spot nearby where there were places for the police to conceal themselves. The answer had come straight away. It wasn't really my dad's birthday next week – he was born in October – but it seemed highly unlikely Rowland would know that or be able to check the facts quickly. The police were confident that as soon as he heard I was on my own, away from police protection, he would make haste to my location.

That's nice of your dad, came the response. So where is this place?

It's like some boring old farm outside Bridgnorth. Grandad grew up there. It's just like these creepy old buildings in the middle of nowhere. It's called Hofland Farm coz it was in our family for years.

That's very cool.

I suppose. Dad took me there once when I was a kid and I cried coz it was like really spooky LOL.

LOL. You wouldn't cry now though, would you?

No way! Like I said, I'm not a baby.

All of this had been dotted through with numerous emojis. Rowland had sent a smiley face back, followed by Chat later.

Imogen had placed the phone on the kitchen table. 'I think he's going for it,' she'd said.

'Hmm.'

I'd been half-hoping he would run. Run and never come back.

'Ben, I promise you,' Imogen had said. 'We won't let you come to harm.'

I'd picked at the toast on my plate. 'I hope not, Detective . . . Imogen. Because I'm literally putting my life in your hands.'

Now, I turned off the road where I lived, glancing in the rear view mirror at the cottage, wondering if I would ever see it again.

ळ

The part about my dad being born and brought up on a farm just outside Bridgnorth was true. Hofland Farm was originally built by my great-great-grandfather in the nineteenth century. They were sheep farmers, and the farm thrived until the Second World War. My dad was born there and often talked about his happy memories of growing up in this place, though he never missed an opportunity to tell me how hard it was, how the kids were expected to muck in from an early age. I wasn't sure exactly what had gone wrong – I only half-listened when I was a kid being told my family history – but by the time he was a teenager, my dad and his family had left the farm, his father having sold it on. Later, the farm went bust and was left to rot. Most of the surrounding land had been bought and absorbed by neighbouring farms, but the buildings were still there. I didn't know who owned them now, but there was no sign of the land being redeveloped. This was where, at his request, we had scattered my dad's ashes after he'd died. And for years after, Mum and I had visited the site every October to pay our respects.

I had missed the visit last October, absorbed by my domestic drama and because Mum was too sick. I felt guilty about that, and felt guilty again now for using Dad's happy place in this way. I was sure he'd understand, though. He was a very practical man, my dad. He didn't believe in allowing emotions to interfere with a good solution.

I drove out of Ironbridge, glancing in the mirror to ensure the police were still behind me. At first, I didn't spot them, and had to fight the temptation to hit the brake, but then they rounded the corner. Imogen was in a black, unmarked Ford Focus, along with two of her colleagues. They kept their distance so the tail wasn't too obvious. Another car, a silver Golf, trailed a little way behind that one.

I headed south along Ironbridge Road, past Broseley, before a roundabout took me on to the B4373. From here it was a straight road to Bridgnorth. The tarmac was almost dry now following the thunderstorm that finally broke at midnight and rumbled on for most of the night, clearing the air. The sun was out again, but it was still cooler than it had been yesterday.

Driving gave me time to think. The last couple of days had been so frenetic that I'd barely had time to reflect on what had happened, on the sickening fact that all my supposed fortune had been manufactured by a murderer. After the hysterical laughter of the previous night, nothing seemed funny this morning, especially what had happened to Michael. Sure, I hadn't liked him. How could I feel anything but hatred towards a man I'd caught screwing my wife? He was a smarmy, conceited, duplicitous arsehole. Perhaps, in my darkest moments, I had wished him dead. But to think that the Viper might have done it to please me . . . It made every part of me go cold.

He was clever, a twisted puppetmaster who had been pulling all our strings. Had he really had Pixie debarked and manipulated Shelley into killing Ross? Imogen was convinced that was the case. He had pointed a gun at my mother, terrified my son. And on top of the terrible murders he'd committed, the other things he'd done made me feel not just horrified, but foolish. Dealing with Ollie's bullies when it should have been something I took care of. Making me look like a hero via the river rescue. Posing as Robert Friend and giving me work. The thought of him exchanging texts with Ollie for the past few weeks filled me with anger, aimed both at him and myself for not realising what was going on. He had made me look like an idiot. And that was one of the reasons why I'd agreed to go along with today's set-up.

It was his turn to be fooled.

ϖ

A long, narrow lane lined by tall hedgerows took me up a hill towards the farm. Imogen had warned me that at this point they would not be able to follow me because, if the killer was watching, it would be too obvious I wasn't alone. There was another route into Hofland Farm, from the west; Imogen and the other police car would drive around and take that road. They were also going to station a vehicle at the end of this lane to ensure that both roads out were blocked.

'There will be armed police waiting there, though,' Imogen had said. 'You won't see them, but they'll be there.'

The road was bumpy and dotted with potholes. The car lurched and rattled as I negotiated them, grinding the gears as I cleared the crest of the hill and found myself at my father's birthplace. I pulled up at the side of the road beside a rusty gate and turned off the engine.

Silence.

The abandoned farm buildings stood at the centre of a small, overgrown pasture, with a concrete yard choked by weeds immediately surrounding the old stone farmhouse and dilapidated barn. A wire fence had been constructed around the pasture and a 'Keep Out' sign, itself rusty and mottled by age and bad weather, was attached to the gate.

There was no indication of life at all, apart from a few crows pecking at the ground in the next field. Where were the armed police – inside the farmhouse? The grey stone building was crumbling, its windows long boarded up, the front door falling off its hinges. There were holes in the roof and moss covered the exterior walls. Every time I came here, I wished I were rich so I could buy the place and renovate it, turn it into a home again, a place that could stand proudly in my father's memory. I wished Dad had asked for his ashes to be scattered somewhere else, but when he'd made his will he had no idea what a terrible state his childhood home would be in when he died.

I stayed in the car, unsure of what to do. Imogen had told me to act naturally, to do what I would normally do on a visit here. I started to open the car door but froze, seized by second thoughts. What the hell was I doing here, allowing myself to be used as bait? I should get out of here, go home and lock the door. Botched police operations were in the news all the time. Inquiries into how things went wrong. An inquiry wouldn't be much use to me if I was in the morgue.

But if I didn't go through with this I would never be safe. It was up to me to be courageous, for the sake of all the people Rowland had hurt and killed. I swallowed my fears and got out of the car. The day was growing hotter and there was no shade here. Putting my sunglasses on, I approached the gate and pushed at it. It opened with a low, groaning creak. I entered the yard, treading on stinging nettles and sticky weeds, trying to 'look natural'. I was finding it increasingly difficult to believe the police were really here, that they could hide so effectively. What if they'd got the wrong farm? What if he, the man who wanted to kill me, was waiting inside the farmhouse or the barn, with its collapsed roof and the surely imagined smell of ancient sheep shit? The sun blasted me, but a chill ran across my flesh. I felt no familial connection to this dead place today. All I wanted was to get away.

And then I heard an engine.

I turned. A white van was coming slowly up the lane towards me. Automatically, I clutched at the phone in my pocket, wanting to call Imogen. I couldn't see her car anywhere, or the Golf that had accompanied hers. My heartbeat accelerated and my mouth went dry. I couldn't help but stare at the van as it approached before coming to a stop beside my car.

The sun shone on the windscreen so I couldn't see inside.

'Hello?' I called.

I could feel his eyes on me from behind the glass. What were the police waiting for? Did they want him to attack me before they acted? Were they even here? I took a step backwards towards the house, then two forwards, trying to see through the windscreen.

At that moment, the sun went behind a cloud and the glare from the glass disappeared. I locked eyes with the man inside the van.

It was him. The man I'd pulled from the river. The man from the photofit. Craig Rowland.

The van door made a clunking noise as he pushed it open and climbed out, coming round the front of the vehicle. He held a shotgun in one hand.

'Ben,' he said. He was smiling. 'Get in the van.'

'No way.'

He raised the barrel of the gun towards me. 'Just get in.'

I looked around. Where the fuck were the police? They should be storming out right now, a dozen of them at least, guns trained on this man, shouting at him to drop his weapon and get on the ground.

'What's the matter, Ben? Are you expecting someone?'

I backed away. Imogen had assured me that the Viper didn't want to shoot me. That would go against his whole MO. He wanted to get me into the van, take me to my happy place, inject me with morphine. But I wasn't sure if I believed this. Not right now.

I stared into his eyes. Last time I'd seen him he'd been drenched, his hair stuck to his head, and the whole scene had been frantic and surreal. This was my first chance to get a proper look at him. He was young, at least a decade younger than me, probably more. He was tall and slim, with a strong jaw. His sandy hair stuck up, ruffled by the breeze that blew across the countryside. He reminded me of a young farmer or rural labourer.

'I'm getting bored,' he said. He had a local accent, a country burr. Levelling the shotgun at me, he moved closer.

Suddenly, I became convinced the police weren't here. I was on my own. I glanced up the lane in the direction Imogen should have been coming in. She had abandoned me.

Rowland strode towards me.

I walked backwards, glancing over my shoulder.

'They're going to get you,' I said, my hatred of this arsehole giving me strength. 'They know who you are. They know everything, Craig.'

He smiled. 'Yeah. They think they know.'

He raised the shotgun.

'Drop your weapon!'

I threw myself to the ground, as Imogen had instructed, and suddenly armed police officers were everywhere, rising from the long grass behind the farmhouse, pushing their way out of the house itself, emerging from the barn, and they surrounded the man who wanted me dead, a dozen guns pointed at him, a dozen voices demanding that he lay down his weapon, give himself up.

He remained frozen, only his eyes moving, left and right. His expression was weirdly impassive. He wasn't scared. The sun was in my eyes so I might have been mistaken, but he looked faintly amused.

He dropped the shotgun on the ground and in the next moment the cops swarmed over him, grabbing him and pushing him face first to the floor.

I pushed myself into a sitting position, breathing hard, and when I looked up, Imogen was running towards us across the adjacent field. She hurdled the fence and glanced at me as she ran past, but her focus was on the huddle of cops on the ground. They parted and one of the armed cops pulled their handcuffed prisoner to his feet. Rowland appraised the panting Imogen coolly, watching her as she struggled to get her breath back.

'Congratulations,' he said in a smarmy voice, and from the look on her face I thought Imogen was going to punch him.

Instead she said, 'Craig Rowland, I'm arresting you for the murders of Danni Taylor, Nathan Scott, Fiona Redbridge . . .'

I tuned out, closed my eyes and got to my feet. A huge wave of relief washed over me. I was alive. I was okay.

They'd got him.

I pushed away the voice that told me it had been too easy.

Chapter 50

The sense of triumph that had accompanied Imogen back to the station while following the black van in which Craig Rowland was being transported didn't take long to evaporate.

Now, as evening drew in, Imogen looked through the one-way glass into the interview room. The offender sat stiff-backed by the table, handcuffed, a uniform watching him from the corner.

'Is he still not talking?' Emma asked, joining her.

'No. The bastard hasn't uttered a word.'

'Not even to ask for a lawyer?'

'Nope. Not a single word has passed his lips. The only time he's opened his mouth is when we took a cheek scraping for DNA. I want to shake him. We need him to tell us where Janet Burgess is, if she's still alive. Adrian Morrow and Eileen Rowland, too. I also want him to confess to poisoning Alan.'

They both knew there was little chance Janet was still breathing. But Eileen? If she was his adoptive mother, there was a sliver of hope that he'd hidden her away somewhere.

'And I want to know why,' Imogen continued. '*Why* he did it. There's something else, too – what he said to Ben. "They think they know." What did he mean by that?' There was another question, as well. Where had he come from, this man with no history? They had been through all the reports of missing children from the appropriate timeframe and hadn't found any who could be him.

Inside the room, Rowland turned towards the glass and his lips curled upwards. It was hot in the interview room and the offender's sandy-coloured hair stuck to his forehead. He stared into the glass with sleepy, heavy-lidded eyes.

'He makes my flesh crawl,' Emma said.

'He just makes me want to throttle him. Where's the duty solicitor?' Imogen asked.

'On her way.'

Cally Johnston, the duty solicitor, arrived ten minutes later, more ruffled than usual, with pink spots on her cheeks. The prospect of representing the Shropshire Viper, at least temporarily, had clearly excited her. It irritated Imogen. The Viper was a celebrity. With his youthful looks, she could imagine him being inundated with mail from desperate women once he was in prison. She could also see how his innocent appearance might have helped him lure at least two of his victims into the open.

Cally went into the interview room first, to introduce herself. Imogen watched them confer through the one-way glass, then went in.

Rowland studied her, seemingly amused. Oh, how she would love to slap that smirk off his face.

She went through the motions of starting the tape and announcing who was present, the time, et cetera.

'Are you ready to talk to us yet?' she asked.

He smiled.

'Where's Janet Burgess, Craig? Have you killed her?'

He raised an eyebrow.

'And what about Eileen Rowland? And Adrian Morrow? We know you set him up. You posed as him too; told Michael Stone that your name was Adrian.'

He gestured for his solicitor to lean towards him and whispered in her ear.

'What did he say?' Imogen demanded.

'He said he needs to visit the toilet.'

'Oh, for God's sake.'

When Rowland returned from his visit to the bathroom, he said something else into his solicitor's ear.

Cally ran a hand through her hair. 'He says he has something for you. Something that will explain everything. He's willing to tell you what it is on one condition.'

Imogen looked directly at Craig. 'What is this condition?'

He spoke into Cally's ear again and her eyes widened with shock. 'I'm not repeating that.'

'What did he say?'

'I can't—'

'Just tell me, for God's sake.'

'He said the condition is that you show him your tits.'

It took all of her mental strength not to leap across the desk and punch him. Instead, she silently counted to five and then said, 'You're wasting my time. It's over, Craig. Come on, tell me. Make it easier for yourself.'

He leaned towards his solicitor. What the hell was he playing at? Why wouldn't he speak to them directly? The little shit was still playing games.

Cally's eyes had widened again. 'He said you need to look in the van.'

ω

Thirty minutes later, during which Imogen had paced so much her knees ached, one of the forensics guys came in holding something in a gloved hand. He opened his palm. A USB stick.

'We found it hidden in a compartment in the back.'

She snatched it from him and rushed to the incident room, plugging it into a computer that she had disconnected from the network, just in case this was a trick, with the stick containing a nasty virus.

She opened the folder that appeared on the desktop. There was a single audio file in the folder. She clicked 'Play'.

There was the sound of someone clearing their throat, and then a voice familiar from TV said, 'This is Michael Stone, reporting for *No Stone Unturned*.'

There was a scratching noise before Stone continued in a shaky voice. 'I'm here with the man the media have dubbed the Shropshire Viper. He has . . . he has agreed to give me an exclusive interview.'

Chapter 51

'So you're sure it's okay for Ollie to stay with me for a few days longer?' Megan asked, her voice small through the phone.

'Of course. Like I said, he'll enjoy it. And it'll be good for you, too.'

'Thanks, Ben.' She fell quiet and I was about to say goodbye when she said, 'Listen, I'm so sorry about everything that happened. About us . . .'

I sighed. 'Meg, you don't need to keep apologising. It's all fine. *I'm* fine.'

'That's . . . good. But if you want to talk, talk about us, I mean, have a proper conversation about . . . everything . . .'

I took a deep breath. 'We don't need to have a conversation about it, Meg. We'll always have Ollie, always be his mum and dad, but you and me, that's over. We can't go back.'

'I ruined it.'

'No. Well, it's not that straightforward, is it? I see that now. It must have been broken already, or you wouldn't have done what you did.'

I could hear her breathing. I wondered if she was crying.

Through the front window, I saw Kyle's van pull up. He sat there for a minute, staring into space, then got out and walked up the front path. He must have felt my eyes burning into him as he glanced over and waved before going inside.

'Relationships run their course, Meg. Marriages don't survive by magic. I probably didn't do enough, took you for granted, whatever. I don't want to go over it all again. I just want to move on. I want us both to move on. I'm not saying we're going to be best friends, but we can be civil.'

'I've got to go,' she said. 'Ollie's come into the room and his ears are flapping.'

I laughed. 'Okay. So, I'll come and fetch him on Monday.'

'See you then.'

I ended the call feeling curiously light. I drifted into the kitchen, unsure what to do with myself. It was weird being in the house by myself at night. I opened the back door and went out into the garden. It was a beautiful evening, the sky clear and glowing with stars, and for the first time in goodness knows how long, I felt free. No one to look after. No one to answer to. No hidden police around the cottage, keeping an eye on me.

I re-entered the house. It still smelled of the lager that had sprayed me and the sofa the night before. I wanted to call Imogen, ostensibly to ask if there had been any progress, but not much time had elapsed since my last call. It was niggling at me – what Rowland had said about the police not knowing everything. Imogen had tried to reassure me, telling me it was almost certainly bullshit.

As I was deciding what to do, I heard a bang. I stopped. Had it come from above? Surely Kyle wasn't in the loft again. That was something I needed to get sorted out. I'd have to talk to Frank about it.

I waited for a moment, but there were no other noises. Deciding I was being paranoid, I went to the fridge and grabbed a much-needed beer. Why worry? Rowland was in custody. I was finally safe.

Chapter 52

Imogen called the rest of the team into the incident room before listening to any more of the recording.

'Why aren't you in that interview room?' Greene was sweaty and red-faced. 'I've had the Commissioner on the phone wanting to know what the blazes is going on.'

What the blazes? Imogen assumed Greene had used his posh voice to talk to the Commissioner and hadn't switched back into normal mode yet.

Imogen clicked 'Play' and realised she was holding her breath. What else would be on the recording? She had clicked back to the beginning so the assembled cops could hear the whole thing.

Stone's voice, as he introduced himself, was wobbly, dry, a shadow of his normal, brash self.

'Sounds like he's reading from a script,' Greene said.

Imogen agreed. She had been in that cold basement, could picture the scene. Stone, seated at the rickety table, opposite the killer, a script between them. Emma began to speak and Imogen hit 'Pause'.

'Do you think that's why he abducted Stone? So he could be interviewed?'

'No. I'm certain he abducted and killed Stone because of his relationship with Ben's wife. This must have been a . . . well, a bonus.'

'Let's just listen to it, shall we?' Greene said.

Imogen hit 'Play' again.

'First of all, would you like to start by telling us about yourself?' Stone said.

There was a long, tense silence and then a voice said, 'Yes, I would, Michael.' Something about his voice made her ears prick up. But she was too intent on listening to what he had to say to think about it.

'Let's see . . . I've lived here, at the Homestead, for a long time. But I wasn't born here. I was a runaway, a foundling, you could say.' He chuckled. 'A kind woman found me wandering in the woods, took me in and cared for me.'

'Eileen Rowland,' Imogen said quietly.

'That woman educated me. I don't mean in maths and reading and all of that stuff. I'm talking about ancient wisdom. Philosophy.'

'Here we go,' said Greene, rolling his eyes.

There was a pause in the recorded action, then Michael said, 'Oh. Sorry. Um . . . Do you want to tell us about that? About your philosophy?'

Imogen could picture Rowland nodding and settling back in his seat. 'I am a student of Epicurus. Your viewers may not have heard of him, so I will give you a brief outline for those too lazy to look it up online.'

He went on to outline who Epicurus was, his life and death, talking for five minutes about ancient Greece and how the philosopher had set up his own school, called The Garden, and attracted followers. Imogen could sense Greene growing impatient, but she found it fascinating. She wanted to understand why Rowland killed, what drove him.

'Epicurus taught us many essential lessons. But the most important ones are these. One, we should not fear the gods. They will not punish us for our bad actions. It is down to us humans to seek justice, to carry out punishment. When I first heard that, I wanted to go back and kill my father. He was an evil man. A cruel, violent bastard who tortured my mother, who made her and my life a living torment. But my father was already dead. It was too late for me to seek justice.'

There was a silence before he continued. 'I can't tell you how angry that made me. It consumed me. He wasn't around to take his punishment. And I'm not exaggerating when I tell you this, Michael, I lost my mind for a while back then. But others, well, they lost more than their minds.' A grim laugh. 'The first seven or eight I killed—'

'Sweet Jesus,' Greene said, as everyone in the room exchanged glances. Imogen shushed them, but had missed a little of what Rowland said.

'But do you know what? It didn't make me feel better. Less angry, for a while. But not better.'

'What about the second essential lesson?' Michael asked, a catch in his throat. Imogen guessed he was deviating from the script.

'I'm glad you asked that. Because it was this that taught me that my rage was harming me, that I needed to let it go.' There was another long pause, a click and a brief burst of white noise. Perhaps he had edited this part of the audio. 'Happiness. That is what life is about. And do you and your viewers know what creates happiness?'

'Please tell us.'

'The first thing is the absence of pain – in the soul, but also in the body. I . . . she taught me how modern medicine could be used to eradicate physical pain.'

Imogen paused the recording again. 'He's edited it there. He didn't say "I". He started to say "Eileen", I bet you. He was being careful. Maybe he hadn't decided yet if he was going to kill Michael.' The room was silent, all eyes on Imogen. 'Eileen taught him about using medicine. Eileen, the painkiller addict. What we don't know is if she took morphine to try to achieve this state of happiness or if she chose her philosophy to justify her addiction.'

'The whole thing sounds out of whack to me,' Emma said. 'I've been reading up on Epicurus, ever since we found out that was the name he used to communicate with Ollie. I thought it might give us some insight.'

Imogen was surprised but pleased. If she hadn't been so busy looking out for Ben, she would have done the same.

'It seems massively simplified,' Emma continued, 'like he got it out of some pocket guide to philosophy.'

'He probably did.' Imogen started the audio again.

'As well as the absence of pain,' the man went on, 'we achieve happiness through tranquillity and freedom from fear and worries. Combine those things and you can achieve a kind of immortal state. You become a god among men. And then I thought about my mother . . . the way she lived her life. In constant pain from the injuries my father inflicted upon her. The opposite of happy. Fearful all the time. Not just sad, but *wretched*. And that's when it came to me – one night, after the woman who took me in gave me some of her medicine – how I could make amends for my failure to save my mum from my dad. It was blissfully simple and direct. I could seek out good people who were suffering and make them happy.'

'And kill them?' Michael Stone asked. He was definitely deviating from the script now.

'Yes, Michael.' The killer didn't sound annoyed at this deviation. 'What better time to die than when we are at our happiest? To be fulfilled, free from worries and pain. It is almost impossible for all but the most enlightened of us to maintain that state. So Danni, Nathan and Fiona. I made their lives perfect. I made them happy. And I sent them from this world in a state of bliss.'

There was a pause. 'I couldn't save my mother. But I saved them.'

'You're a fucking psycho,' Michael said.

There was a muffled thump and the recording stopped.

'It's all twisted,' Emma said. 'His idea of happiness, I mean. Epicurus didn't—'

'All right, all right.' Greene cut her off. 'We don't need to know exactly how this arsehole has muddled up his philosophy lessons. There's nothing new here. Send it to the CPS and get back in that room, find out where the fuck those missing people are. And I want him to go down for DC Hatton's death, too. That's the most important thing of all.'

He left the room, and the others followed, leaving Imogen alone with Emma.

Imogen was deep in thought. There was something about the tape, about the voice, that was bugging her.

'Come on, let's go and talk to the bastard.'

Chapter 53

The police will have listened to my interview with Michael by now. How I wish I could be there, in that room, to see their reactions.

Next time I see DI Imogen Evans, I know there will be new respect in her eyes. And maybe understanding, too. I believe she is intelligent and open-minded enough to realise that I am not an evil man.

Yes, she is a servant of the law, and I have broken these modern laws many times. I know I will be punished.

And that's fine.

I'm worried about Eileen though. How will she cope? I am already concerned about her, alone in her little flat. I left a decent supply of Jasper's heroin behind, and I showed her how to prepare and inject it. I cooked up another batch too. Everything is ready.

'Why? Where are you going?' she asked, opening her heavy eyes.

'There's something I need to do,' I replied, stroking the papery skin of her cheek. 'I will be going away for a while.'

She was so dosed up, she accepted this news calmly.

'But you'll come back?' she said.

I kissed her forehead. 'I love you. Thank you for saving me.'

Chapter 54

Imogen played the recording to Craig Rowland. His eyes sparkled while Cally sat there with an open mouth. She was used to representing drug users and the occasional shoplifter. This was way out of her league.

'Where are your real parents? Where did you come from? We're going through all our missing children reports, Craig. We'll find where you came from. Find out who your real mum was. You say you did all this to make amends for not saving her. If she was a good woman, she'd be appalled. Ashamed of you.'

He rolled his eyes.

'Or maybe it was all Eileen's fault. It sounds like she filled your head with nonsense. All this crazy talk about Epicurus. Why don't you tell me, Craig? Explain it? Perhaps the jury will understand. After all, you didn't want to *hurt* anyone, did you?'

He stared back, that irritating little smile playing on his lips. This was unbelievably frustrating, like dealing with a three-year-old.

'I thought you wanted to spread happiness? You're not making me very happy right now. Go on, Craig. I want you to make me feel blissful.'

Nothing.

She changed tack. 'I bet your birth name wasn't Craig, was it? You look more like a Kenneth to me. Or, no, a Dave or an Adam. Something ordinary. Boring and common. Adam Smith.'

He showed her his dirty, yellow teeth. He didn't appear to ever have been to a dentist.

'Oh, fuck this,' Imogen said, switching off the tape machine and getting up from the table.

'Soon,' he said.

She turned back. 'What did you say?'

He was still staring at the space where she'd sat. 'Soon,' he said again, in a whisper. And then he made a zipping motion over his lips and dropped his head to stare at the table. A shudder ran down her spine.

Imogen instructed the uniform outside the door to take Craig back to his cell, then found Emma waiting for her outside the interview room. The DS fell into step beside her as she strode towards the empty incident room.

Once inside, Imogen said, 'There's something not right.'

'What do you mean?'

'The voice on the recording. Listen.' She opened the laptop and hit 'Play'.

'I've lived here, at the Homestead, for a long time. But I wasn't born here. I was a runaway, a foundling, you could say.'

Imogen paused it. 'How old would you say Craig is?'

'I don't know. Twenty-eight? Twenty-nine?'

'Late twenties, definitely. The voice on this recording sounds older, wouldn't you say?'

Emma pondered this. 'It's hard to tell.'

Imogen paced the floor. 'Craig spoke a minute ago. Only a single word, repeated twice. But the voice sounds different. And I'm sure I've heard that voice before . . . recently.'

'I think you're trying to make it more complicated than it is. We've got him.'

'He told Ben that we don't know everything. What did he mean by that?'

'I don't know. Do you want a coffee? I need one.'

'Sure.'

Emma left and Imogen returned to the audio. She needed to get it analysed. If only Rowland hadn't waited until she turned off the tape machine before he spoke, though she was sure he'd done it deliberately, and that made her even more suspicious.

Because if the voice on this recording did not belong to Craig . . . that meant . . .

That meant there were two of them.

Oh fuck . . .

She jumped up from her seat, grabbed her phone and dialled. If Rowland wasn't acting alone, Ben was still in danger. It was just before eleven. Ben should still be up. But he wasn't answering.

Two of them. There were two of them. Rowland – and someone else. The man on the tape. Was that why the offender at the church had been wearing a balaclava even though his face was all over the TV and he'd already been seen by Ollie?

Was that why Rowland had allowed himself to be caught? So they'd stop guarding Ben?

She sucked in air.

This was not over.

Ben was not safe.

'Come on, come on.'

He still wasn't answering. Maybe he *was* in bed. He hadn't slept much last night. He must be tired. No need to assume the worst.

Except . . .

She barrelled through the control room doors and grabbed the duty inspector, Phil Kane. 'I need an officer, no two officers, to go to Ben Hofland's place, check he's okay and report back to me.'

'What? Haven't we got the—'

She didn't let him finish. 'Just do it. *Now*. I'll explain later.'

She hurried from the room and trotted down one corridor then another until she reached the cells, where she asked the custody sergeant to open Rowland's.

Craig lay on the bunk. She stood over him, casting a shadow across his body.

'There are two of you,' she said.

He smiled as he sat up, then clapped, slowly and mockingly.

She couldn't help herself. She grabbed him by the front of his shirt and pushed him up against the wall. He didn't resist. With her face two inches from his, so she could smell his rank breath, she demanded, 'Who is he? *Where* is he?'

'What time is it?'

She took a step back. His voice was definitely not the one on that recording. It was lighter, clearly younger. But his question had thrown her.

'Come on, Imogen,' he said with a sneer. 'Don't *you* go silent on *me*. It must be, what, eleven o'clock?'

She pushed him again, holding on to the front of his shirt, her face inches from his. 'Tell me where he is.'

'If it's eleven, he'll be with Ben right now,' he replied. His breath was warm and stale. 'It's too late, Imogen. By the time you get there, it will all be over.'

She let go of him and pushed the door open. As she was about to leave, Rowland spoke to her. She turned round.

He wore a sickening grin. 'You made Ben happy, DI Evans. Laughing away together, so happy, so at ease.' He clapped his hands together. 'It's because of you that Ben is ready. Happy enough to die.'

Chapter 55

It was quarter to eleven and I wanted to talk to Imogen. I weighed my phone in my hand, trying to come up with a good reason to call her until, finally, common sense gave me a slap. What was wrong with me? I was acting like a love-struck teenager.

But I couldn't stop thinking about her.

Was it possible that something could happen between us? I remembered what she'd said the night before, after we'd calmed down. *Not now. Maybe when this is all over.*

I was a witness. By 'all over' I had to assume she meant when the court case was finished and Rowland was in jail. But how long would that take? A year?

Maybe that was a good thing. It would give me time to sort my life out, find work, get Ollie properly settled here. And if Imogen was still interested in a year's time – because I was pretty sure I would be – then we could give it a go. Even just the idea of it gave me something to look forward to.

I yawned. I had hardly slept the last two nights, and though I was tempted to stay up, drink beer and watch TV, I knew I should be sensible and go to bed.

I went into the bedroom and plugged my phone in beside the bed, then went into the bathroom to clean my teeth. I thought about

Imogen again, remembering how we'd laughed together, the way she'd tucked a strand of that glorious red hair behind her ear after we'd got a hold of ourselves. I pictured her sitting in my kitchen at the table, drinking coffee. I imagined her in my bed, lying beneath the duvet in just her underwear, smiling up at me as I crossed the room towards her . . .

I spat out the toothpaste. Maybe I should take a cold shower before getting into my lonely bed. Laughing at myself, and yawning again, I came out of the bathroom into the dark hallway.

Someone grabbed me from behind.

Shocked, I fought to pull free, but my assailant was too strong. He had one arm around my throat, pressing against my windpipe, and was twisting my arm up behind my back with his other hand, sending white shards of pain into my shoulder. The more I struggled, the more he twisted my arm. Blinding pain immobilised me. From my bedroom I heard my phone start to ring and finally fall silent as my voicemail kicked in.

The intruder pushed me face first against the wall and whispered into my ear. 'Don't fight it, Ben. It's all good.'

I recognised the voice, but couldn't place it. As he relaxed the pressure on my arm, I tried to turn my head, to see his face. He shoved me harder against the wall.

'I said, don't fight it. Relax, Ben. It's all going to be fine.'

How had he got in? The front door was double locked, as was the door that led into the kitchen from the garden. All the windows were secure and I hadn't heard any glass smash. All I'd heard was that thump earlier.

That was it. He'd come through the loft.

Kyle. Was it him? I tried again to twist my head, but he held it in place.

'It's your lucky day, Ben,' he said. 'You're going to die happy. Isn't that what everyone dreams of? To leave this world peacefully?'

I struggled again, but he had hold of both of my arms now, my face pressed against the wallpaper.

'Stop it,' he said, like someone trying to calm a frightened animal. 'Don't spoil it.'

I struggled until he increased the pressure on my arm, twisting it and sending fresh, white spasms of pain into my shoulder. I gasped and stopped struggling.

'Relax,' he said in a soft voice. 'I don't want to hurt you.'

I felt metal against my wrists, then two clicks. He had handcuffed me. He let go and put a hand on the back of my neck, pushing me along the corridor towards the stairs. I threw myself forwards, trying to reach the stairs before him, but he tripped me and I fell on to my face. Unable to use my hands to protect myself, I was just able to turn my head in time, my cheek scraping against the carpet. A great weight struck my back and I realised he'd thrown himself on to me, straddling my back, pinning me in place beneath him. At the exact same moment, a light swept across the hallway window, accompanied by the sound of an engine – a car pulling up outside. He must have heard them coming, or seen the light before I did. The police?

'Help!' I yelled at the top of my voice, but he pushed my face to the floor, mashing my lips against the carpet.

In another moment, the doorbell rang. I struggled, trying to turn my head to see him, but he kept me pressed against the floor.

'Stop struggling or I'll fucking kill you right here, right now.'

I knew the voice well. Why couldn't I place it? I was panicking, unable to think straight. Was it Rowland? Had he escaped custody? I couldn't make sense of what was going on.

I let myself go limp, praying the police would bash the door down, come inside. But a minute later the car door opened and closed, and the engine started. I listened in despair as they drove away down the hill.

Chapter 56

Imogen sprinted into the control room and found the duty inspector, Phil Kane, as he was ending a radio call.

'Just had a call from the officers I sent to Hofland's place,' he said. 'They said there's one light on in an upstairs room, but they can't see or hear any signs of life.'

Imogen tried to control her breathing. 'Tell them to bash the door down. Ben Hofland's life is in danger.'

'But I thought—'

'There are two of them. And the guy we've got in a cell just told me his partner is going to murder Ben tonight.'

Kane got back on the radio immediately and instructed the two officers to do as Imogen had asked. Emma joined them, holding two mugs of coffee that she set down on the side.

A male voice crackled through the radio. 'But we don't have an enforcer.' That was the name given to the battering ram police used to force doors open.

Imogen grabbed the radio. 'Just kick the fucking door in! No, wait. The next-door neighbour on the right-hand side, Mrs Douglas – Ben told me she's got a spare key. Go and wake her up.'

There was a pause at the other end as Kane took the radio back.

'Sir?'

Kane sighed. 'Do it and get back to me immediately.'

Imogen chewed her nails as she waited, and tried to get through to Ben on his mobile again. It went straight to voicemail. She saw Ian walk past the room and gestured for him to join her and Kane.

'Are the rest of the team still at the pub?' she asked.

'I guess so.'

'Drunk and useless, I expect. Brilliant.' She quickly explained what was going on.

The officer she'd instructed to get the key from Mrs Douglas came back on the radio. 'We've got the key. We're going in now.'

The wait was agonising. Eventually, the officer said, 'There's nobody here. The house is empty.'

Imogen wanted to scream. She grabbed the receiver. 'Did you see any vehicles pass you as you approached the house?'

The two officers conferred and said no, they hadn't.

'He must have taken Ben before you got there.' She handed the receiver back to Kane again. 'Can you get me a trace on Ben's phone? And I need an armed unit, as many officers as you can lay your hands on. Medical backup, ready to deal with someone who's been given a morphine overdose. I know where he's taking him.'

'Where?'

There was a map of Shropshire pinned to the wall. Imogen's finger hovered over it as she searched for the location. She knew exactly where Ben would be taken.

'Here,' she said, jabbing the spot. 'His happy place.'

ᴔ

As she and Emma sped out of town, Imogen said, 'It's about fifteen miles to Ratlinghope. The others are going to have to catch up with us. He could be pumping Ben full of morphine right now. He's probably already done it.'

Imogen's phone beeped with an incoming message: Kane confirming that backup was on its way. At Imogen's estimation, driving at her current speed, she and Emma would beat the other police to the farm by at least ten minutes. But it had to be done. She couldn't risk waiting.

'Ratlinghope's the place Ben names as his happy place on his questionnaire, right?'

'Right. Have you ever been there?' Imogen drove fast, as the landscape around them became green and hilly. There were no streetlights here, and beyond the beam of Imogen's headlights it was pitch-black. There were no other cars on the road.

'Yeah, it's a beautiful place,' Emma said. 'I come walking here quite often.'

'Why? It's desolate. There's no one around for miles.'

'That's why I like it. Honestly, you live here now. This is your landscape.'

Imogen squinted at the dark road ahead, at the nothingness beyond. 'God help me.'

Emma prodded the screen of the satnav. 'Is this where we're going? The Stiperstones?'

'Yes. What is it exactly?'

'It's a hill. A quartzite ridge, to be precise. It's an impressive place.'

Imogen gripped the wheel tightly as something darted in front of them. A rabbit, barely escaping with its life.

'There's an interesting myth about the place,' Emma went on. 'There's an outcrop called the Devil's Chair. According to local legend, the Devil was carrying a load of rocks across Britain. He sat down here for a rest, and when he got up, the rocks tumbled out of his apron.'

'His *apron*?'

'Yes. And the Devil apparently still uses the outcrop as his chair, hence its name, but only on the longest night of the year.'

'Shame. We've missed that particular Devil.' Imogen concentrated on the winding road. 'Well done, Ben. Why couldn't you have chosen somewhere else as your happy place, eh? Like a nice, brightly lit shopping centre.'

Imogen's phone rang. She answered it via the hands-free system. It was Kane.

'Have you got a trace on Ben's phone?' she asked immediately.

'Yes, it's in his house. But listen, I've got a woman on the line. She called in, said she's just seen the Viper's picture on TV.'

'Phil, I've got other things to worry about right now.'

'Her name's Eileen Rowland.'

The hairs went up on the back of Imogen's neck. 'Put her through, but stay on the line. I want you to listen in. And put a trace on the call. We need to know where she is.'

There was a click as the call was transferred. She put the phone on speaker so Emma could hear, too.

'Hello? This is DI Imogen Evans. Is that Mrs Rowland?'

'Hello?' The line was terrible.

Imogen checked the screen of her phone and saw the signal was wavering between one and two bars. 'Mrs Rowland? Can you hear me?'

'Yes. I was just asking the police officer why you're saying these things on the telly.' She sounded woozy, spaced out, but angry, too. 'He would never hurt anyone.'

'You're talking about Craig Rowland?'

'Yes,' she snapped. 'I just told the other officer. He's my son. My beautiful boy. And I thought he was on holiday. He told me he was going travelling. Why are you saying these terrible things about him? That he's murdered people, that he's dangerous? Yes, he's always been a little . . . moody. Erratic. But we gave him a strict upbringing. A *moral* upbringing.'

We? Imogen would come back to that. 'Mrs Rowland, when did you adopt him?'

The old woman seemed confused. 'Craig? I didn't adopt him. He's mine.'

Imogen and Emma exchanged a surprised glance.

Eileen's voice had taken on a steely tone. 'Is that what he told people? That he was adopted? Too ashamed of his old mother, living alone in the woods like . . . like a witch, that's what he said to me once.'

Imogen interrupted her. 'Mrs Rowland, who is Craig's father?'

'His father? He . . .'

Eileen's voice broke up so Imogen couldn't hear what she said. She thumped the steering wheel in frustration. The signal came back and Imogen stopped the car, pulling over by the side of the road. It was pitch-black, the few stars dotted in the sky providing the only light.

Imogen concentrated. Eileen was halfway through a monologue. She sounded like she was drunk – or high on morphine, most likely.

'. . . He was my foundling. When he was nineteen . . . I shouldn't have done it, but . . .' The line broke up again. '. . . Shocked . . . pregnant.'

Imogen shook the phone, as if this would improve the signal. But it was no use.

Cursing with frustration, she restarted the engine and drove on into the darkness.

ω

They passed the village of Ratlinghope and headed out towards the Stiperstones, which, according to the map, was indeed very close to the Devil's Chair. The road was bumpy, severely testing the suspension on her beloved car, but that was the least of her worries right now.

As a policewoman, she had a duty of care for the public. She was here as a professional. It was her job to find Rowland's partner, to stop him and arrest him. Ensure justice was served.

But there was more to this case than that. Ever since she'd arrived in Shropshire and found herself thrown into this case, she had been obsessed with it. It filled her days and haunted her nights. The faces of the victims, their stories and the grief of those they'd left behind haunted her. Every time the killer struck, every time he got away, it was like a personal affront, especially when Alan Hatton had been killed.

And there was yet more to it, if she was honest with herself. She couldn't admit it to any of her colleagues, but she cared about Ben. He wasn't just a civilian she needed to protect. Something had happened between them when she'd stayed at his house – a spark – that had caused him to keep creeping into her thoughts in idle moments. She wasn't the kind of woman who got crushes or butterflies in her stomach over a man. At least, she never had been. But she knew if anything happened to Ben now, she would be devastated.

And she would blame herself.

She could now see The Devil's Chair, its dark, jagged silhouette like giant shark teeth rotting against the blue-black sky. She flicked the headlights on to full beam and turned the car slowly so that they swept over the land.

Nothing.

She stopped the car and turned it off. She and Emma got out and jogged towards the hill, holding torches.

'Ben?' she called. Then, 'Whoever's there, this is Detective Inspector Evans. It's not too late to stop this.'

Her words were swallowed by the night.

'They're not here,' Emma said.

She was right. There were no vehicles. There was nobody here, just a cluster of sheep grazing on the hillside. As she and Emma looked around, the backup vehicles arrived, rolling to a halt beside Imogen's car. Wind whistled eerily across the nature reserve.

'Then where the hell are they?' Imogen asked.

Chapter 57

As soon as the police gave up ringing my bell and left, the man who had handcuffed me hauled me to my feet and said, 'Stay quiet.'

I definitely recognised his voice. And I knew it wasn't the man I'd saved from the river, the man who'd pointed a gun at me. This man's voice was older. I twisted my head so I could see into the mirror that hung at the end of the hallway. The only light in the hall came from the bathroom, but it was enough for me to see the shape of the man who had hold of me. He was stocky, dressed in black – and wearing a balaclava.

'Who are—?'

'Shut up,' he muttered darkly. His head was cocked, like he was straining to listen. He must have been concerned about the police coming back. While he wasn't concentrating fully on me, I kicked out at him, catching him on the thigh. He staggered backwards and I tried to run into the bedroom, but he was too fast. He grabbed my arms and pushed me up against the wall again.

He reached up and opened the hatch to the loft. All I could think about was how I'd caught Kyle in the loft and my stomach went cold. My next-door neighbour? The guy who I still remembered from years before, hanging around the river, trying to chat up tourists. Was he involved in this? A friend of Rowland's? In a flash, I remembered:

Imogen had told me that the person who set Adrian up must have known him. And Adrian and Kyle were friends. I had seen them exchanging a complicated handshake.

Were there two of them working together? Craig Rowland – *and Kyle?*

I had no time to work it out, as he pulled the metal ladder down and gave it a shake to ensure it was locked in place. I thought about running, but how far would I get with my arms secured behind my back? I was sure the police would be back, hopefully with reinforcements, and the intruder must have thought the same because he hauled me to my feet and said, 'Climb.'

'No way.'

He grabbed me between the legs and squeezed. Pain ripped through my body, settling in my stomach. My eyes filled with tears.

'Want me to ask again?'

He shoved me towards the metal steps. After struggling up them without the use of my arms and toppling face first into the loft, I rolled and kicked out at the open hatch from my side, trying to slam it on him, but he was too quick. Then I tried to kick his covered face as his head appeared through the gap, but he blocked my foot, hissing with irritation. Moments later, he pulled the ladder up behind him and shut the hatch. He flicked the switch and the space filled with light.

'You're starting to piss me off,' he said, standing hunched over me. The loft's ceiling wasn't high enough for either of us to stand up straight. I looked around for something to use against him, but I hadn't lived here long enough to accumulate much junk. The loft was empty apart from a couple of suitcases, a box of DVDs and some camping equipment. There would be metal tent poles among that equipment, but there was no chance of me finding them, let alone using them, unless I could get these handcuffs off.

'My shoulder's cramping,' I tried.

He looked around us. 'I bet you forgot that the lofts were adjoined.'

'How could I have forgotten?' I said. 'I caught you up here a few weeks ago.'

He stared at me through the holes in the balaclava, and then he laughed.

'Who do you think I am, Ben?' he asked. 'Not that fucking loser next door? I'm offended.'

He laughed again, and reached up to pull off the balaclava.

ʊ

'*Frank?*'

He grunted.

Frank Dodd, my landlord, the old friend of the family? Hope flared in me. This must be a mistake. Frank couldn't be a murderer.

'I believe you met my son earlier,' he said. 'Good-looking boy, isn't he? Just like his old dad.'

'What? Craig? Craig's your son?' My mind spun in wild circles for a moment before finding a place to land. 'Is that what this is about?' It was the only thing that made sense. Frank was planning on taking me hostage to try to persuade the police to let Craig – his son! – go. 'The police will never let him go, Frank. Whatever you do.'

He laughed. He was pale, sweating with exertion, his quiff flattened by the balaclava.

'You still haven't got a bloody clue, have you?' he said. 'Craig's not getting out. Not ever. But that doesn't matter. Because I'm here, and so are you. And we're the only ones who matter.'

'You're the Viper,' I said, hardly able to believe the words that came out of my mouth.

He frowned. 'Can't say I'm keen on that nickname. Makes me sound like some bloody superhero.'

Frank was the Viper and Craig had been helping him. I struggled to process this new truth. The police had been fooled. We had all been fooled.

And I was going to die.

Perhaps if I made enough noise, it would alert Mrs Douglas and Kyle. Perhaps Kyle would come up into the loft, see what was going on. Yeah, and get himself killed.

A few feet behind Frank was the hatch that led into Ross and Shelley's house.

His plan was clearly to take me into that cottage, where the police wouldn't look for me. I needed to slow him down, keep him talking.

'What happened with Ross and Shelley?' I asked.

He barked out a laugh. 'It was a shame about Ross. I liked him. I didn't actually expect Shelley to kill him. I thought she'd chuck him out and then she wouldn't be able to afford the rent on her own, so I'd be able to chuck *her* out.'

'And you had the dog's vocal cords cut?'

'That's right.' He knelt beside me. 'I put this boarding in myself. Did a good job, didn't I?'

Beneath us, I heard the front door bang open. The police! It had to be.

But before I could shout out Frank put one hand over my mouth and the other on my balls, indicating with his eyes that if I made a noise he would squeeze. Hard.

'I'll come back for Ollie, too,' he whispered. He didn't need to threaten. He was kneeling on my legs now, my arms pinned behind me. I couldn't move, couldn't make a sound.

I listened helplessly as the police – it sounded like there were two of them – moved about below us, searching the house. After a few minutes, one of them, standing directly beneath us, said, 'There's nobody here. The house is empty.'

I listened to their footsteps as they went back down the stairs. Shortly after that, I heard their car engine and the sound of them driving away.

Frank let go of my testicles and removed his hand from my mouth. He grinned. 'Bet you wish it was Imogen touching you down there, eh? Can't say I blame you. She's lush.'

'You're an arsehole,' I said.

He crouched beside me. 'Come on, Ben. There's no need to be aggressive.' His voice had softened to a croon. 'When you're leaving this world, I want you to picture her, Imogen. Picture her making love to you. That soft skin, that lovely ginger hair caressing you, her nice tight—'

I kicked out again, striking his legs, and he lost his balance, falling on to the hatch and banging his head against one of the wooden beams that ran diagonally from floor to rooftop. He lay still for a second and I managed to get to my feet and run, Quasimodo-like, towards the hatch into Mrs Douglas's cottage. But I couldn't open it without my hands.

Frank pushed himself into a sitting position. I stamped on the floor, called out, kicked the wall. I tried to jump on the boards, thinking my body weight might break them, that plummeting through the ceiling would be an acceptable escape method. But it didn't work. Frank was upon me then, grabbing me by the throat and hissing at me to shut up. I tried to headbutt him but he dodged me, then punched me in the face. My nose crunched and blood splattered us both.

He kneed me in the groin and I dropped to the floor, curling into a ball.

Frank was panting. 'You stupid twat,' he muttered.

I watched as he returned to the hatch into my cottage and opened it. Then he came back for me and dragged me, his hands in my armpits, back across the loft and pushed me head first through the opening.

I landed on the carpet beneath, shoulders striking the floor a split second before my head. The world went white. When I came to, after what must have only been a few seconds, Frank was standing over me. My head throbbed, I was sure my nose was broken and I snuffled blood. Worse than all that was the pain in my balls.

Frank grabbed me and pulled me to my feet, then dragged me down the stairs and into the kitchen. He opened the back door and peered out. I prayed that Kyle would have heard the commotion, but there was no sign of him.

Frank hauled me to my feet and pulled me into the garden. His van was parked in the cul-de-sac behind the cottage. He pushed me through the back gate.

'Where are you taking me?' I asked as he unlocked the back of the van.

He smiled. 'Your happy place is out of bounds,' he said. 'So we're going to mine.'

Chapter 58

Imogen had broken the speed limit in her Pagoda plenty of times before, but had never really pushed it to its limits. Now, as she left the dark countryside behind and hit the main road that led to Ironbridge, she floored the accelerator, roaring past a Land Rover that was doing seventy, thankful the roads were so quiet at this time of night. They were heading back to Ben's, to try to pick up the trail from the only place where they knew he'd been that night. When she hit a hundred she became aware of the bodywork vibrating around her. Emma had gone white. But Imogen couldn't slow down.

The other police vehicles and the ambulance were behind her, sirens wailing, unable to keep up.

As she drove, she talked, her thoughts and sentences coming out in staccato bursts.

'Eileen Rowland said Craig was her son. So who was his father?' They had tried to call Eileen back, but she wasn't answering. Right now, Phil Kane was trying to trace the call. 'What did she say? *He was my foundling.* She must have been talking about Craig's dad. A boy she took in . . . And then he got her pregnant. When he was eighteen. That's what she said.'

'So Craig's dad must be about fifty,' Emma said.

'The voice from the interview was about that age. Oh my God. Craig's partner is his father.'

Her mobile rang. It was Phil Kane.

'We've traced the call from Eileen Rowland. It came from an address in Shrewsbury, on the southern outskirts of town. The flat belongs to Dodd's Property Manage—'

Imogen interrupted him. 'That's it! How did I not get it?'

Emma stared at her with alarm. 'Get what?'

'The voice on the recording. I've heard it before. I've met him. He owns Ben's house, and the place next door. And now we know he owns the place where Eileen Rowland's living. Frank Dodd.'

'The landlord? The one with the cowboy boots?'

'It's him. He's got Ben.'

Imogen drove into the road where Ben lived. It was half past midnight. She pulled up outside Ben's address and she and Emma got out of the car. The lights were off in both of the houses on either side of Ben's. They strode towards Ross and Shelley's old place and Imogen hammered on the door. There was no response.

Imogen turned to see an upstairs light come on in Mrs Douglas's house. A face appeared at the window and a minute later Mrs Douglas came through her front door, wearing a heavy dressing gown.

'I heard shouting,' she said. 'All sorts of crashing and banging. Sounded like it was coming from the loft.'

'What? When?'

'About an hour ago. I was going to get Kyle to check it out, but the silly sod was drunk and wouldn't wake up.'

Imogen marched up to her, Emma following. 'I need the spare key,' Imogen said.

'I don't have it,' Mrs Douglas said. 'Those policemen didn't bring it back.'

'Oh, for God's sake.'

At that moment, the police convoy rolled on to the road led by the black van, with the ambulance at the rear. The head of the armed unit, DS Ludwig, jumped down and Imogen rushed to him. She briefed him hurriedly.

'So we think he's in there?' Ludwig asked.

'Yes. We need to hurry.'

Ludwig barked orders to his team of half a dozen officers, the same men and women who had apprehended Craig at the abandoned farm. They approached the cottage silently while Emma ushered Mrs Douglas back into her own home. DS Ludwig stood to the right of Ben's front door. He gave the order and one of his men swung the enforcer at the door, bursting it open, and they went in. Imogen hovered outside the door, sweating with anxiety.

Unable to wait any longer, she entered the house, ran upstairs and found armed officers standing around a metal ladder that led down from the loft. One of them poked his head through the hatch.

'All clear.'

Imogen ran back down to the ground floor. Outside, Ludwig was ordering more officers to break down the front door of Ross and Shelley's former cottage. Imogen waited, but she knew Frank and Ben wouldn't be in there. She sank to her haunches on the front lawn and, unthinkingly, pulled a handful of poppies from the earth. She let out a howl of anguish and frustration, unaware she was doing so until she saw everyone staring at her. She dropped the flowers on to the lawn and got to her feet.

She marched to her car, got in and screeched away from the kerb, leaving Emma on the pavement, staring after her.

Chapter 59

The van doors opened with a bang and Frank climbed in, grabbing me beneath my arms and sliding me across the floor of the vehicle. He hauled me out, and I landed on the ground with a thump. With my arms still cuffed behind my back, it was impossible to run away or fight him. As he pulled me to my feet and began to march me forward, I tried to reason with him.

'Frank, come on, you don't want to do this. Ollie needs me.'

He appeared not to hear me. His eyes were fixed on a point in the near distance.

'I know you're a good man,' I tried, words tumbling over one another, my tongue thick and clumsy. 'You helped Ollie. I know that. You helped me. Maybe I can help you, too. Spare me and I'll be in your debt forever. I'll do whatever you want.'

He wasn't listening. He continued to push me forward.

It was so dark that it was difficult to make out where I was. It appeared to be a patch of overgrown wasteland on the edge of a wood. The ground was flat. The moon came out from behind a cloud and revealed a stream running along one side. Behind us, a wall of trees, standing silent in the darkness.

My own happy place, Frank had said. Where was that? In the back of the van, it had been impossible to see or tell where we were going, but the journey had lasted about half an hour, maybe slightly more.

Frank stopped, still holding on to me with one hand, and looked around. He nodded, seemingly satisfied, and told me to kneel.

I stayed still.

'Get on your knees,' he said.

Reluctantly, I obeyed. The cold concrete was choked with grass and damp, moisture seeping through my jeans.

Frank dropped into a crouch and unzipped the bag he was carrying. I knew what he was looking for.

This was my only chance. I had to act. Fuelled by rage and desperation, I sprang to my feet and kicked the bag so it flew from his grip, contents spewing out and scattering across the grass. As he rose I charged him, colliding with him while he was halfway up, sending both of us sprawling. His head hit the ground, momentarily dazing him.

In an instant I had jumped to my feet and begun running towards the line of trees. Running handcuffed is not easy, and I stumbled once, twice, but determination kept me upright.

I looked over my shoulder and saw him get up, start to run after me, then hesitate. He sprinted back to the van and stuck his head through the back doors. When he emerged, he was holding something long and straight. A shotgun. He ran after me, catching up with every stride.

I increased my pace, praying that I wouldn't trip, wouldn't fall.

Chapter 60

Emma had called Imogen as she sped towards Eileen Rowland's flat to tell her everything they had been able to find out about Frank Dodd in the short amount of time they'd had.

'We've got a birth certificate for a Francis Dodd, born 1967 to a Mary and William Dodd. According to the records, she died in 1980 and he died two years later. I found their marriage certificate – they were both agricultural workers.'

'Where did they live?'

'I can't find an address. But a lot of agricultural workers are itinerant – they go wherever the work is. A lot of them live in caravans or mobile homes. Anyway, that's all I can find on Frank until 1988, when he bought a property in Craven Arms. There's a newspaper article about him from a few years later, an interview in the *Star* about this young self-made man who was making a fortune buying wrecks and doing them up, renting them out. He's a well-respected member of the community now, has won all sorts of awards, there are various photos of him appearing at charity events. He's a member of the Rotary Club and is always on the Shropshire rich list. He's worth millions.'

'And his parents never reported him missing?'

'No. At least there's no record of it. I can't find any record of him going to school. I guess, officially, he was home-schooled. Systems were less strict in those days, so no one noticed when he went missing.'

Imogen would ask Eileen about that.

'Father and son, working together,' said Emma. 'It's going to be a nightmare, working out who did what.'

'The CPS can worry about that. My guess is that Frank committed all the murders and Craig helped out where he was needed. To be honest, I don't really care which of them did what. We need to find Frank. And Ben.'

Imogen, who had done ninety miles an hour all the way there, pressed the buzzer of Eileen's flat and waited. No response. She stepped back and looked up at the building, tapping her foot. There were no lights on inside. She pressed all the buzzers on the panel and waited until a sleepy voice said, 'Hello?'

'Police. I need to get into the building.'

The person she'd woken up buzzed her in and Imogen ran up three flights of stairs to flat nine. She hammered on the door. Again, there was no response. She banged again and pressed her ear to the door. She could hear someone moving around inside. She shouted through the letterbox, 'Eileen? It's the police. I need to talk to you urgently.' She paused and added, 'Frank's in trouble, Eileen.'

The door opened.

Imogen had been wondering where Eileen Rowland had been for so long, convinced for ages that she was dead, that she could hardly believe the woman standing before her in a long white nightgown was real. She looked like a Victorian ghost, and much older than her sixty-eight years. She was almost as pale as her nightgown and her hair stuck up like she'd been in bed for days. She was leaning heavily on a cane.

When she spoke, her voice was weak. 'What kind of trouble?'

Imogen pushed past her into the flat. It was small, a couple of armchairs in front of a TV, food congealing on a plate on the floor.

'I need to find him, Eileen,' she said, as the older woman limped over and slumped into her armchair. 'It's urgent. He's going to hurt someone if I don't.'

'When you do find him, send him here. He promised to bring me more medicine.'

'Morphine? Don't look so surprised. We know everything, Eileen. We've been to your house, found all the tablets. We've talked to your doctor.' The doctor who was going to be struck off for dishing out painkillers like candy. 'We'll arrange for you to get help.'

Eileen coughed. Her eyes were half-closed. Was she on medication now? She didn't appear to be in pain, but was spaced out, groggy. Perhaps she was always like this.

Imogen took a step closer to her. 'I need to know where Frank came from.'

Eileen blinked at her.

'I know he ran away from his family and you took him in. I need to know where his family lived.'

Imogen crouched beside Eileen and opened the maps app on her phone. She zoomed in on Hopton Wood, where Eileen had lived.

'What makes you think I'd know that?' Eileen said.

'Because Frank must have told you.'

Eileen lay back in the armchair, eyes shut tight, and Imogen was afraid she'd passed out. She was about to shake her back to awareness when the older woman said, 'He didn't tell me.'

'Surely—'

'I found it myself. It wasn't hard – it was on the edge of the wood. I knew there was a camp there where some of the fruit pickers lived. I had a feeling he was one of theirs.' Her lips curled into a smile. 'So I went there a few days after he turned up at mine.'

'What happened?'

'His dad wasn't there, but I found his mother. His beloved mother. Do you know what she said to me? She told me to keep him.' Eileen slipped into what was presumably supposed to be an Irish accent. '"He'll be better off with you. It's not safe for him here." I pressed her, tried to persuade her that a boy needed to be with his parents, that I didn't know anything about raising an eleven-year-old boy.'

Imogen waited.

'She said, "If he comes back here, his dad will kill him."' Eileen opened her eyes. They were glassy, focused on the past. '"And I don't want him anyway. There's something rotten about him, something he got from his father. Do you think I want two of them ganging up on me? Keep the little bastard. Tell Frankie if he comes back here he won't be welcome."'

'Did you tell him this?'

'Like hell I did. It would have destroyed him.' A cruel smile. 'But recently, the way he's been behaving, I was tempted.'

Imogen lifted her phone bearing the map of Hopton Wood to Eileen's line of vision. 'I need you to look at this map, Eileen, and show me where the camp was.'

Eileen squinted at the screen, a shaky finger hovering over the map.

Imogen had to pray that she was right. She knew Frank hadn't taken Ben to Ben's happy place. He hadn't killed him at home, even though he'd had plenty of time. So where else would he take him? Not back to Eileen's house in Hopton Wood.

Craig had told the police where to find the USB stick containing the interview with Michael. Why? Surely he wouldn't have done that unless his father had wanted him to. And that meant Frank must have known that the game was almost up. He wanted the world to know why he was doing it. He was no longer the silent killer, hiding from the police. He was a wounded soldier, getting in one last kill before he went down. His last act of glory.

To a man guided by a twisted philosophy, everything would have extra significance right now. Including the place in which he killed his final victim.

The place where this all began.

'Have you found it?' she asked Eileen.

'Right there,' the old woman said, pointing a shaky finger at the phone.

Imogen ran for the door.

Chapter 61

'Ben? Come out. I'm not going to hurt you.'

Bullshit. I flattened myself against a broad tree, praying he wouldn't hear my breathing or my hammering heart. He was close. I could hear him pushing branches aside, rustling the undergrowth. If I wasn't handcuffed, I would fight. He was armed, bigger than me and had far more experience with violence, but I was fighting for my life.

The woods were dark and all I could see was the beam of Frank's torch flitting between the trees. I had been hiding for what must have been half an hour, maybe longer, creeping from tree to tree, deeper into the woods. But he was closer now. His voice was clear.

'I'm losing patience, Ben. I'm going to find you. And I really don't want to hurt you. I don't want to have to do what I did to Michael.' He laughed. 'You should have seen his face when I went into the basement, when he realised there were two of us. I wish you'd been there, Ben. You would have enjoyed it. I did it for you.'

The narrow shaft of torchlight touched the ground a foot in front of me. He was close. So close.

'Oh, fuck this,' I heard him mutter. The light swept away.

Was he giving up? No. Surely it was a trick. He wanted me to come out, show myself. I stayed frozen to the spot, back pressed hard against the tree trunk, metal handcuffs digging into my wrists. But I could hear his footsteps rustling amongst the trees, which made it clear he was heading away from me.

All fell silent.

I waited, straining to hear, but there was nothing, no noise except a bird stirring in the higher branches. I realised I'd been holding my breath and relaxed, thinking about what to do. Where was the nearest main road? If I skirted the edge of the wood, surely that would take me to civilisation.

I stepped away from the tree on to the path.

An arm wrapped itself around my neck from behind.

'Gotcha,' Frank said.

ϖ

He marched me back towards his van, poking the barrel of his gun between my shoulder blades, urging me to get a move on. I pleaded with him until he snapped, 'If you don't shut the hell up I'm going to shoot you right here, right now.'

I shut up.

The moon came out, casting light across the wasteland. We reached a spot close to his van and he told me to stop.

'Get on the ground,' he said. 'Lie on your side.'

'Fuck you.'

'Just do it. Otherwise, it will be Ollie next.'

Reluctantly, moving as slowly as I could, I knelt on the dry, hard ground then lay down on my side. My shoulders were cramping and my wrists hurt. But the pain was meaningless.

I was going to die. I wanted to scream at Frank, to tell him what a piece of shit he was, how much I despised him. I only cooperated because I believed him when he said he would go after Ollie.

Frank knelt on the ground next to me. He set the shotgun on the ground beside him, knowing there was no way I could make a move for it, and pulled his bag towards him, delving inside it again. He must have collected the contents from the grass while I was hiding, because he took out a syringe. It was already full.

I tried to get up, my handcuffed wrists stopping me before I could start. But then they were impeding him, too, preventing him from getting access to the veins on the underside of my arms. Laying the syringe gently on the grass, he pushed me on to my front so my face was pressed against the ground.

'I heard you the other night,' he said. He inserted a key into the handcuffs. 'You and that cop – laughing, laughing so hard. It was glorious. And it made me remember.'

The handcuffs clicked open and he pulled them off me. Relief flooded through my wrists and shoulders. 'My mum used to laugh like that. When she and Dad were locked in their room, when they'd had a drink. When he wasn't beating her. She was happy sometimes. Happy in this place.' He glanced at the air around us like he was seeing something else and smiled a soft smile. None of it made sense to me. 'That's the last time I remember being truly happy.'

He pulled me back over on to my back. I tried to punch him, but he caught my wrist. My arms were weak from being cuffed behind me, full of pins and needles. He knelt on the wrist he'd caught and held the other firmly, the underside of my arm turned towards him.

He picked up the syringe. A droplet of liquid glinted in the moonlight. He turned to look at the sky, staring straight at the moon, then turned back to me and stroked my forehead. His eyes were glazed, like he wasn't seeing me but someone else.

'Now you'll be happy forever,' he said. 'You won't suffer any more.'

He positioned the tip of the needle against my left arm, just below the crook of my elbow, and I felt a prick as he jabbed it into the vein. He pulled on the plunger, drawing a little blood into the syringe.

'Frank,' I said. 'I'm not happy. I'm *not happy*.'

But it was as if he couldn't hear me. His eyes were far away. I had no idea who he was seeing, but before I could say another word he depressed the plunger . . .

. . . and warmth enveloped my body, a rush of bliss. All the pain that racked my body – the cramps in the shoulders, the pain from falling from the loft, the soreness in my wrists – and all the pain that scratched at my soul, it went away, and I surrendered to the feeling. I let myself go, floating, floating back into the womb, back to peace, lying on my side and staring across the wasteland through the newly shimmering night.

There was a woman running towards me in slow motion, auburn hair bouncing around her head. An angel, it must be an angel, and behind her were lights, bright and shining, and she, the angel, was crying out, getting closer and closer until she was there above me.

She threw herself at Frank, a blur of limbs and hair and fists. Frank barely moved as she leapt on him, raining punches down upon him. Something crunched, he gasped and she let out a roar, a cry of fury as she rolled off him and grabbed the shotgun that lay beside him. My eyes were almost closed, but through the slits I saw her turn it around and slam the buttstock into his face, once, then twice, yelling without words, before she turned to me and called my name.

I saw her beautiful face and tried to say her name, to tell her it was all right, that it didn't hurt, that nothing hurt any more.

I sank into the warm darkness.

Epilogue

1

It was a bright October morning, three months after I'd almost died, and the park was quiet apart from a couple of dog walkers and some young mums pushing buggies. Ollie had returned to school a few weeks before. There had been talk, while I was in hospital, of him staying with Megan permanently, going back to school in London. But he had decided he wanted to come back here to live with me. Megan was disappointed, but she understood. The deal was that Ollie would spend school holidays with her and term times with me. It was all very amicable.

I watched Imogen walk towards me, leaves crunching beneath her feet. She was wearing a green coat and her hair was loose. She wasn't an angel, but she *was* beautiful.

'We must stop meeting like this,' she said as she sat beside me, both of us facing the big old horse chestnut tree under which conkers lay in their spiky shells.

'We could always meet at my house.'

'You know that's not allowed.'

'Until the trial's over.'

She checked no one was looking and quickly squeezed my hand. 'Until the trial's over.'

There was something tantalising about it, this strange, old-fashioned courtship. We couldn't kiss. Were barely able to touch. Sex was completely out of the question. Of course, we could have done it in secret. The chances were that no one would find out. But if they did, Imogen's career would be over. It was dangerous enough meeting like this.

'It'll be worth the wait,' I said.

'Got a high opinion of yourself, have you?'

We both laughed.

The first thing I remember after I'd floated away into oblivion is waking up in the ambulance. Imogen was sitting beside me and as I'd opened my eyes, she'd gasped and clutched at my hand. I'd seen the paramedic raise her eyebrows at this, but Imogen hadn't seemed to care. I'd smiled at her, but before I could speak, I'd slipped back into sleep.

They had given me a save shot, the same drug they'd given Annette. Apparently, as the nurses told me in the hospital later, it attached to the same receptors in the brain as the heroin Frank had tried to kill me with, blocking the effects and making me breathe again. Thankfully, they said, I'd only stopped breathing for a minute. Two or three more minutes and I would have suffered permanent brain damage.

A few more minutes after that, and . . .

Imogen had saved my life by working out where I was going to be and calling an ambulance on her way there.

'So tell me,' I said. 'How is everything going? With preparations for the trial, I mean.'

She shrugged. 'Pretty well. Craig is talking now, singing like a bird, as they say. I think he's actually enjoying the attention. You know, he spent his entire childhood with just Frank and Eileen for company. He never played with other children. He barely encountered other people at all until Frank asked Janet Burgess to give him a job at the museum. Turns out Frank and Janet used to go out together, years ago.'

I nodded. The museum had suddenly become one of the busiest attractions in the county: the place where the Shropshire Viper had found his victims. All of them except me. I had been there – but I was already on Frank's list. The moment I'd started renting the cottage from him he'd decided I was someone who, as he would put it, 'deserved to die happy'.

'Craig told us where to find the other bodies. Janet Burgess and Adrian Morrow. They buried them both in the woods, not far from Eileen's house.'

'Poor Adrian,' I said. Frank had murdered him and tried to set him up in order to buy himself more time. He was already dead when Imogen found the shrine to serial killers at his flat. And it was Frank who'd added the smiley faces beside the pictures of the victims.

'Craig told us he posed as Adrian just in case Michael spoke to the police before they abducted him, which was what I'd suspected. Craig also told us about how his dad tried to poison me. Again, that was intended to buy himself some more time. I'd be flattered if it hadn't led to Alan's death.'

She sighed.

'Has Frank recovered from his injuries?' I asked.

'Oh, he's fine. Face isn't as pretty. Nothing to be done for it. It was self-defence on my part, wasn't it?'

'Don't ask me. I was out of it.' We shared a conspiratorial smile.

'Frank is barely talking at all still,' Imogen continued. 'Not to us, anyway. And he's refused to hire a lawyer – he's going to represent himself. The guards at the prison say he's a model prisoner. The younger convicts like him – see him as a kind of father figure. Anyway, we're confident Craig will testify against him. But Mrs Rowland's not around any more to contradict what Frank says.

When the police had gone back to Eileen Rowland's flat after Frank had been arrested, she was dead. She'd injected herself with a huge dose of the heroin Frank had left for her. I wondered if she'd felt at peace in her final moments. It seemed unlikely. She had just discovered what her son and the boy she'd rescued from the woods had been doing. It wouldn't surprise me if her overdose had been deliberate, her way of both dealing with the pain and avoiding any repercussions.

'Anyway,' Imogen said. 'Let's not talk about that any more. How are you bearing up?'

'I'm okay, actually.'

Mum had died six weeks before, still reeling from the shock of my near miss. Finding out that Frank Dodd, her old friend, was the Viper had been the icing on the cake.

'That's why he was wearing a balaclava,' she'd said when I'd told her, her mind still sharp. Because if Mum had seen his face and spoken his name aloud, Frank would have had to kill Ollie, too. And we knew he didn't want to do that.

I was there with her when she slipped away, sitting by the bed, holding her hand. Like Eileen, she hadn't been in pain when she went. Unlike Eileen, she had nothing to regret or worry about. She'd led a good life. A *just* life. And, as she'd hoped, the sun had shone at her funeral.

Her last words to me, brushing the tears from my cheek with a warm hand, were, 'Be happy.'

I intended to. Because if recent events had taught me anything, it was that life is dreadfully, ridiculously short. And after everything that had happened with Frank and Craig, I had read up on the philosophy they claimed to adhere to, a philosophy they had warped and changed to suit them. I liked a lot of what Epicurus had written – about inner tranquillity, about pursuing simple pleasures, about not concerning oneself with death. When I told Imogen about this, she'd teased me, asking me if I was going to build a pleasure garden and wander around it in a toga and sandals. But I think she got it, too.

'Except I have to be concerned with death,' she'd said. 'It's my job.'

'Imogen, this is Shropshire. You've just caught the only serial killer this place has ever had. The only death you're going to have to deal with now is the death of excitement.'

'That's fine by me.'

'Yeah. Me, too.'

We sat in the peaceful park, fingertips touching, and watched leaves drift down. A dog dashed after a squirrel. The sky was clear and the sun bright above us.

'Not such a terrible place, this, is it?' I said.

'I guess not.'

Sometimes, when I closed my eyes, I saw Frank's face, grinning down at me. I felt the jab of the needle. I clung to my recollection of that pain, but stopped the memory right there, not wanting to think about the bliss that had enveloped me afterwards. Because a little pain . . . we need it. It reminds us we're alive.

I got up from the bench, waded into a pile of leaves and began kicking them, laughing as they sprayed up around me. I picked up handfuls and threw them above my head.

'What are you doing?' Imogen asked, coming over to join me.

I smiled as red and gold and orange leaves rained down upon us.

'Living,' I replied.

2

Funny – I actually like this place. Yesterday, I went to the warden and suggested he let me make myself useful around here. I can do carpentry, plumbing, electrics, you name it. I've always been good with my hands.

He told me he'd think about it, but that he liked the influence I had on the younger cons. A calming influence, he called it. I guess he can see I'm a natural leader. A self-made man who can teach these young no-hopers – most of them from shit families – a thing or two.

And I do have a few things to teach them.

I sit in my cell and wonder how Craig's getting on. Fine, I'm sure. Doing what he's told, just as he always did. I saw him at Eileen's funeral, standing on the other side of the grave. We were both cuffed and surrounded by cops. There was nobody else there – Eileen never had any friends – but they wouldn't let us talk to each other. Before we went, I winked at him and he smiled. That was our goodbye.

Craig never really understood my long-term plan. He didn't need to. All he had to do was follow instructions: let them catch him, tell them where the USB stick was. Buy me the time I needed.

My cellmate, Steve, comes in and hands me the newspaper I asked him to smuggle up from the common room.

'You're in there, Frank,' he says. 'Page eleven. Nice picture of you.'

'Page eleven? I'm disappointed. I'm getting less famous.' Till the trial at least. When I get my day in court, the whole world will be listening.

Steve laughs and his eyes shine. I'm a celebrity in here, even among all the other murderers. Steve, though, he's only in for assault. He'll be out in a year. By then, I intend to have taught him everything I know.

By then, he'll see me as the dad he never had.

He peers over my shoulder as I read the news story. There is, indeed, a flattering photo of me in my best gear, looking not unlike the Man in Black himself. And there, on the other side of the page, is the lovely Imogen.

My face still hurts from where she beat me. But it's okay. I forgive her. She was only doing what was right. She was saving the man she was destined to be with.

'Looks like a real bitch,' Steve says, his grin fading when he sees the dis-approval on my face. He still has a way to go before he understands, before he's ready to continue my work.

'She's a good person,' I say.

He nods, unsure.

It struck me when I looked round her flat how lonely she was, how sad. At that point, I thought she needed to go, but afterwards – when she survived – I reconsidered. And when I knew they were closing in on me, that it was going to be almost impossible to finish Ben without checkmating myself, it struck me. Ben didn't have to be the end.

There could be another lucky one.

When Imogen flew at me out of the darkness, I was surprised. I wasn't expecting her to find me there, in my own happy place. I should have chosen another location, but I knew Ben would be the last person I helped with my own hands, so it felt important to me.

Afterwards, I had planned to turn myself in, hand myself over to Imogen herself. Because I knew how happy arresting me would make her.

'Oh, Imogen,' I say, touching her photo. I continue the rest in my head, visualizing her before me, listening to my words, drinking them in.

Imagine how good you'll feel, Imogen, when I'm sentenced, and you can walk out of that court and be with Ben. Successful in your career, successful in love. Not missing London. Not lonely any more.

Perfectly happy. And ready to die.

I look up at Steve and smile. Maybe it won't be him. Maybe it will be one of the other young men in here. One of them, maybe more, will be willing to be my new apprentice, to continue my work beyond these walls. And when I've taught him everything I know, and all the wisdom Eileen taught me and Craig, he will walk out of this place towards his destiny.

Towards Imogen Evans. And as he carries her to her happy place – wherever that is – and prepares to send her from this world with a smile, I hope she'll think of me.

Letter from the author

Dear Reader,

Thank you for reading *The Lucky Ones*. I'd love to hear what you thought of it. You can email me at markcity@me.com, find me on facebook.com/markedwardsbooks or follow me on Twitter: @mredwards.

Please note, the rest of this letter may contain spoilers, so please don't read it until you've finished the book.

Books can originate in many ways. In this case, it started with a conversation overheard in a cafe where I was working on a previous novel. Two young women were talking about a colleague, saying how much they disliked her and wishing aloud that she would disappear. I tweeted about it and, after a conversation with fellow author Steve Cavanagh, came up with an idea: what if someone psychotic overheard and decided to carry out that wish, believing they were doing these women a favour?

That book never got written – the story wouldn't quite come together – but that idea, of a twisted 'guardian angel', stayed with me. And that's when it hit me: I could write about a serial killer who tries to make his victims' lives perfect before he kills them. Within days, I had the basis of the plot . . . and started writing.

I decided to set the story locally to me, in the rural environs of Shropshire, one of England's most beautiful and sparsely populated counties. Woods and farms and ancient buildings – where better for a serial killer to roam? You could say the whole county is the Viper's happy place.

Thanks again for reading – and remember, when you have a piece of good fortune, a stroke of luck, that's almost certainly what it is. Enjoy it.

It's *probably* not an evil guardian angel.

Best wishes
Mark Edwards
www.markedwardsauthor.com

Acknowledgments

I was lucky enough to receive help from a number of people while writing this book. I owe everyone here at least several large drinks.

Sarah Lotz, genius writer, who helped me figure this book out and told me where I was going wrong before I'd even started, as well as advising me on some great places to dump bodies in Shropshire.

My brother-in-law, Ste Gray, who answered all my questions about morphine, save shots and ambulances with great patience. Also, Andrew Parsons and Jonathan Hill, who helped me when my pharmaceutical knowledge failed, which was often. Thanks, too, to Cally Taylor for putting me in touch with Andrew.

Alexandra Benedict, for coming up with a nickname for my serial killer.

Clare Mackintosh, for assistance with police procedural conundrums.

Once again, I owe a huge debt to my superb editor, David Downing, who pointed out exactly how to make this book better and allowed me to ruin his trip to New Orleans with my endless, stressed-out questions.

Thank you to everyone at Amazon Publishing, especially Emilie Marneur, Sana Chebaro and Hatty Stiles. And to my always-enthusiastic and wise agent, Sam Copeland.

Much gratitude goes to Erin Mitchell and Tracy Fenton, particularly for helping me out with my event in Harrogate in 2016.

To everyone on my Facebook page, facebook.com/markedwards-books – your endless cheerleading and support make being a writer even more fun and rewarding. Thanks to everyone who came up with ideas for lost property items. Four readers have their names in this novel after winning Facebook competitions – Alan Hatton, Emma Stockwell, Tracey Snelling and Camille McDaris – only one of whom is killed off horribly.

Finally, as always, an enormous amount of love and thanks goes to my beautiful wife, Sara, for being my first reader, my best friend and the most supportive partner any writer could hope for.

Free *Short Sharp Shockers* Box Set

About the Author

Mark Edwards writes psychological thrillers in which scary things happen to ordinary people, and is inspired by writers such as Stephen King, Ira Levin, Ruth Rendell and Linwood Barclay.

He is the author of four #1 bestsellers: *Follow You Home* (a finalist in the Goodreads Choice Awards 2015), *The Magpies*, *Because She Loves Me* and *The Devil's Work*, along with *What You Wish For* and six novels co-written with Louise Voss. All of his books are inspired by real-life experiences.

Originally from the south coast of England, Mark now lives in the West Midlands with his wife, their three children, a ginger cat and a golden retriever.